Where?

Where?

An Allegorical Novel

MARGARET M. BLANCHARD

iUniverse LLC
Bloomington

WHERE?
An Allegorical Novel

Copyright © 2014 Margaret M. Blanchard.

All rights reserved. No part of this book may be used or reproduced by any means, graphic, electronic, or mechanical, including photocopying, recording, taping or by any information storage retrieval system without the written permission of the publisher except in the case of brief quotations embodied in critical articles and reviews.

This is a work of fiction. All of the characters, names, incidents, organizations, and dialogue in this novel are either the products of the author's imagination or are used fictitiously.

iUniverse books may be ordered through booksellers or by contacting:

iUniverse LLC
1663 Liberty Drive
Bloomington, IN 47403
www.iuniverse.com
1-800-Authors (1-800-288-4677)

Because of the dynamic nature of the Internet, any web addresses or links contained in this book may have changed since publication and may no longer be valid. The views expressed in this work are solely those of the author and do not necessarily reflect the views of the publisher, and the publisher hereby disclaims any responsibility for them.

Any people depicted in stock imagery provided by Thinkstock are models, and such images are being used for illustrative purposes only. Certain stock imagery © Thinkstock.

ISBN: 978-1-4917-2275-6 (sc)
ISBN: 978-1-4917-2276-3 (e)

Printed in the United States of America.

iUniverse rev. date: 01/28/2014

Cover Paintings by S.B. Sowbel:
Front: The Path of the Talpidae, Back: Trailing
Author Photograph by Kathleen A. Herrington

TABLE OF CONTENTS

With gratitude to my creative companions, first readers, superb editors, photographer and artist:
Kathleen Herrington and S.B. Sowbel

Revisiting G.M. Hopkins

"Each mortal thing does one thing and the same:
Deals out that being indoors each one dwells;
Selves—goes itself; myself it speaks and spells,
Crying what I do is me: for that I came.

I say more: the just one justices;
Keeps grace: that keeps all her goings graces;
Acts in god's eye what in god's eye she is—"
Divine. For divinity plays in ten thousand places,
Lovely in limbs, and lovely in eyes not ours—
To the Source through the features of our faces.
Where? In our faces.
Where? Through our eyes.

Where?

An Allegory: "Allegory is a literary device in which characters or events in a literary, visual, or musical art form represent or symbolize ideas and concepts . . . . An allegory conveys its hidden message through symbolic figures, actions, imagery, and/or events."—From *Wikipedia,* the free encyclopedia.

Chapter One

WHO?

Who? The voice on the phone was familiar. Someone from my past, someone calling my old nickname. "Xavy, it's *me*."

Despite the long silence between us, I of course recognized her voice. "Who?" I asked out loud, stalling to overcome my shock.

"Grace!" Her tone was so recognizable, that pitch so confident. Only now the tone was a little tentative, slightly plaintive.

Grace, one of the loves of my life. Long gone . . . Now returned? I became wary. Why was she calling me? After all that'd happened . . . . Some of which I couldn't quite remember anymore.

"Where *are* you?" I asked.

"Vermont."

"Ah, good old Vermont, home of the hippie commune and the civil union." I found myself slipping into my old persona—breezy, irreverent, laid back, on the fence nonchalance. Even though that mask no longer fit, I found myself trying it on again. That old facade gave me some breathing room as I tried to grasp the prospect of having Grace back in my life, after this long separation. Back, at least, within calling distance.

"Where are *you?*" she asked.

"Boston" I replied. How glamorous that might have sounded. If only she knew where in Boston. South of South Boston, trying to distance itself from its working class roots, welcoming gentrification with open arms—the mistress to wealth and power, not the wife. Yet greedy enough now to charge an arm and a leg for this condo I'm subletting from a colleague on assignment in Afghanistan.

"I figured that by your area code," she said.

She obviously wanted more. But I was reluctant to divulge any further personal information. I was immediately propelled back to our breakup. Even though it'd probably been my fault, as so many such things are, I was surprised to discover I still felt hurt. Funny how the past just sits there, like some prehistoric animal preserved in ice, waiting for animation into the same old primeval context. So instead I asked, "What's up?" I knew Grace well enough to know she wasn't just looking me up for old times sake.

"I was just thinking of you. I miss you, Xavy. It's been too long."

Too long indeed. Despite our annual exchange of birthday cards, I hadn't *really* spoken to Grace in at least ten years. Whose fault that was I cannot say. A mutual hiatus, it seemed. But of course I felt guilty for not reaching out to her. I doubted Grace blamed herself for the chasm. Her guilt seemed to focus on social and political issues. When it came to personal relationships, she appeared almost always blameless. I, on the other hand, was a walking *mea-culpa*.

"Yeah," I said. "It has." To stop myself from launching into a litany of excuses for not contacting her, I just repeated, "What's up?"

She was too savvy to protest any further. "I could use your help." As I suspected, she needed something.

"What kind of help?" I said suspiciously. At the moment I couldn't think of anything I could do that she couldn't do better, or just as well. Even then it would be a short list.

She cut straight to the chase. "I'd like your help finding a lost child."

I was flabbergasted. "Are you kidding? Why me?"

"You did such a great job looking for Iris." She was referring to an ill-fated venture on my part, an attempt to play the role of private eye when a good friend of ours disappeared many years ago in Baltimore, in the backwash of the women's movement, during one of my frequent lay-offs. In those days we were still clinging to remnants of the diverse, inclusive community which had formed around our initial, revolutionary push for equal rights. These days, while we are astonished by the strides women have made collectively, we miss that old camaraderie—at least I do.

"I never found her—remember?"

"I know, but you left no stone unturned. You're a great investigator."

2

"Well, that's because I'm an investigative reporter. Not a private investigator." As a matter of fact, I was neither at the moment, but identity lingers. I was curious, of course, about the story of the missing child, but I wasn't about to bite.

"So, is that what you're doing now, Xavy? Do you have a job as an investigative reporter?"

I was so, so tempted to lie, to tell her that I was a hot shot at the Boston Globe covering international spy stories or something just as glitzy. Grace was the last person I wanted to know that my future as a journalist was in the toilet, given that we'd broken up, at least in part, over my "careerism" versus her marginalism. But lies, I had discovered, had a way of snaking around you and then biting when you least expected it. "Sort of." I decided the best defense was, as they say, a better offense. "How about you? What are you doing these days?"

"We're—I'm helping run an alternative pre-school."

"Oh?" Immediately, of course, I was curious about the "we." But I wasn't going to ask, so I shifted back to the missing child story. "Is that who's missing—one of the kids?"

"No—the daughter of a friend of mine."

I wondered if this friend was the "we" she'd just retreated from describing. I backed off from hearing more. I wasn't sure I wanted to hear all about Grace's exciting new life in Vermont. My curiosity, I knew only too well, provided a slippery slope into engagement, and I wasn't sure I wanted to get burned again. Although, as I now recalled, my futile search for Iris had been my idea, not Grace's. She'd actually been quite suspicious of it.

As the pause grew longer and more awkward, I stared out my living room window. Because my condo was in the basement, the window, at eye level, opened onto the parking lot, with a splendid view of various tires under various cars. The only other window, in the bedroom, opened onto the same grim lot. Needless to say, I felt like a mole. My life in Baltimore had been grimy but not quite this grey.

"So, where are you living?" Grace asked, filling the silence by reading my mind, as she was wont to do.

"Oh, it's really interesting—an old church converted to condos," I said, about to quote the promotional materials which had lured me into this catacomb.

"What kind of church?"

3

"Catholic. I'm in the church part and the rectory—priests' home—that's now apartments for the elderly, while across the street the old school is being converted into luxury condos. A different kind of conversion these days. Catholicism has, obviously, fallen on hard times." I waited for the predictable rant against celibacy, predatory priests or the wealth of the Vatican, but surprisingly none was forthcoming. Had Grace changed, regarding hierarchies of any kind, or was she just being careful not to offend me? "And rightly so," I added, lest she assume I'd rejoined the Church.

"Sounds interesting," she said tentatively.

"Lets me relive my old Catholic school days," I said blithely. "Where are you living?"

"Oh, out in the country. In an old farmhouse. In the middle of nowhere, I guess you might say." It sounded stark, but I suspected it wasn't.

"Oh, with sheep and cows and chickens?"

Her hearty laugh sent me into a spasm of nostalgia. "No, just the usual assortment of cats and dogs. It's not a farm, just a farmhouse."

I took the plunge. "Who do you live with?"

"My friend Marcy."

"Friend?"

"Soul companion."

When Grace said, "soul," she didn't mean "sole." For her, I already knew, a Soul Companion was the most exalted of relationships, akin to sainthood in Grace's pantheon of relationships. I knew what she meant: one who accompanies one in the process of soul creation, usually a lifelong friendship. I, alas, was simply an "x." I had apparently failed to make the transition from lover to soul companion. Little did my parents know that when they named me Xavier, they were labeling a cipher. I sighed and focused on a white stone embedded in the elaborate tread of the nearest tire.

"How about you," Grace asked carefully. "Are you living with anyone?"

Not only wasn't I living with anyone; the someone I didn't live with wasn't even here. "Nope," I replied. "I'm on my own these days." The implication was that this solitary state was a temporary situation, but I knew all too well it was pretty much set in stone.

She paused just long enough for me to wince at what was coming. "Are you with men or women these days?" That old bone of contention. The truth was I wasn't "with" anybody, male or female. My old sexual adventures or, more precisely, longings for adventure, had pretty much dried up to the size of a pea. But how much of that did I want to confess? "Does it matter?"

"No, it really doesn't. I was just curious." She laughed nervously, something the old Grace wouldn't have done. Someone must have impressed upon her how unnerving her probing could be. Even though I was the investigative reporter, Grace was a true private eye. She, I'd discovered, could worm the truth out of anyone. But she was the last person I was going to tell about my lack of relationship or my lack of a job. Odd though, how she showed up every time I found myself at another dead end. "My primary relationships these days are with four year olds," she added with a smile in her voice.

I watched as the tires facing me pulled away, leaving a plume of exhaust to curl toward the window. Through the space left empty I could see a spray of yellow forsythia blossoms on the other side of the driveway. I agreed with T.S. Eliot: April is the cruelest month. Here it was spring, I was still buried underground, with neither a partner or gainful employment, and Grace shows up out of the blue to tempt me into another fruitless search.

"I hear it's challenging to be a journalist these days," Grace said, as if hot on the trail of all my sore spots.

"How so?" I asked innocently, as if I didn't know that print media was in free-fall.

"Oh, you know, the ways papers are folding, everybody getting their news on line and all."

"Well, there's still radio. And blogs. And some people still prefer the old fashioned newspaper." I thought of my own ill-fated blog. Somehow everybody with an opinion, however ill-informed or inarticulate, could blog away. Not only did this deplete any potential audience, the income from blog ads amounted to pennies on the hour. While waiting for free lance assignments I churned out column after column for practically nothing while I watched my savings vanish, counting the days until my former colleague returned from the war zone to claim his condo back, and I was homeless again. How could I possibly convey all this to Grace who, despite her own ups and down, invariably landed on her feet, often in some cushy territory. Last I heard she was companion to some heiress. Was that who she was living with now?

"How's Yuggie?" Grace asked, apparently deciding to shift from this tooth-pulling exchange to more spacious conversational territory. Yuggie was my sister, also, through me, a friend of Grace's.

"She's great," I replied, secretly relieved to hear that they hadn't been in contact. Yuggie had a way of drawing in the loves of my life and making them her own, starting, of course, with Mom.

"Where is she these days?"

"Hawaii."

"Hawaii?"

"Yep. Living with Nancy."

"Nancy?"

"Dad's wife." I enjoyed sharing this news with Grace, who'd been the recipient of my multiple complaints about my step-mother and her lavish lifestyle.

"Oh, my, Xavy, how did this come about?"

I felt a slight pang that I hadn't contacted Grace to tell her about the major fault lines that had transformed the landscape of our family dynamics, but how could I have told her once we practically stopped speaking to each other? "Dad died suddenly—a heart attack—after declaring bankruptcy. He lost almost everything when the dot-com bubble burst." I felt overwhelmed at how things had shifted since the movement days when I was a refugee from the upper middle class, ashamed of my father's driving ambition and ostentatious wealth, myself proudly downwardly mobile with disdain for his success and my step-mother's luxury, yet secretly relying on a possible inheritance for backup. It was only when I stood at my dying father's bedside that I realized that he was never as well-off as I'd assumed and that he had been motivated mostly by a desire to provide for his daughters a more secure future than he'd had himself. "He was a humbler man by then. But at least he had a loving farewell."

"Oh, Xavy, I'm so sorry to hear that." Finally I felt a touch of real warmth in Grace's voice. She'd sounded friendly enough earlier, but this, I realized as memories flowed back with this more sympathetic tone, raised the temperature between us by several degrees.

Grace's empathy was so palpable I felt moved to tell her the whole story. "Dad and Nancy had retired in Hawaii, but once he died and there were no funds to speak of, she was stuck there. She proved herself surprisingly resourceful and soon established a real estate business which paid her bills. But then she had a stroke, so that's when Yuggie decided to go over there and take care of her. Now, of course, they're thick as thieves."

"I know Yuggie is a generous soul but it's hard to believe she's sacrificed her life like that."

"Yes, she is. I'm sure it's not easy caring for Nancy, but Yuggie couldn't be happier. Nancy is slowly recovering and Yuggie has a new honey in Hawaii after pining so long over what'shername." It was symptomatic of my state that I really couldn't remember that name, despite weeks and months of listening to Yuggie moaning and groaning about her infidelity. "She loves the culture and the climate there."

Yuggie was a died-in-the-wool lesbian, not some fly-by-night like me. For that reason, or perhaps others, she'd never been subject to the paralysis of political correctness as I had been. Not that I *was* politically correct. But I'd certainly agonized over not being. Now, I suppose, all those judgments had evaporated into the contemporary fog of economic expediency and conservative backlash. I wondered how Grace, who had more progressive integrity than most, was navigating these new tumultuous waters without a women's movement for guidance. Living in Vermont, like living in Hawaii, didn't seem exactly like "manning" the barricades of poverty, discrimination, and oppression. But with this current economic "downturn," I suppose, every place has its share of deprivation.

"If you take this job, Xavy, it will mean some income," Grace offered tentatively.

How did she know I was practically on my last dime? "What kind of income?" I asked warily. I felt hooked.

"The child's mother—she just inherited a lot of money from the other mother, and she's desperate to find the missing child. She'll pay you to investigate, I'm sure."

All these mothers was confusing. It sounded like a tangled web to unweave. "What would that mean for my life? Do I have to come to Vermont?"

"For starters, yes. And then it might involve some traveling."

"Where?"

"Wherever the trail leads you."

I thought about it. My sublet was almost over. Without the reduced rate for house-sitting, I couldn't afford to rent in Boston anymore. The only person likely to miss me was my therapist, but with funds quickly depleting, my time with her was running out anyway. I suddenly decided to come clean. "How did you know?"

"Know what?"

"That I'm at another dead end."

"Oh, no, Xavy, you're not vanished again, are you?" I smiled ruefully at that old term for my tendency to decline into obscurity, shadowed usually by lack of a job and lack of relationships. Due to excessive self-reliance, I had trouble asking for help when I most needed it. Grace knew this better than many.

"I guess I am," I confessed. *"I've fallen into desuetude,"* I joked, evoking the line from a song written by singer-songwriter S.B. Sowbel with whom Grace once had a brief fling. Enough said. At that we both broke into song, "Falling into desuetude, never wanted to, what am I to do? I'm useless." Chuckling together lifted the gloom from my basement surroundings. "No job, no relationship except with my therapist."

"Is she good?"

"She's great. Of course I'm madly in love with her."

"And she's straight," Grace added.

"But of course. Happily married with children." We both laughed. My zest for the unattainable was legend.

"Why don't you come for a visit, Xavy, and we can talk about it? I'm not that far away."

"How far?" I asked, warily, feeling the pull yet reluctant to be so easily drawn in.

"Three hours drive. It's easy and pretty."

Sure, I thought. Nothing with Grace was easy, even though she herself was pretty. I smiled, thinking how scornfully she'd dismiss "pretty" as an acceptable adjective for herself.

But I'd had the sense, when I was still working as a stringer for the *Globe* and earning a decent income, to buy an Accord. It was the only thing in my current life that was still running. And a drive in the country might be just what I needed.

"A change of scene might be just the ticket," she said, again reading my mind.

"Do you still have snow up there?" I said, resisting.

"Oh no, we're having an early spring this year. Global warming, y'know. But it is mud season, so bring along an extra pair of hearty shoes."

Mud season? I imagined stepping out of my car and sinking into a slough of despond. "Let me think about it, and call you back." I pictured my mobile unit disappearing into a Vermont bog.

She acquiesced to this delay more easily than she would have in the past. Maybe she's changed, I thought as I pulled out my pipe, pinched a bud from my precious but dwindling store of weed and lit up. Do we ever change, I wondered? Suddenly I felt awash with the realization that all my own talk in the past with Grace herself about mending my ways had gone up in a puff of smoke. Well, she might as well know that I'm not going to give up *any* of my bad habits, never again. After all, she no longer has any clout over me that way.

As my perspective began to lighten with each inhale, I contemplated the prospect of a change of scene. At first I felt quite resistant. Reconnecting with Grace stirred up all sorts of guilt and regret. Vermont seemed so remote and rural; I'm a city girl *par excellence*—from my stylish crop to my array of silk scarves to my designer boots. I didn't know one end of a silo from another; I knew only the vore in "localvore," as in *voracious*. Tracking some kid who probably just ran away seemed like another wild goose chase, and I wasn't sure if I could bear another failure, in work or in love.

Suddenly though, everything switched perspective, as it sometimes does when I'm high, and I told myself, "Who are you kidding, kiddo? This is that lifeline you've been longing for. This is the hand reaching down to pull you out of the pit. What are you waiting for?"

Rod would be back from Afghanistan in ten days. I couldn't leave until then, but maybe by that time the mud in Vermont would have dried out. And somehow, it seemed, looking for a missing person might be just what I needed to turn my life around. Hadn't Grace just *found* me? Maybe I could do the same for her friend's child. I mulled over the many reruns of *Without a Trace* I'd been watching in my ample downtime. Without the resources of that special unit of the FBI, my prospects were somewhat diminished, but the possibility of again having Grace as a sidekick had some appeal.

Chapter Two

VERMONT

Within ten days, my bags were packed and I was ready to go. Rod was due back that evening, dead tired, no doubt, after an all night flight from Afghanistan. I left the place cleaner than it had been when I moved in—considerably below my step-mother Nancy's standards but much higher than Rod's. Much as I might have liked to hear about all his adventures covering the war for the Globe, hanging out with the courageous young female journalists now *embedded with* U.S. troops (a practice not even conceived of in my heyday), and hobnobbing with visiting American dignitaries, I felt it would be better for my pride and for his exhaustion if I saved that de-briefing for later. Much later.

After our brief fling, my connection with Rod had been tenuous at best. Had it not been for his need for a house-sitter, and mine for a roof over my head, I doubt if our bond would have stretched this far. He was a nice fellow, but at this point of my life much too young, self-congratulatory, and ambitious to become a durable friend. Instead I left him some fresh bagels, a warm note welcoming him home and thanks for his hospitality.

As I drove out of Boston, up through New Hampshire, and into Vermont, I could feel the traffic easing off as the smell of exhaust gave way to fresh air, and the grey of industrial buildings yielded to green landscapes. I recalled my mom's evoking in our childhood "the many shades of green" of her ancestral Ireland. There was the lime green of the fields newly liberated from their snow cover, the golden green of spring leaves, the blue green of fir and spruce, and the multiple green hues of other growing things: emerald, jade, olive. All this fertility combined into curves and hills set against a brilliant blue sky, and, as

I cruised up the Connecticut River Valley, lined and criss-crossed with the azure and cobalt of rivers and lakes.

Soon, as the traffic dwindled down to a few cars and trucks, I turned off the broad expanse of river valley and headed up into the hills, guided by Grace's directions. Haunted by the specter of Mud Season I prayed the roads would remain paved. They did. At least, until I headed up the circular drive to Grace's house. Fortunately my auto's momentum carried me through the ruts of the graveled entry and deposited me at the foot of a long wooden staircase that led up to a bright yellow house which looked like it had stood there, perched on that edge of hill, for a long time, though probably not in the past with the ochre and plum trim it now sported. I had a moment to look around and catch my breath before Grace appeared on the porch, waving. The clapboard house had a large slanted tin roof and dormers, with a duplicate but smaller house attached to it.

At a distance, she seemed like the same old Grace, vibrant, expressive, warm and welcoming. As I looked up at her, standing there in the sunshine at the top of the stairs, some words from Leonard Cohen's *Hallelujah* sang in my head: *There's a blaze of light in every word. It doesn't matter which you heard, the holy or the broken Hallelujah . . . I did my best, it wasn't much. I couldn't feel, so I tried to touch. And even though it all went wrong, I'll stand before the Lord of Song with nothing on my tongue but Hallelujah.*

Closer up, after we'd hugged, I could see she was aging in ways similar to mine. Her body was slightly thicker, her face was creased, her auburn hair was silvered with grey and white. Ykkes, I thought, as I often did when looking into the mirror these days, we're *melting*. That scene from the Wizard of Oz came to mind, even though we weren't wicked witches, at least Grace wasn't. Wicked or wise, it seemed, we all were destined to this melting, those of us lucky enough to live this long. Looking again into Grace's lovely face, I felt even this melting as a blessing.

Soon she had me and my meager belongings scooped up and deposited in the lovely old farmhouse. She settled me upstairs in the guest room, a simple, rustic, comfortable room with a double bed, chest of drawers, cozy chair and a desk which looked out on a fallow garden. This was such a warm welcome I began to wonder if I could possibly *not* accept the assignment she was offering me.

I declined the temptation of my usual afternoon nap and joined her downstairs in the kitchen at a round table next to a window which looked out into what seemed like an orchard. As she served us tea, I commented on the trees. "Apples, I presume."

She nodded. "One's a crabapple. It'll bloom and produce fruit first. The other two take turns each summer."

"Really?" What I knew about trees was even less than I knew about apples. "That's convenient."

"Wait'll apple blossom time, Xavy. It's one of the most beautiful times of year around here."

I doubted I'd still be around for apple blossom time, Operation Search or no. "How long have you lived here?"

"Five years."

Questions flooded into my head about Grace's life during the past fifteen or so years since we'd been together, but just as suddenly they were dammed up by my guilt for having abandoned her and my jealousy about her relationships since then. Instead I asked her about some of the folks we'd both known in Baltimore. She seemed relieved not to have to relive our break-up and its fallout, and we launched instead into a spirited round of gossip and analysis of other people. I, who'd lost touch with just about everyone by this time, was amused, amazed, puzzled or saddened by the trajectories of our various acquaintances, some predictable, some surprising. Who would have imagined, for instance, that a talented feminist member of a working class commune would end up in Saudi Arabia as personal artist for some sultan? Or that one of the most strident of local separatists would now be heterosexually married with four children and five grandchildren?

As we made observations and chuckled together, I felt a pang. Although Grace and I were so different, we'd had such a deep bond of shared interests in people's quirks and mysteries, in social and political dynamics, in fringe movements and obscure adventures. How could I have let that go? A familiar wash of guilt suddenly reminded me I hadn't told my therapist I wouldn't be there for my regular session the next day, that, in fact, I might not be back any time soon.

"Uh oh!" I leapt up and rummaged in my purse for my cell phone. When I turned it on, it got stuck on "Looking for signal." I looked around, baffled. My cell phone never stalled.

"Sorry, Xavy, cell phones don't work here."

It was like someone had just chopped off one of my ears. I was mystified. How could I function without my cell phone?

"Here," Grace said, "handing me a portable land phone. At least it wasn't attached to a cord, preventing me from moving out of earshot. I shifted out to the front porch to make my call, keeping my voice as low as possible. Fortunately I got the message answering service so I didn't have to explain in person. "Ellen, this is Mary," I said quickly lest the machine cut me off. "I've been called out of town on an assignment so I have to cancel our appointment for tomorrow. Sorry for the late notice. I'm not sure when I'll be back, but I'll call when I know. Thanks." I wasn't sure what I was thanking her for, but it just seemed like the safe thing to say.

"Mary?!" Grace asked when I rejoined her. So much for privacy. "Are you incognito with your therapist?"

"You know *Mary Catherine's* my birth name, Grace," I snapped. "Xavier is my last name, remember?" I was in no mood for jokes about my name. I felt sad about separating from Ellen, probably for good, unless by some miracle my ship came in while I was in landlocked Vermont.

"Oh, of course. That's how I tracked you down. But all I could find were the initials, M.C. Nobody calls you Xavy anymore?"

I shrugged. "Formally I'm called Mary now." Formally, I realized, was mostly how I was known these days—at work, in therapy, even by acquaintances. Nobody really knew the real me, the Xavy me. "Not 'M.C.' You can forget the Catherine. My mother wanted it to be Kathleen, the Irish version, but Dad won out because Catherine was his mother's name." I sighed, feeling suddenly abandoned by Ellen, even though, of course, I was the one leaving. I turned my hurt into a joke even as I recognized, as a result of my therapy, that was something I habitually did. "I can just imagine what she'll think, given the issue we've just been dealing with."

"What's that?"

"Impulsivity." We laughed together. How many times had we joked about such psychiatric labels? I felt better. Now it was time to get down to business. "So what's the story about this missing child, Grace?"

"Her name is Liza. She's been gone for several months now, and her mother is very worried about her."

"Several *months*? That sounds ominous. Haven't they called the police?"

"No, she doesn't want the police involved."

"Why not? If she's been missing that long, they should probably bring in the FBI," I said, thinking of the kind and intelligent agents on *Without a Trace*.

"She's not exactly 'missing,' Xavy; she's gone."

"A child? How old is she?"

"Thirty-one," Grace replied without a qualm.

"What?! Thirty-one? Of course she's gone; she should be gone. She's a grown up. You mean, she was still living at home?"

"It's complicated, Xavy." I could tell that Grace was feeling some anguish about this, so I decided to keep my cynical mouth shut and just listen. But what I was thinking was, *Do you mean you're sending me out to search for a missing child who's really an adult?* "Her mother died a year ago. Of breast cancer. Liza had come home to help care for her those final few months. Then a month after she died, Liza disappeared."

"Maybe she just went home. Where did she live?"

"Los Angeles. She did go home but only to move out of her apartment and sell all her belongings. Nobody there seems to know where she went after that."

A chill ran across my shoulders. If Liza's mom had died, whose mother was it who was now worried about her? Was Grace dabbling again in the paranormal, talking to Liza's mom in spirit? I wondered, recalling our previous sojourn into séances and such in our search for Iris. If so, how could that ethereal missing mom pay me for finding her missing child? "You said, her mom was worried about her . . . ?"

"Her other mom."

"Oh!" The two Moms script. "Which one was her *real* mom?" I asked, venturing clumsily, I knew, into uncharted conversational territory. Fortunately, Grace didn't seem intent on correcting my political faux pas. A nice change in our relationship—I hoped it would last.

"She was adopted."

"By both of them?"

"No. Sheila adopted Liza as a baby thirty years ago, as a single mother. Durga didn't enter the picture until about six years ago."

"When Liza was already grown?"

"Yes, but still in graduate school, still financially dependent to some extent."

"Well, I'd hardly call her a mother, then."

"Maybe not, but now that her partner is dead, Durga feels responsible for at least keeping in touch with her daughter. Besides, she's very fond of Liza."

"Durga? What kind of name is that?"

"Indian. She's a Hindu goddess."

"I assume you mean the original Durga," I said with a trace of my old smartaleckyness. "So she's from India?" I imagined a reincarnation of the goddess.

"No, it's a chosen name." Grace was suddenly looking very uncomfortable. "I have to tell you, Xavy, that she's someone you know from Baltimore, someone you didn't care for, to say the least."

My mind was a blank. Somehow although I could recall feelings of irritation or mistrust—certainly not *hatred*—I couldn't remember anybody specific who'd ignited those feelings. Ah, the convenience of an aging memory. "Who?" I asked.

"The point is, she's changed so much she's almost another person."

I was getting alarmed. "Who?"

"Sandra."

"Sandra?" A face loomed up in memory. A rival for Grace's affections. A worm in the apple of Iris's academic career. A thorn in my side throughout that investigation. Of all people I didn't want to see again, please, Grace, don't tell me my prospective employer is Sandra! What kind of karma was this? "Sandra of the haughty 'a' Sandra?" I asked with a neutral tone. "What happened to her hippie husband? What about her and whatshername?"

"Things change in twenty years, Xavy. Her husband ran off with some bimbo singer in his band. What'shername—I've forgotten it too—went straight and became a major union organizer, married to some macho union organizer. Sandra retired from her successful academic career after encountering some Hindu guru, and now she's Durga by way of some spiritual initiation." I detected a slight quiver in Grace's lower lip, as if she were trying not to smile. I knew she was waiting for me to make some joke, but I was still aghast at this development.

"Oh my!" was about all I could manage. I loved Grace dearly, still, but here she was asking me to traipse around the country looking for someone who obviously did not want to be found for someone who used to be my archenemy. *Oh brother!*

"She's really a different person, Xavy. She turned out to be a marvelous caretaker for Sheila, from the first diagnosis to the last days of hospice."

I was beginning to sniff out the rest of the story. "So how did she happen to land up in Vermont?" I asked lightly, trying to keep my suspicions out of my tone.

Grace looked sheepish. "She followed me up here."

"So you and she had become an item?" I felt a curiously irrational flare of jealousy. I assumed that I'd succeeded where Sandra had failed, but now, it seemed, *au contraire.*

"Oh, no. I loved her not too much but too little. At least, not enough."

"So you encouraged her out of guilt?" I tried not to sound judgmental. Guilt wasn't something that usually snagged Grace, but it was an all too familiar hook for me.

"Oh, no. but I did feel sorry for her when her husband ran off and she was left all alone. I was with Marcy then."

Ah, the mysterious Marcy. I felt myself getting mercifully distracted from the transformed Sandra-Durga. "Where is Marcy? Doesn't she live here?"

"She's in Maine with Kara."

"Who's Kara?"

"Marcy's honey."

I was feeling overwhelmed by the complexities of Grace's circle. "I thought you and Marcy were 'partners.' Don't you live together?"

"I thought I told you—she's a dear life companion."

"Yes, but that's a fairly nebulous term, especially in these days of marriage rights. So she's an ex but you live together? And is she the one you run the pre-school with?"

"No, that's Ariel."

"And she's your current . . . ?" I was at a loss for what to call Grace's liaisons.

"No, another soul companion," Grace acknowledged without embarrassment. Rather than being ashamed of her multiple connections, Grace seemed proud of all these bonds. And if they all got along, then I had to agree: it was a miracle. Nonetheless, my mind was reeling with this list of names. It was hard enough these days to remember names I knew, much less ones I didn't. I took out my special leather bound notebook given to me by my sister Yuggie last Christmas, saved throughout my recent unemployment for just such an occasion, and started making notes. Grace looked pleased, assuming, I realized, this signaled a commitment on my part. Yet I was far from persuaded.

"Liza with an 's' or a 'z'?" Names, I felt, were significant clues. I wanted to get them right.

"Z."

"Good."

"Why good?"

"Well, it would be really good if it *started* with a Z, like Zora or Zuta. End of alphabet is easier to find than the beginning."

"And being an X, you have an affinity for W, X, Y, and Z." Grace smiled. One thing I'd always liked about Grace; she enjoyed people's quirks. "Nonetheless you'll probably like Ariel."

I wasn't at all sure I'd like any of Grace's 'soul companions,' having apparently squandered my claim to same. But that wasn't the point. I wasn't on this scene to sign up for lifetime membership. I was just there to help Grace help them. "Do all these soul companions of yours get along?"

Grace smiled. "More or less. I introduced Durga to Sheila through Ariel, who was Sheila's best friend."

"And how do Marcy and Kara fit into that network?"

"That's part of the less. After we broke up, Marcy was jealous of Ariel, just as I got jealous when Marcy got involved with Kara. But we're all good friends now."

"I didn't think you had a jealous bone in your body."

Grace just grinned at me, her lips sealed.

My head was reeling. I decided to get back to the mystery at hand. "So how did Liza—the so-called child—get along with Durga?"

"Well, she'd had Sheila to herself for most of her life, so of course she was jealous when Sheila got involved with Durga. And Durga isn't exactly the easiest person to connect with."

"I thought she was a whole different person."

"Yes, well, under the surface she's changed, but on the surface . . ." Grace paused, searching, I suspected, for the most flattering description.

"Abrasive, bossy, and supercilious?" I offered.

"Not supercilious, but, yes, still a bit abrasive, though so well-meaning, and still, on occasion, bossy."

"Poor Liza. What's she like?"

"Well, she's challenging in her own way. Very bright. Very loving, but also elusive. You can't always guess what she's feeling or thinking. She can be very out there one minute and very guarded the next." Grace took a deep breath, then continued. "She also was a wonder of compassion while her mother was dying. She and Durga really worked well as a team under some very trying circumstances. But I'm not sure they ever bonded deeply, and once Sheila was gone, their reason for being together apparently evaporated."

"Which seems natural to me. Why is Durga so intent on tracking Liza down?"

"That's a bit of a mystery to me too. But Durga is nothing if not persistent, once she's taken on some responsibility. I don't know if it was some deathbed request from Sheila or what. I'm not exactly privy to Durga's inner life. Maybe it's some spiritual quest, or dictum from her guru."

"So she still follows a guru?" I asked. For all my Buddhist meditation retreats, I was, like many wayward Catholics, wary of spiritual hierarchy. I was no more inclined to bow down to a Buddha than I was to a Christ, much as I admired them both.

"Well, I guess, but not in the body, not anymore."

In the body? Was this some kind of tantric practice that has passed me by? I looked quizzical.

"Her guru died about ten years ago," Grace explained. Oh no, I thought, back to the séance mumbo jumbo. I decided not to explore that line of questioning any further at this point. I just nodded. If I agreed to do this, I could inquire directly from the so-called Durga.

"So," said Grace. "Are you willing to take this on, Xavy?"

I scrunched up my face. I couldn't imagine working for Sandra, nee Durga. I couldn't bear the thought of even seeing her again, much less accepting an assignment from her. I recalled that haughty voice she used with her college students, and with me. On the other hand,

I hated to let Grace down. Although it didn't seem that she herself was all that worried about Liza, I could see that she did want to help San . . . Durga. By some quirk of her own, Grace was unreasonably susceptible to feeling sorry for this particular person who, in my experience, had been totally self-centered and mean. But pointing this blind spot out to her at this juncture was probably fruitless. *What to do? What to do?*

Stepping back from this abyss, I turned in my mind to face an even deeper chasm: poverty and unemployment in my seniority just as the housing bubble had popped and the economy was heading over a cliff. I had run out of unemployment compensation, and my savings were just about depleted. I no longer had a father I could count on for subsidies, and my only sister was living a hand-to-mouth existence (in Hawaii, it's true, but nonetheless . . .) My mobile lifestyle and former ambitions had left me without a community, without true friends, without any sustainability at all in my now declining years. *Where to go? Where to go?*

I sighed deeply while Grace watched me anxiously.

"What am I supposed to do if I find her? I can't drag an independent adult back here. What if she resents my looking for her?"

"I think you'll know what to do when it comes to that," Grace said, her large golden brown eyes full of trust. Suddenly I was reminded of my old pooch Phunky and I grabbed a detour.

"Grace, why didn't you tell me, when you gave me Phunky, that dogs don't live very long?" I credited the loss of Phunky for sending me spiraling into the funk that precipitated my abrupt departure away from Baltimore and my life with Grace.

"Oh, Xavy, I'm so sorry. I thought you knew."

"I didn't know," I complained. "We never had dogs. Dad was allergic." This old shock, of course, was one more reminder of the ties that Grace could bind me with. What kind of life lesson was she plotting for me with this proposed adventure? Did I really want to discover that poor Liza had committed suicide or run off with a misogynist circus clown? "I still miss her," I added, about Phunky.

"Then you can empathize with how Durga feels about Liza's departure."

Grace's ability to turn the tables on me never ceases to amaze. This was such a sideways leap that I didn't even bother to argue against the logic of comparing a child to a pet. I certainly couldn't maintain that Phunky wasn't a person. It was time to run up the white flag. "Ok, ok," I said, "I'll meet with her—Durga, that is—but only if you're there too, and only after I've gotten a moment to catch my breath." Grace looked enormously relieved. I guessed she'd oversold my investigative skills to win SanDurga over, and now didn't want to disappoint her friends. I, on the other hand, knew only too well the limits of my sleuthing abilities. Apparently, though, other options for a solution were remote. They didn't want the police involved, and now I could understand why. There was no crime. It wasn't even clear there was really a missing person. But if this newly minted Hindu goddess was willing to pay me, I was willing to search. If for no other reason than to avoid what my grandmother used to call "the poor house."

Just then a large white cat strolled into the room, jumped into my lap, curled up and started purring. Grace smiled. I tentatively reached down to scratch behind his ears, like you do with dogs, and the cat rewarded me with an even louder purr. "He likes you," Grace exclaimed. "He doesn't like everybody." That, I suspected, was flattery. I couldn't imagine this cat rejecting any warm lap. Still I felt somewhat honored.

"What's his name?"

"Zoom."

"Ah, no wonder. A 'Z,'" I said. We both laughed. Not only a Z but a fat cat of the white persuasion—even more politically incorrect than yours truly.

"Somehow he doesn't look like a 'Zoom,'" I said, maintaining my skeptical demeanor. "How did he get that name?"

Grace gazed fondly at him. "He was a lively kitten."

Chapter Three

MEETINGS

I woke in a panic from a dream where a very large, elongated Sandra Durga was lifting a rather small me up in the air. I dangled from her fingertips like a piece of used tissue or a dead mouse, about to be tossed into the trash. The sheets were tangled and sweaty despite the chill of the night (Grace and the missing Marcy apparently believed in turning down the furnace at night) and Zoom, my new bedmate who'd been curled up in the crook of my knees, providing warmth as well as companionship, had leapt away from my thrashing legs. Relieved it was only a nightmare but fearful of the dream's prophetic dimension, I leapt up to go to the bathroom down the hall, my bare feet curling from the frosty air. I hadn't figured Mud Season would be quite so frigid. The other side of bucolic Vermont.

As I sat on the cool toilet seat (and I don't mean "kool"), I wondered if Sandra Durga knew that the private eye Grace was bringing in for the search was me, and if, when she found out, she would reject me as the interfering snoop who'd suspected her of murder in the first degree. She, in fact, had been my Prime Suspect, followed by her deadbeat, although interesting, husband. Thus, her treatment of me in my dream. It's so hard to tell the difference between fears of one's own making or genuine threats.

Snuggling into bed, I tried to coax Zoom back onto the comforter, but, now ensconced in a comfy chair, he'd have none of it. As I warmed up, I began to wonder about Marcy and her honey and whether they too would reject me. Then, suddenly, as I tried to reproduce in my mind a chart of Grace's local entanglements, I realized that once you accounted for the "soul companions": Marcy, Ariel; and dismissed the ones who were probably never-to-be's: Sandra and Marcy's current honey, whose name I couldn't recall—Grace wasn't "with" anybody. Grace was free. Grace was partner-less. Could it be that this missing child business was really just a pretext for getting together with me? Again? Was that possible? Hmmm.

Over a healthy breakfast of granola and yogurt, I tried to map out the extent of Grace's Vermont network.

"So how did you and Marcy get connected?"

"She and I were in the same book club."

"Where?"

"Baltimore."

"I don't remember any Marcy in Baltimore."

"She came after you vanished."

"So how did you get to Vermont?"

"Marcy got a job up here and I followed."

"And you both lived here?"

"No, we both had separate apartments in Burlington. Then we drifted apart and I met Ariel. Then I eventually started the school with Ariel not far from here, and since Marcy had moved out here, where there was plenty of room for both of us, I joined her. Then Marcy met Kara, who'd recently moved to Vermont after breaking up with her partner."

"Ykkes. How do you manage to combine such entangled relationships with such stable community?"

"Well, I guess it's because, at least for folks like us who experienced the women's movement, if friendship can survive the various entanglements, that's what lasts."

"Yeah, I guess now that marriage is legit," I observed neutrally, "monogamy is in fashion for lesbians. No more of the old free love days."

"Of course now that we're older and have, more or less, outgrown the sexual revolution of our twenties, that's easier. It's really not about gay or straight—it's about aging. Most of my lesbian friends these days, married or not, are quite monogamous," Grace said. "Marcy and Kara were both in long-term relationships before they got together with each other."

Which left me wondering what was wrong with me. Fickle, I guess, but still pretty loyal. My life mission did not seem to entail long term commitments, at least not of the sexual variety—that seemed obvious. But what about Grace? "I thought Marcy was with you before she connected with Kara."

"Well, before me, she was in a committed relationship for many years. And Kara was practically married for many, many years. They were both devastated when their partners ran off with new lovers. It's one of the bonds between them."

I nodded, recalling that she'd never left me for another person and that I'd left her not for another lover but for a lousy job.

"Really," she opined, "there's no better friend than an old lover."

While I felt this was meant to be comforting, it nonetheless dashed my wan speculation that Grace might want to renew our status as lovers. Even if she did, I wasn't sure it was possible. In my experience, obviously limited, sexual passion rarely lasted more than seven years, much less a lifetime. And renewing such a passion after years of separation seemed like a pipe dream.

Speaking of which, I was about to wander out to my trusty auto, reach into the glove department for my stash and light up for a moment of ecstatic reflection when Grace went to the phone and called Sandra.

"Hi, Durga. She's here. When shall we come over?"

Facing Sandra so soon, even though it had been years since we'd last snarled at each other, was daunting. No way was I going to smoke now. I had to have my wits about me. I gritted my teeth, then brushed them and tried to poof-poof my short do which was sticking up in the back and sagging down in front. Sandra had been nothing if not well-groomed.

After we'd driven along the main road, which was already windy enough for my delicate stomach, we turned off onto a graveled road which twisted and turned like my intestines. Fortunately Grace is a cautious driver, so she rode over the bumps slow and easy. "Mud season," she explained. "Once all the snow melts, these back roads get filled in so they're more or less smooth until next winter."

As we rose higher and higher, I spotted patches of snow under clumps of evergreen trees. Trees of all shapes and sizes crowded up next to the road, many still leafless. Soon the sky opened up, a brilliant blue laced with puffy clouds, the woods dropped back and we entered a high valley with views of mountains stretching off in all directions. "Wow," I commented.

Expecting to see Heidi and her grandfather strolling past their quaint cottage with a flock of sheep, I was surprised when we turned into a curving pasture and Grace hopped out to open a large metal gate set over a cattle guard. I started thinking big rancher instead of simple shepherd. We crawled along a circular drive at the apex of the hill and dipped down toward a long modern house stretched out just below the crest, its entire front a blaze of glass absorbing the morning sun.

"Jesus Christ!" I muttered. "San-Durga must've really fallen into clover."

"Well, yes," Grace said modestly, never one to envy another's good fortune. "Sheila was pretty well off."

"Well off?" I exclaimed, never one not to envy another's good luck. "This looks like a million dollar baby!" I was eager to get a look inside.

Such was not to be, however. Emerging from a simple circular structure behind the house was a tall, heavy set woman with long grey hair pinned back at the neck. She was dressed all in white, white boots, flowing white trousers, and a loose white knee length shirt over a white turtleneck. Wrapped around her and flapping in the chilly breeze was a bright orange shawl.

Breaking into a bright smile, she waved and called out, "Isn't it a glorious day? So warm and sunny!"

It might be sunny, I thought, but it's not my idea of warm. As she strolled closer, I was taken aback to realize this vision of whiteness was Durga. At least sixty pounds heavier than the old Sandra, and, apparently, a whole lot friendlier. Realizing she was about to hug me, I stuck out my hand. She grabbed it with gusto yet still managed to curl her other wrist around my resistant shoulder. "Xavy! How great to see you again!"

Realizing I too was rounder and greyer, I smiled back. What the heck? Everyone deserved a second chance. One shouldn't eschew anybody who knows one's name. Nonetheless I didn't quite believe she was really glad to see me again, given our history. All this good will was being put on by both of us for Grace's sake—as well as, possibly, in anticipation of my willingness to act as a private eye.

She led us into the circular structure which she called her meditation hall. It looked like an adobe hut right out of the southwest, but she explained it was built of straw bales covered with some sort of white plaster. The simple interior was decorated with various altars and statues of Hindu gods and goddesses along with photos of white bearded or bald gurus, all male. In one corner, or cubby, since corners are hard to come by in round houses, was a small table with a tea kettle on it. Around the table scattered on the floor were various sizes and shapes of cushion. Durga invited us to sit down and offered us what she called yogi tea. While they chatted away, I struggled to settle comfortably on one of the largest pillows which resembled a bean bag chair. Finding my balance without sinking down to my neck or feeling lopsided was a real challenge. I finally managed to anchor myself in some sort of yogic posture, my legs pretzeled into a kind of tripod effect. If this was meditation, I was ready to return to the pews of my childhood and just plain kneel.

"So what are you planning to do with it?" I heard Grace ask as I focused my attention back to their conversation.

Durga shrugged. "Sell it, I guess."

"In this economy?"

"Believe me, Grace, there are plenty of rich folks still out there. They're just lying low." But then she groaned. "Why did she have to buy the whole mountain?"

I was still trying to figure out what "it" was. The mountain? Was it actually possible to buy and sell a whole mountain? I thought of the Waltons, but somehow that wasn't quite the right image for what Durga and Grace were discussing.

Then suddenly they both pivoted toward me, as if, somehow, I was the answer to this quandary. Grace sat down with perfect balance on one of the fat pillows. Durga checked the tea pot, then carried it over to the tiny table with three small cups and poured us each some tea. Only when we'd all been served, did conversation resume.

Leaving her cup on the table, Durga went to a small drawer and pulled out some photos. First *Sheila*: a handsome woman with salt and pepper hair closely but fashionably cropped, a penetrating gaze, and a shy smile. Or was it sly? In any case, I found it attractive. She didn't look like a millionaire, that's for sure. She looked like one of us. *Liza,* a slender, lovely girl with long dark hair, straight to her shoulder and a steady but unsmiling demeanor. I was slightly surprised to see she seemed at least part Asian. She didn't look like somebody who'd easily get lost, at least not in Vermont. She looked like somebody, though, who might want to hide. I began to speculate where she might be able to hide easily.

Rather than commenting, I just listened as Durga, now settled in lotus position on another pillow, spoke about her relationship with Sheila (apparently the love of her life), Sheila's character (apparently a saint), and Liza (apparently a devoted daughter). From time to time, Durga choked up and Grace reached over to pat her hand. I didn't doubt her grief. But I did have questions about her relationship with Liza. So after much nodding and admiring of photos, I asked a few.

"When did Liza go missing?"

Durga looked puzzled. "Go missing?"

It was my turn to look confused. I glanced at Grace.

"She left on her own, Xavy," Grace explained, as if she hadn't described Liza to me as "missing."

"When?"

"About a month after Sheila . . ." Durga said, tearfully. I assumed the tears were about Sheila, probably not Liza.

"So when was it you . . . felt . . . she was *missing*?"

Durga started to speak, then broke into sobs. Grace quickly and subtly shook her head at me. Apparently I was coming off as the Grand Inquisitor. I sighed, then hoped it sounded more like sympathy, which it wasn't, than like impatience, which it was. I thought they wanted me to investigate Liza's disappearance. How could I do that if I wasn't sure when, or even if, she had disappeared? Shades of Iris, I thought.

"Durga hasn't heard from Liza in nine months—she left here about this time last year," Grace explained. Somehow her referral to "Durga" in the third person, right in front of her, was meant to clue me in about something, but what I wasn't sure.

I nodded, wondering if I really wanted to take this case, remuneration aside. What if Liza didn't want to be found? What if she was glad to get away from Durga? I thought of my eagerness to escape the clutches of Nancy, my stepmother, after Mom died, and Dad remarried.

"May I ask," I said gently as Durga blew into a tissue. "if you and Liza were on good terms just before she left?"

Sandra looked surprised at the question. I glanced at Grace, expecting her disapproval, but she looked both neutral and curious, herself, to hear the answer. Sandra nodded. "Yes, of course. We really bonded at the end." This reference to Sheila's death set off another round of sniffles.

I understood how hard this must be for her, I really did, but she'd had more than a year to grieve, and, after all, she'd brought me in to start these inquiries. But, once again, as in my search for Iris, I felt like an unwanted intruder in her life. Nonetheless, I persisted.

"So you and Liza were close?"

"Not at first. Not when Sheila and I first got involved. Liza was jealous," Durga said earnestly. "But later we became very close." Something about the way she blinked at this point set off alarm bells. Being myself an accomplished liar, I'm quick to detect prevarication by others. But this was not the time for confrontation, so I just blinked back.

Soon after that, Grace suggested it was time for us to go. I still hadn't committed to taking on this assignment, but I suspected Durga assumed I would. This irked me.

Chapter Four

NETWORK

As soon as we'd gotten past the cattle guard, I began to pummel Grace with questions.

"I still don't get why she wants to contact Liza."

"She feels responsible for her. I'm guessing she promised Sheila on her deathbed that she'd take care of Liza."

"Why would a thirty year old woman need to be taken care of? Is she retarded or something?"

Grace looked at me in that chiding way she has, letting me know that "retarded" was, to say the least, out of fashion. But she didn't, as she would have in the past, enlighten me as to the current correct label.

"Intellectually challenged?" I guessed.

"Not at all. She's very bright—smarter than Durga, I'd guess."

"Smarter than Durga how?"

"She knew to get out while the getting was good."

A puzzling expression—"while the getting was good"—I paused only briefly to ponder it. "Do you really think she's missing?"

"You know that David Wagoner poem about being lost?" I shook my head. "Well, one line says, '**Wherever you are is called Here.**'" I didn't get it. Smiling at my obvious perplexity, Grace added, "Just because Durga has lost Liza doesn't mean Liza is lost."

"So why, if they were so close, hasn't Liza been in contact?"

Grace pursed her lips. "I'm not sure they were ever as close as Durga would like to think they were."

My eyes lit up. "Durga was lying?"

"No, Xavy, she wasn't lying. But she may be deceiving herself, out of loyalty to Sheila. Besides, Liza, after Sheila's death especially, wasn't always easy to read."

Thinking "inscrutable" but reluctant to voice yet another prejudice, I avoided the stereotype and asked straight out, "I gather Liza was adopted from another country?"

"Korea. When she was a baby."

Aha! Immediately I began to speculate that Liza had been caught up in the recent furor from Korean born adoptees about the circumstances of their adoption. A first lead? Uh oh, I was getting caught up in the drama.

Grace didn't notice. "And when I first met her as a child, she was very lively, very verbal, fairly emotional, then became somewhat hidden, as adolescents tend to be. No," she said, answering my unasked question, "even in her early twenties, Liza wasn't shy—that is, until Durga showed up. Then she withdrew. I remember Sheila's regrets about that—wondering if she should have waited to get involved with somebody until Liza went off on her own." Grace sighed. Whether out of empathy with Sheila or from her own single distress, I couldn't tell.

"Well," I announced, shifting gears, "I'm not sure I can take this assignment after all."

Grace slowed the car down to a crawl so she could look steadily at me, something only possible someplace like a back road in Vermont. "Why not?"

I gazed out across a field, its furrows still dotted with old corn stalks. Around it the newly unfurling leaves of birch trees were vibrant in their greenness. "It's against my principles to track down somebody who wants to be on her own—free of interference from her elders." I was expecting Grace to make a disparaging remark about my principles, which in the past had been remarkably fluid, particularly when mixed with moolah, but she didn't. Instead she shrugged, as if I had a point.

"Besides," I added, "I'm not sure Durga's so easy to read either."

Grace stared at me, then focused on maneuvering the car around a particularly vicious series of potholes.

"Why," I asked, "do you suppose she *really* wants to contact Liza?"

Grace pulled up at a crossroads and stopped to rub her face with her hands. "My guess is that she wants to unload the estate."

"Really? Why would she want to do that?"

"Well, she's supposed to renounce wealth, according to her yogic practice."

"So why doesn't she give it all away?" I asked, rather too eagerly. As if I would qualify as a recipient!

"Because of her responsibility to Liza, I guess," Grace said with another sigh. I didn't remember Grace as a sigher, but these were hard times, economically and spiritually, and possibly even sexually.

Resisting the temptation to ask what the estate was worth, I sailed out into previously charted waters. "What happened to our embrace of poverty, downward mobility, equitable distribution of wealth and all that?" My recall of our movement rhetoric on this subject was a bit rusty, but I figured Grace would know what I meant.

She sighed again. "Well, for myself, it was upward mobility. Remember, I was the first and only person in my immediate family to graduate from college? So I, of course, was all for equitable distribution, but, yes, we did embrace simplicity as a lifestyle, didn't we? 'Poverty' sounds like one of your religious dictates."

Ah yes, I recalled: poverty, chastity and obedience, the vows nuns took. None of which took to me, except, perhaps—off and on—poverty.

"I think we were rebelling against excessive consumerism, being slaves to the market. That was before the boom years, when opportunities opened up, even for women, and some of us decided to climb the career ladder."

The "some of us" referred, of course, to yours truly. Grace herself renounced the high life, gave up her college teaching job (albeit as an underpaid adjunct) and took up child care.

"Before all the bubbles burst," I added. "But I gather Sheila's bubble never burst. Did she earn her fortune under the glass ceiling then?"

"No, she inherited it. Her family was rich, rich, rich, for generations apparently."

"Not exactly the kind of person I'd expect you to hang out with, Grace."

"Oh, she was the black sheep of the family, being gay." Grace always had a soft spot in her heart for black sheep—fortunately for me. "And she was remarkably generous. She gifted or hired others on a regular basis, in addition to supporting many worthy causes. And this wasn't just abstract donating. Once she spied a homeless woman wandering the streets and befriended her, bought her meals, new clothes, a couple of rolls of film, and a bus ticket to her hometown."

"Rolls of film?"

"The woman, apparently, was an itinerant photographer."

I wondered if I could be characterized as an itinerant journalist.

"And Sheila never acted like she was better than the rest of us," Grace continued. "Her own lifestyle was simple and unpretentious." That's not how I would describe Sheila's, now Durga's, home, but perhaps it was modest inside.

Now it was my turn to sigh. I used to imagine myself inheriting millions or, just as unlikely, winning the publisher's clearinghouse sweepstakes and beneficently bestowing oodles of it on friends and strangers alike, freeing people from the burden of debt, fulfilling their life dreams, lavishing them, like Oprah, with trips around the world. Bringing myself back down to earth, I observed, "That house didn't look simple and unpretentious."

"Oh, that was after Durga entered the picture—'Sandra,' actually, before there was a Durga."

"Before her conversion to the simple life?" I asked, not without a modicum of irony.

Grace nodded. "Sheila, I guess, was trying to impress Sandra."

"Did she really buy the whole mountain?"

"Apparently." Grace said, then paused, as if contemplating such a move. "For motivation she took a notion to provide sanctuary for other lesbians, particularly single mothers—high up on a mountain top. She wanted to provide light after years in dark closets, visibility and ownership after being disowned, opportunities to scale the heights after being low folks on the social hierarchy."

"And, after isolation, complete remoteness," I murmured. Fortunately Grace didn't hear me. "Totem pole," I said instead, thinking "low woman on."

"A kind of temple to inclusivity, I guess," Grace concluded.

I thought of my recent basement digs: dark, subletted, lonely. I'd nominate myself as a prime candidate for that hilltop retreat, except for one drawback. "So Durga doesn't want to devote her life to making a sanctuary out of it?" I guessed.

Grace nodded in affirmation of this hypothesis. "I gather she doesn't want the responsibility. She's devoted to keeping her life simple and pure, without a lot of entanglements."

Internally I began to scoff at this obvious ploy to avoid hard work when I realized I'd probably feel the same way myself. So, instead, I imagined the devoted daughter Liza taking on the responsibility of fulfilling her mother's dream. Then I recognized a potential fly in that ointment, the same fly which threatened to spoil my own aspirations. "By the way," I asked, "is Liza a lesbian?"

Grace glanced at me as she guided the car through and around the bright green hills. She shrugged.

This led to a long, winding discussion about the roots of gayness—whether it is, in any way, hereditary—causing us to speculate about aunts and uncles who might or might not have been in the closet—environmental, biological or accidental? Were people gay because their parents wanted a boy instead of a girl, or attracted to *like* rather than *different* because of some birth anomaly, or with that penchant because they'd been closer to their sister or mother than their father or brother when they were young? Was gayness a choice or was it, as some theory insisted (especially in opposition to homophobic condemnation), as out of our control as the color of our eyes or skin? Bisexuals like myself, I argued, have a choice between male and female lovers.

"But do you have a choice about being bisexual?" Grace countered.

Despite this discomforting observation, I felt relieved she no longer regarded me as a renegade lesbian, or worse, a coward, as I suspected Yuggie did (my own sister!). I felt relieved she recognized my genuine propensities, messy as they were. It wasn't that I wasn't a lesbian; it was just that I was both, tro then mo, at different times. Probably more mo than tro, but not entirely.

Secretly, of course, I believed almost everybody was, at least potentially, bi-sexual—as well as dual gendered, excluding those whose obvious aversion to the opposite sex was carved in stone. But I wasn't going to share this theory with Grace whose own sexual preference had never been in doubt. Instead I launched into a reflection on women we'd known who'd been married before they came out.

"I kinda wish I'd done that," Grace said wistfully. "One way—maybe the only way in those days—to have children of my own."

The reason I myself had avoided marriage was just the opposite. Lesbianism had been a convenient, safe form of birth control. But I could feel for Grace; she would have been a great mother.

In the old days, I recalled as we drove along, choosing as a single mother to have a child on your own wasn't much practiced. In fact, at that time, children were being taken away from mothers who'd come out, lest their children be indoctrinated into their perverted lifestyle. They were snatched from devoted mothers and given to their mostly indifferent or overworked fathers and taken care of by underappreciated grandmothers or underpaid childcare workers. Now it's quite common to have a child on your own, or with a same sex partner, but in those days, with job prospects for women so scarce, a husband seemed essential for comfortable motherhood.

Steering away from Grace's regrets, I headed for the topic of women we'd known who'd come out, then gone back in to marry men, sometimes to raise families, sometimes, not to. Grace and I both relished the particulars, especially the personal ones. Whereas in the old days the personal was political, in our current lives, the political was personal. This exploration led us along a stream of gossip which carried us back to Grace's place.

As we drove up the driveway, I relished the opportunity to spend time alone with Grace. I was eager to investigate her current romantic or sexual liaisons. But first I was even more eager to have a date with my pipe. I needed some time to consult my intuition, and nothing works better for that than a good smoke. What meditation is for Durga, service is for Grace, ritual is for many folks, is a deep inhale for me.

Imagine my surprise to see a blue car parked at the top of the drive.

"They're home!" Grace said with surprise. "I'd forgotten they'd be back tonight." Did I hear a pang of regret in her voice. Was she simply bemoaning her memory lapse or had she hoped to spend some time alone with me?

Pulling bags out of the blue car were two attractive women. Marcy and Kara, I assumed. With them were two dogs, one black and white with an ear which stood up and an ear which flopped over, and the other a golden with large, luminous brown eyes. The women each gave Grace a hug, while the dogs wriggled in for pets all around. Then the women turned toward me as I unwound myself from the front seat and settled my stomach from the twisty drive. The tall, slender one with short hair, glasses and radiant smile strode over and shook my hand as Grace introduced her—Kara. Apparently shyer and slower, the other one, who looked somewhat older, smiled graciously and took my hand. Her hooded blue eyes twinkled as she said, "So this is the mysterious Xavy. Welcome."

Mysterious? I liked the sound of that. "Marcy, I presume," I said solemnly, feeling like Stanley encountering Livingston (or was it the other way around?) in the sub-Saharan jungle. Her penetrating gaze was somewhat disconcerting. I guessed she'd heard a lot more about me than I knew about her. After all, she'd been close to Grace for a long time and had, no doubt, ample opportunity to hear all about Grace's litany of former lovers, whereas I had been ignorant of her existence until just a few weeks ago.

So, my pipe and ponderings put aside for now, and my hopes for a tete-a-tete with Grace dashed for the moment, I found myself sitting with them around the kitchen table hearing about Marcy and Kara's trip to the coast of Maine.

"We had to have our periodic hike along the marginal way," explained Kara, "being of the marginal tribe."

"The Marginal Way," explained Marcy, "is a popular trail along the ocean. It looks out over beach and rocks and crashing waves, and sometimes you can see cormorants, seals, and, if you're lucky, whales from there."

"Sounds lovely."

"Did you stay at the gay boys' B&B?" Grace asked.

Kara shook her head. "Too expensive. No, we got an off-season deal at the same motel we stayed at last time."

For the next hour Grace and I listened companionably while Marcy described the incredible sunsets over the ocean and how she sometimes missed that phenomenon she'd grown up with in Arizona of watching the sun set under the horizon.

"In Baltimore, it disappeared behind buildings and in Vermont it goes behind the mountains," she explained. "You don't get that effect of watching it slide down beneath your feet so to speak. That's only possible in the desert or by the ocean."

I drifted off into speculation about how the early explorers realized the earth is round when Kara started waxing poetic about a book on bees she'd been reading. "It's amazing how they've evolved from a small band of insects which got wiped out by winter almost every year into such sophisticated colonies. Eventually they used the embryonic sacs in which they raised their infants as storage containers for their honey and pollen. They actually learned how to protect their food from spoiling by sealing it in with the wax."

"Sweetness and light." Marcy quoted some dead poet on the contribution of bees: honey for sweetness and wax candles for light.

And stings, I added to myself. Ever since I discovered my allergy to bee stings, I had a healthy respect, if not a great appreciation, for their power.

Conversation buzzed about how all the worker bees are female, how the Queen mates in air with several "lucky" drones, who then immediately expire. Kara explained how the drones had evolved from the princes of the hive—fat, lazy, and spoiled, waited upon by the females—into drones driven out of the hive by starvation when their procreative potential failed. Much as I could revel in their comeuppance regarding status, I could also empathize with the fate of those unemployed or retired bees, cast out for no longer performing productively for the larger collective. At that point, gender was irrelevant.

"Sounds like the Borg," I ventured.

"No," replied Kara, picking up my Star Trek allusion. "The Borg are only separate cogs in the larger machine. The bees are more individualized. They develop different skills according to different capacities. Some are remarkable foragers, others, amazing navigators or dancers. Their dances are actually messages about where the best sources of pollen are."

"Still it raises that old question of matriarchy versus democracy," commented Marcy. "Must our human society have queens, workers, and drones in order to survive? Is a matriarchy a fitting substitute for patriarchy?"

"I'm opposed to any archy," Grace said. "I'm for diversity *and* equality."

At that point Grace and Marcy veered off into an all too familiar analysis of why our country is going to ruination and decadence, while Kara, whose bent, I suspect, is more scientific and environmental than political, and I, whose bent is more investigative and quirky, started to fall into separate stupors.

"Opps," Grace finally said when they started bashing twitters and tweets. "Sounds like old fogeydom is setting in."

We all laughed, stretched and went off to our respective beds.

The next day, over breakfast, Kara, who was a writer, started quizzing me about my purpose for being in Vermont. I treaded carefully, avoiding pitfalls of unemployment, the sad decline of journalism, and the dearth of long term meaningful relationships in my life. I tried to downplay my experience as a private eye as well as my need for financial support. Friendly and gentle as her questions were, they were nonetheless probing. She left no stone unturned in exploring every angle of this potential assignment. In terms of investigative skills, I'd met my match. No matter how deftly I deflected the questions back on Durga or flipped them over to Grace, Kara persisted. She wasn't just curious about Durga's quest; she wanted to find out who I was. I felt both flattered and disconcerted.

When I finally acknowledged that Durga did indeed want to hire me to track down Liza, Marcy who'd been quietly standing at the stove frying turkey bacon, snorted. I immediately started back-peddling, explaining that I wasn't sure I wanted that job.

"She should just let that child alone," Marcy muttered.

Why does everybody keep insisting Liza was a child?

"Aren't you worried about her?" Grace asked as she measured out spoonfuls of coffee into the coffee maker.

"She'll contact us when she's ready," Marcy said. "She needs a break. First she had to lose her mother to Durga. Then she lost her mother permanently."

"But this is her home," Grace countered.

"Yes, but if I were of Asian descent, I might prefer to be someplace where I looked like other people." This produced a collective sigh. Even in liberal Vermont, apparently, being a minority made you stick out like a sore thumb. I made a note to talk to Marcy later about where Liza might have gone to find such solidarity. And I wondered how, if I took the assignment, I might enlist Kara's help. Meanwhile talk turned to food and the "eat local" movement in Vermont. As they waxed poetic about it, I ticked off in my head all the things I love to eat which are not grown in Vermont, starting with avocados.

After breakfast Marcy slipped out to walk her dogs. I asked if I could tag along. Everyone cautioned me to wear the sturdy boots Grace had loaned me. We headed up a muddy path through a meadow, the dogs dashing here and there, sniffing and digging at various spots.

"So you don't think Durga should be looking for Liza?" I eventually asked.

Marcy looked me over, wondering how far I could be trusted. Then she shook her head. "She and her mother were very close, as you might imagine." I nodded. As a motherless child I could only imagine. By the time I was Liza's age, Mom and I had both been long gone. "They'd been each other's prime support for most of Liza's life. It was hard for Liza to break away. She only went as far as Burlington to attend UVM." University of Vermont I assumed she meant, noting that in local eyes "Ver" and "Mont" must be separate words, if each was entitled to a separate letter in university parlance.

"Didn't Sheila's relationship with Durga helped free up Liza?"

"You might think so, but no, it just made Liza more clingy." Marcy paused to call the black and white dog away from rolling in what must have been some irresistibly pungent detritus. "Liza was devastated when Sheila died, but that also propelled her out of here."

"So why do you think Durga wants Liza back?"

"I don't know. Maybe she just wants to know where she is. We all would, actually. But once Durga gets an idea, she's like a dog with a bone. She won't let go of it, even when it's a bad idea."

"Why is it a bad idea?" I asked, gingerly stepping over some deer pellets.

"The child needs to find her own way. There's nothing Durga can give her that she wouldn't be better off finding on her own."

"Money?" I suggested.

"Exactly," Marcy said. I waited for more explanation, which was not forthcoming. I began to see how understated she was. She made Grace look like a burbling fountain. I wondered what their relationship had been like. Was still like, for that matter, since they now lived together.

"I'm wondering, if you don't mind my asking, why you all keep calling Liza a child. Isn't she a grown woman?"

Marcy smiled. "I've known her since she was six years old. I guess—"

"So you've known her longer than Durga has."

"Yes, I helped take care of her. Before Durga came along, I was one of her extended family. For all her financial security, Sheila was somewhat clueless when it came to raising children. As the eldest in my rather large family, I knew a lot about childcare."

"So in some way she's your child too."

Marcy glanced at me, surprised at this display of empathy. Don't I look like the empathetic type? "She's more our child—me, Grace, Ariel—than she is Durga's, that's for sure." There was a flash, but only a glimmer, of bitterness in her words. "When she was a sullen teenager, difficult for Sheila to manage, Liza often fled to us. When Durga came into Sheila's life, and more or less pushed Liza to the sidelines, we were Liza's refuge."

We hiked along the path in silence as it rose toward a wooded ridge. The dogs had vanished, but Marcy seemed to have a sixth sense where they were. From time to time she whistled at them, as if to draw them back from some steep ravine or neighborly trespass.

"So aren't you worried, or hurt, about Liza's disappearance?"

"Hurt maybe. Worried, no. Liza is more than able to take care of herself. When she finds her own path, I just hope it leads her back this way at some point. We do miss her."

At this point I decided to drop all my snooping and just enjoy the hike. At least to me it was a hike. For Marcy and the dogs it seemed to be just a morning stroll. When I found myself puffing at the top of the ridge, I decided for the umpteenth million time that I better get myself into shape. Trouble was, at this stage of expanding middles, it was hard to know what that shape was supposed to be anymore.

Chapter Five

FOLLOWING

I woke from what felt like a message dream. Some mythic animal like a unicorn or a lion was giving me a clue—but what? All I could remember when I woke up was "Follow . . ." Follow what? "Come, follow, follow, follow, come follow, follow *me*"? In which case who was "me"?

Did Liza secretly want me to find her? Or was it "follow the yellow brick road"? Did I really want to go to Oz, having already been zapped by the wicked witch ("I'm melting too!") and having already been disillusioned by multiple wizards? Wouldn't I rather just settle down in Kansas? No, the yellow brick road wasn't it. "Follow the money"! That was it. That old saw of investigative journalism. How could I have forgotten it so soon my unconscious self had to remind me?

I waited eagerly for Grace to recover from her morning stupor which could easily turn grumpy when disturbed too early. I'd woken too late to accompany Marcy and the dogs on their morning walk, Kara was apparently sleeping in, and Grace was still stumbling around in the kitchen, so I bundled myself up to ward off the chill and wandered out to the barn where I discovered a workshop full of various pieces of colored glass, a few small machines for cutting and grinding the glass, and a colorful array of houses, vehicles and landscapes constructed out of bottles, plates, glasses and other found objects. Who was the creator? I wondered.

Then poking around the rest of the cluttered barn, I discovered, behind an old barn door, a hidden room within what seemed like an old animal stall, with walls of rough cut lumber, windows looking out onto a meadow, and a small wood stove. Inside was a tiny desk, a rocking chair, a few books, objects from nature, and several candles. Someone's secret hideaway for meditation or writing, I suspected.

Finally from the barn I saw Grace step out on the front porch of the house and glance around as if looking for someone. When I moved out of the shadow of the barn, she looked pleased and waved to me. Pleased she was pleased, I strode up the hill toward her when she called out, "Durga just phoned. She wants to know if you are going to take the job."

In a flash, simply on the basis of my fuzzy dream, I made my decision. If somebody, even just my own psyche, was telling me to "follow," follow I would. But I waited until I was standing on the steps looking up at Grace before I made my announcement. "Yes, I am," I said. Surely if I follow the money, I thought, I'll find Liza. "but I need to ask Durga something first."

Grace looked pleased. There's nothing she enjoys more than helping friends help other friends. She gave me Durga's phone number then vanished, I suspect, to loiter in the hallway to listen.

"Durga," I said when she answered, "I'll take the job. First thing I need to know is about the money."

She launched into what seemed a well-rehearsed contractual negotiation for paying me, along with a generous expense account. I was pleasantly surprised.

"No, no, I mean Liza's money. Did she get a lump payment from Sheila's estate or did she inherit by some other means?"

"She's got a trust fund. Sheila set it up for her when she turned twenty-one, before I entered the picture. I really don't know the terms of that fund."

"Do you know how she gets paid?"

"No, I don't. As I recall, there's a limit to how much she can withdraw each year."

"Do you know which bank?"

"No, but I suspect it's the same bank where Sheila did all her banking—Vermont National."

"What I'm wondering is whether we could trace her whereabouts from where she made her last withdrawals."

"That's a good thought, Xavy, but I don't have the account number or any information about what kind of account it is. Sheila and I never had a joint account or anything like that, so there's no reason the bank should share that information with me."

"Are you her . . ." I hesitated to be so crass as to remind her of Sheila's death and her wealth in the same breath, but it's not as if she hadn't been dealing with this reality for the past year, "heir?"

"The estate is all in another trust and I am the key trustee." I had no idea what that meant. "Even though Sheila and I did have a civil union, we never had time to get married before Sheila got sick. Vermont didn't allow gay marriage until about a year ago. So Sheila stuck with her other strategy, setting up a trust with me as the prime trustee, mostly to avoid my having to pay exorbitant inheritance taxes but also to protect me legally."

This was all over my pauper's head, but I was canny enough to ask, "And you're the sole trustee?"

"No, Liza's included, as well. That's one reason I . . . ."

"You want to contact her," I finished for her in a neutral tone. "Of course." I didn't want Durga to suspect I suspected her motives. But clearly, to her credit, absconding with all the money wasn't one.

"Well, I'll check with the bank and see if I can find anything," I said woefully, out of respect for this morbid context through which I was trying to follow the money. Without a bank account number and some sort of authorization, I doubted very much if the bank would give me the time of day. Even if I were in the F.B.I., I'd have to have some clearance. Where were those fine folks from *Without a Trace* when I needed them?

"You may have to go to L.A., Xavy," Durga said. "All expenses paid, of course."

"Los Angeles?" I said without much enthusiasm. I had only been there once before and had freaked out driving on the mega multi-laned freeways. "Why?"

"That's where Liza went when she left here. It's the last place we heard from."

"Ok," I said. "Let me think about that." After I hung up, Durga's use of the word "we" hung in my mind like "follow" had earlier. From the way she said it, I guessed the person Liza contacted from L.A. wasn't Durga. Otherwise she would have said "I."

Sure enough, I found out from Grace over breakfast that the person back home Liza had contacted once she got to L.A. was Marcy.

"Why L.A.?"

"Liza was an actress. She wanted to give Hollywood a try."

"An actress? Where'd I get the impression Liza was shy?"

"She was. But on the stage she was transformed. She had tremendous capacity to enter into the lives of others."

That made sense. She'd been entering the lives of others ever since she was adopted. But somehow I'd been hoping she'd gone off to enter her own life.

"When's the last time any of you heard from her?"

"About nine months ago."

"What do you think happened to her—I mean the reason she hasn't written?"

"Well, I can't imagine it's easy to find work as an actress in Hollywood, so maybe she just didn't want to confess she's working as a waitress or something." I thought of the trust fund but decided not to evoke it. "Or maybe she's just like all young people, involved in her own challenges and not likely to think much about the old folks at home."

Either or both scenarios seemed valid. But neither offered much assistance in tracking her down.

"You have an address for her?" Grace nodded. "Phone number?"

"Phone was shut off last time we tried it. Maybe she switched to a cell."

"Know that number?" She shook her head.

Just then Marcy came in with the dogs. They whirled around their bowls, whimpering in anticipation of the crunchies she swiftly served. Then she turned toward us with a smile, her face ruddy from the fresh air.

"Xavy's decided to help Durga find Liza," Grace announced. Marcy's smile faded to a grimace.

I shrugged. "I'm not going to drag her back here against her will, you can count on that. I may not even share her whereabouts with Durga if Liza wants privacy. But at least I can find out for all of you if she's ok. Or try to."

"I doubt if she'll pay you if you don't tell her where Liza is," Marcy said. Her tone was neutral but the observation was not.

"Oh, Marcy . . ." Grace protested.

"That's ok," I said. "At least I'll get a free trip to California—land of my dreams."

"Really?" Marcy said.

"Not." I clarified. "I almost had to be institutionalized last time I was in L.A."

Grace and Marcy both looked at each other, then exclaimed simultaneously, "Scoop!"

I assumed this was the journalistic equivalent of "Eureka!" and waited to hear what their shared revelation might be.

"Scoop lives in L.A.," Grace explained, "or somewhere nearby."

"She could pick Xavy up at the airport and help her find her way around."

"Maybe she could even put Xavy up," Marcy said, joining in this planning of my trip, despite her resistance to its mission.

"All expenses paid—remember?" I joked in protest. They laughed. "Who the heck is Scoop?"

"An old friend from Baltimore," Grace said.

"I don't remember anybody . . ."

"Before your time, Xavy."

"Is she some kind of reporter?" I asked. They looked puzzled. "Scoop?" They smiled.

"No, I met her when we were both in college working part time in an ice cream shop," Grace said. "She was so good at it, we called her 'Scoop'. We've been friends ever since."

"How'd she land up in Los Angeles?"

"She's teaching out there," Grace said.

"Antioch College," Marcy added.

I assumed Scoop wasn't one of those abused adjuncts, but I figured I'd find out more about her later. Now I had to start planning my trip. One good thing—it was bound to be warmer there. Maybe when I got back to Vermont, spring would actually be here—apple blossom time and all that.

Suddenly, though, I felt reluctant to leave this cozy group. Soon Kara came down with dreams to share, and Grace started talking about her pre-school nature hike and Marcy, after I'd confessed about discovering her barn studio, told us about a new stained glass flower she wanted to make. With the focus off me for the first time, I began to observe their complex interactions—the playful rivalry between Grace and Kara, the unspoken bond between Marcy and Grace, as if they could read each other's minds, the easy physical affection between Kara and Marcy. I just wanted to snuggle in and be part of a pack again.

Chapter Six

WILD GOOSE CHASE

But before I had a chance to snuggle in, I found myself whisked off. On the basis of my flimsy acquiescence Durga bought me a plane ticket from her ample store of frequent flyer miles and I was on my way, driven at first by Grace, to the west coast. I barely had time to repack my small travel bag before we rushed off to the airport. On the way, I saw a V of geese in the sky, honking their way north for the summer. Oh, I mused, would that I had a flock to fly with.

We drove through a late winter (I thought it was supposed to be spring!) snow storm, the white covering the mud, coating the ruts with thin membranes of ice so that just getting to the car without sliding and falling felt like a survival course. All the new green was muted by a thin layer of snow. I hoped it could survive the chill. Over the frozen, silent tundra (I don't know what a tundra is, nor do I really care, although I'm sure someone would be pleased to let me know there's no tundra in Vermont) we sped, zipping into an edge of the Montpelier oasis to stop by the Coop to buy me a "Phoenix" sandwich (a futile wish, I suppose, for me to rise again from the ashes of my former self and take on this mission like the savior I am not) and a "healthy" chocolate bar (to stave off, I'm guessing, although Grace gave no hint of concern for my health, my penchant for less than healthy Snickers bars). This was to supply me for the flight, given the state of airplane food (if one can call it that) these days. Then, plummeting through blowing and drifting snow squalls, we bypassed the mecca of Burlington in the distance and zipped into the airport, just in time for me to encounter a "ground delay" due to weather which guaranteed I'd miss my connecting flight in Chicago.

Graciously parking the car so she could stand with me while they rebooked me through Philly, Grace effectively blocked me from buying a back-up Snickers bar at the newsstand. As she waved me through security, I looked back at her sweet face with some longing. After all we had just reconnected and here I was, being whoshed off, as if trapped in some alien time machine, to another place, another time (Pacific Coast time) and another season—which, come to think of it, had some appeal. I emerged relatively unscathed through the obstacle course of security, having slid past a white-haired woman in a wheelchair who was getting the federal once-over, her crocheted bag no doubt a cover for a bomb hidden in her Bert's Bees dry skin salve. I felt lucky to survive this time without the indignity of a pat-down (In my previous rounder days the guards apparently assumed my extra bulk concealed weapons and ammo, thus necessitating an inspection which proved embarrassing for all concerned) or the anxiety of a suitcase inspection. Needless to say, I wistfully left my stash of smoke behind, safely tucked into bags within bags within bags within my larger suitcase, now lodged under the bed in Grace's guestroom, safe from the prying noses of Marcy's dogs.

Once within the waiting area, I was pleased to discover another kiosk which sold candy bars. Unfortunately they didn't have any Snickers, so I settled for a Milky Way, hopefully a good omen for a successful flight, as long as we didn't end up there. My capacity for the munchies has diminished considerably over the years. Oddly enough, once I discovered my father was not the wealthy capitalist I assumed he was, and finally grocked that it would probably not be my fate to fall into clover any time soon, certainly not by the usual means of heritage, matrimony or hegemony, I realized I better learn to curb my appetites if I wanted to survive into the current century, and as it turned out when the economy went belly up, survive *in* the current century. Thanks to a healthy round of poverty, stomach aches, and some meditation, I actually managed to slim down some, not to the point of svelte, mind you, but enough so that I could look in a full-length mirror and not gasp. This slenderizing, along with deep interrogation of the consumerism ripe, as well as rife, in our society, however, occurred just about that point in my life when we older folks begin to start melting. So despite the trimming, and even though my own melting hasn't been as bad as it could have been, it's not exactly a pretty picture, if you want to be ageist about it. Which I'm sure you don't. Being snarky about old folks is at least as unsatisfactory as being snide about children. I mean, who needs to feel *that* superior, especially given how aging, as opposed to class, gender, or race, is something we're all heading for eventually?

Anyway, after purchasing and consuming the Milky Way as a way of dealing with the stress of rushing to the airport only to miss my connection, I whiled away the time before my flight to Philly by buying another candy bar, then reading trash magazines (I never buy them, heavens forbid, but fortunately none of the good folks who work at these tiny newsstands seem to care how much browsing people do), catching up on my two favorites—Angelina, one of the most unjustly trashed actor in Hollywood as she jets around the world with her stalwart star of a husband and many multi-rooted kids; and spunky Sandra, with her trashy ex and her cute new one. I suppose I'm soft on both of them for several reasons which have nothing to do with their acting ability: they're both great to look at, rebellious in their own ways, and, icing on my ambivalent cake, they've both had their flings with women (Sandra, perhaps, only through very public sexy kisses, since she seems drawn to some very macho men). As I scour the magazines for new gossip, I'm crushed to discover that Sandra's new date, recently voted most sexy man in America (although I doubt Mexicans or Canadians were included in the voting), whom I'd just seen in some witty romantic comedy, is still in love with his ex and so not available to Sandra and her newly adopted son from Africa. *But it was so promising!* And I don't believe a word of the slander awash around poor Angelina, about her affairs, her drug use, her neglect of her many children. *Nonsense!* I muttered to myself, startling a man next to me reading the Wall Street Journal. I shuffled a bit to the left and read on.

Finally, becoming weary of the trials and tribulations of the rich and famous, I looked for a paperback to read on the plane. Something mysterious but not violent. But unfortunately blood and guts screamed from every cover. I searched in vain for a new John Grisham or a novel which promised to be warm and heartfelt. Fiction, I'd discovered, is more likely than non-fiction to be reassuring that way. You can crawl into fantasy and settle down in ways you can't with facts—as long as it's not a thriller. Then I recalled the book Grace stuck in my bag at the last moment, something light, she said, to read on the journey, assuring me it was not "too" violent. When quizzed, she admitted there was some "brutality" toward the end, and of course a rather unpleasant murder at the beginning, but the latter was unavoidable and the former, justifiable, and in between was all thoughtful reflection and witty conversation. So I settled for that option, which meant saving a few dollars, figuring I could skip the beginning and end and focus only on reflection about events I'd skipped and conversation about people I'd avoided meeting.

Then, as the crowd thickened, I grabbed a seat near the gate's check-in counter and surveyed my fellow passengers, trying to spot people I least wanted to sit next to: a woman with a cute but constantly whimpering dog trapped in a tiny carrying cage; a quarreling middle-aged couple; a very large, very square man wearing a bulky plaid hunting jacket. Glancing around, I was amazed to see lively groups of tanned youngsters attired in mere t-shirts, while I was bundled in at least four layers of clothing. Their lithe bodies and bright smiles suggested they were on vacation. Who, I wondered, would come up north for vacation when the Caribbean beckoned so temptingly this time of year? Then, when I noticed some fancy boots on one fellow, I got it: skiers. No wonder they looked so cheerful. It had just snowed. One person's blizzard is another person's adventure. A good reminder to stop feeling so put upon and start looking forward to this new quest. *California, here I come!*

To get there, however, was more like going steerage than luxury liner. Because I'd been rebooked, my seat selection was limited to the rear of what turned out to be the tiniest of puddle jumpers, one row of single seats on one side of the plane and two seats across the aisle. The last row, I need hardly remind you, is right next to the one tiny bathroom, source of a constant flow of passenger odors. Not only that but when you're in the last row you can't push your seat back; you're stuck at a right angle for the entire flight. And to top it off, my seatmate (no, despite all my fervent prayers, I didn't get the single seat in my row) was the large, square man I'd spotted in the waiting area. And since my seat was next to the window there would be no escape. He turned out to be, inside this skinny plane anyway, even larger and squarer than he'd seemed in the waiting room.

I couldn't help but feel sorry for him as he bumped his head on the luggage rack and surveyed the shrunken target of the seat. Once he wedged himself in, pressing his mammoth arms into the limited space between us as he fastened his seat belt, there was no way I could get out, much less breathe easily. Even though it was close to noon by this time, I decided to forgo eating my lunch until I got to a place where expansion was an option. So for the duration of the flight, I sat back, tried to relax and enjoy the flight as both the flight attendant and later the pilot exhorted me to do, and glued my eyes to the paperback Grace had given me, squinting through the murder until I could enjoy the witticisms of the detective, fortunately a woman, and fortunately rather good-humored as well as remarkably sharp and gutsy. If in my days as a "private eye" I had ever been as plucky and perceptive as this current crop of female detectives, who knows what my future (now my present, alas), would have been? Surely not my current state of indolence, insolence and insolvency . . .

But as the plane bumped and shook in the frosty air, buffeted by winds that seemed intent on pushing it backwards or hurtling it to the ground, I felt thankful just to be alive, and even grateful for the bulky presence next to me who, if in the unlikely event of a water landing, might be able to pull me out of the wreckage, as well as keep us both afloat.

To secure his engagement in such a rescue effort, I switched from alienated traveler mode to interviewer, asking him about the book he was reading on the green economy only to find out he was an environmental engineer. Soon we were talking about peak oil and alternative sources of energy. I told him about the boy I'd recently heard about on the internet who'd figured out, in a school science project, that trees get energy from the sun by arranging their leaves in a Fibonacci sequence.

He was intrigued. "Like in a sunflower. Wow, that might make a good design for a solar collector."

"Yes, that's what the boy realized. If you could make the panels as flexible as leaves, so they could shift as the sun moves, that might allow for an optimum input of sun energy. That's how trees survive, even in a forest with a lot of competition from other trees."

"What we need to do is marry the micro chip to the solar collector," he observed. I was impressed with his openness to new ideas. I'd somehow assumed engineers, especially large, bulky engineers, were rather hidebound. I decided to share with him my idea for a mini-alternative energy device for each household (a chicken in every pot, a car in every garage, a computer in every home, and a mini-collector on every roof—the American dream in technology). Eventually, playing around with this vision, we agreed this device would have leaves like a tree to collect solar energy, a windmill or windsock on top to harness wind energy, and maybe even water running through it to generate steam heat for the house. And inside, a wood pellet stove to use the energy from trees themselves, once they've passed their prime.

"A wind, sun, water tree house," I exclaimed, as if this were a new invention, as if trees hadn't already been doing all this for eons.

He laughed. "A solar, wind, geo-thermal home energy source. Actually that's what some bioneers in Vermont have been saying we need. Only they haven't connected it like this to the design of trees."

"Well, maybe you'll just have to invent one first," I said.

"But it's your idea," he teased.

"That's ok," I said modestly. "If you can make it happen, you can have almost all the credit—as long as you promise to share the credit, and rewards, with that boy on the internet."

"Will do," he said with a smile. "Although he's probably way ahead of us." And to think this was a person I had tried to avoid sitting next to! One more life lesson. Then he pulled out a business card to give me, so we could keep in touch. I had no such card to exchange with him, but I told him I'd contact him when I got back to Vermont. I couldn't imagine actually doing that, but it seemed a friendly thing to say at the time, and maybe, if he did invent our energy treehouse, I might actually send him a congratulatory email.

Just then a huge gust of wind pushed the airplane sideways, producing a shudder of steel and moans from yours truly. I just closed my eyes and tried to breathe for the remainder of the flight, which was mercifully brief.

Finally we landed in Philly and I was eventually liberated, after an interminable wait in the back of the stuffy plane while some tardy agent tried to get the jet bridge in place during which time some passengers waited stoically, some joked, some complained, and I sighed loudly, unable to stand up and flee the accumulated odors to my rear (the rear of the plane, I might clarify) until my seatmate finally started slowly to move up the aisle while we wished each other good luck with the rest of our trips.

At least with the jet bridge we didn't have to, as I anticipated with such a tiny plane, clamber down the rickety stairs onto a icy tarmac in the middle of some bleak parking lot for small planes, miles away from the terminal, and climb into a crowded bus which then deposited us in a proverbial heap at the bottom of a series of steps with our heavy carry-ons. Inside the terminal, I discovered from the monitor that my connecting flight was only two terminals and fifty gates away and supposedly on time. The last time I flew through Philly, however, I'd sat contentedly at the gate which had been announced on the monitor, with my flight destination and departure information still posted at that gate, congratulating myself on getting there in plenty of time, only to discover when I finally pulled my nose out of my book and observed no activity there, that they'd changed the gate without notifying anybody or revising the monitor. Needless to say, I missed my plane and had trouble getting rebooked since it was supposedly all my fault.

So, even though I arrived at this announced gate in plenty of time after dashing through the airport, floating above the moving walkway, riding a couple of escalators, and hopping onto a go-cart when I felt winded, I couldn't relax—no eating or reading of any kind—until I'd bugged everyone I could find who wore a uniform, checked every monitor, asked other passengers, and scoured the area for active agents. Finally feeling assured by a helpful elderly gatekeeper, who promised me he would let me know, in the unlikely event they changed the gate, when my plane touched the ground. At that point I relaxed and ate my Phoenix sandwich, which was delicious. And, having already consumed my second Milky Way on the plane, maneuvering with miniscule movements in the cramped space so I could pull the then soggy bar out of my pocket and unwrap it without nudging my bulging seatmate, I decided to try the "healthy" chocolate bar. My experience of healthy dark chocolate is simply this: The bitterer, the healthier apparently. But one craves sweetness with one's chocolate. This one, however, sprinkled with fruit and nuts, was surprisingly yummy. Hmmm. Maybe Grace understood my tastes after all. Just as I decided to purchase another Milky Way so I could compare the ingredient labels to see why this chocolate bar might be healthier, the kindly attendant called my name to let me know the gate had, indeed, been changed. This necessitated another rapid fire hike through the terminal within a limited amount of time to arrive puffing at the new gate, thus precluding any further purchases, for the moment.

The rest of the flight was uneventful. I declined the opportunity to ride in the middle seat of a three person setup, between two glowering strangers, and leapt into an empty seat in the exit row where I declared with hearty sincerity but very little certainty that I was indeed willing and able to pull open the heavy steel door and be the first person to slide down the emergency chute. This particular row had only two seats per side, more leg room, and easy access to the TV monitor which showed to my delight during the long flight a feature film of Angelina leaping around in some tough but revealing outfit, dispatching what I supposed were the bad guys, even though she didn't exactly seem like the corresponding good girl. I might actually have preferred one of Sandra's romantic comedies, but . . . instead I wondered how many of those gymnastics Angie actually did herself.

When the flight attendants finally served their lackluster snacks, way past the cocktail hour, I checked to see how many squares of my chocolate bar were left and declined everything but a stiff drink, which I paid for with the money I'd saved from not buying a paperback at the airport. (This frugality, despite the dubious promise of a generous expense account, has become second nature, until, at least, I discover some new indulgence.) Eventually the film wound down, to be replaced by stale sitcoms, the lights dimmed, and the next thing I knew we were landing at LAX.

Chapter Seven

SCOOP

At the baggage claim I scooted past several folks holding up signs so I could search for a person who looked like someone Grace would have been serving ice cream cones with during the sixties in Baltimore: a little pudgy, working class roots probably of eastern European heritage, although her last name, Valore, was of mysterious origins, blondish hair going grey, probably wearing glasses, I assumed. Most of the sign holders were mainly men of various ethnicities, probably taxi or limo drivers. After circulating several times, I glanced at one woman holding a sign, a tall, slender, gorgeous—some might say handsome—African-American woman with short cropped salt and pepper hair and a furrowed brow. She was wearing a scoop necked maroon top covered with a gauzy light blue shirt, tied at the waist, over jeans, black sandals and light blue socks. Not particularly fashionable but, after the bulky unisex outfits Vermonters seemed fond of, rather attractive.

Then I did a double-take. On her small sign was neatly printed my name, with the correct spelling. "Scoop?" I asked, pausing in front of her. "Xavy?" she asked tentatively. We both nodded. I'm not sure which one of us was most surprised, but I was too busy castigating myself for my Euro-Centric bias to question, at that moment, why she'd be so surprised. I wondered later who she was expecting. Perhaps someone more overtly mo?

Anyway, as soon as this mystery was solved, her face softened into a brilliant smile. "I just tried to check if your plane had landed," she explained, holding up a cell phone, "but I couldn't get through the maze of the airline's phone system." After a slight tussle over who was going to carry my larger carry-on bag (I absolutely refuse to pay extra to check bags, despite my promised expense account), which she won,

I followed her out into the fresh air of California, clinging to my other bag, which I never let out of my grasp since it holds my baby computer, my cell, my driver's license, and my credit card.

Once outside my first challenge was adjusting to the change in temperature. I felt the heat as a blast, even though it was only 75 degrees, which Scoop described as mild. After snowy Vermont anything over 70 felt like a heat wave. Once I'd peeled off a couple of layers I began to breathe more easily. Fortunately it was still possible to breathe. Last time I was in L.A. the smog was smothering. Either they'd been cleaning up or the wind was blowing the haze out to sea.

She led me out to a shuttle which took us through a massive parking lot to a spot near her car, a sensible maroon sedan which was impeccably clean. I have learned not to judge people by their cars. Or at least to have a more nuanced analysis. Not everybody with a red car is reckless, for instance. Some such drivers are compensating for a rather torpid lifestyle. And so on. Even though I've heard cops stop more red cars than any other color, either because they are actually speeding or because the cops are operating from the same prejudices as I used to. And lately I heard that red cars are in more accidents, but that might be because of the color red, which jumps out toward the eye like no other color, not the skill of the drivers. What maroon stands for, I'm not sure. A tempered fire? Something close to purple (the gay color) but not quite? Anyway, since its interior was a light blue, I decided to stop such idle speculation and concentrate on getting to know Scoop.

She seemed to be an excellent driver, for one thing, which I found enormously reassuring. But as we headed out onto one of the multi-lane highways for which L.A. is famous, I found myself cringing. (When it comes to speed, I'm more comfortable with twentieth century, maybe even nineteenth century mphs.) Panic makes it hard to carry on a normal conversation.

"You teach at Antioch?" I asked, knowing this was true. She nodded. Guessing she was one more exploited, underpaid and overworked adjunct, I waited for the inevitable torrent of complaint about the university, the administrative salaries compared to faculty pay, and so on and so forth. But instead she turned out to be a full-time professor with very few complaints. Her students were half college-age and half adults, most all working during the day and taking classes nights and weekends. She loved serving this particular population.

"What do you teach?" I asked, trying not to notice other cars whizzing around us, to the left of us, to the right of us, zipping in front of us, bearing down behind us, all going at least 85 miles an hour, some crossing as many as six or seven lanes to reach an exit, maneuver toward a split in the highway or just indulge in the fruitless sport of getting ahead of everybody else. I didn't even care that several of them were red. Suddenly I longed to be back in Vermont, bumping over pot holes at 10 miles per hour.

"Mostly post-colonial literature from English speaking countries," she said. "Also creative writing." She made a gesture that was somewhere between a shrug and a strut, complex to follow but easy for me to empathize with. "And women's lit every once in awhile."

Post-colonial? I thought, trying to figure out what countries that might include: African, Asian, Indian—ykkes, I realized, the English really did get around in their day . . . and maybe not just the English. "Does that include the American empire?" I asked, rather smartly I thought, despite my initial wince.

She nodded. Of course.

I dredged my brain for something more intelligent to add. All I could recall from the old days of hanging out with college professors in the women's movement was "post modern" this and that. Everything seemed to be "post"—post colonial, post modern, post racial. I suppose that's because it would be hard to study anything "pre," given as it didn't yet exist. "Do you use a post-modern analysis," I asked.

"Probably more po-po," she said, quite seriously. I was torn between making a joke and wisely shutting up. I decided to shift to a more personal past.

"I hear you were one of the fastest scoopers in the ice cream shop," I said. She smiled. "Somehow after hearing that, I just assumed you'd be a little rounder."

She laughed, a pleasant chuckle which managed to stay low and still sound lilting. "I was even skinnier then. Anyway we never had much time to eat ice cream during regular working hours. Since then I've lost my taste for dairy."

"Lactose intolerant?" I asked.

"I don't think so. No, just fussy, I guess. You know, as we grow older, it just seems sweets and fats don't help us much."

So sensible, and yet I cringed, all hope of stocking up on Snickers, much less organic chocolate bars, dashed, at least as long as I hung out with Scoop. It wasn't clear how long I'd be staying at her place, maybe just overnight. It depended on where the trail to Liza might lead.

The closer we came to L.A. the heavier the traffic and the more suicidal the drivers. Although Scoop wasn't reckless in how she maneuvered the car, she did drive fast, just to keep up with the other vehicles, I assumed, since going slow would be equally dangerous. If I'd known her better, I would have hopped into the back seat and curled up on the floor with my hands over my face, but since I was there in my guise as Private Eye, I didn't think it would behoove my reputation or my investigation to reveal my true feelings so precipitously. So instead I put on my dark glasses, congratulating myself on having the foresight to pack them despite the snow in Vermont, and squeezed my eyes shut for the remainder of the drive, managing at the same time to keep up the chit-chat, even while being driven blind, so to speak, mostly by asking her what Grace was like in those days—apparently a lot quieter and more hidden than she is now, but at times, as Scoop put it, "a real hoot."

When next I opened my eyes we were parked in front of an old time diner, complete with chrome trimming and rounded ends. "I thought you might be hungry after your flight," Scoop said. It was all I could do not to kiss her hand. I was ravenous.

Over a hearty breakfast of omelet, home fries and, sorry, my vegan friends, bacon, sitting across from Scoop who was eating a sensible meal of fruit and yogurt, I began to wonder if she was involved with anybody, some talented starlet perhaps, or maybe some other professor of women's studies? By the time I'd polished off my last bite of potato and munched through the half slice of orange which garnished my plate, I wondered if this was why Grace seemed so eager to connect me with Scoop. Was she trying to fix us up? I felt torn between disappointment at the likelihood that Grace wasn't longing to re-bond with me romantically, after all, and some frisson of excitement at getting to know Scoop. To cover up all this confusion, I decided to go professional and ask Scoop about our missing person, Liza.

"Yes," she said, "Liza stayed with us when she first came to L.A."
Us? I took a sip of coffee and nodded, encouraging her to continue.
"She hoped to become a film actress. I think Grace thought my
partner, Tony, could help her out." *Tony? Toni? Tanya?* At the word
"partner" my short-lived hopes of getting to know Scoop more
intimately immediately evaporated. But what about that potentially
androgynous name? How many ways can you spell "Tony"? Could it
possibly be that Scoop was not, herself, gay? Oh, my, I thought, what
has happened to my gaydar? Have I buried myself in the bowels of
South Boston so long that I can no longer trust my instincts?

My hopes perked back up when, after climbing back into the car
and speeding along another highway, we finally began to slow down,
cruising past the boardwalk of Santa Monica, before winding through
a cute neighborhood of tiny houses, some adobe, some stucco, some
gritty clapboard, some suburban glass and chrome, all featuring petite,
colorful gardens surrounded by friendly walls and distinctive gates.

This place, for some reason, reminded me of *The L Word.* Not
that any of those folks lived in anything this funky, at least not so
far as I got in the series. As I recall, they either lived in gritty urban
apartments or expansive luxurious homes somewhere in the foothills,
even though, oddly enough, this discrepancy in class did not seem to
divide them, at least not as much as all the sexual shenanigans did. But
still, this neighborhood felt like the kind of place that might welcome
a marginal yet thriving gay crowd in search of the American Dream.
How many of my lesbian friends, especially from the mid-west had
escaped to L.A. to find community? Probably half of them, the half
that hadn't fled to Greenwich Village or San Francisco. One more
reason to hope beyond expectation that Scoop was a lesbian (even
though, I needn't remind you, I'm not sure I would call myself a
lesbian. Why I hold the objects of my attraction to a different standard
is worth investigating—later.)

As you might imagine, my hopes were completely dashed when
Tony met us at the door and, before I could recover from the shock,
managed to walk off with both my bags, depositing them in the guest
bedroom (which, heaven be praised, had its own tiny bathroom). Tony
was one of the most beautiful men I've ever seen. He wasn't exactly a
"Tony" type. But I could imagine calling him Tone or even Tune. He
was decidedly male yet had a grace, a gentleness to him that made him

all the more attractive. His short black hair tinged with grey matched his luminous dark almond eyes smiling from beneath expressive eyebrows. His clean-shaven look allowed chiseled features to frame plush lips which added a hint of rose to the bronze of his skin. I'm so weary of that scruffy, unshaven look so many young men aspire to these days. I'm not sure how they manage to keep it from growing into a full beard, which would be more attractive. Looking fashionably unkempt probably takes a lot of grooming. But Tony wasn't a young man; I'd guess he was in his fifties, younger than Scoop by a few years but not a lot. Still quite strong, I guessed, from the way he lifted my book-laden bags without the slightest effort, even though, unlike Scoop, he was a little thick around the waist.

What a roller coaster this meeting of strangers can be. One minute you're locked into trying to figure out X. Then along comes Y and you're completely captivated. Not to mention what's going to happen with Z, for whom you're supposedly searching.

Anyway, I was glad to escape from this quandary when Scoop suggested a nap. After sleeping upright on the plane, I was more than delighted to lie horizontal on the guest bed. When I woke, the sun itself was starting to recline, its golden rays slanting through the window and playing upon the closet door. Groggy for a moment I found myself wondering where I was. Then I remembered: Scoop and Tony's house in L.A. After freshening up, I wandered out into an area I'd only glimpsed from the entry hall earlier—living, dining, kitchen space intertwined, all open to a patio where Tony stood in a t-shirt and pair of shorts at a barbeque, flipping pieces of chicken and vegetables.

He greeted me casually as I strolled out to survey the water feature in the back yard, a fountain burbling over a dramatic array of sea rocks and shells, then following a variety of paths down to a quiet pool next to the patio flagstone. Some water features can sound like dripping faucets or, even worse, make you want to run to the bathroom far too often, just from the power of suggestion. This one sounded quite melodious. Tony confessed he'd worked hard to get that effect, shifting rocks and stones around until they served as harmonious instruments. "Something to remind me of Hawaii," he added.

"You from Hawaii?"

"Yeah," he said with a boyish grin.

I started to ask if he was a native Hawaiian, then hesitated, wondering if that would sound post-colonialist. "Were you born there?"

He nodded. I still wasn't sure if that meant he was actually Hawaiian. "My sister lives on Kauai," I said. "I'm hoping to visit her there sometime . . ." *when my ship comes in,* I thought to myself. "I hear it's really beautiful."

He nodded, then sighed. "It sure is."

"So how did you end up in L.A.?" I recalled what Scoop had told me about Liza. "Acting?"

He nodded. So far, he was turning out to be a man of few words. "But there aren't that many roles for someone like me, especially an aging someone like me, so now I'm in film school. I'd rather be behind the camera these days than in front of it."

"As a director?" I asked, wondering what kind of movies he might want to make. But clearly he was torn between being hospitable to me and cooking the meal. So instead of bothering him more, I just asked if Scoop was out teaching a class.

"Scoop?" He turned from the grill with a puzzled expression. "Oh, you mean Sela?"

"Sela?" Of course, I realized, not everybody calls her "Scoop," in fact, probably not anybody but Grace.

"Sela—the African Eve," he explained.

Now he had me puzzled. "Sela . . . Sela," I repeated. "How's does Eve fit in?"

"Sela is the name, in Kenyan anyway, of the first woman."

"Oh! What about her last name, Valore?"

"Valore is Sela's middle name—she dropped her slave surname, which I believe was Wallace."

I nodded, thinking of the racist governor of Alabama during the Civil Rights era. Who wouldn't want to distance themselves from such an owner/possibly ancestor? I'd heard of this practice before, but only knew women who'd taken their mother's name as last names, like Nelliechild. I wondered about dropping my own patriarchal last name, Xavier, then realized I was more than a little attached to it since it was now, at least in this context, also my first name.

Shortly after that Scoop (aka Sela) arrived with a bottle of wine and a report to Tony about her afternoon class. Over dinner I heard more about Sela's students (I couldn't call her "Scoop" now. It might be affectionate, but it evoked her wage-slave past.), Tony's film aspirations (To my surprise he wanted to create a movie musical based on Moby Dick), and Liza's sojourn in L.A. (Alarmed at how naïve and innocent she was after being raised in Vermont, they tried to protect her from some of the worst pitfalls of Hollywood competition and sleeze). Tony, who was currently unemployed, promised to take me the next day to meet an acting coach, James, with whom he had trained, and who, thanks to Tony, had also mentored Liza. James might have a better idea where Liza had gone.

Chapter Eight

LA LA

The next morning when I woke, the sun was high in the sky and the house was very quiet. Nobody seemed to be home. I was so exhausted I couldn't move. I don't know if it was jet lag or just the strain of adjusting to so many new venues in such a short time, but I realized, once again, that I'm no longer my bouncy, indefatigable self. I got dressed, then dropped back onto the bed and soon fell asleep again. I dreamt I was being chased by a gang of hoodlums through various Hollywood stage settings, one minute dashing through an ersatz Tombstone, past saloons and corrals, the next, in faux outer space, dodging rockets and comets.

What finally got me up and moving swiftly through my morning ritual was the smell of onions and garlic wafting in from the kitchen. Once again Tony was at the stove, cooking us an omelet, full of chopped squash, peppers and tomatoes. Sela, ala Scoop, was off to her office for the day, and he had apparently taken charge of showing me around.

After breakfast we climbed into Tony's little red Nissan pickup about which he seemed to be inordinately proud (What is it about folks and their trucks? No, don't tell me—it's just a rhetorical question.) Once again, I was treated to the terrors of L.A. highway driving as we zoomed up past Hollywood and various canyons toward Studio City. There in a fashionable but not ostentatious condo complex we stepped into James' pleasant living room where he greeted us with a tray of green tea and ginger cookies. As soon as I saw him, I felt a shock of recognition—but from where? He was tall, slender, still handsome with curly blonde hair greying and receding, as well as a surprisingly thick, dark mustache. Had he been a regular on some old

TV series like Magnum? Or maybe he played the villains in films of the 70's, when being blonde, unless you were Robert Redford, made you seem suspect, part of the establishment, obviously a WASP with a dark streak (played by the mustache). He must have been used to this tentative identification because he shook my hand with a kind but resigned twinkle in his deep blue eyes. Noting that, I decided not to go into the predictable, "Don't I know you from . . . ?" I could ask Tony later.

Tony introduced me as if I were, instead of James who really was, some kind of celebrity, a genuine private eye. I felt warmed by the kindness of these men, and stimulated by their curiosity about my investigation. I was tempted to make my search sound more mysterious than it was, more Hollywoodish, but resisted the temptation to play the drama queen. Instead, as I've found it prudent to do, I downplayed both the plot and the skills of the investigator, explaining I was just an agent for a mother who'd lost contact with her grown child.

"I thought Liza's mother died," James replied. I realized then he'd known Liza well enough for her to confide in him. So, a lot better than I did. I shrugged, muttering something about "the other mother," then let him take the lead, asking him instead about her experience as an actress, his forte.

"Liza was talented, as many of the young people who come to me for coaching are," he said with a smile for Tony, who was obviously in awe of his former mentor. "Her experience was slim, but her skills were natural: deep empathy, subtle expressions, nuanced tone and gesture. She was shy in the spotlight, as many actors are." When I looked surprised at this, he added. "Most people don't know that about us, how many of us suffer stage fright or dread personal exposure."

I nodded. "No, I guess we assume that Hollywood is populated by publicity hounds. All mega Leos."

They both laughed. "It is," Tony said, "But celebrity isn't the same as acting achievement."

"The celebrity thing, then, must be torture for the real actors," I observed.

"It kills some of them," James said. "But others learn how to deflect the publicity and pretty much maintain their privacy. After all, even legitimate fame is pretty fleeting." I wondered how much of this ephemeral spotlight he'd experienced himself. Again I racked my brain to recall where I'd seen him. Was it on the big screen or my little TV monitor? "If you're wise," he added, "it becomes a meditation on the transience of things."

"You sound like a Buddhist," I commented. He smiled. A dazzling smile. I was even more charmed as he went on to describe one of Liza's successes: an acting job on ER where she played a doctor. "She was thrilled to get this part, even though it was only for one show. It's rare for an Asian American woman to get such a plum role. She studied doctors, read up on the heart surgery, prepped for days, imagining herself an accomplished medical professional." He obviously enjoyed telling a good story. "Of course, with those TV shows and their last-minute scripts, you never really know what's going to happen until you're on the set. And you can't really improvise without the director and the writers getting upset. So it wasn't until she was about to go on camera that she found out they'd just decided to kill off the patient. Despite all her research, her only patient is going to die. Suddenly she's playing the part of a woman doctor who's either incompetent or very unlucky. Yet there's nothing much in the script to allow her to respond to this loss, no opportunity for any real acting. Liza was devastated, not over the twist in the script which she laughed about, but about how little control an actor really has in this system."

"'Alone and afraid in a world you never made,'" I quoted from some anonymous, to me anyway, poet.

"Exactly!" said Tony. "That's why I want to make films rather than star in them—not that anybody has ever asked me to star."

"It's a very hierarchical system," James agreed. "And pretty cut-throat if you don't have the right connections."

"But you've done very well in it yourself," I said, hoping that I hadn't missed some major scandal about this successful yet surprisingly humble man, whose name I couldn't quite place among the vanishing faces I'd seen on various screens.

He nodded. "But much as I enjoyed acting myself, my greatest fulfillment has come through mentoring young actors like Tony and Liza. I just wish the roles for them were more diverse. But that's changing."

"James is personally responsible for at least 20 Oscars," Tony said.

"Hardly," James replied, as he stood up to refresh the tea pot, disappearing into the kitchen for a moment. I was tempted to whisper inquiries to Tony about James' previous roles, but refrained. We both sat there in reverential silence, contemplating the vicissitudes of fame. Not that I've ever had the opportunity to experience them—but we can all dream, can't we?

When James returned with a fresh brew of tea, I asked him if he knew where Liza went.

"Well," he replied solemnly, "when it became clear to her that she wasn't going to be able to make a living as an actress without some major transformation in our culture or some very lucky break, she contemplated several options. Her mother's death really shook her up, shifted her priorities. As such events can," he added.

I leaned forward, sympathetically. I'd never actually recovered from the shock of my mother's death, even though it had occurred ages ago.

Noting my response, he continued. "She was very drawn to social action like helping the hurricane victims in Haiti or volunteering with Habitat for Humanity. But none of that would provide a living. She also felt pulled to a spiritual practice. So I told her about the Metta Monastery where I've done some sitting."

"Is it Vipassana meditation?" I asked him, reminded of my weekend retreat at the Insight Meditation Society in Massachusetts, which had been an old Catholic monastery.

"No, it's more in the Tibetan Buddhist tradition—with a lineage connected to the Dalai Lama."

I nodded as if I understood what tradition this was. I knew of the Dalai Lama, of course, but I had trouble sorting out the various lineages, which seemed as diverse and tangled as the orders of Catholic nuns, brothers and priests, about which, despite being raised Catholic, I was also woefully ignorant. I recognized the difference between the Jesuits and the Franciscans, but that was the limit of my esoteric knowledge. That distinction might be akin to the difference between Vipassana and Tibetan Buddhist traditions, but I wasn't about to discuss any of this, especially in a place as hip as L.A., lest I reveal myself as unsophisticated about current spiritual practices.

"Is there any chance she might still be there?" I asked.

"Well," he replied, "that was about nine months ago. It's possible, I guess, but not probable, unless she decided to join the staff. I haven't heard from her since." He ran his slender fingers through his thinning hair. "If she'd gone somewhere more exotic, I think she would at least have sent me a postcard." His tone was poignant. The tinge of sadness seemed sincere to me, not acting—but then, I realized, that's probably a false dichotomy. Acting is expression, not pretension even though it usually involves pretending you're somebody else. Durga, I realized, wasn't the only parent substitute who was wondering where Liza had disappeared to.

To cheer James up, Tony asked him to demonstrate for me his remarkable range of dialects. Reciting something from Kipling, James swiftly moved from Irish to East Indian to South African to Chinese to Yiddish to Mexican with a seamless flow of words and tones, without missing a beat, without exaggeration or parody.

"Remarkable!" I exclaimed, delighted. What a skill that would be for a private eye. You could talk to different peoples as if you were one of them. "You must have quite an ear."

He smiled. "Want me to decode your dialect?"

Me? I thought. I don't have a dialect!

"Born in Missouri, probably St. Louis, lived as a child in Atlanta, then moved north, probably with your family to Philly, then as an adult lived in Baltimore, and more recently in New York City, probably Queens, then Boston. Am I right?"

Awed and humbled, I just nodded. Untypically, I hadn't even talked that much. "Kansas City, not St. Louis; Brooklyn, not Queens," I finally added.

"Ahh. "As a fellow from the Bronx I should have recognized the difference," he said modestly, as he wrote out a phone number for the Metta Monastery. Before I departed, I promised I would let him know if I ever found Liza.

On the way back Tony stopped at a dispensary to fill a prescription. Or so he said. Much to my surprise, and hidden delight, the dispensary was a medical marijuana clinic, or so they said. When I looked inquiringly at him, a neutral expression covering my intense curiosity, he mumbled, "Glaucoma" as he hopped out of the car. Not to miss the fun, I jumped out too and followed him into a rather sparkling showroom with an glorious array of gorgeous, green and growing five-fingered plants and buds, all labeled with a variety of creative names and range of prices, graded like Vermont maple syrup from top quality to ordinary by an ascending / descending code of letters and numbers.

Just looking at them put me in an altered state. What a relief to have it all out in the open like this, legit, recognized as medicinal after all. I almost collapsed on the polished floor in relief. Tony, seeing this, buoyed me up, entreating me to breathe deeply while whispering in my ear, "Isn't it fabulous?!"

From that moment on, we were comrades. With the help of my whispered questions he purchased some medium to high grade pot called "The Great Turning," after showing his certification card, which he explained later he'd obtained by getting a letter signed by his eye doctor. I hung back among the display cases lest they suspect he might, as I devoutly hoped, share some with me, despite my almost 20/20 vision and otherwise fairly good health, unless one counted anxiety and stress. Although this openness was very cool, I think I might have preferred the Dutch system by which anybody over a certain age could purchase whatever they want from something more like a café. That way nobody felt like a criminal, even though, I was surprised to learn, even in Holland, smoking marijuana is officially illegal.

Legalities aside, we hopped back into the car, swung by a Deli near Tony's house to stock up for a late lunch, and headed back to the sunny patio, the water feature, and a good smoke. It didn't take long before he was telling me all about his half-written script for the Musical Moby Dick. I almost lost myself in blissful visions of his Polynesian ancestors carving out the long boats which carried them across the Pacific Ocean to places like Hawaii, maybe even as far as the west coasts of North and South America. It was easy to imagine a whale becoming part of this tale, but hard to imagine a Captain Ahab commandeering one of those boats. Maybe that shift in magnitude was what turned the whole plot into a musical, rather than Melville's tragedy. The larger the ship, the harder the fall.

Somehow, as we spoke more about this particular brand of highly intuitive sailors, we ended up talking about gender stereotypes and bi-sexuality. His Polynesian ancestors on one of his many sides sounded more androgynous than one expects from the conventional western sailor. Don't ask me to explain that conversational change of course, but it seemed to flow naturally. Oddly enough, even though I'm wary of smoking with anybody I don't know because the intimacy can feel intense, there wasn't even an itch of desire between Tony and me. It was more like hanging out with the brother I never had. As for bi-sexuality we discussed it only abstractly, him being so solidly tro and me, supposedly, entirely mo. And yet, it was as if we secretly understood other possibilities.

He confessed to me the difficulty of being unemployed, hoping for a call-back from an audition, waiting for some elusive break, taking film classes without feeling particularly challenged—but at least he was learning the basics. Sela never complained, he grumbled, about him strolling around at his leisure while she was running around so stressed out.

"Well, she's probably grateful for all you do around here—cooking, shopping . . ."

"mowing the lawn and keeping the fountain running . . ." he chimed in.

We both sighed. I know the woes of unemployment all too well. No matter how busy, useful, anxious or eager for a job you make yourself, it's hard not to fall into decrepitude, and equally hard not to attract the envy of the employed.

Somehow from there we started discussing our favorite TV shows—*Bones, Without a Trace, the Next Generation* of *Star Trek.* Tony was quite taken with *Dr. Oz.* He asked me if I'd seen the session on medical marijuana, then gave me the blow by blow—another boost to my pothead self. Three-fourths of the studio audience, plus Dr. Oz, believed medical marijuana should be legal. I couldn't agree more.

We spent so much time talking about all this that by the time we actually turned on the TV, the Dr. Oz Show was gone, and news was starting to come in about the earthquake and tsunami in Japan. When they announced that the tsunami was heading for Hawaii and the West Coast, we both pulled out our cell phones and called Hawaii. I couldn't reach Yuggie, but Tony got assurances from his family that the waves were very high but not so far threatening the Big Island. Then we started worrying about the West Coast which wasn't far from where we were actually sitting.

Sela was full of the disaster when she arrived home later that afternoon, having heard all about it on her car radio. As Tony and I sat there glued to the TV, she handed me an envelope with Durga's name on the return address label. I turned away from the heart-breaking scenes scrolling across the screen and opened it. Inside was a blank piece of paper and a new credit card with my name on it. The so-called unlimited expense account. Grace must have talked Durga into it, empathizing as Durga apparently could not, with the difficulty of having to ask every time I needed more money.

With that financial burden out of the way I decided to call the Retreat Center at the Metta Monastery and see if I could come up there for a weekend retreat. That way I could kill two birds with one stone (an expression I hate): see if Liza was there or find out where she'd gone, and possibly get my own life in order so I'd be prepared to face any further global disasters. Then I turned back to watch re-runs of that terrible wave deluging the vulnerable coastline of Northern Japan and listen to stories of the heroic forbearance and kindness of the survivors, wondering what was going to happen when the Tsunami reached us, me suddenly having been transformed into an active "us" by my having flown right into the American edge of maximum impact—other than Hawaii, of course, where Yuggie was.

That, of course, was only the beginning of the disaster stories. Soon followed the nuclear reactor disaster, echoing Hiroshima, the rebellion in Libya, echoing the American Revolution, the wars in Iraq and Afghanistan echoing the Crusades. Proud of the American military helping in Japan, mixed about them bombing Libya, and tired of them occupying Afghanistan and Iraq, my identity as an American couldn't find a reliable compass. But one thing was clear: my own small concerns, the dynamic between me and Tony, the state of my addictions, even my search for Liza, suddenly became miniaturized by those larger spheres of action. If young people in Egypt were ready for democracy, this old gal was ready for redemption. Time for me to move on. Time to go meditate so I could weather these global shudders with more equanimity. Time to face the Mayan end of the known calendar, Humanity's Last Chance, whatever the future might deliver.

Chapter Nine

METTA

On Friday morning Tony drove me to the train where I sat in a back seat by a grimy window watching the golden hills and crowded suburbs of southern California fade away as we wound up along the coast toward Santa Barbara. There, as advised by Sela, I rented a car to drive up to the Monastery which sat on a promontory further north facing the blue Pacific, high above the remnants of the Tsunami which had roared up against the coastline without causing as much damage as some feared. Not here anyways.

On the train I decided against trying to contact an old college friend who lives in Santa Barbara, unwilling with my current dearth of enlightenment to share the dead-ends of my own life in the context of her long term marriage to a corporate lawyer, her lovely and successful children, her own reputation as a sophisticated art dealer. How we ever survived as roommates now escapes me. She's a good person, but my tolerance for other people's *schadenfreude* at my expense has dimmed considerably over the years. So I contented myself with admiring the Spanish architecture, splashes of green, picturesque harbor and mountain embrace as I putted through the town in my red compact (having resisted the temptation to take advantage of my "unlimited" expense account to hop into a silver Lexus convertible).

The coastal drive, once I turned off onto Route 1, was lovely, with glimpses of blue sky, aquamarine water, red-barked pines dancing with the wind, and sandy beaches. Driving toward San Luis Obispo, I recalled it was considered "the happiest place in the United States," so I stopped there for lunch, disappointed to discover the only waitress at the small café where I stopped didn't seem particularly happy. Her smile was friendly enough, but it didn't beam out contentment. Maybe, like me, she was just passing through? Happiness, after all, is not really ever a place, it's a state—of mind, that is. And that, after all, was what I was in search of—although such a search is always marred by the realization that everything flips over into its opposite. Maybe equanimity would be a more fitting goal? Somehow though it was easier to imagine myself being happy than to imagine myself being serene.

Harmony, the place where I was supposed to turn off to get to the Monastery and where I stopped to ask directions from a cranky gas station attendant, didn't exactly live up to its name, but names are even less reliable than reputations. Perhaps, whatever concord engendered by its title emerged only on Sundays? I was sorry to discover that this juncture was still south of the Hearst Castle, so any hope I had of dropping by for a quick tour was dashed. Maybe after the retreat—depending on my next destination. Curious as I was to see the opulence of this American royalty, I had to remind myself that all his wealth came down at the end to one childhood memory: "Rosebud." And I couldn't quite remember now who or what Rosebud was: not a person as anticipated, but an object—a sled, maybe?

Although the Monastery was hardly a castle, its location was every bit as spectacular as the photos I'd seen of the Hearst citadel. It sat high above the waves, atop a dramatic cliff which plunged toward rocky beaches lit with sun as it slid down toward the horizon. A network of trails twisted down from the parking lot toward the beach, past mammoth boulders and stunted scrubby trees. The large grey building sat solidly on the only available flat surface, its stone walls blending into the rock foundation of the cliff as if they had been carved out of the same mountain. A former Franciscan stronghold, it had been purchased by an up and coming Buddhist enclave about twenty years before.

After following the signs for retreat participant parking, I lugged my suitcases up the drive and into the entry of the first building, to be greeted by a perky staff person with long red hair who assured me she'd watch out for my bags while I registered. The length and legalities of the registration forms, assuring MM (Metta Monastery) I wouldn't sue them for any injuries sustained while meditating, and that I was healthy enough to sit for two days, and that I'd pay if they had to take me to the nearest hospital (which obviously wasn't anywhere nearby), and that my shrink approved of my undertaking this venture made me feel I was committing myself to some institution. Which, I suppose, I was, albeit only temporarily. It was amusing, for me anyway, to imagine the possible scenarios which gave rise to each of these directives. I hated to start out by lying (my shrink might have approved my making this retreat if she only knew where I was), but it was only a white lie—fortunately having been raised Catholic I knew how to parse out every little venial sin, like how far outside the church one could stand and still get credit for attending Sunday mass. As I filled the forms, I looked around for Liza. Was it possible she was still here?

Next I got in line behind other arrivals to run the gauntlet of greeters sitting behind a long table ready to orient us to life at the Monastery. The first was a young woman with a pretty face, a bright smile and a buzz haircut. I might have jumped to the conclusion from her do that she was a dykeling, but unlike the old days when most of us of the persuasion either hid our identity or flaunted it, being gay or even bi these days seemed to inspire copy cat hairdos and dress. Whether or not she was gay, she was obviously a goody two shoes, but that didn't bother me in that moment as much as it might have at some other time. Her cheerfulness, albeit rather too fixed to convey real warmth, was a nice antidote to my last encounter with a cranky stranger, and when she assured me I could have a single room because of my prodigious snoring, I felt well taken care of. It was her job, apparently, to provide us with maps of the complex, and directions to our rooms. I may have exaggerated how much I snore, but it was worth not having to share a room with a stranger. I was alarmed to discover I was supposed to have brought my own linen, but when I explained my transient situation, she assured me there were extra sheets, towels and pillowcases, and gave me directions to the linen closet.

The next greeter was quite a bit more matter-of-fact, trying to ascertain what chores I might be best at performing. She introduced herself as one of the cooks. Now she really did look like a dyke in disguise, but she probably wasn't. Chores? I thought. I really hadn't planned to do any chores. We were paying for this retreat, right? I didn't, of course, say this out loud but she read it in my face and sternly muttered about the importance of karma yoga. I wasn't sure what karma had to do with chores, but if sweeping the floor would relieve me of some of my past karma, I was ready, so I smiled at her gamely, hoping my graying hair and somewhat pudgy physique would dissuade her from assigning me to scrubbing the floors on my hands and knees. With some apparent impatience, she passed me on to a tall, lean young man with a bald head and goatee, who, without even looking at me, appointed me to the dishwashing brigade. I was handed a slip of paper with the time when the brigade would be shown how to wash the dishes, shortly before our first meal. I slipped it into my pocket and went back into the hallway to retrieve my bags.

My room, alas, although cozy enough in its spare, institutional way, did not have an ocean view. Instead it looked out on a clothes line in the back yard. I scurried to the linen closet and picked out some green sheets and matching pillowcases. As soon as I made my bed, I had to try it out. The next thing I knew a bell was ringing for the evening meal, and I was late for my dish washing orientation. I arrived at the dishwashing station just as the bald goateed man was giving the last instructions to a group of eager looking people. Surveying the set-up I realized this system wasn't going to be like doing the dishes at home. I tried to slip in unobtrusively, but as the group dispersed, a slender woman in her thirties, very competently put together, asked if I was "Mary Catherine," and when I nodded, stuck out her hand to say we were to be partners for the noon meal dishes. I smiled as I shook her hand, praying she had followed the instructions, apparently quite elaborate, judging from some of the stunned expressions on the people around me. Having entered late, I felt relieved, embarrassed by my lateness but free of burdensome institutional expectations, for the time being at least.

After the evening meal of soup and bread, we had our first large group orientation to the principles and practices of the Monastery. One after another, staff members—none of them Liza—got up to describe the procedures required for everything we would be doing at the place, from meals to showers, from silence to chores, mostly in the form of "do nots." I felt propelled back to Catholic school, as if these were nuns in sheep's clothing. Not only did we have to swear not to violate certain precepts, like no killing, sex, or drugs during our retreat, we also had to pledge everything from silence and eschewing cell phones to removing our shoes and wiping up after our tea balls—and, probably, not picking our noses. I was beginning to feel trapped in a world made for obsessive-compulsives. If I'd asked, they probably had a process for correctly scratching our behinds. By the end of that hour I was ready to flee, having concluded that religion itself was created for obsessive compulsives. All faiths probably started with genuine insights about the divine, but as they became established, they fell prey to more and more fastidious rule-making. Every impulse, every twitch was monitored for optimal spiritual and communal dispensation. Spontaneity was anathema, individuality was to be shunned, figuring anything out on your own was heresy. Such seemed the fate of any institution, no matter how holy. No wonder Liza had fled the joint (assuming she had).

Fortunately I was mollified by the meditation session that followed. Once I found myself the right chair under a window, so I could look out at the ocean, padded with pillows for my tush, my back and my feet, and once the woman in front of me finally got herself settled, I was able to relax and enjoy the two young teachers, a young woman with a Boston accent and a youngish man with an Italian name. As soon as I saw him bowing down to the statue of the Buddha on the platform in front of us, I figured him for a former altar boy. As soon as I heard her voice, I decided her father was a Harvard professor and her Buddhist propensities, a retreat from her family's intellectual predilections. She won me over immediately by reading that Rumi poem about the Guesthouse, leaving me to imagine all my sorrows and meannesses clamoring to be allowed in. "The dark thought, the shame, the malice, meet them at the door laughing, and invite them in."

She went on to share her observation, when she'd done a long retreat somewhere in or near Tibet, that people in Buddhist cultures seemed so much more relaxed than us Westerners. She thinks it's because Buddhism teaches that people are like gems, naturally full of light but maybe just needing a little polishing, whereas Western culture is obsessed with the notion of original sin, that we're all somehow deeply flawed and thus in mortal and constant need of improvement. She hit my particular nail on the head. Even though I realize that within Catholicism all sins can be forgiven, by God anyway, except despair, which is the failure or inability to ask for forgiveness, somehow the sin story usually trumps the redemption story, especially for those of us who no longer go to confession.

So I welcomed the meditation instructions, strove to keep my body still, having already discovered from a previous retreat my restless torso syndrome. I also endeavored to stay awake, my eyes open but fixed on a spot on the floor, my breath steady, my mind on my breath instead of every stray thought that came sailing by, grounding myself in the present moment. What a relief when they finally rang the bowl gong and I was able to retreat to my single bed and glorious sleep. I woke up in the morning with the wisp of a dream about Liza, wondering how, if I was supposed to keep silent, I'd ever be able to find out where she was—obviously not here. Which of the staff persons I'd met might know? Maybe the perky one with the red hair?

The next morning before and after a breakfast of oatmeal, yogurt and prunes, there was no dharma talk (Buddhist teaching), just alternating sitting and walking meditation. Walking meditation for me consisted of walking down the hallway and up the stairs to my room where I then did lying meditation (Don't laugh—there is such a thing) or tried to reach Yuggie in Hawaii by cell phone (I still hadn't heard from her, and despite the fact that the Tsunami had apparently passed by without much damage, I was worried.) By the time the noon meal came around I was well rested and ready to tackle the dishes, after a gaseous meal of cabbage, kale and tofu, bound to make the afternoon's meditation even more challenging, if you know what I mean.

Since we were all supposed to eat "mindfully," mealtimes turned out to be rather grim. Everyone was straining to chew meditatively, placing our spoons or folks down between each bite so we could fletcherize with full awareness. We looked like a field full of discontented cows. Plates greedily piled high with fibrous vegetables sat bulkily in front of solemn faced folks who were not supposed to communicate with each other. It felt a bit lonely. Last time I was on a meditation retreat was with a group of friends who managed all sorts of non-verbal communication and high jinks from exchanged notes on the message board to eye gestures and hand signals. Here there was absolutely nobody with whom to exchange glances or raise eyebrows. I finally stopped eating and sighed loudly.

By the time I arrived at the dishwashing station, my competent teammate was already attired in long rubber apron and green rubber gloves. As I started to help her move dirty dishes from the counter to the sink, she looked distressed and gestured skillfully that I wasn't supposed to touch those dirty dishes, but instead had to don my own separate rubber gloves and touch only the clean dishes, after they'd been sterilized in the washing machine, a huge square metal tank which had to rise to some phenomenal level of heat and steam before the dishes were ready. She pointed to some instructions on the wall, but I never had time to read them as the dishes piled up on the counter and she worked like Charlie Chaplin on an assembly line rinsing dishes and piling them on the racks while I pulled out the steaming, slippery bowls, plates and utensils and stacked them on a cart to be pushed precariously, when full, into the dining room and returned to their assigned places. Quite a system, I thought, with both admiration and intimidation.

Soon, of course, I found myself inventing ways people could get by with fewer dishes—another institutional "improvement" to add to the multiple brainstorms which had probably given such precise rigor to the current routine. The rigidity of institutions, I realized, is built from individual contributions to the overall organization. Maybe that's why we need the occasional disaster, I opined, to return us to more natural behavior. Civilization can really be confining after a few centuries. Yet it's so tempting to add another original layer to those now ossified innovations.

The meditation after the dish washing seemed particularly peaceful. I was only too happy to sink, sweaty and breathless, onto my padded chair and just pay attention to my breathing. The focus for this session was on silence and sound, as well as our own breath. All we had to do was pay attention, stay in the present moment, be mindful of *whatever* happened.

Suddenly a new sound entered the room—ringing out as neither the songs of the birds outside or the shuffles of the people inside could. A cell phone? *Uh oh*, a fundamental *no no*. And it was blaring out from my pocket, playing my own somewhat customized cell phone tune. I'd forgotten to turn it off after my last call to Hawaii. *What to do??!!* If I ignored it, it would go away eventually, but not until everybody around me had traced its source. I considered joking, saying aloud, "Another opportunity for mindfulness, folks," but that would violate the rule against speech. As the phone kept ringing, I could feel in my mind one infraction piling up behind another. Oh, how I wished I could just go to confession.

I tried ignoring it. I felt everyone in the room trying to ignore it. Finally there was silence. A deep collective breath. A bird song outside. Then it started ringing again. Casting down my blanket and pillows, I leapt up and rushed out of the meditation hall as if my life depended upon it. Seeking someplace where I could safely talk, I bounded out of the front door of the monastery and stood on the steps while I answered the phone. It was, of course, Yuggie.

"I wasn't sure if I had the right number or not. Where are you, Xavy?"

"At a silent retreat," I whispered loudly.

"Oops," she said. "I got all those messages from you. I just wanted to let you know we're all right here. Where are you?"

"In California."

"Oh, great. Why don't you come for a visit?"

"I can't. I'm on a job."

"A journalism job?" she asked. I wasn't taken with her skeptical tone.

"No, an investigation."

"Oh?" Normally Yuggie was one of my most enthusiastic fans. But she's never been enamored of my pretentions toward privateeyedom.

"What kind of investigation?"

"Oh, I'll tell you about it later. Grace got me into it."

"Grace? You've seen Grace? How is she?"

Even though I no longer had any claim to Grace, and even though the Pacific Ocean, plus the whole North American continent now lay between Yuggie and Grace, and even though my jealousy of the friendship between Yuggie and Grace was what had pushed me into a deeper commitment to Grace, I was still reluctant to disclose the whereabouts of either to the other. "She's fine," I replied briskly. "But what about the Tsunami? Didn't it hit you all?"

"No, it sort of flooded around us. Just higher than usual waves. These islands are pretty tough."

"Yes, they've been around for a long time, I guess. Climate change is just another challenge. Nancy ok?" My interest in Nancy's welfare was close to nil, but I knew Yuggie would be pleased I asked.

"Oh, she's just fine. Says to say hi."

"Hi back," I murmured, then took a deep breath. "Well, Yuggie, I'm relieved you're doing ok. I better get back to the retreat. I'll call you when it's over."

"Ok, Xavy. Think about it—we're just a hop, skip and a jump from where you are. I'd love to see you."

"I'll think about it." And I did. I wondered if there was any case to be made for Liza having fled to Hawaii. Maybe then I could go for an all expense paid visit.

After that, I had a choice: either creep quietly back into the meditation hall, looking as if I'd just received a distress call of some sort. Or just wander around outside until the next walking meditation, hoping nobody had noticed what the cell phone culprit looked like. I chose the latter, even though I suspected at least one other meditator would not only remember who I was, but would have developed an illogical aversion toward me, not unlike what I had begun to feel about the large man in front of me who compulsively readjusted his sitting bench throughout every sitting.

I wandered out to a bench overlooking the ocean and marveled at the fact that only a few weeks before I had been confined to a basement apartment in sooty Boston yet here I was on the far edge of the western coast facing the remnants of a Tsunami as it washed over the restless waters of the Pacific.

The rest of the retreat passed peacefully enough. The food, despite a heavy emphasis on beans (and me without my Beano!) and vegetables like broccoli and cauliflower (and other such greenhouse gas emissioners), was tasty enough. The talks were inspiring. And I developed a crush on a woman about my age, slender with short brown hair and kind, green eyes, sitting to my left. A Vipassana Romance they used to call it. Even though this wasn't Vipassana meditation, it was close enough. When I wasn't concentrating on my breath, the pressure of my tush on the chair or the twitters outside, I found myself imagining who she was and why she was here. I was also able to scout out the most likely staff person to provide me information about Liza, once the retreat was over.

But I did find myself questioning the point of all this mindfulness. What good would it do the rest of the world for me to be aware of my every breath? What good, in the long run, would it do me?

True, it's good to slow down, to rest, to take time, as they say, to smell the flowers, but wasn't this that fruitless naval-gazing radicals used to eschew? Aren't we all, with this contemporary world in crisis, doomed to anxiety and tension? Isn't that the least we can do for our brethren, particularly those who have the least? Don't we who have indulged in so many transgressions, some public, some private, all selfish in their own way, owe it to our fellow humans, particularly those many who've suffered terrible losses through greedy bankers, natural disasters, and tyrannical dictators, to suffer with them?

As if I'd asked these question aloud, the teachers gradually answered them. The former altar boy spoke of forgiveness, starting with forgiveness of self. Plunging into my habitual well of self-flagellation, I found plenty of things for which I should forgive myself. The real challenge, though, was, forgiving all those who'd injured me. As I ticked them off, I began, slowly, mindfully, to begin to understand why they might have done so, starting with my mother who had the gall to die too early, continuing with my father who had the gumption to remarry somebody I didn't like, and moving on through Yuggie, who had the nerve to be genuinely nicer than I am, to Grace, who'd simply chosen to move on with her life once I'd evacuated from it, and so on and so forth. I found it relatively easy to forgive those I actually love. It's harder to forgive people I don't really like. But even there, thanks to the encouragement of this teacher, I could find reasons for people doing what they did: fear, envy, anger, misunderstanding. I could hardly let myself off those hooks without releasing those who'd hung there with me. Although it might have been a transitory act, all this forgiveness felt like a great relief. It's a burden carrying grudges, especially as they pile up higher and higher. To forgive is to become lighter.

Then as if to explain why mindfulness is important, the other teacher read a poem by Naomi Shihab Nye: *Before you know what kindness really is, you must lose things, feel the future dissolve in a moment like salt in a weakened broth . . . Before you know kindness as the deepest thing inside, you must know sorrow as the other deepest thing . . . . Then it is only kindness that makes sense anymore."*

Yes, I thought, tearfully, only kindness matters anymore. Not success or fame or money or even romantic love. Only kindness.

Loving kindness. Metta. To be kind is to become full of light. I guess.
I hope.

Once the retreat was over, and the whole place started buzzing
with conversation, at a decibel level which suddenly sounded raucous,
I fled from the dining room to find the red-haired staff person whose
name was Melissa. Yes, she knew Liza, but she didn't know where
she'd gone. Liza, she told me, had served a standard six month stint on
staff, but didn't re-up. They hadn't been close though. I might find out
more from Nan, another staff person. Nan, it turned out, was the pretty
one with the buzz cut, the one who'd greeted us so pleasantly when we
registered. I found Nan out in the vegetable garden, weeding. Without
her bright smile, she actually wore a rather pensive look, which made
me wonder what her story was. She didn't know where Liza was either,
but they'd talked about going to Haiti to help with the earthquake relief
effort. Liza, she said, wanted to work with kids, to use the arts to help
them recover from trauma.

Haiti? I thought. *Not Hawaii?!* Hopefully, Durga wouldn't take it
upon herself to send me there. But, still, didn't I have a duty to report
that information to her?

I thanked Nan, wished her well with the rest of her life, and
scurried to my room to clean it up just so, as per regulations, for the
next retreat—with this special cleaner for the sink and that polish for
the mirror. Instead of troubling myself with a vacuum cleaner, which
was in high demand, I settled for a broom and, rather than wrestle with
my next door neighbor for the dustpan, I swept my few grains of sand
into the closet, with the secret message, "Ashes to ashes, dust to dust,"
for the next retreatant's meditative pleasure. Then I quickly repacked
my bag and exited the Monastery, leaving a generous offering for the
teachers.

As I drove out of the grounds along the cliff, I spotted a bench
alongside a trail overlooking a cove, so I pulled the car over and
hopped out to locate in the bottom of my suitcase, hidden in a vitamin
jar, the joint Tony had given me for my adventure. Then I dug a lighter
out of my purse and made my way down the path to sit and smoke
as I gazed out, like an ancient explorer, onto this other side of my
world. Soon I felt full of light, as well as much lighter. This retreat
hadn't gotten me much closer to Liza, but it had gotten me closer to

myself—hopefully now a kinder, gentler self. Maybe perhaps, though probably not, a more mindful self.

Behind me the moon began to rise as before me the sun began to set. A magical moment, this meeting of gold and silver.

Then, hearing a sound, I turned away from the ocean toward the trail, just in time to see the woman of my vipassana dreams tootling along the road above, alone, in a yellow convertible. Had I not stopped here, would I have spotted her sooner? *Would we have connected?* Had I not been here, would I have even seen her and her yellow car?

I turned back to the fluid dance of sunshine and moonlight.

Chapter Ten

UP IN THE AIR

By the time I arrived back in Vermont, my kinder, gentler self felt a bit frayed. Flying these days offers such a plethora of opportunities for violating the practices of loving kindness that it was all I could do to keep a civil countenance. Nonetheless, there were no unforeseen delays, no unfortunate re-routings, and only the usual sardines-stuffed-in-a-can claustrophobia. In Chicago, however, while I waited, crammed in a corner of a crowded downstairs waiting room for small planes as multiple flights arrived and departed, we were all treated by CNN to multiple re-runs about the Southwest plane whose roof ripped off, leaving passengers staring at the blue sky above (I assume it was blue) and clinging to strangers in the next seat. Some even mercifully fainted. Fortunately I wasn't flying Southwest, but still—it could be the same kind of plane.

I glanced surreptitiously at the strangers surrounding me. *Nobody knows my name*, I realized. Nobody would notice if I vanished into thin air. From there my mood was all downhill. If I got sucked through the roof of some airplane, I could count on one finger anybody who might miss me: Yuggie. Maybe Grace. Sure I had multiple acquaintances, people who seemed to enjoy my company, but dear, deep friends, I don't think so. Nobody who would really *grieve* my passing. I'm sure this sounds crazy, but it really made me meditate on the meaning of life, particularly my life, and come to some firm resolutions about changing it. *More about that later.*

I was pulled out of this tailspin by two men, one on either side of me, all of us, it turned out, catching the same puddle-jumper to Vermont, all of us alert to every announcement, every possible gate change. In the midst of such a milling, murmuring crowd, with multiple destinations, it was a relief to have something in common with these two others—that we were, at least, going to the same place. One man was a native Vermonter, youngish, friendly, and hearty. The other was a distinguished looking Frenchman, possibly from Montreal, who, he later revealed, was a world business traveler. They commenced, across my lap so to speak, comparing airplane disaster stories, mostly and obviously near-misses: the plane whose landing gear stuck, the missed plane which later crashed, the fire on board one flight, the emergency chute on another plane.

You'd think all this lively recounting of potential tragedy would really send me into the doldrums, but in fact it cheered me up. Survival stories, assuming you have lived to tell the tale, can be adventures recalled with gusto. Once I announced that I too was flying to Burlington, they included me in their exchange, even though all I contributed to the list of potential mishaps were meaningful nods and smiles of encouragement, an all too familiar routine when I am in the company of men. Aside from one terrifying moment years ago when the plane suddenly dropped down what seemed like several hundred feet, I really didn't have much to share. But still, it felt comforting to be sandwiched between one hearty youngish fellow and one sophisticated globe trotter, especially when our gate change was announced and I felt swept, within the companionship of fellow travelers, up the escalator to our new gate, as we all dragged our suitcases behind us. Of course, as soon as we entered the jet bridge, we became strangers again, each anxious to make sure there was enough room in the overhead bins for our carry-ons.

By the time we landed and I rushed past security at the Burlington airport, I was delighted to see Grace's dear familiar face as she greeted me. At last, again, someone who knew me. Maybe even loved me. I breathed a deep sigh of relief, resisting the temptation to throw myself into her arms. On the hour's drive in the dark to her home, I regaled her with a full account of my California adventures, omitting only a few details, like my trip to the dispensary with Tony. Although she was interested in hearing about my retreat, her focus was fixed, laser-like, on Liza's whereabouts. So, prompted by the dearth of information to report (nothing, essentially, she didn't already know), I divulged the suggestion from the staff person that she'd gone to Haiti to help with earthquake relief efforts. Once that cat was out of the bag, I couldn't exactly stuff it back in and order her not to tell Durga. Even though I made it very clear that I seriously doubted that rumor, I could see the wheels spinning in her head, propelling me south across the Atlantic, deep into the Caribbean Sea. *No way, Jose!*

By the time we arrived "home," the house was dark, so I whispered "goodnight" to Grace, crept upstairs to the guest room, and tumbled into the warm bed. Toward morning, as the sun slanted in through the dormer window, I dreamt I was back with my family in church, Mom, Dad, me, Yuggie all kneeling there together, in the good old days before everything fell apart. It felt rather peaceful, until I woke up and found I was still dreaming—or at least couldn't shake the Gregorian chanting out of my head. It was even in Latin, as the Masses used to be in the old days before reforms in the Church turned everything into the vernacular. *Uh, oh*, I thought, I've got that hearing disorder, *tinitus?* or whatever it's called—where sounds in your head have no equivalent in external reality. I've read it can drive you nuts—as if I need such triggers.

I quickly washed up, got dressed and crept downstairs, hoping to find Grace so I could tell her what was happening in my head. Maybe she'd know a solution, from Dr. Oz or somebody. But instead in the living room I passed a sleepy looking Marcy staring piously at the TV. It surprised me that the apparently solemn and artistic Marcy would be watching TV this early in the morning. Even I, in my most indolent days, rarely turned it on before noon. Not wanting to intrude, I waited until I was deep into the kitchen to turn around and see what she was watching. To my amazement, it was a Mass, complete with a priest, a choir, and a congregation. They were all saying the "Our Father" in Latin. I stood there translating, surprised at how much of the Latin I still recognized. Latin, the bane of my freshman and sophomore years of high school. As it turned out, I'm not adept at any languages except, I suppose, my native tongue. Something gets mistranslated between my ears and my mouth. The reverse of tintinis, perhaps.

Anyway, I barely had enough time to feel relief that the music wasn't only in my head, before Grace, looking intense, whisked me away to a local diner so we wouldn't disturb Marcy's worship. Over some scrambled eggs and home fries with onion, Grace told me that when Marcy's mother died the previous fall, among the papers discovered in her security deposit box was a request that all four of her children attend daily Mass and communion during the Lenten season after her death.

"*Daily* Mass?!" I exclaimed.

Grace nodded. "Marcy's mother was very devout—and yet, still a lot of fun."

"Communion? So Marcy is still an active Catholic?"

"She went to church with her mother when she visited her. I assume she did communion too."

"So she's not excommunicated?"

Grace looked at me puzzled. "Excommunicated?"

"Kicked out . . ."

"No. I think she left of her own volition."

"But how can she—"

"I don't know. There's much about Catholicism or Christianity she still respects."

"Except for the gay thing," I offered.'

"And the man thing."

"And the abortion thing."

"And the patriarchal thing."

"And the sin thing." I chimed in, with my new found Buddhist blessed be.

"Not to mention the Crusades and the Inquisition thing," Grace concluded. I remembered then how much more upset about the Crusades and the Inquisition she'd been than I ever was. Somehow those gruesome events were never much emphasized in Catholic schools. But being Jewish, she certainly had a different take on the Dark Ages than I had, in those days. Since then, of course, I've been tortured with enlightenment.

"But why is she watching the Mass on TV, *in Latin*? Every day!"

For Grace who studied Hebrew as a child, a foreign language (if Latin counts as a foreign language anymore), was not a stumbling block, but for me it was a clue: not only were the priests celebrating these TV Masses probably what she'd call "conservative," they were indubitably to the right of "orthodox."

"Actually I went to temple every morning for a year after my mother died to say the Kaddish," Grace murmured.

Oh no, I thought. Grace's mother died? Not only didn't I know and so hadn't been there for her, I certainly would never have guessed she'd go to worship at a synagogue every morning. I resisted the impulse to fall into paroxysms of regret and self-loathing and tried to focus on what Grace had just told me. She didn't seem to notice my discomfort and perhaps didn't even remember I hadn't been around (a different cause for self-flagellation).

"It was somehow comforting," Grace said. "Gave a place for grief that's hard to find in our regular daily routines. Also, helped me feel closer to my mother." The formal way she said "my mother" was a clue to me she did realize I hadn't been there. She used to talk quite freely about her "mom." Now I felt distanced from that intimacy. I sighed and switched the topic, wondering aloud what was next—in the day, in the search for Liza, in my life.

"I don't know," she said, "but I'm going to the school today to help out with preparations for All Species Day. If you want to come along . . ."

"All Species Day?" I asked.

"It's a local celebration of all the world's various species. People dress up like birds, plants, animals, fish. It's very festive and lots of fun—a great spring awakening."

I was hooked.

*   *   *

The school was another old farmhouse, but this one was located on a hill with views of western mountains in the distance and a pasture which ran down to a pond. Grace led me into a converted barn full of children listening with rapt attention to a sturdy looking woman in her early sixties or late fifties. She had intense golden brown eyes and a mane of multi-shaded hair, ranging from gold to soft grey to pure white. This, Grace whispered, was Ariel, her school partner, her work partner. Ah, the many shades of "partner."

"So when the Buddha decided it was time to retire," Ariel was telling the kids, "he contemplated who his successor would be. Not, as it turned out, the efficient Hue who expected to be appointed, but the quiet Quang. Buddha could see that while Quang wasn't bossy, the other monks respected him more than they did the sometimes bullying Hue. When Hue got word of this, he was bitterly disappointed. Instead of accepting the Buddha's decision, he vowed revenge. He decided to use the most powerful force in the village for his weapon: the elephant Maliwa, who was known for his fierce temper and enormous strength."

Ariel's voice had become so menacing at this point that some of the kids shivered and looked around for protection.

"So Hue went to one of the elephant minders, the one he knew loved to gamble and was always in debt, and he bribed him to release Maliwa from his chains the next evening just when the Buddha took his daily stroll among the villagers. The minder agreed, reluctantly, after Hue assured him it would look accidental. But unbeknownst to Hue or the elephant minder, they were overheard by a little mouse who lived in the elephant enclosure with the elephants—she lived mindfully, of course, so she wouldn't get squashed by their humongous feet. Her name was Li Li.

"As soon as it got dark, Li Li scurried out of the enclosure and ran and ran—because of course it takes a mouse a lot longer to get somewhere than a person or an elephant—to find the Buddha who was meditating under the Bodhi tree. When she found him, she climbed up on his peaceful shoulder and whispered in his ear what she'd overheard. The Buddha nodded, asked the little mouse to meditate with him, and continued to sit there serenely. When finally he was ready for sleep, he asked the mouse to stay with him, sharing his mat on the floor of his hut, which little Li Li did gladly, even though she missed getting some of the leftover scraps of elephant food."

As Ariel paused for dramatic effect, I surveyed the room, full of kids' drawings, a variety of animal masks, costumes of all sorts, and natural objects. This was a school I wished I had attended. There were about 30 kids, four or five years old, sitting around on the polished wood floor, listening quietly for the most part. Any squirming seemed to be from tension over the story, not boredom.

"That evening, as the Buddha set out on his evening stroll, with Li Li tucked in his pocket anxious about the outcome, the quiet of the village was shattered by the trumpeting of an elephant. The elephant minder had released the chain which bound Maliwa's foot and the elephant was charging through the village knocking over carts and buckets in his rush to freedom. His anger at being chained and confined knew no bounds, so everybody quickly got out of his way. Everybody, that is, but the Buddha. Strolling calmly toward the raging elephant, the Buddha peacefully looked him in the eye and spoke his name. Puzzled, the elephant paused in front of the Buddha, then bowed his massive head.

"Seeing this, the traitorous Hue ran off into the jungle in despair. The Buddha then reached into his pocket and pulled out Li Li. 'Courage comes in small packages," said the Buddha. "This is the hero,' he told Maliwa, 'who saved both of our lives.' For everybody knew that if the elephant had harmed the Buddha, the elephant would have been severely punished. 'It's not always the largest among us who is the most powerful. Sometimes the least of our brethren are those who do the most good."

Isn't that from the Bible, I wondered: "the least of us . . ."?

"Li Li, not used to either exposure or praise, tried to scurry out of the Buddha's palm, but the Buddha instead handed the trembling mouse to Maliwa, now as calm as a cow, who took her in his trunk and placed her on his back in a place of honor. The end."

The children clapped enthusiastically, then scrambled off to the next activity behind two younger women, while Ariel smiled a dazzling smile at Grace, signaling that she'd join us soon. Grace took me into the farmhouse kitchen. She loaded the wood stove, which was down to embers, with more wood from the nearby stack, then filled a kettle and placed it on the top. By the time Ariel joined us, the water was boiling. Ariel's firm handshake and direct gaze suggested someone not easily intimidated. I complimented her on the story and she modestly told me it was a version of a tale she'd heard from some Buddhist source. She admitted the mouse was a new addition. She asked me some penetrating questions about myself, while we sipped cups of herbal tea, but it felt more like a quiz than deep interest. Clearly she wanted time alone with Grace to consult, I assumed, about some school business. I wasn't quite sure what Grace's role in the school was—not like a regular job apparently since she seemed to come and go as she pleased—but I got the hint and left them alone while I wandered about the premises, peeking into various out buildings, guessing their original purpose and observing what they were now used for. A silo for instance had been transformed into an art gallery.

When Grace finally rejoined me, she seemed to be somewhat agitated. As we walked down toward the pond, through the muddy pasture, she muttered, "Get over it?"

"Get over what?" I asked.

"Oh, that's just Ariel's idea of advice. Such things might be easy for her, but . . ."

"What things?"

"Oh, Xavy," she said with a tone of dismissal. Suddenly this felt as if it were all my fault.

"What did I do?!" I asked defensively, quick to sense blame yet pretty damn sure I was innocent in this instance, so innocent I didn't even know what she was talking about.

"Ok," she said, stopping and looking me in the eye, "but this is strictly confidential."

Confidential between you and me, I wondered, but not between you and Ariel? But I didn't say anything; I'm smart enough not to sabotage a budding revelation.

"Ariel's partner, Willow, is still jealous of me," she confessed. "She thinks Ariel and I had an affair when they split up, briefly, years ago. And for some reason Ariel doesn't want to disabuse her of that notion. But Willow doesn't take it out on Ariel; she takes it out on me."

I responded with all the sympathy I could muster, thoroughly confused. Of course, I had to admit, jealousy is never that rational. "Oh," I said, wondering what I could ask that wouldn't inspire Grace to take it out on me. I had assumed that all Grace's Soul Companions were X's, but with Ariel that didn't seem to be the case. Perhaps building the school together was all the affair they needed. A venture like that could certainly bond folks more deeply than some brief liaison.

Grace sighed deeply and sat down on a large rock, leaving me to stand in the mud. I sat down on another rock, wishing to be at eye level with her rather than looking down upon her. I'm the last person to claim superiority about the dregs of jealousy, whether caused by me or suffered by me.

"Well, how do you feel about Willow?"

Grace muttered gloomily. "She's adorable."

"Your innocence makes it even harder, I suppose." Grace was looking so down, I began to wonder how innocent she really was. But, unlike me, Grace was less likely to be distressed by guilt than by rejection.

My sympathy wandered toward Willow. I recalled my jealousy of what seemed an innocent connection between Yuggie and Grace.

"I wonder if jealousy is a primary emotion or just a cover-up for something else."

"Fear of loss, maybe? A reminder of how she almost lost Ariel?"

"Yeah, plus some kind of insecurity, I guess, some doubt about how loveable you are."

Grace nodded. The rock I was sitting on was cold and hard; my tush ached for some movement. I stood up and she joined me. The field was so muddy we decided to explore the pond some other time, and trudged back up to the car.

Once we were on our way home, I asked Grace about Ariel.

"We call her the Sleeping Lion because Ariel means the "lion of God" in Hebrew. That's also the name of one of the most prominent mountain peaks in Vermont—at least what the native Americans called it. It's now called Camel's Hump, which seems odd in a climate where camels are not exactly native."

"Are lions?" Upon reflection I could see Ariel's golden grey hair as a lion's mane.

She smiled. "Just the elusive, and perhaps extinct, catamount or cougar. Maybe Moose's Hump would be more appropriate, but I like the Indian name."

"So Ariel's like a sleeping lion?"

"Yes, often she purrs like a kitty, but watch out when she wakes up and starts roaring!"

"Was she roaring at you about Willow's feelings about you?" That, it seemed to me, would be the height of arrogance, something I'd already suspected of this divine lion.

"No—but she's such a hero type she doesn't seem to understand how the rest of us mere mortals sometimes feel. 'Get over it' is probably one of her mantras. And, mostly, she does."

"It's probably what she tells Willow too." I wondered, if Ariel wished them both to get over it, why she didn't just tell Willow the truth? Seems she wanted to have it both ways—the delicious "secret" and the claim of innocence. Some fantasy she hadn't yet gotten over? "How is she like a hero?"

"Oh, in every way imaginable. She's apparently fearless. She's generous. She loves a challenge, and will put 150% of her strength behind every obstacle. She's noble in her aspirations, honorable in every way."

Every way but telling the truth to her partner, I thought. "Is she religious?"

Grace shook her head. "Completely secular. Grew up in a family of artists and intellectuals. No religion—just some traditional feasts."

"Sounds like she's Buddhist now."

Grace shrugged. "More eclectic—like me."

"What's Willow like?"

"Willow? Well, I don't know her so well, but they're a funny pair. Ariel relishes the challenge, while Willow embraces sacrifice. They seem to work together like a pair of eyes in terms of doing copious good for others, yet as the hero, Ariel thrives on congratulations and eschews anything like condolences, whereas Willow thrives on condolences and rejects anything like congratulations."

"Willow sounds like the martyr type. Is she an ex-Catholic by any chance?"

"Catholics don't have a monopoly on martyrdom," Grace growled. "No, it feels more like a Gertrude and Alice type of relationship—like traditional hetero actually. Willow is no martyr."

Grace sounded so grumpy about this that I decided to globalize the whole conundrum. "Sounds a little like our current international dilemma—two interlocked archetypes: the Muslim martyrs sacrifice themselves while the American heroes try to save the world."

"Hopefully that's changing now with what's happening in Egypt. More Arab heroes, fewer martyrs—and maybe less need for American 'heroism'."

"One can only hope."

"But that analysis might explain the dynamic between Ariel and Willow. Interlocking archetypes."

"What my therapist calls 'conjoined complexes,'" I observed. "How long have they been together?"

"Oh, ages," replied Grace. "More than twenty years."

"And where do you fit into that time line?" I blurted out.

"Oh, Xavy!" replied Grace in a tone which made clear this topic was over and done with. Another confidentiality I wouldn't have privy to. At least for the moment. Then she added, "You know the maddening thing? Ariel's usually right. I *should* get over it."

The way you got over me? I thought.

Chapter Eleven

PASSOVER

Somehow, while waiting for the next shoe to drop, I was able to spend the week recuperating from my California adventure. At least until Grace shared with Durga the rumor about Liza being in Haiti. Fortunately, as it turned out, Durga had flown south to avoid Mud Season, so I was safe for the time being.

Mysteriously I found myself rising to share the daily TV Mass with Marcy. By mutual consent, we muted the fiery sermons by supposedly celibate priests admonishing us sinners to curb our passions while yet giving birth to all the poor "unborn." During that lengthy homily period we prepared our different breakfasts in companionable silence, then sat respectfully during the consecration and ate together during communion. We rarely commented on the proceedings although we did exchange a few glances after some of the more orthodox prayers. And one time after the priest said in Latin, "The Lord be with you," we both responded in unison, "Et cum spiritu tuo." After the Mass I often joined Marcy and the dogs for their daily trek up the mountain, which seemed as spiritual in its own way as the liturgy. Is it better to be an unborn, I wondered as we trudged silently up the steep path, or an unwanted, neglected, abused kid who still suffers from not having been wanted?

After that I usually spent the morning at the school with Grace, helping out by providing individual attention to any kid who seemed to need it, either for academic or for emotional reasons. Sometimes, with the little ones, it was just a matter of letting them sit in my lap while I read to them. I found myself getting attached to a little boy named Oscar who had been adopted from Ecuador by a single mother. Oscar was, in turn, attached to a baby salamander named Riddle. Although amphibians have never really been my thing—I prefer fur—I tried to share Oscar's enthusiasm by telling him stories about Riddle's past life in a warmer climate, based on my assumption that Ecuador was bound to be warmer than Vermont.

In the afternoons I sat with Zoom on my lap watching Dr. Oz, picking up all sorts of healthy tips which I announced to anybody around for dinner, and then promptly forgot. There seemed to be no formal routine around meals, or any obvious schedule. Grace spent much of her time at the school (I was wrong at first—it was a job, just one with very flexible hours) and Marcy, a retired teacher, spent much of her time in her barn studio working with stained glass, and both of them made frequent trips into Montpelier. Kara, who had a full-time job in some environmental advocacy agency, was rarely around except on the weekends, but Marcy spent several nights at Kara's house.

One night Grace announced to me that preparations were underway for an annual Passover/Easter celebration at Kara's house. In attendance would be Marcy and Kara, Ariel and Willow, Durga, Grace and yours truly. All I had to do, for some reason, was "be there."

Since Grace had to arrive early to help Marcy and Kara with the cooking, I drove alone, having mastered the twists and turns from Marcy's house to Montpelier. I stopped at a local florist to buy some Easter lilies for the occasion. This, as it turned out, was not such a hot idea since Kara's cats went bananas over flowers. Oh well.

During the flower flurry I was able to scout out Willow, the only one of this august company I hadn't met. She was tiny, tiny, more like a mini-willow, very slender, girlish in one way, tough looking in another, her long wild hair like the branches of a young willow, but she was my age at least with a lively, intelligent face expressing a range of emotional responses. This I observed as she communicated with Ariel in very articulate non-verbal language how she was feeling about the present company—which happened to be us. Wondering who or what might be making her squirm I stepped out of the scene, metaphorically speaking, to observe the dynamic so I could figure that out. The source was Grace, I finally concluded, judging from Willow's frequent but surreptitious glances at her. Made sense, I realized, if Willow is jealous of Grace.

Yet I could also see why Ariel might prefer Grace at times. There was something about Willow that made one wary. Me included. A baby femme with nerves of steel? The dark side of sacrifice, perhaps? I can't quite say what, but I could see that Grace might want to watch her back.

Next we were all treated to the breathless arrival of Durga nee Sandra with her flow and flutter, all enlivened and bronzed from her week away. *Where? The Bahamas. So near and yet so far from the fated Haiti.*

Why, I wondered, while she's jetting all over creation doesn't Sandra herself search for Liza? She's sending me on a mission she herself should be conducting. Isn't she, merely by the fact of hiring me, condemning this inquiry to failure? To get someone else to act for you goes against the principles of transformation. If she wants to find Liza, I realized, she's the only one who can do it because she's the one who really cares about tracking her down. *Not me. I don't even know Liza. My only motives are inherently suspect.*

As soon as she'd settled down in an easy chair with her bulging bag, Durga started distributing gifts to us from her vacation, even something for me that looked like a telescope. Somehow this display of generosity brought us all together, each wondering what we'd get, each pleased for the others because there seemed to be enough to go around.

My telescope turned out to be a kaleidoscope. Later I wondered if this was a message from Durga. Something about patterns shifting constantly? A code, perhaps, for our exchange of, or change in, roles? She used to be my prime suspect, now I was her agent. But I'm afraid I lacked agency without her fuller participation. I knew, however, I still didn't trust her so was hesitant to invite her to join this search in a more active way. This recognition, in turn, exposed, to me at least, my commitment to continue the search for Liza, even if it meant I had to go to Haiti. But I wasn't going alone. Nor was I going with Durga . . .

Both Kara and Grace were in high cooking gear, shifting around each other in Kara's tiny kitchen like two magicians while Marcy hovered helpfully on the sidelines, ready to take orders. I noticed how, despite her apparent interest in the food preparation, Marcy was actually focusing on the interaction between Grace and Kara, with obvious fondness for them both. When she caught me observing her enjoyment of their display of cooperation, she smiled a little sheepishly.

Dinner was a great success: roast chicken and vegetables, with all the trimmings using every lovely bowl on the premises, preceded by prayers from multiple traditions: the Hebrew blessing of the bread and the fruit of the vine sung by Grace, a Hindu chant from Durga, the traditional Catholic grace before meals spoken by Marcy, a Buddhist blessing from Ariel, and a here-and-now giving of thanks from Kara's Protestant background, along with Kara's lighting of the candles and selection of background music. Only Willow and I had nothing particular to contribute. This, however, did not create much of a bond between us.

Conversation during the meal was also somewhat traditional— at least within groups such as ours. It featured our own four Seder questions, which asked (1) How is the exodus of the Jews from Egypt parallel to the movement for liberation among contemporary Egyptians? (2) How are women today more liberated than women when we were born (and how much credit can we take for that progress?). (3) How much more needs to be done on both fronts? And (4) how connected is the Mass, based on the Last Supper, originally a Passover Seder, to the issue of liberation? This last question was perhaps mostly of interest only to me and Marcy. Although the others listened politely to our ruminations on the subject, they seemed relieved when Grace brought in dessert, her special apple pie with chocolate sprinkles, apparently a perennial favorite.

After dinner Marcy and I did the dishes while everyone else retired to the living room to listen to Durga tell about her vacation, which sounded from a distance quite exotic, judging mostly from the oohs and ahhs. Then, with everyone slightly high on the ritual wine, and me, as usual, longing instead for a good smoke, Kara, Marcy and I found ourselves in the midst of a spirited discussion in the kitchen about the mysteries of Christianity, while Durga, Grace, Ariel and Willow (who seemed velcroed to Ariel's side) conversed in the living room. Marcy was trying to plumb the depths of her mother's faith, Kara was trying to reconnect with her family's religious beliefs, and I was just along for the ride. We all agreed we could appreciate the Biblical messages about loving one's neighbor, but as Marcy pointed out, most religions follow some sort of Golden Rule. We speculated how Christ, as opposed to many churches, would treat gay folks, given his kindness toward lepers and outcasts.

"What strikes me now," Marcy said, "after listening lately to so much of the New Testament, is how much the message from Christ's life is about resurrection, about life after death. It was as if he came to show us that option. I hope he's right, for Mom's sake."

"But don't the Buddhists believe in many lives after many deaths?" Kara asked.

"I thought the Buddhists didn't believe in life after death," Marcy said. "Isn't it the Hindus who believe in reincarnation?"

"Maybe Jesus was a Bodhisattva," I suggested, imagining such an enlightened being who reincarnates in order to save others. He certainly was cast in the role of savior.

From the living room rose the indignant tones which usually accompany discussion about politics, especially when fueled by the fruit of the vine. I decided to stick with religion.

"What intrigues me," I said, "is the Trinity: Father, Son, and Holy Ghost. When I was still practicing, it once came as a revelation to me that God is not a person but a relationship." In a more blissful state I could almost feel in touch with the divine three-in-one.

"Where is the feminine in all this though?" Marcy asked.

"I would think," said Grace, just passing through the room to get some coffee, "that Mary, being the Mother of God, might have more divine power than she seems to." We all shook our heads. Even though she'd ascended into heaven without, apparently, giving up her body, she wasn't part of the Trinity, that's for sure; she was just a "handmaiden of the Lord." Not God in a body, like Jesus, not God in Spirit, like the Holy Ghost, just a body full of divine spirit.

"Well," said Marcy, from within her own mystical inner dialogue, "from the way we mirror, or project, this energy in, or from, our real lives—the Trinity parallels the nuclear family." She paused a long time as we all pondered this possibility, then she announced. "That means that the Holy Spirit, 'giver of life,' must be the feminine principle.'"

"Wow," exclaimed Kara. "So if the Virgin Mary was conceived by the Holy Spirit . . . and Joseph didn't have anything to do with it . . ."

Grace, pouring out her coffee, looked amused.

"Then," Marcy continued, "that means that Jesus' parents were both female: Holy Mother Mary *and* the Holy Spirit!"

I gasped. "Jesus had two mothers!"

Kara, Marcy and I burst out laughing.

"Christ is the son of lesbians?!" I howled.

Grace eyed us sceptically as she put a dollop of milk in her coffee, then returned to her political discussion.

Eventually all this hilarity led to a need for further refreshment. Our spirits were willing to keep contemplating, but our flesh was all too weak. Soon the last of the pie was almost gone, and we were rotating back through the main course, nibbling on remnants of the roast chicken and the salad.

Hearing the three of us rustling around in the kitchen drew the others back into the dining area, where a discussion ensued, over the sharing of leftovers, about the whereabouts of Liza. Obviously Grace had already revealed the Haiti rumor, not just to Durga but to everybody, because suddenly each one of them was busy giving her opinion—pretty much all at the same time—about whether or not Liza was the kind of person who might have gone to a kind of place like Haiti. I listened carefully. Ariel and Grace were the only ones who could imagine Liza taking on such a challenge, Ariel because of courage, Grace because of compassion. Willow couldn't fathom it. I suggested Liza might have gone to Hawaii instead, since it was closer to California than Haiti. "Why?" Grace asked, with more than a dose of skepticism. Kara wondered if she'd gone to Japan to help with the latest disaster. Marcy pointed out that there was no evidence Liza had gone to any of those places. If she wanted to help kids suffering from trauma, there were plenty of them all over the country and throughout the world. Me, I was hoping they'd say she was the kind of person who might, for some reason, go to Hawaii. I wouldn't mind following her there so I could see Yuggie.

The group's speculation about Lisa's character and personality was soft, subtle, and kind—challenging each other when any too-fixed notions began to incarnate, at the risk of getting locked in consensus or group judgment. Some thought she was impulsive, others, that she was cautious. Some felt she was too generous, others said she was frugal. The only thing they agreed on was that Liza would be great working with kids using the arts as therapy. But characterizations of Haiti, and Hawaii, once I threw that place into the pool of speculation, were soon subject to endless projections and inventions.

Someone knew enough about Haitian history to explain how it had been colonized, and exploited, by a series of countries, including, shamefully, the United States. I wondered what Scoop might have to say on the subject.

Hawaii, we all agreed, although it too suffered its share of colonizers, has such a lilt to it. Both are potentially tropical paradises but one was fortunate to be located in the middle of the Pacific Ocean, somewhat but not entirely remote from foreign intrusion, while the other was unfortunate enough to have been the end point of a long hard voyage toward Empire. None of us had been to Haiti while several had vacationed in Hawaii. Those who had seemed eager to describe her pristine beaches, rocky cliffs and spectacular waterfalls, to counter, I assume, those TV and newspaper images of disaster burned into our psyches after the devastating Haitian earthquake. Not to mention the more recent cholera epidemic.

Since I've never even met Liza, I just listened for any clue, any hint about where she might be, from these folks who knew her best. What they offered told me some about her but more about each of them. As we talked I noticed who were more worried than others and who seemed to know her better than others. Grace, Marcy and Ariel staked a claim to greater intimacy than Durga, her so-called mother or Willow—which didn't stop Durga or Willow from having their own strong judgments. I'd run away too if I were the lone screen for so many projections from the older generation. I felt grateful for having at least one sibling—even though I was the recipient of the mostly negative projections, and Yuggie, of the mostly positive, or at least that's how it seemed to me at the time. Listening to all their speculations, I tended to trust the folks like Marcy and Grace who knew Liza better and who were also less worried. But, still, it wasn't easy to dismiss the concerns of the others.

At the same time I appreciated collective recognition of my reluctance to go to Haiti, their willingness to let that slide for the moment. After all, it wasn't like any of them wanted to go in my place. Durga seemed particularly reluctant, but she wasn't the only one.

Another reason I was hesitant to leave again was my growing fondness for this new group of potential friends. After our shared religious revelation, so to speak, I felt close to Marcy and Kara. My encounters with Ariel at school intrigued me. Willow I had yet to appreciate, but she too held some interest. And Durga, well, I was beginning, in this new context, to recognize her as, if not a friend yet, no longer my nemesis.

So you can imagine my surprise to hear, as people departed toward their separate abodes, that almost everyone was heading out of state for the next week. Marcy was going to visit her sister, Grace was going to a workshop on non-violent communication, Kara was off on a field trip for work, Ariel, to a conference on early childhood education. That left just Durga and Willow. Willow, fortunately, expressed no interest in getting together with me. And Durga I was hoping to avoid as long as possible, lest she try to twist my arm about going to Haiti. I knew her well enough to know she rarely deviated from her appointed course and that she was stubborn and willful enough to disregard the group consensus which had temporarily relieved me of that pressure, especially now that the group was dispersing.

Fortunately, when Durga telephoned the next day to see if she could set up a meeting, I was sick as a dog, if you know what I mean, and could barely speak to her over the phone, much less meet in person. Unfortunately, I had overdone it on the refreshments, encouraged by the plethora of goodies and inspired by the sharing of consumption. I was only too glad to be left alone by humans. I had agreed to take care of the animals while Marcy and Grace were away, but in many ways, it felt like they were taking care of me, especially Zoom whose warmth against my aching tummy felt like a hot water bottle.

Chapter Twelve

DOWN IN THE DUNGEON

Did I say sick as a dog? Well, I was sicker. Dogs just upchuck whatever's bothering them and that's that. Even after I was emptied out, I still felt lousy. I must've picked up some intestinal virus on the plane. All that healthy food from the Monastery must've turned off my immune system, usually on high alert due to a steady consumption of sugars and chocolate. Of course, there was that festive Passover indulgence a few days earlier.

Fortunately I was all alone, no one but the animals left here to suffer with me or from me.

All I could do was lay around the house sipping chicken soup (made by Grace from the Passover leftovers), watching TV, from Bones to Dr. Oz, hopefully following a sort of death-to-life scenario. I also maintained my vigil with the TV Masses, for Marcy's sake, since now that it was Holy Week, Lenten season was close to an end. Zoom's warmth on my lap kept me anchored in comforting reality while I explored diverse dimensions of the spirit.

One day the doorbell rang while I was watching trash on TV. I wondered if I could escape to the back of the house without detection. Not that I feared a serial killer was on the loose, not really, even though the image did flash through my drama-ridden brain. But the sounds from the TV gave me away, so despite the fact I was dressed like Oliver Twist, I figured I better answer the door.

On the front porch stood two women, one resolute older one and another younger timid one. The pamphlets in their hands gave them away and too late I realized I had been trapped by the Jehovah's Witnesses. But it's not in me to be rude to strangers unless I'm in the New York subway or standing in line for a seat on a Southwest airline flight, so when I saw that one of the pamphlets was about "Coping with the Loss of a Loved One," I accepted it politely, remarking that a friend of mine had just lost her mother. They expressed sympathy, then handed over a *Watchtower*. Jesus on the cover, looked like an Anglo-Saxon movie star with a graying beard, which seemed a stretch given that he couldn't be more than 33 (although maybe with reduced life spans in those days, that was old enough for grey hair). I recalled how glad I'd been to make it to my 34th birthday, having identified with Jesus so thoroughly in my religious youth. I was relieved my feeble imitation of Christ hadn't led to premature death.

As I stood there awkwardly holding the pamphlets in my hand at the open door, wondering what the pitfalls would be of inviting them in, the older woman started telling me kindly about the Second Coming, when Jesus would rule as king over the whole world for one thousand years. *Hmmm*, I thought, doesn't this contradict everything Jesus said about his kingdom not being on earth? I felt resistant to their simple faith.

Then she pointed out the prophesies and how they are now being fulfilled: earthquakes, famine, disease, "lack of natural love," (I wondered if this was heterosexual code for homosexuality but in fact I learned later upon reading the handout it referred to domestic violence), and ruining of the earth. This point was hard to contradict, since these events did, indeed, seem to be bursting all around us these days. The prophesies, however, were mostly from the Old Testament. I couldn't help wondering if they hadn't already been fulfilled. There had been plenty of disasters before the modern age, even though contemporary society is busy perfecting the last prophesy, destruction of the environment, after which, I assume, there will be no more prophesies. It was hard not to hope with these earnest folks that "better times are just ahead," when hunger would be no more, disease would be eliminated, and the earth would be renewed. I just wished, somehow, it could be achieved by human cooperation and shared governance rather than divine intervention, especially in the form of a kingdom. Isn't monarchy a outdated institution? Isn't dictatorship one cause for the Arab Spring?

But I didn't see any point in arguing with these sincere women, so I continued to smile and nod, murmuring that it would indeed be wonderful if there was no more hunger, etc. Finally as my politeness began to fray, I confessed I was a Catholic, which isn't quite accurate anymore (if you go by Church doctrine), but true enough. This didn't stop them in their tracks as I hoped it would. The older one, as persistent as a squirrel, told me I could still learn something from the Bible and invited me to join them for home bible study. The younger one nervously awaited my response. To fend off this offer, I replied that I was just a visitor to the area and probably wouldn't be around long enough to participate. This got me off that hook, and it's not even a lie. Finally, I smiled at the younger woman to help calm her nerves, called their attention to the improved weather, and closed the door, clutching the pamphlets which I commenced to read during commercials.

Little did I realize at the time that this incident would sparked a Jesus Obsession which would last until the pagan rituals of All Species Day. It wasn't just that I'd been empathizing with Marcy's attempt to understand the spirit of her mother's devotion, it was also the fact that my own name Xavier means "savior," referring, I assume, to that same Christ. Was I meant, somehow, to save someone? Someone besides myself, surely. But who? If so, I'd better get at it, since time, or at least my time, was running out.

Meanwhile on TV the readings about Christ's passion became more dramatic, more intense: the hints of betrayal, the Last Supper, Christ's agony in the garden, his three disciples falling asleep three times (count me as a fourth because I fell asleep listening to the priest drone on about this human frailty), the treacherous kiss followed by the deep regret followed by the despair of suicide (ah, poor Judas), Jesus' cry on the cross, "My God, my God, why have you forsaken me?" And nobody around for me to talk with about all this. Marcy, come home!

I finally called Yuggie, despite the fact that my cell phone didn't work and so I had to pay higher long distance charges, but she was not at all interested in discussing Holy Week or the New Testament, even though in our youth she had been far more pious than I was. Oh well. It was nice to hear her voice. Instead I was treated to a story of the nature hike she'd taken with her new girlfriend through some tropical rainforest. All this while here it was almost snowing outside!

Far from the many shades of green greeting me on my initial entrance into Vermont, upon further intimacy I was now being introduced to her sundry greys: snow, sleet, fog, freezing rain, even the noisy drumming of hail. April, and it was still very chilly outside!

For some reason it seemed much colder than Boston, maybe because in the city there were lots of houses and people around to block the wind. Fortunately Marcy and Grace had a bundle of warm coats, boots, hats and gloves for me to borrow.

This weather, however, did not dissuade the dogs from demanding their usual morning walk, any more than my weakened condition did. Neither rain, snow, sleet nor wind seemed to deter them from their appointed smells. The dogs, I was discovering, were not just good at taking care of me, solicitously, and possibly sympathetically, following me around the house as I moaned and groaned.

They were also experts at getting me to take care of them. The black and white one, with her floppy ear, seemed to be the great communicator, jumping up and down and barking at me, then leading me to their bowls on the exact dinner hour, as if she were watching the clock with one eye and me with the other. But it was the dark one, who lay there staring at me with those soulful golden eyes who really got me moving toward the dog food.

On one of our morning walks we crossed paths with the mailperson, who doggedly entertained me with the story of how, in the nineteenth century, because of some volcano erupting in the Philippines, Vermont had no summer. It never warmed up. It even snowed in July. That was the year all the crops failed and there was a mass migration from Vermont. This tale did little to cheer me up. I had just been playing with the idea that here was a place where I might finally settle down, where I'd discover *my people*, where I might actually, and finally, belong. Just my luck to root myself somewhere right before another evacuation. In this season of Passover, might I hope for my own dollop of liberation or, at least, redemption, without, I hoped, the necessity of an Exodus?

About that time I woke up in the middle of the night to a funny noise which sounded like gargling. I finally tracked it down to the furnace. I turned the thermostat down, went back to sleep, then in the morning phoned Marcy at her sister's house and described the sound. "Call the oil company," she advised. "The number's on the bulletin board in the kitchen. Meanwhile, better turn off the furnace. The emergency switch is in the hall closet." I flipped the switch while she was still on the phone. So far, so good, except for the fact that it would now be cold inside as well as out. "Build a fire?" she suggested.

"Where's the furnace?" I asked, embarrassed that I didn't automatically know.

"In the basement," she replied. "Don't go down there. It's a dungeon."

So we hung up and I called the Oil Company. They assured me they'd send somebody over right away, and to my surprise, they did. (In the city I could be waiting for days.) Within an hour one baby faced fellow and one veteran whose pants hung on his hips like diapers (in what used to be a fashion statement for young men a decade or so ago, but was probably not in this instance). Fortunately they knew where the basement stairs were—hidden under a trap door in that same hall closet. People talk about coming out of the closet—not about going down into and under it. As I peered down after they'd descended the steep stairs, more like a ladder than a staircase, I heard them splashing around. Dungeon indeed. Then the younger fellow asked me to turn on the furnace so they could listen to its wheezing. I did. It sputtered on, then started gargling again.

"Ok," he called out, "you can turn it off now."

In a matter of minutes they'd clomped back up, their boots muddy and dripping black water all over Marcy's mostly clean floor, to announce that the basement was flooded, threatening to fill up the blower and ruin the furnace.

"Sump pump," the older one murmured.

"What'll I do now?!" I cried out.

"Call a plumber," said the younger one. "And keep the furnace off until he pumps all the water out."

So I called the plumber, whose name was also on the emergency list tacked to the kitchen bulletin board. Then I built a fire in the wood stove to keep us warm. Fortunately there were enough fire starters and dry wood around to get the fire going without too much hassle. The light and warmth of the flames were comforting.

Fire and water, I mused, recalling the candle dipped into the baptismal font for the Easter ritual, I'm getting my full dose of each. All so symbolic, yet also so real. Odd, how the holiest moment of the Catholic ritual of rebirth parallels worship of the Hindu yoni and lingam, both apparently symbolizing the act of sexual union. Is there any message here about my mission as a savior? Unlikely, given my befuddled sexual identity and the current state of my libido.

Within an hour John the Plumber arrived and after a friendly greeting and enough shared knowledge about dire basement emergencies and flooding to assure me he really knew what he was doing, he carried his pumping equipment down into the dungeon to spend the next six hours pumping all the H2O out of the basement through a window, with the aid of two portable pumps and hoses, while he used a long crowbar to clear out the drain through which the spring melt usually flows—according to Marcy who called in periodically for updates. Suddenly I felt like the captain of a sinking ship, trying to keep us all afloat while the bilge, whatever that is, was pumped out. Zoom and the dogs seemed remarkably unconcerned, the dogs entertained by the movements of this emergency worker in his muddy boots while Zoom kept a safe distance away from the flurry, upstairs where he could bask in the warmth emanating from the stovepipe.

At the end of that endlessly busy day, John advised me to check periodically the pump he was leaving set up down there to make sure it was working. To do this, apparently, all I had to do was keep the basement hatch open so I could switch on the light and peer down to gauge the water level. Sure, I thought, I can do that, gazing down into the yucky basement at the thin stream pulsing through its dank interior, my own dark innards still smarting from a continuous, though now subdued, purge of their overindulged contents.

That night, after making sure the dogs and Zoom were sufficiently fed and the fire, sufficiently stoked, I collapsed into the soft guest bed as soon as hazy daylight disappeared into the gloom. I dreamt that in the midst of some communal celebration I encountered a young woman who was weeping. When I asked her what was wrong, she cried out that her mother had committed suicide. I felt conflicted between sympathy for the mother and empathy for the daughter, but since the mother was gone and the daughter, right in front of me, I comforted her, assuring her it was ok to feel hurt and anger as well as loss. She listened, but gave no response. When I woke, I felt awash with grief. Was this my younger self? My own mother with her weak heart had died far too soon. Not from suicide, certainly, but when I was not much older than this young woman in my dream.

As it turned out, that morning was Good Friday. What I remembered about Good Friday was the three-hour Stations of the Cross, that step by step recollection of Christ's crucifixion, with all its embedded stories: his three falls, Simon enlisted to help carry the cross, Veronica's veil, Mary, the sorrowing mother, the beloved friends Mary Magdalene and John, all at the foot of the cross, the good thief and the bad thief, the cruel Roman soldiers. After walking the dogs through remnants of dirty snow not yet melted and fixing myself a healthy breakfast of yogurt and fruit, I decided to check the basement before turning on the TV to see about Good Friday services.

What I discovered as I peered down into the basement was a still pump in the middle of a silent pond which threatened to engulf the furnace again. I heard a voice in my head saying, "Take up your cross and descend into the dungeon." I glanced down at my new Merrills, wondering how I was going to keep my feet, much less these shoes, dry and clean if I went down there into that muck.

Just then, like a bugle call from the heavens, the phone rang. It was Grace, checking in from her workshop to see how I was doing. When I told her about my conjoined health and basement crises, she murmured, "Housebody." This diagnosis implied, somehow, that what was happening in my body paralleled what was happening in the house. That synchronicity, while intriguing, suggested to my stirred up Catholic guilt that somehow I was to blame for the flood.

"Housebody!?" I shrieked. My tone, apparently, was an accurate enough measure of my distress that she moved quickly from theory to practice.

"Near the front door, Xavy, you'll find a pair of rubber muck boots that come almost up to your knees. Put them on before you go down into the basement. They will keep your feet dry."

"Ok," I gasped. "Call me back in about twenty minutes." I rushed to the entrance and found a pair of black boots. Shaking off my precious Merrills I stuck a foot with its world's softest socks into one of the boots and discovered to my relief that it fit. With my feet thus girded, I descended into the dungeon, my feet protected from the thick layer of mud and gook which layered the basement floor beneath the two inch pool of water lurking around the idle pump and seeping toward the furnace. All it took was a slight jiggle with two fingers and the pump leapt again to life. What a relief to watch the water pulse up through the hose and hear it splash out the window.

Sartre might think hell is other people, I mused after I'd emerged from the dingy basement, but hell can just as easily consist of being left alone with a flooded basement and a fussy pump. I pulled my dry feet out of the filthy boots, slid them into Grace's slippers which I found near the front door, and heated up some water for tea while I waited for Grace to call back. When the phone rang again, I leapt to answer it.

Then I proceeded to subject Grace to every detail of the basement crisis with more than a modicum of reporting about my intestinal distress, almost defying her to evoke "housebody" again, (while at the same time probably confirming that diagnosis) until I was generally satisfied with her expressed sympathies. When I tried to draw a parallel between my sufferings and Christ's crucifixion, however, she would have none of it. Understanding how Jesus might not be a priority for her at the moment, I asked her instead about her non-violent communication workshop so she could amuse me with anecdotes about various run-ins, outbursts, and freak-outs during the meetings, and how skillfully or unskillfully the trainers handled them.

Finally I told her about my nightmare, asking, "Who do you think the young woman was?"

"You?" she asked hesitantly. "I know your mother didn't commit suicide, but weren't you about that age when she died?"

After admitting that possibility, we wondered together why I might be having such a dream at this point in my life. Then, to get myself off the hook I suggested that maybe I'd picked up something about or from Marcy or Kara.

"Marcy's mother just died, of course," Grace responded. "But she had a good long life and she was anything but suicidal. And Kara's mother is almost as old and still going strong."

"What about Ariel, Willow or Durga?" I asked, still convinced I'd absorbed this situation by some kind of osmosis. I've been afflicted in the past with a kind of telepathy by which I can sense the unspoken feelings of others, mostly the sad or mad ones. It's both, as Monk on TV says of his sixth sense," a blessing and a curse," but mostly, in my case, a curse.

"Ariel's mother died of lung cancer from smoking, so maybe she's a candidate," Grace answered. "Don't know much about either Willow or Durga's families, just that their mothers are still alive."

Then, finally, I asked Grace about her own mother's death. Of course it turned out that she'd been in her eighties and she'd died quietly at home from complications brought on by diabetes. Peacefully, surrounded by family. Nothing remotely suicidal about it. But I was glad for an opportunity to ask, since I'd missed the whole event.

"Maybe all this—the ailments, the flooding, the dream," she speculated, "are a form of tonglen."

"Tonglen?"

"It's a Tibetan Buddhist term for a practice by which one takes on the suffering of others as an act of compassion. I was just talking about it with someone here. Wait, let me find a quote about it from Pema Chodron. Here: 'In tonglen practice, when we see or feel suffering, we breathe in with the notion of completely feeling it, accepting it, and owning it. Then we breathe out, radiating compassion, loving kindness, freshness; anything that encourages relaxation and openness.'"

Boy o boy o boy, I thought, reflecting upon Christ's passion. If his crucifixion isn't "tonglen," then I don't know what is. He completely took on human suffering, even to the point of feeling despair. "My God, my God, why have you forsaken me?" And he breathed out resurrection, redemption for all of humanity, just as we do in metta meditation. Was Jesus simply another bodhisattva? I recalled suggesting that during our ecstatic discussion last weekend.

All this, of course, I didn't share with Grace who suddenly had to sign off and rush to some workshop on active listening. But I did reflect upon tonglen later as I watched the elaborate ritual from the Vatican broadcast on the Catholic channel that afternoon while I sat there trying to breathe in the suffering of my body, the house, and a world in crisis, and breathe out metta, renewal and resurrection. I'd certainly felt abandoned by my mother as Jesus felt abandoned by his father. Suddenly I got an insight about Liza I was surprised I hadn't realized sooner. I could easily imagine how abandoned Liza must have felt when her mother died.

Was Liza who the young woman in my dream? If so, finding her might involve retracing or recalling my own steps after Mom died. That's when I'd run away—not to some place like Haiti or Hawaii, but to Baltimore. Just a hop, skip and jump from where my family lived in Philly but far enough away for me to discover a new life for myself, at least for the time being. That's where I got caught up in the women's movement, where I met Grace, where my career, such as it was, began. *Hmmm.* What if Liza was somewhere close by, like Burlington?

On Easter Saturday I continued my forays into the yucky basement, clad in my mucky boots, to bring new life to the touchy pump. I took up my boots and headed down, not up, into that dark fount, dipping this candle of self into the obscure baptismal waters, hopefully washing away my multitude of sins. Not only did the pump get stuck on off, it occasionally, as signaled by a high screech, tended to get fixed in the *on* position, which also required intervention. This, I realized, is what caretaking is all about. It takes constant vigilance. You can't leave anything alone for very long. Is this what I would have experienced had my mother lived to a ripe old age? Would I have been up to the challenge?

Throughout that day of liturgical waiting outside the cellar tomb, I mulled over my situation here in Vermont. I was here because I was being hired to go elsewhere. Much as I might like to stay, try to fit in, find some way to belong to this place and these people, my mission was to search all over creation for a missing person. Is this what it means to be a savior? To be the person who must leave in order to save? I wished I knew who was going to be saved in the process: Durga? Liza? Grace?

On Easter Sunday my three day vigil was over with the return of Grace and Marcy within hours of each other. Allelulia!

"You've saved the day!" Marcy cried as she hugged me. "And the house! And the animals."

"Actually it was John the Plumber who saved the house," I modestly told the truth. "As well as the furnace. And my sanity."

"But you kept it saved," proclaimed a grateful Grace, "by reviving the pump," as Marcy rushed to the phone to call John the Plumber even though it was Easter evening. She needed to find out how soon he could install a more permanent, more reliable sump pump in the basement. I was relieved to hand that responsibility over to her.

Meanwhile I rejoiced at my liberation from what had proved a rather gloomy solitude. It's not that I'm not used to being alone or lurking in a basement, but I think I've had enough of loneliness and the subterranean. If finding Liza was going to be the ticket to my particular salvation, then I better get cracking. I had no illusions that I'd saved the house or, for that matter, the housebody.

Where should I go next, if not Haiti? I waited for Grace to provide some helpful hints.

Chapter Thirteen

DOGS AND GODS

Fortunately my sump pump valor in the eyes of Marcy and Grace gave me a reprieve from hurrying off to Haiti. Because I'd been there to save their house from flood and frost, they seemed content not to bug me about finding Liza any time soon. Even though it was quite clear to me, when John the Plumber arrived on Easter Monday to install the bigger, better sump pump, who the hero of this story was, I was content to rest on my laurels for the time being. At least until after All Species Day which Grace was busily preparing for at school as she assisted both children and their parents in designing costumes.

Marcy and I took a break from the daily TV Masses now Lenten Season was over, but I still often accompanied her on her daily walks—a break from my usual lackadaisical routine. As we strolled we often talked about other species, mostly dogs. She confessed to me that watching the dogs eat poop or rub in dead things pushed the limits of her tolerance for how different they are from humans.

"It's their extraordinary sense of smell," I murmured. "Not sure why they want those yucky odors in their fur, but apparently they like it."

"Yeah, apparently their sense of smell is ten thousand times better than ours. They can sense cancer cells before someone even feels sick."

"It's their blessing and their curse, you know." I thought of my own hypersensitivities.

"Their blessing and *our* curse, maybe, but I know what you mean," Marcy joked, then looked at me more closely. "Do you have anything like that yourself?"

"Well, I seem to have this radar that picks up negative feelings other humans are feeling but not expressing. It's a blessing in protecting me from being too naïve or helping me feel empathetic, but it's a curse when I feel mad or sad or bad for no good reason, and those who are actually having those emotions don't feel a thing—especially when I suggest that possibility and they deny it indignantly or matter-of-factly, which makes me feel even madder or sadder."

"Yeah, I know what you mean. At least the dogs don't try to hide their tastes," she said. "And it's not as if humans don't eat shit, metaphorically speaking, or have an appetite for the morbid. I guess in our own ways, we're garbage hounds too. Look at what's on TV."

I confessed internally to indulging in such trash. By this leap Marcy distracted me from finding out what her blessing and her curse was. Not the same as mine, I suspected.

"I wonder if God, if there is a God, or Gods, feel the same way about human beings as we do about dogs," I said. "Fond of, but baffled by our behavior."

"As we do about other humans," she added.

We then launched into a discussion of human nature from a self-styled divine perspective. By the time we tromped back into the kitchen to feed the roiling dogs, we had gone on to compare the death of Jesus with the death of the democracy martyrs in Egypt. We agreed they'd each stood up against tyranny—in his case against both the hypocrisy of the established religion and the occupation of Jerusalem by the Roman Empire. In the case of the Arab Spring, against feudal governance engulfed by American empire building.

"He didn't fight back. In that sense he was more like Gandhi, a non-violent resister." Marcy said. "Innocent. That's why Pilate washed his hands."

Grace stood at the kitchen sink washing her hands. I was worried she might be jealous about my growing connection with Marcy. Or our incessant talk about Jesus. But, I pouted to myself, it's nothing to be jealous about. I find Marcy's calm presence comforting, somehow. And we have this Catholic thing in common. Besides, in my own name, there's this Xavier thing.

"Do you feel left out when we go on and on about Jesus?" Marcy asked Grace. In the past I had described to Grace the many shades of Catholicism, not unlike the multiple Judaisms. I hoped she wouldn't object.

I was relieved and surprised when Grace smiled. "No, I'm intrigued. He was after all Jewish. But I didn't grow up knowing much about him. He sounds like a prophet, maybe even a messiah or bodhisattva, but you know, of course, I believe the divine is not a singularity, not even a trinity, but a multiplicity. Any one person is bound to be a limited manifestation."

I could hardly argue with her. Grace, actually, has always had more faith in the divine than I have, with her beliefs in the life of the world to come and spirit guides and even angels. I looked at Marcy and smiled.

When we all had dinner with Kara that week, she seemed similarly obsessed with life after death. By sharing Marcy's grief, we all were, I guess.

Marcy, of course, since her mother's death, had been wondering where her mother had gone. As I did when Mom died. It's puzzling, I know. There seem to be no obvious messages and yet there are signs and symbols which could be coming from her. Meanwhile, every flight, every set of wings reminds you of her departure.

Marcy nodded when Kara described this. "Yes, but where has she gone?"

"She's there, I mean, *here*," Kara explained. She'd been reading Elizabeth Kubler-Ross on life after death, as well as Raymond Moody's book about near death experiences. "Just in a different dimension.

"Why can't I sense her then?" Marcy asked, with some anguish. We all shrugged sympathetically. Not only W*here is she?* and H*ow is she now?* but also I*s she still who she was?* The puzzle of Liza's missing person seemed like a piece of cake in the face of these so ultimate mysteries. Much less obscure.

"Apparently they can perceive us but we can't perceive them," Kara explained. "Which is odd since we're the ones with the bodily senses, while they are free of all that—apparently."

"It's sort of like the dogs with their sense of smell ten thousand times better than ours, as you said, Marcy, right? With our limited abilities we can't even imagine how they can perceive us. Maybe that's where all the faith stuff comes in—we have to trust what we can't know."

Kara's was the only mother among us still alive, but given her advanced age, Kara was naturally anxious to figure out where her mom would be going. "Kubler Ross says the human body is like a cocoon and the spirit which survives is like a butterfly. It's that different. This life is only a preparation for that more illuminated soul."

"Well, I hope so. It affirms what a lot of spiritual teachers have said, but it doesn't make much sense." Marcy sighed, then smiled. "I guess that shows the limits of sense."

"Speaking of senses," I said trying to encourage this lighter note. "I sure hope dogs also have spirits which survive." Then I recalled that time Grace and I went to a psychic for a séance and I felt our old dog Shadow brush against my knee, almost sending me into a panic.

Next event in this action-packed week (Who would have known rural Vermont offered such adventure?) was The Wedding. I thought, despite all the hype preceding it, I would be the only one watching at the crack of dawn (I *was* the first one to turn on the TV), but lo and behold by the end of the day, all four of us had seen The Two Kisses and, at least, replays of the ceremony, the bow and curtsey to the Buttercup Queen, the procession to and from the Cathedral, and endless re-runs of Diana's wedding to Charles, her tragic marriage, and Kate's "commoner background, up from the coal mines into royalty." I was fascinated with the report that Diana was still calling Charles "Sir" at the time of their wedding and that Charles then and still doesn't brush his teeth without some valet putting the toothpaste on the brush. While bemoaning on behalf of this new young couple, Kate and William, the endless gossip and global scrutiny, contradictorily I relished every detail, from her dress and his red uniform to the spirited musical selections. I celebrated their love, her poise, their simple life together without servants, and the fact that they rode to the palace in a horse and carriage and left in a sports car. A good omen, no doubt, for the future of the monarchy!

Wait a minute—I don't give a hoot for the monarchy. Isn't it an outmoded institution? Aren't I an American? If I can't hark to the vision of King Jesus, why on earth would I celebrate the ascension of King William? And yet the British really know how to do pageantry, and this was a bright spot of love in the midst of a string of horrendous global disasters.

But truth be told, during our group post-mortem of the ceremony the institution we focused upon was not the monarchy but marriage. As a group we had mixed emotions about the marriage equality movement. While we have no problem with "equality," we aren't sure marriage, as between a man and a woman, is the right model for, or fits the relationships we experienced between us. Equal, I reminded myself, doesn't mean sameness. And yet wanting what the majority possesses was proving to be an effective strategy. Coveting thy neighbor's goods may violate one of the ten commandments, but it provides a great argument for fairness. Not that any of us are willing to sneer at some of the potential benefits.

"At least she cut out the 'obey' part," Grace commented.

"I wonder what the British monarchy would do if it were William and Henry rather than William and Kate?" Marcy asked.

"Or Kate and Elizabeth?" I added.

We all burst out laughing. Then collectively sighed. It wasn't just that old prejudice against gays which was getting us down, it was the fact that our own sub-species of human was divided about the issue of marriage itself. Probably more because we were women than because we were lesbians (I included myself in this category despite my occasional ambivalence). Even those of us in the most stable and long term relationships had doubts about the efficacy and structure of the institution of marriage. What form of bonding did we want to hang our authentic lives upon? And yet, why not honor long term committed and monogamous relationships, of which there were many among our friends?

Myself, I can't imagine being married. But maybe that's because I once *got* married. (More about that later, perhaps. It's not what it sounds like.) "Been there, done that"—as Marcy, who previously took that trip down the aisle, observes, Others like Grace, who is as devoted a soul companion as anybody I know, simply couldn't fathom marrying just one person to the exclusion of all those she loves and feels deep commitment to. She claimed she'd probably end up marrying at least a dozen, if not gobs more. (That might be one way to make sure everyone gets health coverage.)

The range of opinions about this strategy for equality also represented a split between older and younger gay women (I can't speak for the men). We older folks, for the most part, built our lives to survive without external validation. We masters of disguise and subterranean movements were now being asked to come out in the open, acknowledge our loves, make it all official. Yet we were so good at moving through the dark, some of us find it more spacious than the fixity of officially sanctioned situations and others still distrust the light, the scrutiny, the exposure. Although we all agreed with Harvey Milk that nothing will change around homophobia if we don't come out to friends and family, going so far as to wed publically seems to some of us a bit too much. We have no illusions that public scrutiny will assure tolerance. And we are smart enough to know that even the most solid love relationship, sacramental or not, can dissolve within the daily grind. Which isn't to say that we each don't long for a one and only every once in a while.

William and Kate represent a matched pair well grounded in the traditional realities, with clear roles, potential for producing future monarchs, and public acclaim. Despite the glamour of royalty, they are as familiar, in a way, as Mom and apple pie. William and Henry, Kate and Elizabeth live romance on the edge and on the sly, our secret stories hidden within private lives. These characters would be as recognizable as our best friends.

"I just can't imagine being that public with my love," Marcy said. I wondered if she meant Grace or Kara, or, from what I've seen, both.

"You can't imagine being public with anything," Grace teased. Yet, she too, would be hard pressed to deny any of her soul companions in order to choose just one of them to honor with her allegiance. For which I am grateful.

Marcy smiled. "That's true."

What we didn't say, but all knew, was that as a group we ourselves weren't exactly divided into couples in that sense of fixed pairs. It's not that we are promiscuous, or polyamorous, just that the connections between us are such a complex weave of friends, lover, partner, friends' honeys, it's difficult to conceive of them within the framework of marriage. Once you set up such a category, then everything has to be reduced to that either/or, if you know what I mean. If things between you change, divorce is your only option.

"Wilhelm Reich maintained that sexual passion lasts only about seven years," Grace opined. I glanced at her. If ever I were to marry a woman, Grace would have been my choice. I even begged her at one time to make that pledge, in an era where actual marriage between us was unthinkable—but she demurred, saying our "higher selves" were already united and seemed to be doing pretty well. And so, I guess, they were. Maybe that's what allowed us to grow apart from each other and what drew us together again.

But during this particular exchange Grace was tuned to Marcy. At this point I was just a background chorus.

"Marriage tries to make it last longer, probably for the sake of the kids," Marcy said. "My parents were happily married for more than half a century."

I wouldn't know myself. It was useless to speculate whether my parents would have stayed together if Mom hadn't died. Nor could I assess from my present perspective the degree of passion or even affection between them. Dad seemed devastated by Mom's departure, but why then did he so quickly take up with Nancy?

I wondered about Marcy and Kara. They seemed to be a couple but their connection felt fuzzy. They acted so independent of each other. And Marcy and Grace—I'm not sure yet. They seemed so well versed in each other, yet here they were, apparently, living very separate lives. How separate? I wasn't sure yet.

And how I, Xavy, fit into this whole dynamic, I had no idea yet. Not only didn't I have a clue where people went when they died, I still wasn't sure where I was supposed to be for the rest of my life. Vermont?

Our next event was All Species Day. I gathered it was some kind of costume party and parade, but as much as I like disguises, I felt reluctant to participate in such public silliness. But Grace insisted I'd find it meaningful, Marcy told me it was fun, and Kara implied that if she was going to make a fool of herself, she wanted company. So, figuring I really had no choice if this group was to be my pack or my flock, I fell in line.

Kara was going as a bear, wearing a mask she'd constructed years ago from paper mache. Marcy was dressed as a moth, with a pair of old fashioned snow shoes strapped upside down on her shoulders for wings. Grace and I debated going as two parts of a horse, but couldn't agree who would be the backside, which would have required a grueling stint bent double for the entire parade. So instead Marcy offered two legs of a table carved by her artistic great aunt as elephant heads, from the days when Asian exotic was all the rage.

"She was very attractive but never married," Marcy said about her Aunt Abigail, the one who carved the elephant head legs. "Mom always wondered why." We exchanged glances. The love life of spinsters was always fair game for speculation, but we refrained from outing her on the basis of absolutely no information.

Going as elephants in the middle of Vermont had its own appeal, despite the misleading political party association. Donkey that I am, I found elephants somewhat more exotic yet potentially just as loveable. Grace had read about how in the past century elephants came to Montpelier as part of the circus, lumbering off the train and marching down Main Street to climb the stairs to the local opera house, site of a variety of entertainments. Up and down those stairs alone seemed an impossible feat. They must have felt as out of place in this rural north country as we did in straight America.

Soon the four of us were climbing up the steep hill to Hubbard Park along with a streaming variety of real and pretend animals of all shapes, sizes, colors and disguises. Our human species, to my delight, wasn't just children, many wearing colorful wings of all shapes and sizes, but also adults dressed as everything from swans to turtles to moose. The real animals were almost entirely canine but included a range of breeds and sizes, most quite calm and amiable. (You could probably say the same thing about the humans, come to think of it.) Marcy remarked she was afraid neither of her dogs would be so well behaved. My old dog Phunky would have loved it, not so much because she loved other dogs but because she loved people. Were the dogs, at the same time, acting human, I wondered, or were we the only "pretenders"?

In the center of a soccer field surrounded by woods, this congregation of all species then formed a great circle. Suddenly, as a hush fell over the gathering and we all gazed at each other, I felt exposed—like I was being "outed." As an elephant? In that large arena, I felt like running into the woods. But, surrounded by the trio of Grace, Marcy and Kara, I figured I had no choice but to stay and participate, whether I liked it or not. It's one thing to watch a Mass on TV, quite another to be thrust into some pagan ritual without a clue.

At one edge of the circle stood two gigantic puppets in watery blue costumes. Opposite were white birds, a flock of gigantic geese held up on poles by people draped like feathers. "Bread and Puppet," Grace whispered reverently.

"Who?" I whispered back, but she was now intent on the next action, a blessing and song led by two women who were either Native American or dressed like Native Americans. This seemed innocuous enough, but I could feel my skepticism rise even as Grace whispered a translation of their chant. Was this going to be another woo woo ritual conducted by bourgeois hippies who didn't have a clue about the real issues of indigenous communities? (Isn't it funny how indignant we non-Native bourgeois can feel about the plight of First Nation folks without ever actually doing anything to address those issues?) Recognizing my ironic self I pushed her aside and waited, patient as an elephant, for further revelations.

Suddenly a human sized bird rushed into the circle flapping huge black wings and squawking dramatically.

"She represents spring and the return of the winged creatures as the sun rises in the east," Grace whispered. The raven then led a flock of folks with wings around the circle. I had to admire the varied feathered constructions and even began to speculate what kind of wings I might like. Marcy wearing her webbed appendages left us briefly to join this entourage.

Then a woman draped in black, like a witch, moving creakily as if she were ancient, carried a torch around the circle from the east to the south and lit another torch held up there by a woman in a costume emulating the sun.

"Time for the four footers," Grace whispered, pushing me into the stream of mostly faux animals emerging from the south to plod around the circle. I held up my elephant head and clutched at Grace's sleeve, it was so hard to see behind our trunks. Talk about exposure. As I blindly creaked along I felt like some ancient mastodon. But when I heard a child admiring our elephant masks, I felt heartened. Perhaps I was taking all this a bit too seriously?

At one point, as we paraded around with the other four footers, I peeked out to see Grace waving to a young deer on the other side of the circle who was walking with another deer of similar design. Since they were both wearing paper mache deer heads, I wondered how Grace recognized the first one.

"Who's that?" I asked.

"That's Hope. She did an internship with the school when she was in college."

"How did you recognize her in that outfit?"

"Well, she told me she was coming as a deer. And besides, I've seen that poncho on her a million times. She and Liza used to hang out together a lot."

"Oh?" This, I thought, falling out of my elephant stride and into a more focused private eye pace, might be an opportunity to talk to one of Liza's peers about her whereabouts.

Having completed our round, we returned to the south and watched the creatures of water with their fins and shells emerge from the west. Then, finally, from the north, the rooted, ersatz plants and trees paraded, waving their leaves and branches.

While Grace tried to explain these mysteries, how the directions corresponded with the seasons and the elements, I found myself charmed by some of the species: a young buffalo on stilts, his father dressed like a warrior, a little frog in her mother's furry arms, a bevy of teenage girls wearing gossamer wings with designs drawn on slender legs, and a sleek male cat pouncing upon invisible bugs. The presence of real dogs made our various constructed tails seem rather limp—although I had to admire the gumption it took for a human to wear one. Actually, even though real elephants do have tails, I didn't have one at all—didn't even think of it until I saw the other tails. Maybe next time, I thought, surprising myself by this concession that a "next time" was a remote possibility while I pondered how to make a more springy tail.

During another part of the ritual I spotted the pair of deer Grace had recognized and decided to seize this opportunity for investigation. But when I headed around the circle to confront them, they startled away like real deer might if approached by either an elephant or a human, and disappeared into the woods just as someone started playing a didgeridoo at the opposite curve of the ellipse to call us to another phase of the ceremony.

As lithesome young women frolicked around inside the sphere performing some ritual dance about burying the winter, and welcoming spring, I surveyed the crowd. Not everybody was wearing a costume but those who did seemed to favor the rustic. At some points it felt like watching a Brueghel painting come alive, with the added incongruity of some of them talking on cell phones or wearing designer boots. The medieval period is not one that has much resonance with me—whether it's nobility on horseback, peasants tromping through streets thick with mud and refuse of all sorts, or nuns confined to ancient convents. To tell you the truth, there is no period of human history I long to live over. So even though the modern age seems to have overdone progress, at least in this part of the world, to the point of decadence, there's no Golden Age I'm hankering to return to.

As the old hag extinguished her lantern and folded her dark body into a pile of straw at the center of the circle, I contemplated the fact that I'm not so much returning to some Golden Age these days as getting closer to departing this gilded one. I felt heartened when the same personage emerged from the straw bales as a youthful dancer in radiant robes.

While taking all this in, I saw the two deer dart past us toward a fire set by the convergence of torches from the four directions, where we were invited to burn an offering and make a wish. By the time we two elephants had plodded with our heavy heads over to that spot to toss our yearnings into the fire, the two deer had disappeared again. I marveled at their nimbleness.

From the fire we all processed from the muddy park down into the tidy town where we paraded through Main St., then along State Street past curious or admiring onlookers. We marched onto the lawn in front of the Capital Building, atop of which is a statue of Demeter, goddess of grain, a favorite of feminist lore in the days of the women's movement. (Demeter or Ceres is the mother who lost her daughter Persephone when she was abducted and raped by Hades, the king of the Underworld. In my mind at that time this myth had been reversed by my mother's death. She'd disappeared underground while I, the daughter, waited in the ordinary world for her return. Only I had no power of pomegranate seeds to trick the underworld ruler into releasing her from spring to fall.)

But somehow this whole ritual, outlandish as it appeared to my urban eyes, did a pretty good job of celebrating the return of light and heat symbolized by that myth, a radiance and warmth all the more precious because of the cold, dark days of a northern winter. It has been ages since I've been part of something much larger, more resonant than my own fragile survival. I hadn't felt this sense of belonging since the women's movement, and even then, I'd stayed on the edges, like the consummate journalist, watching and wondering more than acting and moving. No longer so employed or charmed by that observer role, perhaps my participation in All Species Day allowed for a morsel of transformation. (If not the return of Mom, at least progress toward a more expansive, less grubby self?)

Even behind my elephant head, I found marching down Main Street in that public setting surprisingly exhilarating. It felt like coming out, somehow—only, I guess, as an elephant rather than a woman of questionable sexual orientation. Of course nobody could really see me, but I could see them watching us, if only briefly. For most people, our moments of fame are only glimpses. They never get fixed by celebrity. But such exposure can be enlivening nonetheless. After my solitary sojourn clomping with the muck boots in and out of the dark, damp bowels of the basement abyss, it felt good to be back in the light.

At dinner out that night Kara shared her latest findings about life after death. Apparently the first thing we do in the afterlife is a thorough life review. Kara was convinced this would be a painful process, given her many flaws, failures and foibles, most of which were invisible to the casual observer (me). Grace tried to reassure her that this particular review wasn't about judgment but about learning from our mistakes, no matter how tragic or trivial. So we could, perhaps, she suggested, prepare to become bodhisattvas and return, even after this life is over, to save others. How Grace manages to keep this scenario Jesus-free is a mystery to me. But she knows about a life before the Jesus story, before the male hero-martyr story, a life like Kuan Yin's.

That night I dreamt that I was facing a panel of angelic judges, trying to justify my many peccadilloes and excuse every mortal sin, every indulgent veniality—most of which, alas, are already behind me. There are so many of each I despaired of ever getting into heaven, if such was the goal of this life review. Lordy, Lordy, I thought upon waking in a sweat, I better start making amends right now if I hope to turn my life around in time. What did that meditation teacher tell us about how we're like gems who just need a little more polishing? I'm going to need a jack hammer to grind off some of my dross!

When I turned on the TV the next morning to catch a bit of *Good Morning America*, I discovered Osama Bin Laden had been killed. It makes sense, I thought, that Obama would have to get rid of Osama—the association of their rhyming names, more than he could withstand. How curious both names end with MA. (And frankly, speaking of MAs, I thought, I still don't get why Moslem mothers are willing to send their sons out to commit suicide, or any mother, really, to send her son off to war. What a waste.) But to my surprise, I found out his name is actually Usama, not Osama. How odd that the first three letters of his name are the initials of the country he hoped to destroy: USA.

I was distressed to see Americans cheering in the streets, gloating as if we'd just won a football championship. It was just like the images of cheering crowds in the Middle East after 9/11. I wondered what kind of life review Usama was currently undergoing—he was the 17th child of his father at the beginning; he was holed up in two rooms with three wives and several children at the end. I thanked whatever God anyone believes in that the Special Forces crashed and burned that one helicopter and so they couldn't take the women and children hostage.

Then I switched off the pictures of patriotic Americans draped in the red, white, and blue, cheering for the USA—not unlike the British spectator at the Wedding, who had the Union Jack painted on his grinning face—only this demonstration was about killing, not matrimony.

Oh, God, what a complicated species we are, I thought.

Chapter Fourteen

GOING DOWN

Next thing I knew I was heading down to Baltimore on the train with Grace. I hadn't yet persuaded her to go with me to Haiti, but somehow she'd talked me into going with her to Baltimore to visit an old friend recovering from surgery. She touted it as a homecoming of sorts. At least a return to our old haunts. I knew I'd probably chicken out on my own, so even though a large part of me wanted to just wallow in Vermont, I figured I better grab this opportunity to have her support in revisiting my errant past. She, of course, had been back many times since the heyday of the women's movement so it probably didn't seem as sinful or as past. Especially since Grace doesn't believe in sin or absolute endings, for which I am eternally grateful.

"Maybe we should just hop a plane from there to Haiti," I suggested tentatively as we swayed, click clacking along the edge of the Connecticut River, savoring views of the fresh greens of finally spring sliding past our sight.

"I can't afford to go to Haiti!" Grace protested so loudly I knew she was intrigued.

"Durga will pay for it," I argued, wishing I could be sure. Meanwhile, to assuage our mutual reluctance Grace and I were sending regular donations out of our own shallow pockets for Haiti relief efforts.

"For you, not for me." She had a point. Why should Durga pay for her? If Grace cared as much for Liza as Durga did, Durga's reasoning would assume, Grace'd be out beating the bushes on her own dime.

"I'm not going without you." This, I finally realized, was the formula by which I could avoid going to Haiti. But I really meant it too. Without Grace I'd be sure to get into trouble in any foreign country.

"There is absolutely no evidence—psychic or factual—that Liza is in Haiti. If it turns out that she is, then I'll go with you—but only as a last resort, only if she refuses to come home any other way."

"I'm on it." I replied in my most professional manner. What that actually meant remains a puzzle. Research!? Surely if she's in another country, she has to have a passport with her real name on it. Which means that if she's working down there for some NGO, then they must have some record of her presence. (Research, the preferred alternative to so much activism—with a few tempting exceptions.) Nonetheless, having heard how many different NGO's had rushed to Haiti in the wake of the disaster, I felt a bit daunted. Good thing Durga has deep pockets because this might take some time.

As the green of trees began to give way to the flatter hues of houses, I mulled over my resistance to going to Haiti. From all I'd seen on TV, it was a lush, green country with lovely, lively people. Despite all the hardships of poverty, politics and weather they'd suffered, both the land and the people seemed remarkably resilient.

As I started to nod off I got a flash of my younger self yelling "Go to hell" at my new stepmother—a display of self-indulgence which got me kicked out of my family home and well on my way to a threadbare inheritance from my disgusted and disappointed dad. That was one of the few things—along with "I hate you," "Drop dead," and "Shut up"—our real mother wouldn't allow us to say. I could just picture her distress in heaven when she'd overheard that, even though I can't imagine she'd ever have been any more enamored of Nancy than I was. Fortunately for her, she didn't have to be—whereas I did—at least act polite. So, now, was the message of that one outburst coming back to haunt me? There was nobody here telling me to go to hell. Did Durga's urging me to search all over the world for Liza strike my tender ear like that variation of "get lost," coming back to bite me? The old Durga certainly wouldn't have hesitated to convey such a message. After all, I'd been as fond of Durga in her previous incarnation as I'd been of Nancy—the truth is, they somehow remind me of each other. The irony of all this is that instead of going to hell, Nancy ended up in Hawaii, a paradise of sorts. With Yuggie too! How lucky for her to have been cursed by me. (Not so lucky for me.)

Somehow relieved to have figured this out, I turned to Grace who was eyeballs deep in a novel by an Australian writer about the

American Civil War. After trying valiantly to keep her concentration free from my niggling interference, she finally put the book down with a loud sigh and paid me some attention. Realizing I had a very brief window of opportunity to make this interruption worth her while, I asked about the friend she was going to visit, I'd forgotten why. Some illness, I gathered from overhearing Grace telling Marcy about it with some distress.

"She just had surgery for cervical cancer," Grace said sadly.

"Uuuh. Sounds serious."

"Maybe not. It was what they call a 'surgical cure.' They got all the cancer cells, there was no evidence of any spread, and she's basically pretty healthy."

"Well, that's good. Do I know her?"

"I don't think so. She was before your time." They're always, according to Grace, either before or after my time. My time, in Grace's mind, must've been just a blip.

"What's her name?"

"Sierra."

I gave Grace a look. "No, I mean her real name," I said with a slight snicker. How many people our age were ever named Sierra? The look Grace gave me back was enough to wither a sun god. It implied: Does anybody whose own name was imposed upon her have any right to feel superior? "Well," I murmured, "It sure sounds like a *chosen* name to me." I took a deep breath and started again, "What's Sierra mean?" I asked earnestly, murmuring to myself, *anyway*.

"Mountains, I think. Or maybe a mountain range."

"Odd name for somebody from Baltimore to choose."

"She was from out west, actually. Colorado or New Mexico, I think."

"What was her original name?"

"Faith Hall."

"You mean like the singer?"

"That's Faith Hill. Hall was her birth name. Then she married a Miller."

"*Faith Miller*. I knew her!" I said triumphantly. "She wasn't before my time."

Grace looked surprised. "Tall and slender? Kind of ethereal looking?"

"More anorexic, I'd say," in deference to my former, somewhat chubby, Baltimore self. "Very straight, as I recall." And not without a touch of self-righteousness, I thought to myself.

"Until she came out. More 'traditional,' I would say. Even after she became Sierra."

"Yeah, wasn't she a minister's daughter?"

Grace nodded, obviously reluctant to pursue this inspection of her sick friend just to keep me entertained. Again, I was proving so insensitive that I rued the advent of my life review. I tried to think of a kind thing to say about Faith aka *Sierra*, but I'd known her only from a distance. Doesn't Sierra also mean *saw*? I wondered but decided it was better not to ask. A sawtooth mountain range?

I was also curious whether Grace considered Sierra a "soul companion," which would suggest they'd at one time been lovers. This too seemed best to keep to myself for the time being. Not all Grace's lovers were "soul companions" but it seemed that all her soul companions were, at one time or another, lovers.

Grace went back to her book and I distracted myself by watching a little girl in front of me stick a well-chewed piece of gum on the buckle at the back of her older brother's baseball cap while he played with some electronic gizmo. Every time she glanced back to see if anyone was watching, I managed to avert my gaze lest she think I approved or disapproved. Finally he grabbed the cap, hurtling the gum under the seat. When she crawled down there to retrieve it, she caught my eye from beneath as she checked me out, and I gave her a grin. Although I never had a brother to bother, I could admire her impishness. One of the pluses of not being a parent is an unwashed appreciation for mischief. But once spotted, that little rascal made a point of disappearing.

As soon as we arrived at the splendidly restored train station in the middle of Baltimore, Grace insisted we hop into a cab and go right to Sierra's house where she was recuperating under the care of her longtime partner, friend and currently "wife," Mona. At that point I was ready to hit the sack after twelve hours on the train, but Grace was resolute.

"Wife?" I groaned.

Grace held up a hand. "Please, Xavy, not now." She hopped out of the cab, paid the driver with a sweet smile, then snapped around and faced me sternly. "If you don't want to come with me, I will understand completely. You don't know Sierra, after all. You have no reason to care—"

"Oh, please, Grace, I want to come with you. I want to help . . . you, if not her. Help you help her." *Help me*, I thought. Suddenly I feel compelled to beg to go visit someone just recovering from major surgery out of some misguided assumption that I could be of help? And yet, I knew this compulsion felt right. The right thing to do, for all the wrong reasons. This was already turning out to be an instructive course of action, this coming down here with Grace.

Grace smiled and nodded, slipping her arm around my shoulder as we bent to pick up our bags and march purposefully down the block in search of Sierra's house, a stylish row house in a respectable and integrated middle class neighborhood. Certainly a step up from our old hangouts. No danger of purse snatchers or drug busts in this locale—a good thing since I felt vulnerable enough pulling the suitcase behind me over the cement grooves in the growing dusk.

Reluctant to wake Sierra in case she was resting, Grace knocked lightly on the front door instead of ringing the bell. As a result it took a while before anybody heard us. Finally footsteps approached, then the front door creaked open tentatively, revealing a plump face about Grace's height, a winsome smile and very weary looking eyes. Seeing Grace, the woman opened wide the door and embraced her, sobbing briefly in Grace's arms.

This, I guessed, was Mona. The warmth with which she greeted Grace suggested that Sierra and Grace hadn't ever been intimate in the deepest sense of that word, but that wasn't a sure bet. It depended on how long Mona and Sierra had been together and how much Sierra revealed to Mona about her past dalliances. Be that as it may, it was clear that Mona needed some relief from caretaking.

And soon it became clear—as she ushered Grace upstairs for a private visit with Sierra, who was too wiped out to deal with more than one person at a time, particularly a virtual stranger such as myself—that the one designated to provide solace to Mona in the form of tea and sympathy was me. I started, while the water boiled, with washing the dirty dishes which filled the sink, then sat down at the kitchen table with a sturdy mug of ginger tea to listen to Mona's litany of complaints, mostly about the hospital and the doctors and the whole goddam medical system in this country—nothing, of course, about Sierra who'd been a perfect lamb during the whole ordeal. This I found hard to imagine unless Sierra was a saint—but who knows? In any case it didn't require any special sanctity on my part to sympathize with Mona. All I had to do was ask some pertinent questions, nod encouragingly at her revelations, and tisk with a shake of my head at the outrageous behavior of one night nurse. Against my natural predilections I didn't question anything she declared. I just listened with concern until the venom was all gone and she was able to open up somewhat about the terror she'd felt at possibly losing her partner. I nodded vigorously at this. Even though I had no partner to lose, I could empathize with such a potential loss, marriage vows or not.

Finally, as I felt her venting subside with this slight admission of vulnerability, I addressed her weariness, suggesting that the caretaking itself might be taking a toll. To my surprise, she vehemently denied this. *Uh oh*, I thought, another martyr? What did Grace say about Willow? How they hate to be congratulated—instead prefer condolences? Had I, in my attempt to be kindhearted, crossed the line? It was tricky. Apparently any suggestion that Sierra was a burden on Mona was anathema. But any praise of Mona's caretaking was also heresy.

Suddenly I felt like bursting into tears myself—and I didn't even really know Sierra. It was that thing of mine I was telling Marcy about—how I pick up the unsaid feeling and try to poke it out into the open. However, in this case, short of whacking her over the head with my limp tea bag, I didn't see how that could happen. Fortunately she'd already cried on Grace's shoulder so her need for catharsis was dissipated. My function here wasn't, after all, counseling; it was witnessing.

Trouble is, by this point, I was getting bored. After all, I'd never met Mona before. (I think the ailments of old friends are more interesting somehow when you know the roots of or are surprised by the outcomes of their distresses.) And boredom for me can be dangerous for others. I resolved to keep my big mouth shut: no telling her what she was or should be feeling, no advice, no offers to take over, no analysis, no nothing but nodding and moaning with her. *Sigh.*

Fortunately, eventually, Grace appeared to save me from quizzing Mona more closely about her relationship with Sierra. I prayed she hadn't decided we should spend the night there in order to support the recovering couple. Then I realized Grace already knew that would be a bad move, for so many reasons. It was one thing to be there for Sierra and to sympathize with Mona; it was quite another to impose ourselves upon them. What a relief. Despite the dire circumstances common sense was going to prevail. Grace promised Mona she'd return the next day.

When we got out on the street again, our suitcases trailing noisily behind us, I asked Grace where we were going to sleep that night. It was now approaching midnight and I was wiped.

"At Mia and Ruth's," she replied.

"Good grief," I gasped, "are they still together?" From all our old pairings Mia and Ruth were the most unlikely couple, yet here they were still together. Grace nodded. "Oh, I hope that doesn't mean we have to drive out to the country." Last I'd seen them, they were part of a women's rural commune.

"Oh, no, that venture is long since over. Now they live in the city, not far from here. Within walking distance, in fact."

I groaned. Grace's idea of walking distance and mine are worlds apart. But in fact it didn't take us long, and the exercise felt good after long hours stuck in the train followed by the strain of sitting still listening to Mona in her kitchen. Vermont must be getting me in shape.

"How was your visit with Sierra?" I asked as we trudged along.

"Amazing!" Grace said. This surprised me. I figured it would have been gloomy at best. One reason I didn't mind being left out. "She had an OBE while she was under."

OBE? I wondered. Is that some kind of special operation? Obe, as in "robe"? Or "globe"? Or did it relate to obesity? (Which seemed unlikely unless Faith had really changed *a lot*.) I shot a puzzled glance at Grace who then explained in an overly patient tone, "Out of body experience."

"Like a near death experience?" I asked, recalling Kara's description of the book she was reading, *Life after Life*.

"I think so," Grace said.

"An NDE," I said smartly. With a little heads up I could brandish letters with the best of them. "What's the difference?"

"One happens when you die, the other doesn't require dying."

"So Sierra didn't die and then come back?"

"Not so the doctors noticed."

"Which isn't saying much, given what Mona was telling me about the doctors."

I wanted to ask Grace more about Sierra's experience and why it was amazing, but we were tired and instead got busy searching for the right address. Grace's sense of direction is somewhat compromised, so, even though she'd been there before, I didn't trust her leadership in this respect. I imagined instead us wandering around in circles all night. This neighborhood of old Victorian homes, many apparently converted into apartments, was somewhat funkier than Sierra's neighborhood. But lo and behold we found Mia and Ruth's modest house easily enough. It was painted a variety of colorful but tasteful hues and its wrap-around porch was especially inviting.

We were greeted at the door by a very sleepy looking Mia. She looked much as she had the last time I saw her, maybe ten years earlier, a little greyer, a little rounder but just as luscious looking as ever. She gave me a warm hug as if we'd stayed close friends, then led us to a guest room with a futon, already pulled out and neatly made with sheets, pillows and blanket, told us where the bathroom was and went back to her own bedroom. I hesitated to point out that Grace and I didn't sleep together anymore, but Grace just collapsed onto one side of the bed with a groan and within five minutes was sound asleep. Even though this was hardly the romance of previous incarnations, the warmth of her back, along with her heavy breathing, felt comforting after my long, lonely hiatus from any kind of bodily contact.

When I woke, Grace was gone and the scent of coffee wafted into the guest room. Sun poured through the bathroom window as I took a shower and brushed my teeth. After Vermont's chilly spring, Baltimore's southern warmth felt good. When I joined the group in the kitchen, Ruth, whom I hadn't known well in the past, shook my hand and gestured me toward the coffee sitting out on the counter. We didn't speak lest we interrupt the intense conversation between Mia and Grace. I guessed it was about Sierra's OBE.

"At first she was just hovering over the operating table watching the doctors work on her body."

"Yes, that's pretty SOP for OBE," Mia joked. I was glad to see that I wasn't the only one taking this with a grain of sand, or salt, or whatever.

"But, Michela, listen to this," Grace said. *Michela? Oops. She wasn't Mia anymore? What's this with all these name changes? Are our identities all that fluid?* "After floating there awhile she started heading toward the light, you know the blessed light. And when she got there, she felt this blissful feeling. And then she was greeted by her child."

"She had a child?" I asked.

"She lost a child," Grace replied. "A baby . . . only a few months old."

I was shocked. "How terrible."

Grace nodded. "She was devastated, needless to say. That's probably what broke up her marriage. The tragedy was she couldn't have any more children. She'd taken a big risk just having the one."

"So how did that meeting make her feel?" Mia asked. I could tell from her hushed tone she was now completely into this story. I wasn't sure about Ruth who stood there just listening intently.

"Oh, wonderful. The child reassured her it was ok she'd died, it wasn't anybody's fault. She'd only needed those few months to do whatever she needed to do in this life."

"Wow," Mia said. "She must be a very evolved soul."

Either that or she didn't have much to do, I thought, but didn't say so lest Grace complain I was being too literal. It's just that one wonders about things as such short lives. It's reassuring to think they have a purpose, however fleeting.

"The only trouble is that once this occurred Sierra didn't want to come back to this life. She wanted to go on and be with her child. But the Being of Light who was with the child told her it wasn't her time yet to die."

Suddenly I understood why Mona was feeling so put upon. Sierra would have preferred to stay with her child in the other life rather than return to Mona in this one? How noble yet unrewarding to be taking care of someone who'd rather be somewhere else.

This, for some reason, reminded me of Durga's search for the missing child, Liza. Suddenly I wondered if Liza had decided she'd rather be with her departed mother Sheila than continue her life on earth. Had she taken her own life? Or does committing suicide set up a barrier between the soul and her departed loved ones? Suicide's a sin for Catholics, so one might expect, if one is Catholic, some kind of punishment. They say when you die, you get what you expect. In some cultures, like ancient Greece or Japan, suicide can be honorable. So did the Greek and Japanese suicides get rewarded while Catholics who commit suicide get punished? That didn't seem quite fair.

Somehow this suicide scenario didn't feel right for Liza. It made some sense for older folks to want to join their younger departed beloveds but generally it's expected that younger people have their own lives to live before such ethereal reunions. Besides, if Liza were with Sheila now, then I suspect on some astral plane Sheila would let her partner Durga know so she'd stop paying me to search for Liza. Not that she was paying me at the moment, since I couldn't figure any way of justifying this trip to Baltimore as part of the search. If I had, I would have flown.

"How's Mona taking all this?" asked Ruth matter-of-factly. Exactly, I thought. It's one thing to play around in the afterlife, but meanwhile, back in this one . . . people are still suffering.

Grace looked at me, acknowledging my appraisal of Mona's condition as the freshest. "Not well," I pronounced with some authority. "Looks to me like she's one screech away from a nervous breakdown." Or at least a screaming fit.

"Oh dear," said Grace, looking to Mia for help. But Mia, it turns out, was somewhat estranged from Sierra, and probably Mona too, for reasons I of course was not privy to, although I gathered from a hushed conversation between Mia and Grace and some salient remarks by Ruth that it had something to do with Mia and Sierra both being in the same church choir. I was surprised to hear that Mia, being originally of Italian Catholic roots, as was I, would be going to any church, much less a Protestant one (since I was pretty sure Sierra, being a minister's daughter, would not be going to a Catholic one). While they chatted, I speculated on possible causes for this falling out: a mutual crush on the choir director, an argument over the selection of hymns, someone singing off-key.

Anyway, the upshot of this morning's processing was that Mia would go with Grace back to Sierra's house, both for reconciliation—what better time for forgiveness than right after an OBE? If not a NDE?—and to persuade Mona to take a break somehow while we took care of Sierra. This generosity of "we" gave me some pause, but what the heck, if it was a group action, I might be willing to participate, especially if Mona was both taken care of and out of the way—just to be part of something larger than my own limited self. Besides, in her blissful state, Sierra's recovery might even be pleasant.

Once they'd headed breathlessly out on their mission, I asked Ruth why Mia had changed her name to Michela.

"Oh, that's her birth name. She decided, when her mom died, to go back to her given name, out of respect."

"Oh!" How sad we have to wait until they're gone to honor our mothers.

"Of course, 'Mia' is actually what her mother called her when she was little. It just stuck for awhile too long."

Dear, dear. Does this mean I should stick with "Mary Catherine"? Oh, Mom, why don't you come back and tell me what to do sometimes, as you tried so valiantly when you could? Do I have to have an OBE, or perish the thought, an NDE first?

Trouble is, I've gotten kind of fond of "Xavy." It feels good to be called that again. It's livelier, somehow, than Mary Catherine—more me.

Chapter Fifteen

BODIES AND SOULS

It was my own fault: I was guilty of attention seeking of the worst kind. After having consoled Mona for several days before we shipped her out to visit her sister, I resorted to the competitive illness ploy. I regaled every one sitting around Sierra's kitchen with the story of my most recent conundrum, what Grace called the house/body bowel syndrome. Her theory that houses and bodies sometimes reflect and resonate with each other's conditions proved a more fruitful topic than my bowel distress, leading to more theorizing about whether our cars echo certain psychological difficulties like braking, clutching and steering issues.

But it also precipitated a cascade of stories about various infirmities. Thanks to me, we heard about Mia's knee replacement, Grace's rotten teeth, Lucy's kidney stones, and, in absentia, Mona's diabetes. Only those who had life-threatening illnesses—Sierra still basking in the glow of her OBE and Ruth whose bout with breast cancer she was firmly set against dwelling upon—declined to contribute to what my grandmother used to call the "organ recital."

It was like one of our old consciousness-raising sessions, each person getting, more or less, equal time to connect the topic to her own personal experience. Only with this particular topic I knew from experience it would only speed up in terms of individual miseries while spiraling down in terms of group gloom, like a washing machine on the spin and drain cycle.

Desperately I wondered how to shift the momentum. Lighten things up.

Funny, we used to talk about bodies in terms of sexual liaisons— although only rarely discussed sex itself. Now our contact stories were not about lovers but about doctors, massage therapists and herbal healers. Some of us are completely enthralled by the established medical system; others, wary of traditional western medicine, swear by various alternative therapies.

Unfortunately my sexual liaisons had dwindled down to a precious few flirtations, which I really couldn't offer up as a tempting conversational shift. *What about the erotic dimension of life?* I thought of asking. *Aren't we all still alive to that?* Then I imagined them asking me to explain. The truth is, sexuality in this contemporary culture is so out there, bodies on display, private parts scarcely private, that affairs seem more than ever like trophies, and sex itself, no longer hidden, no longer mysterious, often appears comic. With very little left to the imagination, a certain numbness sets in. Anyway, I wasn't quite ready to serve myself up as the butt of some kind of joke. What other distractions might I offer? How could I shift this conversation to something more redolent of our old edgy, feisty, tough talk? Whether or not sex itself was hush-hush in the old days, relationships were not: we took great pleasure in gossip about flirtations, affairs and break-ups.

Glancing around this circle of friends, desperate for something juicy, I realized Lucy had shown up at Sierra's minutes after Mona headed out to visit her sister. Was there something tantalizing going on between her and Sierra? One more trial poor Mona would have to endure? We'd all known Lucy in the old days. Her freckles were a little wrinklier but her slightly bucktooth smile was just as endearing. Back then she'd been quite the Casanova. Just the person to ground one after an OBE?

This offered a tempting ploy with which to shift the conversation, but, even if it were true, I was the last person to put the spotlight on somebody else. Besides, outing Lucy in this context, on the basis of no evidence whatsoever, except her timing, especially given the out-of-body aura still lingering around Sierra, wouldn't really shift the tone of this conversation. For one thing, gossip doesn't work if the people you want to gossip about are right there with you.

How else to shift the focus? Ask about vibrators? Share exotic fantasies? Catch up on *The L Word*? How about something akin to the auto-erotic? Maybe that favorite old question: If your life was portrayed in a film, which actor would you like to play you? I, of course, was caught between Sandra and Angelina, but, realistically, I'd settle for Meryl or Ellen.

But, as they droned on about their symptoms, my only remedy at the moment was simply tuning out. I found myself recalling images of teams of women practicing "Rhythmic Gymnastics" for the Olympics. For someone who didn't have the foggiest idea about this sport, it looked, with their skimpy, frilly but colorful costumes, remarkably erotic as the women tossed bright balls into, under and around each other, a coordinated group in constant motion. Like some synthesis between an ancient fertility rite and quantum physics.

Eventually, after many a twist and turn, our own conversation turned to sharing various remedies. This held slightly more interest for me, highlighted as it was by conflicting approaches to healthcare which reminded me of our political differences in the old days: a full range, from the more prescriptive and obedient to the more experimental and resistant. I wondered if personal responses to health care could be allied with certain political tendencies, but, looking around, could see no particular patterns. And to complicate matters, some of the most rebellious in our youth now sound like the most compliant.

Finally I saw Ruth stand up and rinse her coffee cup with some impatience, and I suspected we'd gone far enough with the aging body themes, so I switched the subject toward the soul by asking what Mia's writing group was focused on.

"Mostly memoirs," Mia said. "We want to get it all down before it's too late."

Ruth groaned at this, and I had to admit it sounded awfully apocalyptic. Good prep, though, for those life reviews after death Kara told us about. I wondered what I would write about my life if I were so inclined. A career in journalism, ironically, can skew one's approach to one's own biography. Either it's not dramatic enough or attempts to liven it up are automatically suspect.

"The Karen you mentioned, the one with the carpal tunnel syndrome," I persisted, still trying to steer us away from topics of death and decay, "is that Karen Townsend?"

Mia nodded. Karen was a friend of mine who'd ended up on the other side during the famous split in the women's movement in the old days.

"Do you remember the Women's Union split?" Grace asked. She knew Karen had been one of the group we called The Heavies.

"Who could forget it?" said Lucy. In those days she had been on our side, of course.

Sierra, who hadn't been around at that time, looked curious, so we quickly filled her in. This split, which played itself out in a dramatic confrontation over the content of a women's fair, had left the Baltimore women's movement in shock for years.

"So you don't feel any rancor toward Karen?" I asked Mia. Karen had sided with the leftists; Mia, of course, with the feminists.

Mia shrugged. "That was a long time ago. And remember I was on the periphery, because we were out in the country trying to create a women's land trust. I remember that awful meeting when they withdrew from the union, of course, but I wasn't much involved in the aftermath."

Grace and I looked at each other and shrugged. Truly a lot of water had gone over the dam since then. "Who knows," Grace finally said, "maybe they were right."

"About lesbian mothers?" I asked incredulously.

"No. But maybe about lesbianism being a distraction from feminism. Wasn't that really what was bothering them?"

"Uhhn?" I said. I was in no position to take a position. Besides, we're all such unique compounds of identity it's hard enough to sort out the individual strands much less turn a single one into a political imperative.

"Do you remember the Lesbians Against Families," Lucy asked in her harmless yet mischievous way. This kind of teasing had made me wary of Lucy in the past. But after all these years she seemed perfectly innocent.

I remembered. Attacks on the family, even in those rebellious days, felt like anathema . . . even though at the time I wasn't exactly dripping with appreciation for my own family.

"No," Mia said, "Who was that?"

"Some separatists," Grace murmured. "They wouldn't let any boy children attend their events." She obviously didn't approve. I moaned, feeling for my vulnerable little Oscar.

"Male dogs either," Lucy added.

We laughed. Some of us had, as familiars, male dogs. If they weren't welcome, neither would we want to be.

"Lesbians Against Families: LAF," I spelled out with my newfound appreciation for acronyms. "It must have been a joke."

Grace shook her head. "I'm afraid they were deadly serious."

"Sounds like the lesbian equivalent of the Heavies," Sierra said.

"But it's not like they had the option of being, in those days, 'For' Families," I observed.

We nodded as we mused over changes in the larger society. Then we fell into a discussion of how gay couples these days are not only allowed to keep their children, they seem to embody some of the strictest values of traditional family life. This led to a brief but decisive critique of *The Kids are Alright.*

It was only a hop, skip and jump from there, conversationally speaking, to Gay Marriage.

"If Mona and I hadn't gotten married," Sierra said, "it would have really been hard for me in the hospital. You really need someone there to look out for you, even to the point of sleeping in the room with you to make sure you get your meds and who can insist on nursing care when you need it."

"I know," said Lucy. "A friend of mine was in the hospital recently and nobody would answer her call button."

"See, Babe," said Ruth to Mia. "It just makes good sense."

Mia looked conflicted. This, apparently, had been a standing argument between them for some time, even though Maryland had yet to pass gay marriage legislation. Sierra and Mona had gotten married in Massachusetts and somehow the local hospital honored that bond.

I could see that Mia wanted to protest against marriage, but given Ruth's stand, as well as Sierra's married status, she couldn't exactly speak freely. As a total non-participant on so many levels, I could only admire her fortitude. Were I in a committed relationship, gay or straight, would I want to get married? Hard to tell. Marriage still felt a bit like servitude—or, at least, a straitjacket. I suppose it depends a lot on who you marry.

"Did you know," Grace said, "that straight couples can collect 50% more of their social security payments for their spouses, even when the spouse has his or her own social security benefits—as long as only one of them is collecting at any one time?"

This was news to all of us except Ruth, who again nodded toward Mia. It was a moot argument, however, since there were no federal marriage rights for gay couples.

We wandered away from this gloomy topic to discuss various children and grandchildren we knew, including Liza. Grace shared the story of Liza's disappearance without, thankfully, implicating me as the person hired to find her. This led to speculation about where Liza might have gone. Again I was fascinated with the range of options, aka projections, as well as struck by the fact that some of these people actually knew Liza, from visits to Vermont—certainly more than I did. Yet none of their speculations provided any convincing clues.

I was, however, somewhat comforted by Ruth's story of how her own daughter held off communication for almost two years during one long, rambling search for her true self. Now she was living around the corner with two children of her own, the joys of Ruth's life aside from Mia. This suggested a positive interpretation of Liza's absence, as well as a potentially lengthy partial employment *pour moi*.

"Best leave them be until they've found their own firm ground," Ruth said in her sensible way. I couldn't agree more (despite the hook of Durga's checkbook).

From there we returned to the topic of what happened to Sierra during her NDE. Actually she insisted that she hadn't actually died. Even though she'd been separate from her body which lay there on the operating table, she had another body which was full of light and free of pain, and which felt fine.

In that body, she told us, she was able to embrace her child, whose body was smaller than hers, like a child's would be, but somehow not as small as a two months old baby's. This caused me to wonder about the passage of time in eternity, whether the child was still growing—but I didn't ask because I suspected nobody knew, and besides they were all enthralled by Sierra's description of the Being of Light and what s/he said to her. We all wanted to know if the Being was male or female or androgynous, but she said she couldn't tell and that it didn't matter. It probably didn't make much difference either what class or race the Being belonged to. The only things which mattered, according to Sierra, were love and learning. Same as what Kara had been reading about.

Love and learning? Where'd that leave me so far in this life? I never did so well in school and I was at a dead end with relationships.

That night I woke in the darkness to Grace's gentle snoring, feeling very down. I'd dreamt about Liza. She was on the phone saying something I couldn't quite hear. Her tone was hushed and her words were elusive. I wasn't even sure she was talking to me. The fact that she called at all suggested she was still alive, but since I've had messages in the past from people who were probably already dead, like the still missing Iris, I couldn't assume the best or the worst, or, now that I'd heard about Sierra's OBE, I couldn't even assume the worst wasn't the best.

Anyway, the fuzziness of all this, and maybe other reasons, left me feeling very depressed. I just wanted to cry, but I didn't want to wake Grace who was worn out from listening so empathetically to so many sad stories from all her old friends. I didn't want to be just another sob sister. But the fact of the matter was I was all alone in my single, solitary life, without a partner, without a mother, without a daughter or granddaughter, or even a niece or nephew (unless Yuggie had adopted somebody in my absence, which I wouldn't put past her).

Soon enough, or perhaps it was just from the wine that night after coming back from Sierra's house, Grace woke and heard me snuffling into my pillow.

"What's wrong, Xavy?" she asked, her fingers tentatively touching my bowed back.

"I don't know, I just feel so depressed," I moaned. "Everybody has somebody and I have nobody. No wife, no husband, no children, no grandchildren. All I have left is Yuggie and she's all the way across the Pacific Ocean."

"You wanted children?" she asked sympathetically, trying to keep her surprise at bay.

"Didn't you?"

"Not really. I enjoy children, most children anyway, but I never wanted to play the disciplinarian or get so invested in their life success that I pressured them to make certain choices. I wasn't drawn to the role of parent, maybe because I was the eldest and had to take care of the younger ones when I was still young myself. I certainly don't miss some of the conflict and disappointment so many parents seem to experience with their children."

I just moaned, unable in my distress to appreciate fully the common sense of her words. "Nobody cares about me," I cried. "If I were in the hospital with some deadly disease, who would be there to make sure I got my meds and my meals?" *It's not that I am under any illusions that my non-existent children would be there for me, but chances are they'd at least send get well cards.*

"I would," Grace said calmly.

This, for some reason, made me cry even harder. "No, you won't. You've got a beautiful life without me; you've got Marcy and Kara and Ariel and Durga and even Willow. You don't need me."

"Maybe I don't need you, Xavy, but I love you."

"You do?" She was stroking my hair gently as if I were a child, which is what I felt like, young, vulnerable and very much alone. But this time, which I take as a sign of some maturity on my part, I didn't launch into my usual catalog of failures—financial, professional, personal in terms of spiritual growth, personal in terms of relationships, health in terms of addictions, health in terms of lack of exercise, health in terms of diet—milking the catastrophe which was my life for all it's worth—no, instead, I just accepted her comfort for what it was, a generous gesture from someone who needed more sleep, someone who was truly a friend.

In the morning, with somewhat greater clarity, I wondered whether the dream about Liza had set off my depression. Did I, somehow, identify with Liza? Or was I picking up, as is my wont, something she was actually feeling? Given that I didn't know Liza at all, had never even met her, that really seemed a stretch.

After breakfast I was alone with Grace when she said, "Let's go home, Xavy"

"Home?" I replied. I didn't say, but I thought, *home? Where is home? I don't have a home.*

Chapter Sixteen

JUNCTION

The train ride back north was crowded but uneventful until early afternoon when we crossed into Vermont, chugging along the Connecticut River, shifting between New Hampshire on one side and Vermont on the other. At that point, the conductor announced that one of the next stops would be "White River Junction."

This announcement was then picked by a boneless looking, disheveled boy/man seated behind us who had been playing some kind of video game since he boarded the train with his mother and sister in Massachusetts. Aside from some mutterings over his hand held device, he'd been fairly quiet until this announcement, but as soon as the conductor stopped, this young person started chanting, "junction," over and over. At first it was funny. I started to chuckle with him, then realized if I laughed, it might sound like I was laughing at him. Instead I glanced at Grace, her head buried in her book. The sound of "junction" has, initially, a certain appeal and resonance, I thought. Perhaps he's just a poet gone wild. But despite efforts by his mother and sister to shush him up, he couldn't stop saying the word—over, and over, and over.

After awhile, a long interval of silence, he, mercifully, paused, his voice growing fainter as we churned along the track. But the next time the conductor repeated his announcement about forthcoming stops, the chant resumed, over and over and over: "junction, junction, junction." I was hoping that the deeper we got into Vermont, the calmer he would become. But it was as if a switch in his brain had turned on and he didn't know how to turn it off. Apparently nobody did.

I found myself falling into the rhythm of the *junctions* until the words blended and split in novel ways: *Junction* became *junk shun,* then turned to *shun junk, sun drunk, drunk son.* I began to wonder if the word in any of these permutations had some secret meaning for him. Eventually the cadence of the train's clacking and swaying melded with the pulse of his voice, almost putting me to sleep.

His speech had the opposite effect on Grace. Finally, she pulled her head out of the novel she was reading and searched desperately for some place where we, or even just she, could find some place to hide from all the "junctions," but the train was packed—there were even a couple of youngsters with back packs standing in the aisle at the back of our coach. After maybe the hundredth "junction," Grace fluttered her hands in the air and disappeared toward the restrooms, mumbling something to me about saving our places.

"Must be that echolalia," I whispered to her as she left. She just rolled her eyes.

Grace was not alone in her distress. Several passengers looked like they were heading instead toward shrieking meltdowns or an all out physical assault.

I tried to imagine it as some kind of Hindu chant or even like the Hail Marys in a rosary, something even less than innocuous, maybe even spiritually potent enough to put me in a trance. But without the help of some smoke, I soon realized I wasn't going to get there. I tried chanting "junction" to myself under my breath (so as not to encourage him), hoping it would lose its bruising power, but the more I did that, the more it took on deeper meanings: *junction,* the apocalyptic turning point between death and life currently facing the planet; *junction*, a personal crossroads between my life passed without meaning and connection or better options which might lie ahead; *junction*, the crucial decision I should soon make about who and where I need and want to be . . . all focusing on a moment in time rapidly approaching as inexorable as the imminent White River . . . . Was the Universe, as they say, sending us a message through this unlikely prophet? If so, I figured, Grace didn't care—or already knew.

It seemed also, though, that I personally was being called to make some kind of momentous choice. But aside from leaping off the moving train into a shifting array of destinations—none of them necessarily soft or pleasant—I wasn't sure what that choice might be. Should I become a Tibetan monk? Ask Grace to marry me? Adopt a child? Go to Haiti by myself? Or just sit there in solidarity with my sound-challenged fellow passenger murmuring: "junction, junction, junction," wondering what it all means.

Once past White River J, I figured we were in the clear, but soon the conductor announced the approach of "Montpelier Junction," and the refrain began again: *Junction, junction, junction.*

"I didn't know Montpelier was also a 'junction,'" Grace whispered as she returned to our seat once we left White River Junction. Having finally habituated myself to his chanting, I just smiled beneficently. As soon as we arrived in Montpelier she grabbed her suitcase, murmured "What a relief!" and hurried off the train. I took my time, glancing back at the echoing boy as he and his family also gathered their belongings to depart the train. As we exchanged glances I smiled at him. His eyes lit up but he quickly looked away.

Outside the train Grace waited for me at the tiny station, then led us down along the track to a parking lot where Marcy was waiting for us. A homecoming of sorts. Nice.

Most of the way home, Grace in the passenger's seat, me in the back, we regaled Marcy with our tale of the Junction Boy, but before we pulled into the drive, she announced quietly that Liza had called.

"What?!" Grace and I said in unison. She glanced back at me with raised eyebrows. Our missing person had finally surfaced? Was this the mysterious junction the boy had been announcing? The return of Liza?

"She phoned because she'd heard the two of you were on your way to Haiti to try and find her."

"Heard from who? *Whom?*" I asked.

Marcy shrugged. "She didn't reveal her source."

"You didn't ask?"

"I did ask. She didn't answer." Marcy replied primly to my tone of incredulity.

"Hmmm," Grace said. "Does this mean she's ok. Have you told Durga yet?"

Marcy shrugged. "She said she was fine." Then she shook her head. "I wanted you two to be the first to hear."

I smiled in appreciation. Even though I didn't know Liza, I was relieved for her sake and for everyone else's that she was, apparently, not dead or in danger. At the same time I realized this meant my gig was probably up, so to speak. This current source of income would immediately evaporate, along with my excuse for being here. "Did she say where she was?

Marcy shook her head. "But she did admit she was in another country."

"Another country," I mused. "I wonder if that's factual or metaphorical." Like *home.*

"I assume it's factual. Liza's elusive but she's not the dreamy type," Grace said. Her implication, I could tell, was that I am the dreamy type, just for suggesting such an interpretation.

"I wonder why she called you and not Durga," I commented. Grace and Marcy exchanged a glance, then simultaneously shrugged. Neither, apparently, wanted to point out the obvious: that Liza felt closer to Marcy than she did to Durga.

"I want you both to be there when I tell Durga," Marcy said. "I don't want her going ballistic on me alone." Aha, so the new, improved Sandra/Durga was still capable of going ballistic? The fact that generous Grace nodded, rather than protesting, confirmed this possibility. And as long as Grace was there, I was willing to go too, just out of curiosity. "She's traveling at the moment," Marcy added, "so we have a good excuse for delaying. I'll try to set up a meeting by email for when she gets back."

"So this means that Liza is found, even though we still don't know where she is?" Grace asked.

Marcy shrugged. "I think it means Liza doesn't want to be found." I glanced at Grace and she also shrugged. I felt it would be gauche to shift the focus to yours truly, but I couldn't help wondering what this would mean for my current income stream.

Grace and I then dragged ourselves to our respective beds (no more sleeping in tandem) and I fell into a deep sleep full of dreams about junctions, junctures and junk. When I woke, I felt disoriented. Where would I go now? Back to Boston? Back to Baltimore? Any chance I could stay here? Maybe find some kind of job?

The next day I woke feeling both groggy and disorientated. It was too late for the dog walk with Marcy, who didn't seem to be around. I checked to see if her car was still parked in the drive and since it was, I figured she was probably down in the barn working on her stained glass. Grace had left a note on the kitchen table saying she'd gone to the school to catch up.

I spent the day in desultory activities like checking my email and googling everything I'd wondered about in the past week, from OBE's to echolalia, waiting until 4 p.m. when I planned to sneak into the living room and turn on the TV for Ophra's last show. It's not that I was an Oprah regular, mind you—there were times when I just couldn't take all that public soul-searching—but I certainly was an admirer. I remembered her from her last days as the news anchor in Baltimore, during my first days there as a cub reporter and neophyte feminist and I've followed her amazing career ever since. I certainly wasn't going to miss the last show, no matter what Marcy or Grace might think about my weakness for pop culture. It was already clear to them I was a dreamer and a neer do well—I couldn't even find a missing person who was only a phone call away.

Imagine my surprise to find the TV already on and tuned to the right channel with Marcy and the dogs sitting and waiting. All I had to do was smile and join them. When it was over, I turned to Marcy with tears in my eyes. "To God be the glory!" I echoed moistly. Ophra's last quote.

Marcy, I could see, was just as moved. "What a story," she finally said. "It's as if she brought the consciousness raising process of the civil rights and women's movements into a national dialogue."

Then after a respectful silence we launched into a discussion of whether she was or wasn't . . . , about "the triangle," about why Steadman was so obviously present at this broadcast while Gayle apparently was absent, about the trash magazine I'd read on the train which claimed Gayle was offended Ophra was planning to live with Steadman in California instead of her and while Oprah was jealous of Gayle's growing intimacy with the Obamas.

"Interesting that Steadman's a last name and Gayle's a first," I observed.

"Steady man," Marcy murmured. "And I guess he has been. That must have been a comfort to her. Yes, it does seem a bit gendered, doesn't it? But Ophra's only a first name too, and look what she's done with that—turned it into something like *Moses* or *Michelangelo.* Talk about making the most of what you've been dealt."

We left it at that. Neither of us a stranger to triangles (I often wondered how she managed to keep primary connections with both Kara and Grace), we weren't about to grind the gossip into little pieces we could spit out scornfully. Instead we had a healthy meal together with a minimum of cooking and a maximum of nourishing conversation. We talked about our departed mothers and wondered whether they could still follow our lives. We talked about other species and what we had to learn from them.

By the time Grace returned, the bond between me and Marcy felt like a longtime friendship. I felt so much at home that Grace's announcement about Laurel, almost as soon as she stepped into the kitchen, flipped me.

"Who is Laurel?" I gasped.

"She's a friend of mine from New Mexico." I must've looked devastated because Grace added, "I'm sorry to kick you out of the guest room, Xavy, but it's only for a week. Then you can come back."

"Kara said she'd be happy to have you stay at her house in Montpelier," Marcy said solicitously. "It'll give you a chance to hang around town."

But, but, but, but, but I cried out internally. What does this mean that Grace has a special friend in New Mexico? Who is this Laurel? What about "home, sweet home"? Just then, as if to answer me, Zoom jumped up into my lap. So comforting for us both. Home is both a warm lap and a warm kitty in your lap?

Later Marcy told me that Grace had met Laurel at the college library when Laurel was in Montpelier for a residency of the local MFA program for writers. So Laurel was a writer? But wasn't I writer enough for Grace? Oh no, because Laurel writes fiction and poetry and I'm only a journalist. And to top it off, Laurel is exotic Hispanic while I'm just plain old Italian-Irish. And, I gather from what Marcy told me, Laurel is drop dead gorgeous, while I . . . . let's not even go there. No wonder all Grace wanted from me was a little interim companionship while she waited for the return of Laurel. How could I be such a fool as to think she was hankering after me? Of course I hadn't figured she *was* hankering after me until it was quite clear she wasn't.

I sighed deeply. Marcy obviously felt a great deal of empathy. Of course, she knew how I felt. Grace had dumped her for Ariel, I guessed, then again, for Laurel. She probably assumed Grace had dumped me for someone else, although I knew, and Grace knew, the truth was somewhat more complex.

"How do you stand all this shifting around?" I asked her.

"Oh, you know, I'd certainly rather have Grace around than not. She's simply not somebody who is going to stick with just one person. And yet, she's loyal to her friends."

"I'll always be true, darling, in my fashion, true, dearie, in my way," I sang, choosing humor over tears. I had to admit, Grace is nothing if not faithful.

To distract myself from this new distraction I turned to checking my email. I was astonished to find the following message in my in-box: *"Hello. how are you doing? i hope everything is moving well with you. please don't be surprise to recieve my message in your mail box, i got your email address through episody that was forwarded to my email address so i decided to write to you, but before i proceed i will like to tell you my name, I am Miss Grace Juliet Zaya. I will be very happy to have you as my good friend because the warmth of a friend's presence brings joy to our hearts, sunlight to our souls, and pleasure to all of life. kindly write me back so that we can introduce ourself more better as well share thought and pictures with love, honest and faithfullness. thanks for your reply. Yours sincerely Grace"*

By what *episody* or echolalia, I wondered, have I been bounced from Grace to Grace? I began to speculate about the possibilities of many Graces. Who were the Three Graces of Greek mythology? Here, I realized, I have been hung up on Grace's many lovers when in fact there are in the world at large also many Graces. Inclusivity can work both ways. Not only can Grace embrace multiple others, I could welcome other Graces.

Although tempted to embrace this instant friend, or at least to use her as a decoy from my feelings of rejection and competition, I finally decided to delete her, paranoid as we all have become about identity theft and fraud in this age of cyber insecurity and mutant viruses. So much for my diversity of Graces. Despite the competition, I guess, I prefer to clasp the blessing I know than the one I've never met.

And so the next day I packed up my meager belongings, made sure I had my stash of weed and my computer, said goodbye to Marcy, Zoom and the dogs and headed out to Kara's house.

Chapter Seventeen

THE GRANDMOTHERS

Kara's house in town was lovely and peaceful and she was very hospitable, but under some deadline pressure at work (one aspect of employment I don't miss)—not much available for hanging out. So I decided to write a memoir, by way of a life review. After a couple of days of staring at my computer screen trying to figure out where to start, what to say or not say, and how to justify such self-centered activity, I gave up and started wandering around town.

Montpelier is the smallest state capital in the country—only 8,000 residents, but full of visitors from surrounding towns, legislators from around the state as well as tourists from across this country and Canada. It doesn't take long to hike from one end of town to the other. With church steeples punctuating the sky in all directions, it feels like a typical New England village. I sampled treats at every eating establishment and tracked down the best cup of coffee. I lingered in bookstores and conducted a thorough survey of all the small specialty shops. I watched for bear and deer, which Kara told me had been seen in the nearby park or wandering the residential streets.

By the time Grace called to ask me if I wanted to join her at a welcoming ceremony for the 13 Indigenous Grandmothers, I jumped at the chance to see her (and maybe meet the mysterious Laurel) as well as witness the ceremony. I wasn't sure who the Indigenous Grandmothers were, but I was curious.

The ceremony was in the middle of a green in front of the college on a hill above the town. Very New Englandy with its red brick buildings and white pillared facades. But the parking places around the square had all been taken. I tried to squeeze into a spot next to a fire hydrant but thought better of it when a woman about my age frowned upon me. Perhaps she was just frowning, or maybe just squinting into the sun, but I felt intimidated so I moved my car up into a crossing with yellow warning signs. I'd picked up some carryout at the Coop at the bottom of the hill and was eager to eat it before the ceremony began. As I sat there cramming some mac and cheese into my mouth with a plastic fork, a young woman leaned into the window of my car and told me the obvious, that I was illegally parked. "I wouldn't want you to get towed," she said cheerfully, but I suspected she would be happy to see me reprimanded.

So I finished eating, then swung around to another street where a spot stood open just in front of a hand-written "no parking" sign. I squeezed in so someone could still fit behind me. Turning around as I got out of the car I saw a bevy of colorfully attired older woman crossing the street where I'd just been parked—so that's why that young woman wanted me to move, I realized. I'd been parked in the path of the Grandmothers, one of whom was in a wheelchair. Why hadn't she just said that?

I snatched my camera out of the trunk and ran onto the green to take photos of the indigenous costumes. As I was busily snapping away, another young woman with a camera told me I wasn't allowed to take photos of the Grandmothers. When I glanced at her own camera, she explained that there was only one official photographer approved by the Grandmothers, plus her, and she had to sign some kind of confidentiality contract assuring that she wouldn't use the photos for any commercial enterprise. "We aren't *allowed* to take pictures?" I asked incredulously. When she saw my protesting face, she explained somewhat apologetically, "There will be a photo opportunity later."

Jesus Christ, I thought as I marched back to my car with the camera, *rules, rules, rules*. These must be awfully strict grandmothers. I thought of my own grandmother, who was for awhile my best friend. She wasn't so much strict as she was firm. As I was stashing the camera back in its bag in the trunk, I turned to face a woman about my age whose lean, bronze face was full of laugh lines. She was dressed in a colorful costume and accompanied by a bossy looking younger woman obviously trying to herd her along to catch up with the rest of the Grandmothers. This darling Grandmother winked at me and I grinned back. Perhaps it wasn't the Grandmothers who were so strict but their handlers.

As I circled the green, sizing up the crowd while checking out the sky which had been threatening rain, I reflected as I do occasionally on how I happen not to be a mother, much less a grandmother, wishing I hadn't skipped that first stage so I could become a grandmother. Even though I'm now old enough to be a grand, nobody is clamoring to protect my path, shield me from nosy photographers, much less listen to my wisdom, which is certainly not indigenous. I do like relating to children. I'm not so wild about disciplining them. Maybe my reluctance to give birth was Mom's early death—not wishing to inflict such a potential loss on a child of my own, but I know others for whom the loss of a mother was extra incentive to continue the legacy. In any case, I sometimes feel somewhat excluded by celebrations of motherhood and so had mixed feelings about honoring all grandmothers, much as I loved my own Gram.

Grace was there, not with Laurel but with Ariel and they were both shepherding a flock of small children from their school. There was no time for me to complain about all the restrictions, only enough for her to tell me the 13 Indigenous Grandmothers was a council of wise older women from around the globe who were traveling together to bring a message about saving the Earth. Only seven of them had been able to come to Vermont. Once I connected with Grace and her contingent, Oscar, my little charge from the school, found me and took my hand. I began to calm down while the Grandmothers assembled slowly in front of a natural arch constructed in front of a fire pit with wood waiting to be lit.

After another round of instructions and prohibitions from one of the handlers, we all stood around waiting for a young woman to, literally, rub two sticks together to make fire, while thunder rumbled from the distant hills. Behind the diverse group of Grandmothers I saw a flash of lighting, bright and focused. I imagined it plunging down into the fire circle, miraculously igniting the flames. I found myself caught between faith and practicality. One minute I was ascribing to the Grandmothers supernatural powers and the next I was wondering why, if, according to the introduction, the Grandmothers had brought a fire which has been already been around the world without ever going out, we needed to build our own fire. Perhaps it was an empowerment ritual? Around the edge of the circle, between the Grandmothers and the participants a tall, lean man circulated, as if shaping the circle's energies, herding them perhaps into an orderly assembly by which the fire was finally born. Just in time for the thunder and lightning to usher in a brief shower. But the man and two women managed to shield the nascent flames from being doused. Miracle enough.

Because of Oscar's warm hand in mine, I refrained from any smug remarks about fire building in the rain and waited patiently with the rest of the gathering for the fire to flare up and the showers to dissipate.

As I glanced around the circle I saw Grace talking to the same young woman with the nose ring we'd seen at All Species Day, Liza's best friend whose name I now recalled was Hope. Once again I moved around the fire toward them and once again, Hope retreated. This time it was obvious to me she knew who I was and fully intended to avoid me, which only strengthened my supposition that she knows where Liza is and doesn't want to tell me. When I finally reconnected with Grace, I could hardly contain my exasperation. She looked puzzled.

"Grace, it's obvious she knows where Liza is," I complained.

"She's sworn to secrecy, and I have to respect that," Grace replied.

"You knew this all along?" Somehow I felt betrayed. I'd assumed Grace was my co-conspirator in this search, but apparently not.

"I suspected it when Marcy told us Liza had called. How would she know we'd gone off on a trip if someone—probably Hope, who must've heard it from Ariel at school when I was absent—hadn't told her?"

"Why didn't you tell me?" I whined.

She shrugged. "Frankly, I figured the search would be over now that we know Liza is ok and obviously prefers to keep her location a secret."

"I guess we'll find out when we talk with Durga," I said, pushing off the wave of despair which threatened to inundate me every time I realized my reason for being here was evaporating.

"Don't worry," Grace said, reading my mind as she was wont to do. "We'll find something else for you to do."

I gazed across the circle at Hope's departing back. I still longed to interrogate her.

But at just that point the heavens opened and poured down their libations on the gathering. Umbrellas were unfurled and an announcement was made that the whole assembly would move into the college gym so the ceremony could continue. I'd had my fill of ritual so I ran back to my car and, having neither umbrella nor raincoat, took my soaking self back to Kara's house for a shower and a nap.

Kara, I realized, lived a bit like a monk in the simplicity of her home. It felt, once you entered it, like a sanctuary. Entering this peaceful environment I immediately felt at ease, safe from whatever turmoil raged outside. Beautiful objects like feathers and rocks mingled with crafts and paintings which honored the elements. Every surface could serve as an altar, paying homage to and through nature and art. This home, while comfortable, felt like a temple. The crafted products seemed both natural and spiritual. The objects from nature had aesthetic and symbolic appeal. Candles at strategic spots highlighted this reverent atmosphere. Soon I discovered Kara's cd library stocked with a wide range of meditative music.

The next day, encouraged by a phone call from Grace and still curious to see the visiting Laurel, I went to the State House where I expected to find a similar gathering around the Grandmothers on the lawn in front of the gracious capital building atop of which was a statue of the Roman Ceres or Greek Demeter, the goddess of grain. The one whose daughter, Persephone, disappeared into the Underground after being abducted by Pluto. Thank the Goddess the same fate had not, apparently, been suffered by Liza.

I expected this event would be on the statehouse lawn, complete with signs, chants, and random acts of desperate kindness like the many protests I'd covered in my reporter guise. This time, since rain was forecast, I made sure to bring an umbrella. But the wide green lawn was empty. Instead I followed a festively attired crowd, many dressed as other species, through the capital building itself and up the curving staircase into the legislative chambers. I found myself between someone in a bear costume, and someone in a raven costume. When a young person of ambiguous gender and species identity, aside from sporting a tail, asked me who I was there to represent, I recalled my elephant guise for All Species Day. But somehow claiming to be an elephant in the legislature might put me on the wrong side of the aisle, so, recalling the stuffed animal I had as a child (Yuggie, of course, had a lamb), I said, "Donkeys." S/he grinned in a way which made me realize s/he could care less about my political chops. So, if this isn't a political event, I thought, why is it taking place in the Statehouse?

To my astonishment, there in a half circle in the middle of the room, below the speaker's podium, sat the seven colorful Grandmothers, including the one who'd winked at me. As the horseshoe hall filled up, I grabbed a legislator's seat without caring whether it was Republican or Democratic, Progressive or Independent, and sat down to watch the proceedings. I wondered if any of the "grandmothers" were gay. I recalled something Grace had told me about Native American gay folks being called people with "two spirits." This, better than any other labels, fit my own contested identity. Which Grandmother would I want to flirt with? Probably the tardy one with the great laugh lines.

I spotted Grace herding some children from school into a half circle in front of the Grandmothers. I knew they'd been practicing a song to sing for the Grandmothers, but I didn't realize how close they'd be to the action, if "action" was the right word for this mild gathering. Laurel, if she was there, was in the background, and since I didn't know what she actually looked like, I couldn't spot her although I certainly tried. I mean, how many drop dead gorgeous Hispanics were in the audience? Perhaps she was disguised as some exotic bird? Grace's attention was totally with the children, so no clue there.

Someone was playing a flute with mellow music which gave a meditative cast to the ceremony. Then a very tall man with long red dreadlocks, wearing a colorful robe which seemed right out of central casting for the latest film about Merlin, waved a long stick which looked like a cane but must have been a wand, and the buzzing crowd settled into respectful silence. I heard somebody next to me whisper that he was a Druid. I recalled a brief foray into Wicca with someone I'd had a crush on back in the day, and figured he was what they called a Warlock. He certainly had a booming voice to go with the role.

What on earth is this? I thought. It was wild enough to meet with the seven indigenous Grandmothers here in these stately chambers. Now we're going to have some pagan ritual as well? Conducted by some male witch? Whoa!

Sure enough, after welcoming the Grandmothers, the Druid priest solemnly cast a circle in the center of that House of Representatives, evoking the directions which were then poetically described by human representatives of assorted species. The four directions somehow were equated with the four elements and the four seasons, as they had on All

Species Day. But that drama had taken place outside in the park. This ritual was being held in the very seats of power. Other ambassadors also evoked the above and below dimensions, conflating my childish notions of heaven and hell with class divisions in contemporary recession-plagued America, until I realized they were pointing at some very different directions, toward earth and sky. But I still wasn't sure what all this had to do with politics.

As more speeches and music followed, I check out the participants in the crowded chamber: mostly women of all ages, quite a few children, a smattering of men. Some in animal costumes, some hippies in "native dress," some wiccans, but nothing uniform, just the usual eclectic Vermont gathering of nature lovers and eccentrics. I might have expected to find some of them dancing on the lawn or carrying picket signs but certainly not sitting solemnly in the Legislature as if they were about to debate some law.

After the children sang their song and presented crystals from Vermont to each of the honored visitors, the Grandmothers spoke, some in perfect English, some with accents, some with translators. They were from Tibet, Central America, South America, the American West and other countries I didn't catch. One sang a song about gaining happiness by giving back everything one receives. Others spoke of honoring our natural world and all the creatures in it, of the importance of gatherings such as these. None of them preached or ranted or advocated for a particular piece of legislation, but we all, if by including myself I make an "all," felt blessed. There was something magical about this event. Certainly like nothing, in all my years of reporting, I'd ever experienced before. A peaceful takeover of the governmental center of power? It was political without being political, if you know what I mean.

The next day, however, more angst—not the extinction of a species anxiety, but a more personal loss of an animal friend. Marcy called to tell me through tears that Zoom had died suddenly of feline leukemia. I couldn't believe it. He seemed perfectly fine the day I left, curling around my legs and purring as I packed. But he had been lethargic, which I figured had to do with warmer weather and a too wet spring. I was shocked—Zoom, my biggest, perhaps only real fan in this new environment and without a doubt, my most comforting friend.

Marcy had just gotten back from the vet with his body. He'd taken very sick in the past few days and by the time she got him to the clinic, there was nothing they could do but put him down. She was distraught. Grace had gone off on an adventure with Laurel and she was alone. I said I'd be right over.

When I got there I could see that Marcy was even more stunned than I was, but also blaming herself. "I didn't have him inoculated, I didn't know, I'm not used to cat illnesses since I didn't grow up with cats, all my cats have died of old age, I didn't think he'd catch it from another cat because there are no other cats around here, I feel I let him down, I didn't take good enough care of him, I just thought he had hairballs, so I treated him for that and then I decided he had worms so I treated him for that, but I didn't take him to the vet because the tests have gotten so expensive these days, and I let him down when he was dependent on me, and he was such a sweet, sweet cat . . ."

I let her get it all out, then gave her a hug and wept with her. Regret is one emotion I know inside and out. We blame ourselves for the most of reality we have no control over. Would it be worse to realize how essentially powerless we mammals are? I briefly wondered if he'd gotten sick under my watch, while Marcy was away but decided it wouldn't help her if I took the blame, and truly, he seemed fine during that time, bright eyed and playful, despite the surrounding gloom regarding the flooding basement. Instead I helped her dig a grave in the front yard where he liked to sit and watch the birds at the feeder. Together we lifted his body out of the carrier which sat on the front porch and laid him to rest. We placed a cat-shaped candle on his grave and thanked him for all he'd given us.

As we sat at the kitchen table sipping tea, Marcy confided that her grief over her mother's death was reactivated by Zoom's death. "I've convinced myself through readings and through hints of connection with Mom that there is life after death," she said, "but I'm not sure about animals."

I skipped the reminder that we are animals, and instead told her about Shadow's appearance during that séance I'd attended years ago with Grace. Marcy then told me about messages she'd received from people who'd died, about things only they would have known. We pondered this mystery without drawing any definitive conclusions. I missed Grace whose certainty about life after death was so reassuring. And yet I knew, from my own experiences, that belief, no matter how firm, cannot erase the sting of loss. So instead of pondering the ultimate secrets I asked her about her mother and told her about mine. Focusing on those deepest of losses and those particular loves of our lives, we were able through this sharing to feel more grounded.

And this loss provided us both with more empathy for Durga when we met with her a few days later. Laurel had flown back to New Mexico and Grace was ours again. The drive up the winding road was saturated with green and the road itself had been recently filled in so the ride was much smoother than on our last visit during mud season. Nonetheless Grace drove carefully as she and Marcy chatted in the front seat, mostly about whether cats have souls. I sat in the back seat and wondered what a soul really is.

This time we didn't meet in Durga's modest meditation hut but in the house, a sprawling affair which glittered with expensive furnishings and objects d'art. It felt a bit more like a museum than a home, at least not like any home I'd feel comfortable in. Beautiful, for sure, but so polished you slid over its surfaces. In my case probably leaving greasy stains. I'd been nurtured by Kara's temple of a home yet felt like a sightseer here.

We gathered around the kitchen island, its granite top cool to our touch. Sun steamed through the large picture window, misty with rain from the night before. I quietly drank the high octane coffee Durga provided us while Marcy reported on her phone call from Liza.

Durga, I could feel, was mightily peeved that Liza had called Marcy instead of her, but she restrained herself fairly well. Meditation training, I figured.

"No, there wasn't any static on the line," Marcy said, "no indication of where she was calling from. It could've been next door for all I could tell. And of course she didn't say."

"How do you know it was a foreign country then?" Durga asked through gritted teeth.

"She told me, by way of explaining why she thought Grace and Xavy were going to Haiti to look for her."

Durga gave me an inquisitive look. Of course I hadn't told her I'd agreed to go to Haiti because I hadn't agreed. I just shrugged. I figured it might be best to let ambiguity prevail.

"Did she say how long she would be there?" Grace asked.

Marcy shook her head.

"Or why she won't reveal her whereabouts?" Durga asked.

This time the rotation of Marcy's head suggested to me both a shake and a nod: yes, I guessed, Liza did tell Marcy why but she swore Marcy to confidentiality. Which suggested to me Marcy wasn't the reason for Liza's cloak and dagger routine, but that Durga might be.

Durga must've made the same interpretation, because, to my shock and horror, she suddenly burst into tears. This was an entirely new event: Durga weeping. Unimaginable In years past. The cool, the collected, the above it all Sandra never showed a spurt of emotion other than irritation.

Grace was immediately at her side, patting her back and offering a tissue, while shooing us both out. Marcy and I retreated to the rather sterile living room while Grace administered to the distraught Durga. As we settled our tushes tentatively on the white couches, Marcy murmured something I couldn't hear, so I moved closer and asked her *sotto voce* what she'd said.

"I just don't get it," Marcy whispered. "She always resented Liza's primary place in Sheila's life. They never seemed fond of each other. Why is she so bent out of shape now over Liza's trying to live her own life?"

I shrugged. Who was I to translate the so often inexplicable contradictions of human behavior? But I'd been touched enough by Durga's tears to give her the benefit of the doubt. "Maybe Sheila's death changed everything for her? So now she feels responsible?" I thought about it. After all, it takes two to tango. "Why can't Liza just be open about her desire for independence?"

Marcy nodded. "I asked her that, in fact. She didn't exactly say, but apparently she feels some pressure from Durga to do something she doesn't want to do."

"What could that be? She has her own trust fund so she's not dependent on Durga in any way, apparently."

"Yes, Sheila made sure of that. She must've known they weren't a match made in heaven. But you're right—death changes everything. The pressure might not have anything to do with money."

Gazing at the gallery worthy display of paintings and sculpture gracing the living room and at the valley wide view through the glass wall in front of us, I found it hard to believe that money didn't play some role in Sheila's quest. Just then Grace appeared in the hallway to beckon us back into the kitchen/dining area.

In the kitchen a sad looking Durga reached out hands to both of us, encouraging or allowing us each to pat her on the back sympathetically. This vulnerability and receptivity was, indeed, for me a new phenomenon, something the old Sandra would never have tolerated in herself. Good old Grace. Nothing like her empathetic touch to turn somebody around. She'd probably been the one who'd helped Durga through her grief when Sheila died.

I sat there receptively, awaiting word of a significant turnaround, some realization from Durga that she was finally willing to let go of Liza and move on with her own independent life. Even though such a conversion would send me back to the unemployment line, it felt like progress.

"Xavy," Durga said solemnly, looking deep into my eyes, "I'd like you to go to Korea."

What?! I stared back at her.

"I'm convinced that's where Liza is. How dense I've been. I should've guessed this from the very beginning."

I glanced at Grace who looked stunned.

"Why would she be in Korea?" Marcy asked, her voice tight with restraint.

"Of course she wouldn't tell me about it," Durga said, caught in her own internal loop. "It doesn't have anything to do with me."

"Liza was born in Korea," Grace explained to me as if that solved the mystery.

"But she was just an infant when Sheila adopted her?" Marcy said. "Surely she can't remember . . ."

"When Sheila died, Liza felt the need to find her birth mother," Durga announced.

"How do you know?" Marcy asked, trying to keep skepticism out of her voice. "Did she say so at the time?"

Durga shook her head, revealing some of her old impatience. "Isn't it obvious?"

"Not to me, it isn't." Marcy murmured.

Korea? I thought. All I knew about Korea was the Korean War, which my father fought in, the thriving economy of South Korea and the morose situation in North Korea after that war. And all the mixed race children in orphanages as a result of American servicemen stationed over there. She is going to send me to Korea? All by myself? *I don't think so.*

Chapter Eighteen

P TOWN

The next thing I knew I was off to Cape Cod and Provincetown—not Korea, and not alone, but with Grace, Marcy and Kara. This was a vacation trip long planned by Grace and Marcy. Fortunately they let me come along. They were eager to share Cape Cod, and Provincetown, with Kara who'd never been there. Kara drove while Marcy and Grace reported to her about the meeting with Durga, Grace with amused compassion and Marcy with some skepticism.

Grace's soft spot for Durga puzzled me. She could be ferocious in her penetration of people's phoniness, but for some reason, even though she had no illusions about Durga, she tended to give her the benefit of the doubt every time. *Perhaps to balance my inclination toward opposite interpretations?*

"It just seems to me that Liza is more interested in getting away from mothering than in finding more mothers," Marcy said. "Autonomy, not more entanglement."

"Maybe we underestimate the effect of growing up an Asian child in a mostly Caucasian community," Grace replied. "Identity is a big deal when you're that age. Remember how bent we used to get over every label?"

"That was the heyday of identity politics," Marcy replied. "It was the times, I thought, not a developmental stage." Grace shrugged.

I, the one pinpointed for this mission, tried to imagine Liza's possible family as I began sorting through all my stereotypes about Korea: peasants killed by North Korean bombs, mixed race children from affairs between American soldiers and Korean women, the stigma of being an unwed mother in a traditional culture, prostitution your only option, parents so poor they figured their child would be better off in America . . .

"Well, I doubt very much that Liza went to Korea," Grace said authoritatively. Again, I wondered why she sounded so sure.

"I can imagine her wanting to find another mother," I said tentatively. Goodness knows, I found a host of mother substitutes after Mom died, although I'm not sure how conscious I was about it. Grace sighed. I assumed she was thinking about her mother.

Fortunately, for all their speculation, neither Grace nor Marcy agreed with Durga that I should be sent to Korea to search for Liza. At least at that point. Besides, they could hardly ship me off to Korea just as they were about to sail off to Cape Cod.

"If she's gone to Korea, then we'll hear all about it in good time," Grace said philosophically. For all her impatience sometimes, Grace can be remarkably accepting.

"Durga needs to do her own digging at some point," Marcy said. "She can't hire you to do all the dirty work."

Yes, she probably can, I thought. Besides, upon reflection it had occurred to me that a trip to Korea might entail a stop in Hawaii. A chance to visit Yuggie. A sojourn I couldn't at the moment otherwise afford. But still I wasn't convinced I wanted to go alone to a foreign country where I didn't speak the language, couldn't even read the alphabet. My only hope would be to persuade Yuggie to go with me.

Soon we arrived in Wellfleet where Grace had found a cottage for us to rent for the week. I'd been to Provincetown years ago when I first moved to Boston. It turned out to be Gay Pride week and the parade I witnessed there was shocking even to gadabout me. Provincetown, it seemed, was mostly a haven for gay men. Lesbians, except the butchiest of motorcycle riders, were generally absent from the parade which featured every kind of drag queen and every kind of penis symbol. I found myself half apologizing to a young straight couple standing next to me, then shifting in the crowd lining the street to block their children from viewing some of the more obscene displays of sexuality. It had all served to confirm my assertion that I am not "gay" per se. I eschew labels, especially about something so nebulous as sexual attraction. My observation was that male gay sexuality seemed much about display while gay women's was more about concealment—went with the organs, I figured.

This time on the Cape, however, everything felt different. I was with other women, for one thing (Last time I'd come with a gay boy friend from the office who'd also never been there before and you can imagine how that turned out . . .) and we were by the ocean, not in the defining town. There is something so mesmerizing about the sea. So vast that who we are, whether gay or straight, human or seal, gull or dog, male or female, adult or child, seems to blend into the landscape, uniting us as tiny beings confronted by the curves of a whole world meeting between ocean and sky.

It seemed ages since I'd stood on that California bluff overlooking the Pacific Ocean, contemplating a tidal wave. But it had only been a couple of months ago. Now instead of watching the sun set, I was watching the sun rise—over the dunes. And instead of standing there alone, I was sitting on the beach with friends. I'd gone from sea to shining sea, east to west to east—and I still hadn't found what I was searching for.

The cottage had two bedrooms, each with a double, so I hoped to be lucky enough to share a bed with Grace, but she was reluctant, for some, perhaps many, reasons, to sleep with me in front of Marcy and Kara, especially when there was another option—a cot in a small utility room which could only be called a closet. However, since I was a non-paying guest, I kept my disappointment to myself. I could hardly complain. I was vacationing with three attractive, interesting women after eons of a solitary, mostly sterile existence. From my single room, my closet if you will, I could come and go as I pleased, combining, I told myself, the best of independence and companionship. Besides, my willingness to give Grace the best bedroom instead of tossing a coin endeared me in her eyes, an appreciation I hoped would prove profitable in the long run. Sometimes a grateful Grace can be a generous Grace.

This was my first opportunity to get to know Kara more fully. I'd witnessed her inquiring mind and her hospitable self, but she'd mostly been busy when I was around so I hadn't seen her delight in all things natural. She didn't know until right before she came that Cape Cod was this fascinating arm of rock and sand, as Thoreau described it, reaching out into the Atlantic. She didn't know this was the place where one of her heroes, Mary Oliver, lived, this the landscape she often wrote about.

And since Grace wanted to sit on the beach writing poetry herself and Marcy wanted to wander up and down taking photos, I, who hadn't seen much of the Cape aside from Provincetown, became Kara's exploring companion. We headed off first to hike the trails around various ponds, only to find ourselves alone on the paths with swarms of mosquitoes. Fending them off as best we could, having forgotten the bug spray, we ran as fast as possible, collapsing in giggles when we finally got back to the parking lot. "Guess that was the four-minute hike," I observed once I got my breath.

"I figure Mary Oliver knows better than to venture out here this time of year," she replied.

Then we rented bikes and zipped along faster than the bugs could catch us. When it started to rain, we headed for the Visitors' Center where we watched a film about Thoreau's visit to Cape Cod and another about the ecology.

"They're not sure if or how long this piece of land will survive," Kara observed afterward.

"Well, they say with climate change, it's best not to buy waterfront property," I replied—as if buying beachfront property was even an option.

"We'll be long gone, I suspect, before Cape Cod is," she said. "It must be one of the most dynamic ecosystems in the world. Or at least this country."

One day on the beach I managed to light up a pipe under my blue umbrella, then just sat there looking for seals which popped their heads up periodically out beyond the waves. I was trying to observe how long they were under while I imagined what they did while down there.

Watching for the seals I became mesmerized by sunlight caught in the surf, the pattern of green and white in the undercurl of the waves, and by the rhythm of the waves rising and crashing as the tide came in. Marcy had wandered off to take photos of all the dogs who weren't supposed to be on the beach (fortunately this was before the official season started so the rules weren't being enforced), Grace was engrossed in the revision of some long epic poem about friendship, and Kara had taken her shoes off, rolled up her pants legs and ventured into the chilly water. She called me to join her, but I was absolutely stuck in my beach chair, hiding under the umbrella from the sun and from any public scrutiny.

As I stared out at the horizon, shifting my vision from the waves to the seals to Kara, I noticed how she entered that element so sensitively, her bare feet tuned to the splash of the incoming waves, the receding sand beneath her toes. As she moved further and further into the water, I could feel her delight in its flow as she bent to look for rocks and caress the water with her fingertips. Every so often she'd dart her hand down to pull out a rock—like a heron or kingfisher might do in retrieving a fish.

After awhile Kara came back to show us the beauty of the rocks she'd harvested, their shape, color, heft, and glow. I realized the beach was lined with these rocks which either stayed as the waves pulled back or tumbled into the ocean with the retreating current. To catch the ones rolling in between was the mission of the fisherperson. It was, I thought, a task of receiving messages from the ocean.

"Can you hear the silence of the ocean?" Kara asked us upon one of her trips back to our chairs. I listened. Sure enough, every so often—between the roar of the incoming waves and the whisper of the withdrawing water—there was silence. Like the pause in meditation between the in breath and the out breath, only so much more pregnant within this oceanic presence. I've always thought of the ocean as teeming with life, but suddenly it seemed as if this vast body of water was life itself, the lungs of our whole planet, the murmur of the universe. Just then a seal popped up right in front of me, as if reading my thoughts and approving. Listening, as Kara suggested, to the silence from the ocean, I realized, tuned me into the whole of sounds around us, all coming together in those rhythms of silence.

After Kara went back into the ocean, moving closer to the waves until they were up to her knees, dipping her hands reverentially into the water and really, I could tell, feeling it, I noticed a young man slowly advancing onto the beach to my right. He came up to the waterline very tentatively, his movements awkward. At first I thought it the clumsiness of adolescence but then I realized he had some kind of handicap. There was something slightly spastic about the way he held his arms stiff at the shoulders and elbows and pulled his legs forward from the knees, with an effort, perhaps because he was barefoot but probably because he had some neurological condition. My heart went out to him. But what fascinated me was how he seemed to imitate Kara's approach to the ocean, inspired, perhaps, by observing her zest.

At first he seemed shocked by the chill of the water, but as he bravely edged forward toward the incoming waves, his body shifted into what looked to me like ecstasy. And in that mirroring I could recognize what I'd observed in and through Kara, but couldn't quite name, a kind of bliss.

To the left Kara continued her rock fishing, apparently oblivious to her water companion on the right. But to my surprise, when he bent over to dip his hands into the water, she made exactly the same gesture, even though she hadn't looked at him or given any sign she was aware of his presence. It seemed to me, in my altered state, like some kind of psychic empathy, as if her attunement with nature spilled over into a joining together with this young man. I felt privileged to share this moment of inclusivity with them.

Later, reflecting upon this event, witnessed only by me and perhaps some members of the boy's family, I understood why Marcy was fascinated. Kara seemed blessed with some ability to commune with the larger natural world while also staying connected with human nature. As a result she seemed to serve as some kind of transformer. Like a salmon swimming upstream I was hooked.

Realizing now I wouldn't break the spell if I joined her, I decided to take the plunge myself, removing my own shoes and walking across the dry, then wet, then soggy sand into the ocean far enough to shriek at the cold water—approaching each wave boldly, then running away as it splashed behind me. Not exactly communing but still, somehow, getting in touch. I felt like a child. I found a small, round, grey rock into which I projected all my bad feelings of anger, loneliness, jealousy and regret before tossing it back into the ocean, and then I dove for a square red stone which looked like it might make a good foundation for something new.

Later as the sun grew hotter, young people ran out in bathing suits and plunged into the foamy waves. Amazed at this show of uninhibited glee I wondered if I'd ever been bold enough to dash headlong into a wave. If not, wasn't it too late now? Was I doomed to a frugal and feckless, much less fuckless, existence from now on? On the other hand, I simply couldn't imagine at that point diving into the ocean.

For our evening's entertainment we had decided to go to P-Town to see if we could find a gay bar. Grace was nostalgic about the old days of the gay bars, Kara was busy recalling her days at the Chances

R in her hometown and the community generated there, Marcy was indifferent, with some memories but not particularly fond ones, and me, mostly curious. I've been in and out of my share of gay bars, but I can't say one ever felt like home. Which is probably just as well, given all my other proclivities.

So we ventured into Provincetown which was rich with visitors strolling the streets after several rainy days, gay and straight, couples of all sorts, groups of friends, families of all sorts. After bouncing in and out of the shops along Commercial Street, we paid $5 each to get our hands stamped so we could go into one of the gay bars which had advertised a "tea dance." When we got in, we found the bar empty, the pool table deserted, and the deck where the tea dance was being held sparsely populated with mostly men eyeing each other. The music was loud and pounding but there was no dancing. Another bar turned out to be similarly dead, dead, dead. Grace was very disappointed. It seemed that old world which provided such refuge and comfort had disappeared, like Brigadoon. Kara, who'd hoped for some dancing, was also sorry.

It was only when we'd gotten back on the streets and I saw a woman kiss her woman partner, then take her hand and head for an ice cream parlor that I realized what had changed. Everybody had come out—outside onto the streets, into the sunlight, braving the public eye, which here in Provincetown at least was no longer judgmental, at least not that way. There was plenty of scrutiny, still, of course, especially among the young and fashionable, but it was profoundly superficial, not slashing into one's core identity. So even though I could empathize with Grace's feeling of loss of the old tight community, especially among women, I could see that the openness of the blossom had progressed from the tight comfort of the bud.

Still Grace longed for some deeper connections with other gay women. As we ate at an sidewalk café populated by movie stars like Kathleen Turner and directors like John Waters, we realized that the Film Festival currently going on in Provincetown might offer an opportunity to share experiences with other women, so we checked in at the film society office to see what films we might be able to see, and decided on one entitled, *Co-Dependent Lesbian Space Alien*. Sure enough, the movie goers lined up outside the venue were almost all women, probably lesbians, many very friendly and chatty. It was the bar scene outdoors, without alcohol. The film depicted three archetypal aliens with bald heads and cowls to cover their gills, exiled to earth because it was believed their Big Feelings were having a deleterious effect on their planet's climate. It was hilarious, and the audience roared at every in joke. As the director explained later, it was a hybrid between the old space alien films of the fifties and the old lesbian romances from a similar era. At the end of the film we were each given a button which said, "Co-Dependent Lesbian Space Alien," with "Lesbian" in large letters. I put mine on right away and wore it for the rest of the time we were in Cape Cod, although sometimes covered by my vest in more sedate Wellfleet.

It felt to me like a minor key rendition of coming out. I've never wanted to label myself anything, much less a lesbian. I like men, I enjoy sex with a few of them, I appreciate some of them, I find many of them to be very helpful, but the truth is I've only fallen in love with one of them and he quickly figured out he wanted something I couldn't give: a stable, committed, long-term relationship. The truth is that usually when I fall in love, it's with women. My best friends are mostly lesbians. I'm getting too old to pretend that all my options remain open. So why not, finally, come out, at least here in the safety of gay-ridden P-Town? Especially since I'm also coming out as an "alien," which I've always felt like, sort of. I mean, I can't claim the glamour of showing up from some other planet nor the suffering of being a complete foreigner, but I do know what it's like never to quite fit in anywhere.

Grace raised her eyebrows when she saw me putting on the pin— she suspects it means more than just fun, since my not calling myself a lesbian has been a bone of contention between us for forever. Kara and Marcy just accepted it as play on my part, in a very safe context. I take some comfort in the fact that Kara, who has never doubted since her early teens that she was gay, tends to be as hidden, as furtive as I am when it comes to declaring publically anything very personal, certainly anything to do with one's sexual preferences. None of the usual stereotypes fit Grace, and Marcy is so private that the very idea of revelation seems foreign.

Anyway, after the film we wandered the main streets again, popping in and out of various stores. At one point, while Kara and Grace were going gaga over exotic pottery and fountains in one particularly appealing store, I headed over for an ice-cream, and Marcy sat on a bench with a lot of older gay men in a tiny park. When I came out of Ben and Jerry's I saw Marcy chatting with a couple of young women, one of whom was Liza's best friend Hope with the nose ring, the one who keeps eluding me whenever I approach. The other youngster was of at least partial Asian descent, quite lovely. At first I wondered if this was Liza, but judging from Marcy's casual stance, I assumed not. If this were Liza, surely she'd be standing up to hug her.

Rather than approach and possibly spook Hope, I just stood there licking my cone, watching them. Hope was doing most of the talking, while Marcy kept nodding her head as if she was being persuaded of something. Something to do with Liza? I was dying to spy on their conversation. I was beginning to suspect that neither Grace nor Marcy were being entirely forthcoming with me about Liza's whereabouts. They apparently had no compunctions about my continuing to collect fees from Durga while they continued to erase the clues. Did this mean they enjoyed my company? Or was something more sinister going on here? Needless to say it is slightly disconcerting to suspect your old best friend and your fine new friends of subterfuge.

Eventually, Hope, who seemed to be conducting a surveillance of the flowing crowd, spotted me, then rather quickly floated off in the opposite direction, her arm hooked onto the elbow of her friend, propelling her forward.

"Hope?" I said to Marcy as I strolled up to her. Marcy nodded. "She gay?"

Marcy shrugged, then smiled. I knew it was hopeless to find out from her what they'd been discussing, so I didn't even try. Maybe later she'd whisper it to Grace and I'd eavesdrop.

The next day we went for a long hike through the woods and fields past cranberry bogs up onto the dunes until we were overlooking a deserted beach. Kara, of course, headed immediately for the water, pushing down through the sand to join a whole colony of gulls and perhaps a pod—or is it a herd?—of seals, while I sat on the edge of the dunes watching and Grace played a tune on her recorder. Overhead a gull would occasionally fly, its broad wings floating on the air currents as the seals soared through the waves.

It wasn't until we returned to where we'd parked our car that we discovered we were all covered with ticks, large brown ticks with lots of squiggly legs. This precipitated a sudden and frantic disrobing and minute examination of each other's bodies. From a distance it must have looked like a tribe of bonobos. One young woman rode up on her bike, took one look, and kept on peddling. This purging was followed by a rapid retreat back to the cottage and showers for all, accompanied by much reflection about Lyme and other tick-borne diseases and much speculation about various kinds of ticks and the best ways to remove them. I was the only one who had actually been bitten by one of these dog ticks, and it was barely a nibble before I snatched it off and tossed it away.

But by that time I had also been bitten by something more potent.

Chapter Nineteen

FRIGHT OR FLIGHT

As Grace and I drove back from her school. I told her about a painting Oscar had just finished, with my encouragement. "It was entirely his composition. I was just the cheerleader."

This "cheerleading" was not bad for a job, even though unpaid. The least I could do for my free room and sometimes board was help out at Grace's school. Much as we frowned upon "volunteerism" during the women's movement days, I could see now it had its perks. I could set my own hours and pretty much choose my tasks. Playing with Oscar was one of my favorite "responsibilities."

"It was a beautiful painting, Grace, showing a little boy riding on the very broad wings of a rainbow colored bird."

"Sounds like something from a Harry Potter movie."

"He says it's how he got to America. I wonder if he remembers that."

"I suspect it's a story his mother has told him, about how they flew back together."

"You don't think he would remember such a trip?"

"He was only six months old. And wouldn't he remember a plane rather than a bird?"

She had a point. But still toying with the idea of going to Korea I was wondering if Liza remembered her trip to America. It wasn't possible to ask Sheila whether she had flown back with the infant Liza or if someone else had brought her. And I doubt if Durga would know. Or even Grace. Nor was I sure how old Liza had been at the time. "Do you think he remembers his birth mother?" I asked.

"That's hard to say. But I doubt it. I understand from his adoptive mother that he was only a few days old when he was dropped off on the steps of the local cathedral. So if he remembers anybody, it would be whoever took care of him at the orphanage, one of the young nuns I imagine."

I tried to recall my first memory. Standing in my crib crying, I think. Arms lifting me out and holding me against softness. My mother? Probably. But not necessarily. Maybe my grandmother. "I wonder why he's drawing a picture of his flight at this point," I mused.

"Because it was the biggest adventure of his young life so far?" Grace surmised. "I don't think it's because he's stuck there in some trauma loop, if that's what you're wondering. He seems quite happy with his new family and with the school. And with you, I might add." She looked more intently at me as she slowed down to let a lumbering tractor cross the road in front of us. "I hope you're not going to abandon him now, Xavy."

"Abandon him?!" I shrieked, feeling suddenly trapped. Surely Oscar wasn't dependent on me. There was no pattern to our connection—it was always a pleasant surprise for both of us. "No, of course not, but I have to tell you—I can't keep going without a job. So either I fly to Korea to search for Liza, as Durga wants and is willing to pay for, or I find a real job."

"Why don't you go to the local papers and see if they might hire you?"

"Are you kidding? Local papers are dropping like flies; reporters are becoming an endangered species. There are very few jobs left in journalism, except for real hustlers. And as you must know by now, I'm not exactly a hustler." I waited for her to contradict me on this, since she had in the past accused me of being a "smooth operator," but alas, the way she looked at me simply confirmed the fact. Not only am I not a hustler, I'm not even particularly lucky. Somehow I always end up in the hole instead of making a hole-in-one.

"I doubt very much that Liza is in Korea," Grace said. "It would be just another wild goose chase, only this time half way round the world."

I decided it was time for some transparency. "I suspect you know where she is, Grace. You and Marcy know, don't you? And for some reason you're prolonging this engagement with Durga—right?"

She shook her head, but said nothing. That's the trouble with asking too many questions in a row. Was she denying that she knew where Liza is or was she denying she was drawing out Durga's employment of me? Finally she admitted, "I like having you around, Xavy. I don't want you to leave."

So she was the one—not Oscar—who would feel abandoned? This revelation shook me up. The last thing I wanted was to let Grace down again. "What about this Laurel?"

"What about her?" she said, suddenly on the defensive.

I realized I didn't have a leg to stand on, unlike a goose I'd seen in Cape Cod who rested very steadily on just one leg. "Well, how do I know you're not going to go live with her in New Mexico?"

She shrugged. "I can't leave my life and friends here, no matter . . ."

Please don't finish that sentence, I thought: *No matter how much I love and lust for Laurel?* I simply didn't want to hear how enamored of glamorous Laurel Grace was. Nor was I in a mood to listen to her litany of soul companions, in whose august company yours truly never seemed to be firmly enough included.

On the other hand, I knew deep in my heart that my jealousy of Laurel, although true enough, was a cover for the real reason I felt the need to flee. At Cape Cod I had sort of fallen for Kara. Watching her on the beach, communing with Marcy, playing with Grace, her love of nature, her delight in exploring along both the ocean shore and the shops in town, her tall, slender body, attractive face, and luminous spirit—oh my! But this attraction was a direct threat to my growing friendship with Marcy and a possible blow to Grace who, at times, seemed to be suppressing her own jealousy of Kara's relationship with Marcy. Oh, what a tangled web we weave.

"Well, that's a relief," I said, returning to the subject of Laurel. "I couldn't imagine staying here if you disappeared." I hesitated to use her phrase, "abandon," lest I rip the scab off old wounds. "But I'll be back, Grace. I shouldn't be gone more than a month at most. And frankly, it will be a way for me to visit Yuggie. Hawaii is a natural stopover on flights to Asia. I have wanted to see her setup in Hawaii ever since she moved there, but I never could afford to fly there. Now I could."

She nodded. "That makes sense, Xavy. I wish I could go with you. I'd love to see Yuggie again."

"I wish you could too," I said, and some part of me really did. But another part recalled how jealous I'd been when Grace and Yuggie hit it off so well, last time we were all together. I sighed.

"I just can't leave Ariel with complete responsibility for the school," Grace explained, making visible yet another strand in her web. "She's having a hard time lately."

Although I didn't know Ariel very well, it was hard to imagine any responsibility she couldn't handle. I waited for explanation with a quizzical expression on my face.

"Willow wants her aging mother to live with them."

"What's wrong with that?" I asked. One should be so lucky to have an aging mother I thought, but didn't say. I've found it's best not to intrude on Grace's empathetic connections with others. Not only are they somewhat impenetrable, they feel somehow sacred. My more cynical, if that's what it is, perspective, I've discovered, can break the spell.

"Well, I haven't met her, but I gather the mother is rather difficult. Demanding. Dependent. Unable to spend much time alone. Memory problems. Mobility problems. The usual challenges of old age, I guess." She sighed. I nodded without much comprehension. Neither of us had had the privilege of watching our mothers last into old age. Yet still Grace would empathize, and I could not, with those burdened with caretaking their fading mothers. I could, however, empathize with those like Ariel whose partners felt burdened with such caretaking.

Of course, if I did go to Hawaii, I realized, I would have to deal with an aging Nancy, my own demanding stepmother. But that's not the same as having to live with her for an extended period of time. Especially with Yuggie around to meet her every need.

Anyway, the prospect of dealing with Nancy prompted me to delay my trip to Korea for a bit more. Meanwhile, Grace and Marcy decided they wanted to hike a section of the Long Trail, Vermont's portion of the Appalachian Trail, and invited me and Kara to join them. Needless to say any kind of strenuous exercise is not exactly my cuppa, and Kara had twisted her knee so wasn't up for a long hike. Instead she offered to pick them up at the end of their hike and drive them back to the beginning where they'd parked.

"Why don't you come along?" Kara asked me. "We could have a picnic while we wait for them."

This was an offer I couldn't refuse. As I implied earlier, I was smitten.

Grace and Marcy set off on their hike early Saturday morning. We were to meet them at "the Gap" on Sunday afternoon. Assuming this didn't refer to the clothing store, I pondered what gap might be implicated, trying not to focus on the obvious chasm between my desires and my conscience. But what could be more harmless than a picnic shared by friends in a lovely spot?

The Gap, it turns out, was a mountain pass in the highest peaks of the Green Mountains. To reach it we drove through one of the broad green valleys, graced by a sinuous river, typical of Vermont, then we turned and climbed, winding higher and higher until we reached the pass from which you could see the valley on the other side of the mountain range. This opening was where we were to meet Grace and Marcy. From the overlook we could see down around the next bend a beaver pond and since we had plenty of time, we decided that would be a good place to wait, eat our picnic, and, since we are both photographers, take pictures.

After sharing a phoenix sandwich, potato salad and a chocolate chip cookie from the Coop, we started focusing on the lovely pond before us. I was entranced with a kingfisher which circled around the pond in the distance and the large blue, green and gold dragonflies hovering at the edge of the pond, while Kara seemed to be fascinated with the rippling waves and grasses, each of us lost in our zoom lenses.

At one point we heard a crowd of bicyclers chatting as they huffed and puffed their way along the road past the pond and up the steep curve to the Gap. I couldn't imagine even trying such a feat and pictured myself as the little lame boy following the Pied Piper, gasping from a distance as the magical passage closed behind the Piper and his devotees, leaving me behind and alone.

When this intrepid crew reached the Gap, they all stood along the edge of the overlook and cheered. Looking up I applauded them from my ant like perspective. Imagine my surprise when those same voices then descended back down to the small pullover spot where we had parked, and emerged, chatting, along the path to the pond. Three young women racers dressed in black Speedo shorts and matching t-shirts were removing their pointy helmets while leaving on their kerchiefs. Their leg muscles were so honed and toned I felt grateful mine were hidden within my jeans. Several other women and a couple of men followed along.

"Hope you don't mind being witnesses to a wedding," someone called out to us.

"A wedding? Right here and now?" Kara asked.

"Yes!" Someone replied with delight.

Glancing at the assemblage and at the spokeswoman who looked a little like some gay actress (Jody Foster?), I guessed the wedding was going to be between two women.

"Well, may you have a long and happy marriage," Kara cried out to the couple, whoever they were, either the hetero couple looking out across the pond together or two of the lithe women wearing their sleek racing attire.

"Hope this doesn't seem Surreal," said the spokeswoman.

"Oh, no," replied Kara, "it's Super-real." I took this phrase as affirmation of the potential gayness of the marriage.

We reached for our camera bags so we could sneak away from this private rite just as another member of the party called out, "You can be witnesses."

This gesture toward inclusivity, combined with our passion to support the marginal, effectively glued us to that spot for the duration of the wedding ritual. So we sat like bumps on a real log, staring at a huge frog staring back at us while, surrounded by that luminous ring of water set in a steep valley below the deep chasm, we listened to the ceremony as it took place behind us.

The whole time Kara remained focused on the life of the pond, snapping photos of dragonflies and frogs. I, on the other hand, became completely engrossed in the dynamics of the wedding party, even though I could only catch snatches of what was said. I figured the two straight couples included the sisters of the brides and guessed which sister went with which bride. I grew impatient with the attractive "preacher" (as played by Jody Foster) going on too long about the engaged couple as if she felt obliged to explain lesbianism to the straight folks—even though I could sympathize with her attempt to close that particular gap. I was nonplused about the pair's rhyming names—Karen and Erin—and relieved to hear them joking about that later. I wondered what "The Gap" meant symbolically to them as a wedding venue. I was curious about the third young woman in racing attire, also obviously of the persuasion, who joined the couple for many a photo, almost as if she were a third bride, while I speculated wistfully about a potential three-way marriage between Kara, Marcy and me. As they exchanged their vows, I could sense Kara join me in sending mute warning shots across the bow of this newly launched relationship.

Punctuating this drama were tiny beeps of excitement from me whenever a particularly lovely dragonfly hovered right in front of us, as I tried to signal to Kara to snap the photo.

After the ritual was over, as champagne was pulled out and wedding photos taken, I whispered to Kara that she should offer to take a picture of the whole group. As witnesses it was the least we could do. She was reluctant, either to intrude or to be distracted from her own focus. So I hesitated, realizing this might infringe on their dynamic— what if the group was not all that whole?

Suddenly Kara hollered out, "Would you like a photo of your whole group?" Then to my surprise she pointed to me. "She's an excellent photographer." So much for my shifting the task to her! When it comes to "sharing responsibility," I'd met my match.

Once I'd performed this duty with a couple of their cameras, I called out congratulations, and we felt free, finally, to wend our way up the path back to Kara's car, so we could pick up Grace and Marcy back at the Gap. As they trudged down the trail, weary but exhilarated, our intrepid pair of hikers proved the perfect audience for our account of the wedding before they regaled us with tales about their night in one of the Long Trail shelters.

The next day as Grace and I drove to school, she turned with a slight frown. "I want to ask you a question, Xavy."

That tone of voice whistled over my skin & not in a good way. I knew something was up. I assumed an air of complete innocence, something I'd learned from observing Yuggie under parental scrutiny.

Grace looked ahead and asked: "What do you think of Marcy?"

I was caught off guard. "Marcy?" I relaxed a little. "I think she's great—kind, smart, interesting—I love seeing her with animals—kind of gives you a sense of the best of humanity without feeling guilty, you know?"

"Yes, that's a great way to describe her—I would hate to see anyone cause her pain."

I turned toward Grace & said with feeling, "Me too!," happy that we were on the same page.

Then she turned to me & I saw the old Grace who could slice and dice like a gourmet chef, then grill and roast before serving you (aka me) up as humble pie. "Wait," I said, "What do you mean?" even though at that point, I knew full well that the pointedness of her question was aimed right at my Pinocchio nose of interest in Kara. *Sighhh.*

She sniffed. I braced myself for an onslaught. Her interrogations were usually consciousness-raisers, often transformative, and always illuminating about us both. I have these interactions to thank for much of my otherwise limp self-awareness. Nonetheless, I had to steel myself whenever I saw her inquiring mind aimed in my direction. Quickly I threw up all my defenses and counter-attacks, feeling both blameless and indignant that she, of all people, might indict me for my roving eye. Despite her gift for forgiveness Grace is nothing if not exacting when it comes to personal integrity and owning up to anything less than. It is kinda like confession, with feedback. You know you are going to be forgiven, but you might go through hell to get there. Her expectations are tough but more about honesty than about performance, certainly not conventional or prescriptive. "Bad" is not necessarily so, sometimes even welcomed, but "mean bad' is usually frowned upon. "Good" is almost always suspect. Where coveting somebody else's mate falls on Grace's moral continuum these days is not easy to gauge, but I couldn't imagine, given our history, it would be found commendable.

Just then a squirrel ran across the road and she braked to let it get by safely. We breathed sighs of relief, then fortunately our conversation shifted to upcoming events that day at school.

But I knew I had been put on notice. And I was glad. The last thing I wanted was to disrupt this happy "family" I longed to belong to, or, heaven forbid, hurt Marcy. Besides, as far as I could tell, Kara's interest in me couldn't rival her delight in a hovering dragonfly.

But I should have known that Grace wouldn't let this nagging suspicion drop so easily.

One morning after the hilarity of an evening the four of us spent together around a fire pit in Marcy's back yard, with most of the requisite indulgences, Grace suggested she and I hike around a lake north of us, which had some spectacular views. Hiking isn't exactly my sport of choice, but given my lethargic state, I thought the exercise might do me good. It was bright and early, the sun out but the air still cool, so we set off with our sturdy hiking boots, walking sticks and a picnic lunch.

Once we'd admired the lovely lake set between two towering mountains like a hidden gem, we headed robustly up a steep winding path which led around one side of the lake, Grace striding ahead, me puffing behind. At one point after I sat on a rock to catch my breath, Grace asked me, as if she hadn't already quizzed me, what I thought of Kara. Sniffing this out as another potential probe, I acted as non-committal as possible, shrugging and asking *her* what *she* thought of Kara, as I wondered how in the world she could have intuited the faint flicker of attraction I still felt for Kara.

"I like her very much, and I *love* Marcy," she replied with a grim tone.

Caught on the pin of her scrutiny, I was tempted to ask why, if she loved Marcy so much, she'd broken up with her to get involved with . . . *whom?* Laurel? I realized I'd lost the order of Grace's litany of companions. Is dumping somebody any more excusable than falling in love with their lover? Recognizing that while lifetime monogamy wasn't one of Grace's paths, fidelity is definitely one of her virtues, I nobly refrained from this line of defense. After all, I hadn't exactly fallen in love with Kara, at least not yet—I was just attracted, and that's no crime. Even more important, I was much too fond of Marcy to hurt her in any way.

Still Grace's subtle inquisition did have its effect. I'm hardly the one to challenge Grace's propensity toward inclusivity when it comes to embracing diversity. And I'm in no position to tackle the complexities of any intimate relationship with anybody at this point in my life. So, without admitting anything but a mild appreciation of Kara's gifts, I surrendered to Grace's unspoken dictum: *hands off.* Someday there might be a person for me, but first I had to find a place for me.

As we trudged onward and upward, I imagined this hike was Grace's idea not just of retreating to a "higher ground" celebrated as a result of the recent flooding, but her way to inspire *me* to "climb the highest mountain," as the song would have it. Up, up and away from my profligate ways. If only she knew how *un*profligate I felt these days. Decadence was not even on my Bucket List.

Nonetheless I entertained myself, as we plodded along, slowly rising higher and higher, with remembering former lovers, imagining who and where they were now. By the time we reached the top, with a spectacular view of the lake and the mountain peaks rolling back to the horizon, I had decided that instead of lusting after new companions, I should spend the rest of my life celebrating the ones I'd already known. One by one I imagined revisiting each and every lover, having intimate exchanges with them for old times' sake. By *intimate* I don't mean sex, given all sorts of complications, but certainly warmth and closeness, in some cases, perhaps, warmer and closer than they'd ever been in reality, but, hey, my fantasy life was alive and well.

And by the time we sat down in a grassy meadow at the summit, overlooking the lake, to eat our picnic lunch of tuna sandwiches and oranges, my appetite, as well, was working just fine. My imaginative reunions had been refreshing.

On the way back down, we came to a fork in the path. "Two roads diverged," I said aloud, quoting a famous one of Vermont's many poets, "and you'll take the one less traveled by." Grace, whose sense of direction is seriously challenged, never minds getting lost. "Lost" for her is just another way less traveled by. But I hate getting lost. Despite years of taking less traveled by roads, much of the time because of following folks like Grace, I just couldn't get used to not knowing *where* I was, even if it wasn't a place I actually knew or could find on the map. In any case, I was pretty sure we'd come up this way from the right folk, but she insisted we take the left folk which ran along closer to the lake.

"These paths all flow down to the parking lot, I'm sure," she said. "This is just a short cut."

So, of course I followed her. By this time the sun was high overhead and it was getting pretty hot. The lake looked so inviting I wished I'd brought along a bathing suit, even though it has been years since I'd ventured out in public, risking exposure, in a swimsuit. Not only has the muddle of my middle expanded exponentially but my muscle tone looks a bit like ice melting—not a pretty picture.

So you can imagine our surprise when, upon rounding a curve in the trail, we came upon a crowd of picnickers gathered along the shore of the lake, all completely naked. Men, women and children, some lithe and slender, some tubbier than moi, some graying, some even bald. I know the human body is supposed to be beautiful, and at the hands of great painters it certainly can be, or seem to be, but, honestly, I prefer animal bodies covered with soft hair. Not that I would want that much hair or want to make love with a really hairy person, but aesthetically speaking, this crew, at least, left a whole lot to be desired. Or, put another way, the more that met our eyes was more than we needed to see. Nothing was left to my fertile imagination. Not that we saw much, after that first shocked realization. Although these nudists seemed friendly enough in their natural state, I picked my way through their midst as if I had blinders on, focusing only on my feet as I felt my way along the path. I assumed Grace was doing the same, while managing at the same time to exchange friendly smiles and nods with naked people who were more busy watching us than we were watching them.

Once we got past the nudist beach, Grace murmured, "Somebody mentioned a nudist beach around here, but somehow in chilly Vermont, it's a surprise."

"I'll say," I gasped, collapsing on the grass between the lake and the parking lot before bursting into giggles. Grace joined me as we laughed, not at the enlightened naturalists, but at our own shock.

So much, I thought, of my dream of revisiting past lovers. I was pretty sure, much as I'd like to see them, or at least some of them, I wasn't up for that kind of exposure, even with my somewhat fading eyesight. But I'd love to see them, again, those old friends, the almost dids and never coulds as well as the actual lovers. Real reunions, of course, might take some forgiving first—from both sides, no doubt.

"Well," Grace declared as we drove back, "that was bracing."

"Indeed," I agreed, not sure whether she meant the hike, our talk, or the encounter with the nudists.

"Refreshing even," she added.

I wasn't sure about that, but I was curious how she meant it. I am eternally intrigued with how Grace's mind works. Despite the fact the only thing which seems to bring us together is a need to rescue somebody or other (in this case, not Liza but Durga), our friendship is so comfortably furnished with layers of knowing it feels as solid as more conventional connections. We neither mirror nor complement each other, but when we interact, we form a more potent alliance. At least at this point it feels that way.

"They seemed so innocent," Grace explained, "like the day they were born," Grace commented as we drove home.

"Like Adam and Eve in the Garden of Eden?" I replied, wondering how anybody managed to stay innocent in this rotten world of ours.

"We're home," Grace said cheerfully as we drove up the drive to Marcy's house.

Home? I wondered once again. Where is that? For Adam and Eve it was the Garden of Eden. For me, who knows? What is "home" anyway? For most of us, not one particular place, that's for sure. Not anymore.

Grace's suspicions, despite my protestations, apparently encouraged her to bless my trip to Hawaii and beyond. Her support, and assurances that she would be here when I returned, although I did not, and never would, exact such a promise, made it possible for me to head off once again into the unknown. But this time, once again, I would be truly on my own—from coast to coast, and then off across the Pacific Ocean. Alone at least until I got to where Yuggie is.

Next followed a flurry of arrangements, including plane reservations, contacting Yuggie, getting a passport, trying to learn some basic Korean phrases, asking Durga to find out what orphanage in Seoul Liza had come from. I couldn't decide whether to fly through San Francisco, where I knew nobody, or Seattle, where my estranged cousin lived. The prospect of being lonely trumped the anguish of trying to reconcile with Julie (that's a whole other story) and so I opted to change planes in San Francisco, with only a brief layover in a Holiday Inn near the airport—expensive but I couldn't complain, since I had the Durga credit card.

Then it was just a matter of saying goodbye. I spoke to Kara on the phone and our farewell was blissfully breezy. She assumed I'd be back, as I said I would, in about a month. Marcy suspected otherwise, I guessed, from the way she expressed appreciation for my support around Zoom's death and for our conversations about life after death, the spiritual landscape, and living with animals. She was in the throes of trying to decide whether to get a new kitten.

"It just seems too soon, you know. I don't like the idea of Zoom being a replaceable part."

"I know what you mean. I wouldn't want to think I'm easily replaced myself, and I certainly wouldn't feel that way about someone I love. You need time to grieve."

"It's just that Willow was telling me about a litter of very cute kittens her neighbor has. It's tempting."

"I kinda think the new one will find you, one way or another. Maybe she or he is one of those kittens, but not necessarily."

"Yeah," she said gloomily. "Well, I hope you come back, Xavy, it's been fun. But I wouldn't be surprised if Hawaii grabs you. You haven't been through a Vermont winter yet. If you had, Hawaii would certainly suck you in." She chuckled.

What was it about a Vermont winter that warranted a chuckle? I wondered. Would my curiosity about that pull me back? I doubted it, but the lure of this community of women might well do the trick. At this point I had every intention of returning, assuming my crush on Kara had burned out by then. Perhaps even arriving back in triumph, with the reluctant Liza in tow, but probably without much to show for the jaunt except a renewed understanding of Yuggie's current lifestyle. But I also knew my capacity for distraction. And with Grace yearning toward the Southwest, I wasn't sure I wanted to bet on any future for myself in Vermont. On the other hand, I wasn't ready to burn that bridge. Without setting anybody up for disappointment, I also, kinda, wanted them to anticipate my return—leave a space for me in their hearts, at least. I mean, where else could I live at this point in my life? Wasn't I running out of options?

"I don't know if you realize it, Xavy," Marcy said as I turned to go, "but you really saved the day."

My ears perked up. Saved the day? "How so?"

"We were really devastated when Sheila died. It shifted everything in a way, I guess, looking back on it. Then Liza's departure was one more missing piece in the puzzle. We were all discombobulated, if you know what I mean."

Discombobulation, I thought, my chronic condition. I just nodded. I waited for her to get to the part about how I'd saved the day.

"Well, I don't know for sure, I just know your presence has shifted everything level again, somehow. Your relationship to Durga, for instance, somehow rights the picture, if you know what I mean." I think I did. "And your connection with Grace, well, that has been transformative for all of us."

I looked puzzled. As Marcy tried to explain, it just sounded worse and worse. What it seemed to come down to was, if Grace could care for me, who seemed so clueless and unrooted, then it seemed guaranteed she also cared for them who were more together and functional. From my point of view she obviously cared for them as much as she cared for me, probably more, but, to my mind, that wasn't because they were particularly functional and together, at least not more than anybody else. But, compared to me anyway, maybe they were, or felt they could be.

I was disappointed that my "saving the day" amounted to being more of a slouch and a sinner than anybody else, but I could see how just my presence could serve as a distraction from the fact of death, the experience of loss, the expression of grief. Plus, my inability, and reluctance, to find out where Liz was, seemed, somehow, comforting to everybody but Durga—and I wasn't actually sure about her. I suspected that if I really wanted to know where Liza is, I would just ask Grace.

"No, really, Xavy, it has been . . . wonderful, somehow." Suddenly she looked shy. "Somehow, I can't really explain it, but you've brought us all together."

Humm. So I'd been some kind of catalyst? The mysterious stranger?

"I mean, who knows, maybe you did it for an adventure, maybe you were sent by angels, I don't know, but I just want to thank you."

Uh oh, I realized what this was—a final farewell. I'd saved "them." Now it was time to move on to somebody else to save. The "savior" must come from the outside and return to the outside. Inwardly I groaned. Being sent by angels isn't a whole lot of help if you want to root yourself somewhere. Wherefore does a Xavy turn? Of course there are always the angels to return to. I sighed.

"Oh, I'm sorry," she said, reaching out to touch my wrist. "I don't mean to project all that stuff on you, but you got to admit, Xavy, you play that rescuer role pretty well."

"I do?" I said modestly, feeling a flush at my ears.

"Yep," she said with a warm smile.

I refrained from asking for more particulars. She demurred from telling me.

Next it was time to say goodbye to Grace. Last time we separated, it took a decade before we reconnected. Who knows what would happen this time?

"So when's your return flight. Xavy?" Grace asked as we zipped along the highway to the Burlington airport.

"I didn't make a reservation because I have no idea how long it will take to find Liza."

She frowned but didn't say anything.

"I haven't even made any reservations for the flight to Korea," I went on. "Durga can't find the name of the orphanage where Sheila got Liza from, and she seems reluctant to go through Sheila's files to find it."

"Yes, I can imagine that would stir up all sorts of memories."

"Well, without that basic information, it would be like looking for the proverbial needle in a haystack—the only way you're going to find it is if you sit on it."

"Ouch," she said, then shrugged. "So you'll have a nice visit with Yuggie, then come home to us."

Home? Us? Why did Grace always assume that wherever she was, that was home, or that a wanderer such as I belonged to such an "us"? It was my turn to shrug. Who knew what I might discover in Hawaii. And what about the mysterious Laurel of the Southwest?

"Anyway," she added, "I'll lean on Durga to get that information to you. I've got your email address and cell phone number. When you call to check in, you can give me Yuggie's phone number where I can at least leave a message."

"Check in?" I asked with a wry smile.

"You bet," she said. "I'm not going to lose track of you again, my dear. In fact, I'd like you to phone all along the trip, especially to let me know you arrived safely. Ok?"

I nodded, pleased to be the recipient of so much caring, even if not by any means exclusively. Reluctantly, when we arrived at the airport, I got out of the car with my lone bag—no baggage fees for me. Despite the Durga subsidy I didn't want to be left in the middle of urban sprawl with no toiletries. Suddenly seized with separation anxiety, I was ready to fall on my knees and beg Grace to be, once again, the love of my life, sex or no sex, Laurel or no. But instead I nonchalantly kissed her on both cheeks, gave her a brief fierce hug and strolled into the airport as she stood there waving.

Chapter Twenty

WESTWARD HO: JOURNEY TO THE EAST.

The flight west wasn't bad. I had plenty of time to look back and reinvent a life for myself in Vermont. *Try to get some sort of job with the local newspaper, or maybe even other media. Find myself some cheap place to live in town. Jump out into the larger arena somehow. Clarify connection with Grace. Become more independent.*

In anticipation of my reunion with Yuggie, and out of imagined conversation about my current life situation, I began to realize that staying as a guest with Marcy and Grace might not be my best— most honorable as well as most advantageous—option for a living situation should I return. But would I still feel at home if not sustained, if not supported, by Grace and Marcy? I don't mean financially but emotionally. I'd felt so much more less lonely being at Marcy's house and being appreciated by, and able to appreciate, both Grace and Marcy. It's like we made a team of sorts. With Kara the icing on the cake.

At the same time, facing forward, I had lots of time to imagine Yuggie's life in Hawaii. I still couldn't believe how easily she apparently fit in, much less how quickly she decided to severe herself from the mainland. I never doubted that Yuggie hadn't once more landed on her feet, despite various reduced circumstances. Yuggie always had a gift for landing on her feet. She started walking early, apparently, and hopefully she was still nimble. But still it had been so long—a couple of years—since we'd been together, and now she had a whole new life, new relationships (with the exception of Nancy, our stepmother) and a whole new context. I wondered how much Yuggie herself had changed as a result. We're both getting older, for sure, but do people ever really change? Especially sisters.

Guess that's what I'll be finding out, I thought. I reminded myself how nimble I still feel—so hopefully Yuggie did too. Although, these doggone airplane chairs, I also realized, would challenge anyone's nimbility—they seem designed somehow for hunched backs. It used to be that pillows and blankets were provided as wedges, but now they cost money and seemed quite scarce. For all my nimbleness I was beginning to feel like a pretzel, twisting in my seat like a figure 8 while I tried mentally to connect those two poles of my current existence, one where I didn't really belong and one I had only yet imagined. Did I need to turn myself into a Mobius Strip?

Meanwhile, of course, there was the present moment, that kind of suspended animation one experiences when flying, along with a realization that at any moment everything could turn round completely, all with one unexpected nosedive. One tries to keep oneself immune to the sensation of being suspended with a group of strangers high above the deep blue sea, all of us riding inside a large metal bird. To distract myself from that awareness—this was the first time I'd flown over the Pacific ocean—I watched all the available tv reruns and new film releases, listened to a variety of musical styles, and watched my fellow passengers, observing their dynamics, guessing who they were, while studiously avoiding any real contact with them.

On the flight to Chicago, I had a single seat, thank goodness. On the flight to San Francisco, I shared a seat with a young man who never took his eyes off his computer screen which was showing a film of the young-men-crashing-cars-and-picking-up-girls genre, only slightly more appealing than the young-men-hanging-out-picking-their-noses-and-making-poop-and-fart-jokes genre. On the flight to Honolulu I stared out the window while an older couple argued about whether they should try to call their troubled daughter from the plane. It was their first trip out of the country and she, apparently the type who has trouble relaxing, was obviously, to me anyway, very nervous to be so far out of her comfort zone. And he, trying unsuccessfully to calm her down and cheer her up, was growing increasingly irritated, no doubt because this vacation was costing them an arm and a leg. (Another expression I hate. The image of paying for anything with a body part is, to say the least, gruesome.) Any pleasantries on my part would have been a waste of time.

So it was a relief to finally land in Honolulu where I was to take a puddle jumper, with room for about twenty passengers, over to Kauai, where Yuggie lived. By some stroke of fortune for this short flight I happened to sit next to a tall, lovely, friendly native Hawaiian about my age who told me all about Kauai and ended up inviting me to attend a musical event (which she called a *Kahiko*) not far from where Yuggie lives, she said when I told her the address. And, she added graciously, my sister was most cordially invited too. I told her I'd love to, waving goodbye to her on the tarmac as I spotted Yuggie behind the security doors.

Yuggie looked much the same as last time I was with her—her hair shorter than I've ever seen it and grayer but otherwise that same dear face, slightly more worn but looking quite contented, relaxed, and best of all, glad to see me. She, being slightly older (we are what they call Irish twins, born within a year of each other) embraced her role as hostess, whisked me up, commandeered my rollabag, led the way out of the airport and to her car, then swung us out into traffic, zipping around the countryside until we arrived at her abode.

As we chatted on the way, I tried to observe any changes in Yuggie's person that might correspond to her change in lifestyle, now that she'd moved to Hawaii, gotten involved with a native Hawaiian, and taken on a family in the process. But when we are together, just the two of us, our dynamic is pretty well rooted in our shared values, perspectives, and sense of humor. It takes encounters with others or with challenging situations to bring out our differences, which are manifold. Our conversation, at this point in any case, was light and informative, not fraught with conflict or bad news, so any new changes in her personality or perspective were not likely to emerge.

After we parked, she led me up to side by side cottages—on an old sugar plantation no less. Apparently Nancy's stint in real estate had led to some interesting property possibilities. Nancy lived in one cottage while Yuggie and Okalani lived in the other, next door. *Next door!* I shuddered. The cottages seemed quaint, with some kind of roofing material which looked like thatch, each with its own distinctive porch, or lanai, with a palm tree fence between them and their neighbors, all facing, you guessed it, the deep blue-green sea. A far cry from Yuggie's former abode in downtown Philly.

Okalani, Yuggie's new partner, was lovely, younger than Yuggie but not by much, with long, dark lustrous hair, chiseled yet blossoming features, and a plump body shorter than Yug's, a lively personality, and a modest demeanor. She greeted us at the door, then giving us time to visit and me to settle, slipped out to play in the quiet street with her two grandchildren, a boy and a girl about five or six who looked like duplicates of each other. They were cute. She was yet another genuine grandmother, I realized, with Yuggie, once again lucking out, able to be a grandparent even without ever having been a mother.

"Twins," Yuggie observed. "Very special in this culture. Historically the Hawaiians were ruled by what they considered divine twins."

"Ah," I said, wondering what my life would have been like if Yuggie and I had been twins. We were so close that we might as well have been, but I think I prefer having a few distinctive differences, related to birth order and historical context if nothing else. But actually, thinking about it, Yuggie and I are very distinct, even with all we've shared. I won't elaborate on this at the moment, but it doesn't take a genius to note the differences in our lifestyles.

"They live just down the street," Yuggie explained as I settled into the tiny guest room.

I told her about Oscar and about Grace's alternative pre-school and its philosophy of nature-based creativity. This propelled us into an expansive exploration of my so-called life in Vermont, my connection with Grace, and the women's community there, such as it was. Yuggie was disappointed to hear Grace was involved with someone else as she'd been secretly hoping Grace and I would get back together.

"That's a pretty rare event," I observed—people splitting up and then getting back together. It's amazing a romance happens in the first place, but it would take a miracle for it to rekindle again." True enough, that was a miracle I'd also been secretly longing for, but I could tell by now the pizzazz has been replaced by something deeper, more nourishing, more mysterious. Grace still didn't feel to me like Yuggie does, a comfortable old slipper, but neither was she the latest in designer shoes.

"Yeah, I guess," Yuggie said, thinking back to her long relationship with what'shername. "I can't imagine being back with Cleo." Ah, yes, the dastardly Cleo.

"Do you have any link with her?"

She shook her head. "I tried to stay in touch but she just stopped responding."

Guilt, I guessed. "It's not easy to stay close when you're so far apart." I was thinking how hard it has been for me to stay close to Yuggie who is so now far away we've had to forgo our previously frequent back and forth visits. But sisters are different than old friends, much less old lovers. Even with all that ocean between us, it only took seconds for us to reconnect on a deeper level.

First I told her about my adventure in Vermont, including, of course, its *reason d'etre*, the search for Liza. Then she told me more about her life in Hawaii, her private practice as a counselor (surprising how, even in Paradise, people manage to tie themselves into knots of the psyche), Okalani's job at the local food coop, and Nancy's retirement from the real estate business.

"How is she doing?" I asked with as much concern as I could muster. Yuggie's hooking up like this with our stepmother, and my former nemesis, was such a sore spot between us we'd just stopped talking about it. But now that I was in Hawaii, where Nancy reigned, I could no longer avoid the inevitable. This trip would be my High Noon.

"Oh, she's fine, really," Yuggie said, casually as she gave me a hard glance, wondering, I'm sure, how resistant I might be to being nice to Nancy. On one level I was insulted she'd fear my rudeness. On another, I could understand, given past behavior, why she might suspect the worst.

"What about the stroke?" I asked with a modicum of sympathy in my tone. I didn't want this bone of contention to come between me and my beloved sister. It used to be that our opposition to Nancy was one of our strongest bonds. But ever since Yuggie moved to Hawaii, where Nancy and Dad had retired, that common ground had eroded, like the soil of a volcano become lava pouring into ocean. Now that Dad was gone, Yuggie, apparently, was Nancy's best friend.

"Fortunately Okalani was with her when it happened so we were able to get her to the hospital right away. She's recovered almost entirely, but she lost some muscle strength during the recovery so her mobility is somewhat less than it was. She's dying to see you."

An unfortunately turn of phrase I thought, and highly doubtful. I certainly wasn't dying to see Nancy. She'd been the bane of my existence at one point during my torturous adolescence. The dreadful stepmother, so keen on dressing us just right when we were at just the wrong age for adult interference, and constantly leaning on me for all my bad habits from smoking to picking my teeth at the table. It got so I went out of my way to do something innocuous that I knew would drive her batty, like wearing orange and purple or using expressions like "Right on." I suppose it wasn't her fault that Dad married her so soon after Mom died, but I could never forgive her for even trying to take Mom's place, which was, of course, impossible. She was not as fun as Mom, not as charming, and certainly not as intelligent. How Yuggie could be embracing her now was a mystery to me.

But soon enough Yuggie was leading me, inwardly kicking and screaming, toward Nancy's cottage. Inside was dim and surprisingly cool, with the soft drone of a ceiling fan as background music. Seated in a blue recliner with a focused beam of light on a magazine she'd been reading was an old woman, who struggled to her feet to greet me. I couldn't believe this was Nancy, but it had been more than a decade since I'd last seen her. Her hair was almost totally white, with thin pink skin showing through the part, and her brown eyes squinted to take me in. I gave her the obligatory hug, then stood back as Yuggie helped her sit down again. As she settled back into her chair, I was struck by how lovely she still was. Her natural beauty seemed enhanced by the apparent wisdom bestowed by wrinkles, and the twinkle in her eyes was livelier than it had ever been. The years, and probably the care of Yuggie and Okalani, had been good to her. There was no evidence of a stroke except, perhaps, her slow movements.

"Mary Catherine," she said warmly, "how wonderful to see you again." How good that you *can't* see me, I thought callously. Yuggie's warning that Nancy was suffering from glaucoma and therefore blurred vision assured me that Nancy would probably not be casting a jaundiced eye on my outfits, which were much snappier than they used to be, but still—

I nodded in agreement, then receiving Yuggie's encouragement to speak up, since Nancy couldn't see nods, I said, "What a wonderful set-up you all have here, Nancy."

"Yes, isn't it grand? I was able to buy these cottages for a song just before some big conglomerate purchased the whole plantation to develop a mammoth hotel and shopping mall."

"So this was originally a plantation?" I asked. I recalled that Nancy was quite the history buff. This encouraged her, to Yuggie's delight, to launch into a tale about Hawaii's sugar plantations, and how splendid they had been. Probably not for the native workers, I surmised, but refrained from pointing that out lest we go down that slippery slope toward our old political wrangles. I could get the story on that later from Yuggie. Obviously the cottages had been spiffed up since the plantation days. Nancy was busy describing the grandeur of the old mansion which graced the coastline. I tried to imagine the plantation owner who lived there—probably of European descent, no doubt patriarchal. Listening to her tell her story, I could see that, unlike me, she was a detail person, which helped explain our previous clashes. She observed and savored minutiae, details about furniture, menus, and dress, while I tend to invent particulars—not a plus for a journalist, I have discovered.

Soon her story came to a close and she began to inquire about me. Once again I was forced to skip over the unpleasant details of my current situation with a dearth of description and vague hints of possibilities. Yes, I was gainfully employed, conducting an investigation, but no, it was top secret so I couldn't elaborate. Yes, I used to live in Boston, but now I was on the road. And so on. It wasn't as bad as evading Grace's questions had been, because Nancy didn't know me well enough to guess at my prevarications, even though she'd been the recipient of a host of them. And besides, she seemed pleased at my apparent good fortune. She expressed this with a sweetness I didn't recognize. Either she'd mellowed with age or my perceptions of her from the past were skewed. I preferred the former explanation, but was beginning to see why Yuggie's so-called "sacrifice" was something less than that. Nancy might be a step, but she was, still, a mother, after all. Not my mother, for sure, but maybe good enough for Yuggie.

We all—minus the twins who'd gone home to their mother, Okalani's daughter—had dinner together at Nancy's place. It consisted of an array of carry-out items from the food coop, thanks to Okalani. As we ate, I told them about my companion on the plane and the *Kahiko* she'd invited me to.

Okalani was impressed. It's not every day, she explained, that a *haole* is invited to such a traditional native event. Yuggie translated "haole" as "white person" or "foreignor." I wondered if it was akin to "honky." Used by Okalani, anyway, it sounded neutral, not an insult.

When I described the woman who'd invited us, Okalani was even more impressed. She was pretty sure it was a well-known local kumu, or head hula teacher, who was revered, I supposed from Okalani's tone, as a kind of guru. Even though the invitation was totally due to this kumu's tolerance, generosity, and hospitality, somehow the fact that it had been extended to me by such a personage seemed to rub a bit of that exalted aura on me, in Okalani's eyes at least. And Yuggie seemed pleased that as a result Okalani was thus impressed with me.

This sudden respect made me feel a bit giddy, it was so atypical. I wanted very much to bask in the glory, but it was quite undeserved, so I really couldn't wallow for long. I know it wouldn't take much before I entered the ranks of mere mortals once more. Meanwhile I asked Okalani about her own training in Kahiko. I was surprised to learn that the dance and its graceful movements, as traditionally tied to chanting, was not the erotic, exotic swaying western tourists flutter around, rife with pig roasts and rice wine, but a sacred ceremony full of symbolic and aesthetic gestures. I looked forward to the event which was to take place the following Sunday afternoon.

As soon as I got a chance, I called Grace to let her know I'd arrived safely. Unfortunately it was in the middle of the night in Vermont so we had a rather groggy conversation. I asked her to check with Durga about the name of the Korean orphanage. It was the last thing I wanted to think about at the moment, but, hey, I was getting paid for conducting some kind of search.

Chapter Twenty One

TROUBLE IN PARADISE

For at least a week, Yuggie shared with me one adventure after another. We picnicked under spectacular waterfalls surrounded by lush green forests. We hiked along the North Shore to see gigantic waves splashing onto towering rock cliffs along the Na Pali Coast. We snorkeled on the South Shore within a lagoon surrounded by lava rocks to protect us from the force of the waves, as we swam with an infinite variety of colorful little fish. We rode in a small tourist boat along the West Side with its white sand beaches, lush canyons, and sea caves.

I got seasick as I always do in small boats but fortunately Yuggie had some Dramamine which gave a certain sleepy glow to the sightseeing but kept me from making a spectacle of myself as has happened aboard other packed sailing vessels. From the deck we could see gigantic sea turtles gliding along the ocean bottom, weaving in and around huge rocks. We enjoyed a wildlife sanctuary and watched for sea mammals. I was disappointed that the humpback whales only came in the winter and spring, but I saw lots of dolphins.

On weekdays it was usually just me and Yuggie, whose work schedule was apparently flexible, but on Saturday morning we were joined by Okalani to visit *heiaus* (ancient sacred sites) where we puzzled over the petroglyphs and heard from her about some of the local legends. Her daughter and the twins snorkeled with us on Sunday before we all went to a festival to browse through an ethnically diverse row of food stalls. Wherever we went I was fascinated by the multi-cultural nature of this small island. Only in certain sections of Manhattan or San Francisco had I encountered such diversity and never in such a harmonious setting. If there were tensions between the different ethnicities or between *malihini* (visitors) or *kamaaina* (residents), I did not experience them.

I had my own tensions to deal with. One was the fact that despite being surrounded by all this beauty, and welcomed by this loving family, my mind and heart were still occupied with Vermont folks. I obsessed about Kara, I worried about Oscar, I wondered about Grace, and I replayed everything Marcy had told me about my beneficial influence. The other was the fact that, despite their hospitality, I felt left out whenever Yuggie and Okalani dove into one of their private conversations. I knew I didn't exactly fit into their lifestyle, but the private whispering and occasional chuckling made me itchy. I was afraid my disinterest in hanging out with Nancy was turning both Yuggie and Okalani against me as someone who didn't embrace the traditional culture's respect for elders. I was too choosy about which elders I respected and which I didn't. I couldn't exactly escape because I had no means of transportation aside from my two feet which were limited in their ability to map my location in case I got lost. So at times, despite all the people, I felt more than a bit isolated. What's the point of being in paradise if you're all alone, like Robinson Crusoe?

The highlight of the week was the Kahiko, traditional hula dancing led by my friend from the airplane, whose name was Ali'ikai. Hula is taught in schools or groups called *hlau*. The head teacher of the school is the *kumu hula*, which was Ali'ikai's title. Okalani remained impressed by my connection with this august personage, especially after the *Kumu Hula* greeted us with a dazzling smile, even hugged me and seemed pleased I had brought Yuggie and Okalani. The ceremony was held in a bright jade meadow surrounded by high emerald hills dotted with lime green palm trees. It was a perfect Saturday afternoon. When it comes to shades of green Hawaii seems to have every bit as many as Vermont or Ireland. Ali'ikai led the opening chant, a call and response that seemed to be blessing the space. Okalani explained this was the entrance chant by which the haumana (students) asked for permission to enter.

Then as the dancers performed with their intricate but graceful hand gestures, Okalani explained what those gestures stood for—the rolling waves, the swaying coconut tree, bright sun, gentle breezes. Some of these dances were performed by children, some by old women, some standing up, some sitting down, but invariably they felt both graceful and genuine. In the background I saw a couple of instruments I did not recognize. After awhile I understood their gestures as a kind of prayer, a tribute to the movements of nature. I'd never realized before how dancing can be a form of worship.

I was startled when Yuggie started moving with the dancers. She's always been light on her feet, but I'd never seen her so graceful. It was as if she's a native now. I'd been noticing how in other ways she has changed in this new environment. She's still patient, kind, playful, but there's a silliness she gets with Oklani, and a seriousness she gets with Nancy, which feel new to me. This observation was both fascinating and disconcerting. I guess that's true whenever you discover untypical behavior in someone you think you know intimately, but it's especially perplexing in a sister.

Afterward, as we stood there thanking Ali'ikai for inviting us and rhapsodizing over what a beautiful event it was, I caught Yuggie eyeing me. I shot her a quizzical look and she returned with a mischievous grin, glancing at Ali'kai, whose beauty was, indeed, dazzling, especially in her colorful muu'muu. Just then her granddaughter, who had been one of the hula dancers, ran up and gave Ali'kai a big hug.

I raised my eyebrows at Yuggie. It was typical of her to imagine me following her lead and falling in love with a native Hawaiian so I could spend the rest of my life in this paradise. My tastes, however, are not that traditional, particularly since it seemed quite clear to me that Ali'kai was as straight as they come. Been there, done that.

On the way home, I asked Yuggie and Okalani about marriage rights for gays in Hawaii.

In unison they responded, "reciprocal beneficiary relationships."

"What's that?"

They shrugged, then Yuggie explained that gay marriage rights had been voted down and a constitutional amendment passed which limited marriage to opposite sex couples, that a civil union bill had then been vetoed by the governor, but a revised version of civil unions had finally been approved by the legislature but wouldn't go into effect until next year. Meanwhile what prevailed was "rbr: reciprocal beneficiary relationships," which gave a few limited rights to same-sex couples.

"It's really a very traditional culture," explained Okalani somewhat apologetically.

I'd already figured that out, but I'd romanticized it. "But it seems so tolerant," I protested, trying to hold onto that vision of equality.

"In some ways, yes," Yuggie said. "In other ways, not so much."

I didn't ask if they would get married if such were allowed. It seemed too personal. I didn't want Yuggie prying into my relationships any more than she already did, so I better not pry into hers, especially in front of her partner. Nor could I guess how they felt about this issue. They seemed to have their own secret language.

The next day, Okalani buzzed back from her job on her motor bike, but the buzzing tone continued, even after she'd turned the bike off, in the kitchen where Yuggie was fixing dinner. It turned out Okalani was on the bargaining team for the Coop workers' new contract negotiations, and she was fit to be tied. This was a dialect I could grasp.

"He laughed at our requests, then dismissed them," she said indignantly.

When I looked puzzled, Yuggie whispered, "the manager."

"As if 50 cents more an hour were outrageous. All we're asking for is a liveable wage."

"I thought that was part of the Coop's mission—to pay its workers a living wage," Yuggie said in her most reasonable voice, hoping, I guessed, to calm the waters. Yuggie was not "political" in the way I occasionally am. She could be righteous but rarely did she get angry at the powers that be. She tended to assume reasonableness even when it was imperceptible.

"The Council took that statement out last year," Okalani moaned. I was surprised to see her so upset. She had until this moment seemed unflappable, even when the twins were careening off the walls in the living room, chasing each other giggling with glee.

"I wonder why," I said.

She shrugged. "I guess they didn't think it was that important. Maybe it got in the way of his dreams of expansion."

"Are you unionized?" I asked, while Yuggie stood back, in deference, I supposed, to my vaster experience with forms of protest.

Okalani shook her head sadly. "No, but you'd think we'd learn from our own history." I looked puzzled. "The way they treated the workers on the sugar plantations." I nodded. I knew the psychology of victimization intimately.

Yuggie sat there listening expectantly, hoping, perhaps, that I might know something from my reporting days that could unlock this conundrum. All I really knew was that it 's helpful, but not necessarily effective, to have a union so workers are less likely to be played off against each other.

"Who is on the Coop Council?" I asked.

"Coop members elected by the membership," Okalani replied.

"No workers?"

"No—just the manager. They make policy decisions like the promise of a living wage, but he makes the day to day management decisions, like hiring or firing. He handles contract negotiations."

"Do you have a lawyer for your side?"

She shook her head. "Just our rep."

"Well, I think you need to do two things, at least," I announced, as if suddenly I'd become an expert on labor relations. You need to make your needs known directly to the members, not just those on the Council, who've probably bonded with the manager, but also the whole membership. Do you know how large it is?"

"Several thousand at least." Okalani's mood began to shift from defiance to resolve.

At that point I should have just listened. But it felt so good to be helpful—almost like belonging—I didn't want to relinquish that role. So I went on too long. "And you need to have an expert negotiator on your side—doesn't have to be a lawyer but it should be someone who knows how to bargain."

"Doesn't your rep know how to bargain?" Yuggie asked mildly. I should've guessed by her neutral tone that she was no longer finding my input helpful.

But Okalani was, once again, impressed. "Xavy, you're a writer. Could you help us write a press release or some kind of leaflet we can hand out to members."

"Is he going to allow you to do that?" Yuggie asked. I could tell she hated to point out the obvious opposition. What I didn't realize was that she now felt my advice as intrusive, as if my support was escalating the conflict rather than resolving the tension.

Okalani made a face. "Probably not. Maybe we'll need some members on our side who could hand them out." She looked expectantly at us.

Yuggie immediately volunteered, and I followed suit, somewhat reluctantly. Somehow I was more drawn to snorkeling than to campaigning. After all, labor disputes these days were a dime a dozen. A trip to Hawaii was probably once in a lifetime, especially an aging lifetime. But I was more than willing to help Okalani write a draft of the flyer she could check out with her fellow workers. In fact, it felt invigorating to be partisan for a change, instead of stuck in journalistic neutral. It reminded me of my women's movement days.

And, as it turned out, I enjoyed distributing leaflets later with Yuggie, interacting with the wide array of the people who were rushing in and out of the Coop. Some were too busy to stop, some grabbed the flyer to read later, and a few stopped to talk about the issues. Most of those were shocked to hear that any injustice was being done to the workers.

"That's not how a Coop is supposed to operate," one protested. "This is sounding more like a corporation."

"Exactly!" I agreed. Suddenly I was a dedicated protestor, even though usually I complain only about major events which affect me personally like getting fired or facing homelessness.

I later attended a meeting the workers called to explain their plight to sympathetic bystanders. The more they talked, with a variety of voices, some angry, some hurt, some confused, the more I sympathized with their situation. I myself wouldn't mind a steady, liveable wage. My dependence on the whims of Durga was better than nothing, but still it wasn't exactly a secure way to make a living. All the attendees vowed to write letters to the Council members, urging their support of the workers. Okalani felt buoyed by the public support, but I wasn't sure how much difference it was going to make. I was encouraged by the fact that she and her cohorts had located a skilled non-violent communicator to help them in their bargaining with the management. Much as I relish a good conflict, I could see the situation was getting more and more polarized.

Suddenly my peaceful vacation in paradise was beginning to feel a bit like purgatory. Yuggie, deep into supporting the distraught Okalani, was no longer available for our outings. And somehow without her companionship and guidance, my solo sightseeing lacked luster. The only compensation was Okalani's gratitude for my assistance. Once again, I'd acquired a high gloss in her eyes. This was a surprising development. Rarely am I regarded as a hero.

Finally, though, the negotiations were over and, no surprise, management won. They gave a modest raise of 25 cents an hour, but also increased the health care premium, so the workers barely broke even. The manager somehow convinced the Council members during this economic downturn that he couldn't risk overextension in expenses, even though just weeks before, according to Okalani, he'd been crowing about the increased revenues and hinting about further expansion.

Okalani was so disheartened by this outcome that she fell into an, apparently, uncharacteristic depression. Yuggie finally announced that she and Okalani were taking a vacation to Maui for a change of scene and of mood. This left yours truly to man the homefront, including looking out for the twins and for Nancy.

Why is it that whenever someone is needed to provide comfort to the peripheral (Mona comes to mind), it's me who gets chosen for the assignment? Not that Nancy and the twins are marginal, but still . . .

As it turned out, the twins, Kaimi and Meli, were a barrel of fun. In my role as guardian a'lightly (their parents, after all, were just down the street), I felt at times like a triplet. We rode bikes down to the lagoon and swam with rainbow fish. We had water fights in the back yard with the hose. Mud fights, however, I ruled as beyond the pale. I also drew the line at sneaking into the neighbor's lanai and stealing mangos from their tree. Not that I hadn't indulged in such highjinks in my childhood but without adult supervision. Both children, although spirited and athletic, were quite peaceful. They got along so well they seemed to have their own sign language. Either that or they were reading each other's minds. Upon further exposure they didn't look as much alike as I'd thought at first, perhaps because they were girl and boy. But they both had sweet personalities and they took care of each other in all sorts of ways. I usually had them in the afternoons while their father slept from his night shift at a hospital and their mother went to her part time job in a nursing home. Until school started again, their parents needed some help with childcare, and Okalani had arranged her summer hours at the Coop to fit the bill. I was glad to fill in with the kids so Okalani could get a vacation. But I breathed a sigh of relief when her daughter, Maluhia, picked them up in the late afternoon. Childcare, fun as it could be, felt like quite the daily workout.

In the mornings I checked in with Nancy to see if she wanted me to do any shopping for her or drive her anywhere. Since her stroke she'd stopped driving. After going on jaunts in search of just the right earrings or a new pair of stockings, I began to understand what she really was looking for was some company and an excuse to get out of the house. So I would suggest a scenic drive or an outdoor market or just a stroll among the tourists for some people-watching. We often finished these outings with a lunch at one of her favorite places, little cafes with good food and not much noise so we could converse. She sang Clare's praises (Clare is Yuggie's real name—what everybody except me calls her) and even seemed resigned to her unorthodox relationship with Okalani. Turns out Nancy felt quite close to Okalani's daughter, Maluhia. She told me it was like having the granddaughter she'd never had. I had to swallow hard: neither Yuggie nor I had provided anything other than granddogs.

We diplomatically avoided any religious or political discussions since I knew she was a devout Christian and lifelong Republican, but occasionally, she surprised me with some liberal comment on the news. I suspected Yuggie's influence, but I could see Nancy was much more intelligent than I'd ever given her credit for, and some of her more astute remarks could only be from the perspective of age. Although appearances were obviously still important to her—she always dressed up when we went out—she no longer seemed wed to wealth and status. Despite my own relaxed attire, she never, ever made any judgments about my appearance and never seemed ashamed to be seen with me. She had definitely mellowed with age and apparently enjoyed my company. At least she laughed at my jokes.

I found myself remarkably patient with her frailty and poor eyesight, pleased to offer her my arm when we walked over rough spots and to help her read the menu in a dim restaurant. I felt something I'd never experienced with her in my adolescence and rarely since then: needed. Perhaps if this had been a more or less permanent situation it might have become oppressive, but as a change of scene, relationally, it was rather rewarding.

The icing on the cake, surprisingly enough, was taking her to her church the Sunday morning before Yuggie's return. There was no pretense of piousness on my part. Besides she knew we were all Catholic, even my father. But she needed a ride and I was available. What surprised me was how moved I became by the singing, choking up when I tried to join in. I wasn't familiar with any of the hymns, but the words were right there in the hymnal and the music was easy to follow, especially accompanied by a piano and fiddle. The sermon was mercifully short and blessedly down to earth. When I found tears running down my cheeks on the last song, I was touched by her reaching across and squeezing my hand. Never mind that my tears were for my lost mother. Here beside me was the stepmother I had rejected so decisively. A second chance?

After church we went to a local hotel for their splendiferous brunch buffet. I helped her load up her plate with goodies, knowing she probably wouldn't eat but a bit of each. She was so frail and thin like a little bird pecking at her food. The same cannot be said for me, although I did have enough sense to steer away from the two-inch thick pancakes.

I was surprised when at the end of the meal she confided her regret that she hadn't been more of a mother to us. This shocked me.

"I grew up in a very stoic family," she said. "We were on the move constantly, and while there was plenty of tension, and more than enough laughter, there was no time for grief. I just thought at the time that you girls needed to get on with your lives. Your father was doing that."

I winced. Yeah, that was the problem, I thought. He had no time for grief either. He moved on far too quickly. But I didn't want to distract her from what seemed like an apology.

"I tried to fill in as I thought a mother would do, but it's hard to command much authority with adolescents even if you've been with them all their lives. Coming in as a stranger made it almost impossible. I probably shouldn't have tried to socialize you, just be friends."

I accepted her apology with surprising grace. "That's ok, Nancy," I said, noting that I still couldn't call her "Mom." "We're friends now, and that's what counts." I reached over and squeezed her hand. She smiled and started pecking at her cheesecake.

In the evenings I took long strolls on the beach listening to the waves and looking at the stars. I stood outside several tourist traps listing to the Hawaiian singing which is so heartful and melodious. And I thought about my life, where I was, where I was going and where I was going to end up. Should I stay here in Hawaii with Yuggie and her extended family? Should I head on out to Korea for that fruitless search? Should I return to Vermont? Should I go wherever I could find a job? It was all very puzzling.

Chapter Twenty Two

QUANDARIES

Having Yuggie home helped ground me, but rendered me less helpful, which now that I'd had been somewhat useful, felt even more useless. I still played with the twins sometimes in the afternoons and I still took Nancy out to lunch occasionally, but it was silly to pretend I could fill the roles Okalani and Yuggie performed so well and so faithfully. And I really didn't want to compete with either of them. Again I felt like some loose end.

Perhaps it was time to head out to South Korea. I still hadn't gotten the name of the orphanage from Durga. In fact I hadn't heard from Durga at all. Grace told me she was traveling again, this time on a pilgrimage to Tibet. Oh great, I thought.

Finally I shared my dilemma with Nancy. Once I'd explained the whole situation to her (well, maybe not the whole situation—I never revealed I was otherwise unemployed), she became totally engrossed. She found it quite plausible that Liza might have gone to Korea to search for her birth mother in the process of grieving her adoptive mother, but she doubted that Liza would have stayed there. Of course, it was impossible to know when, not to mention if, Liza had gone to Korea in the first place. We pondered that together. She was intrigued with my supposition that the folks in Vermont, other than Durga, actually knew where Liza was.

"You might find it interesting, Mary Catherine, to visit the country which your father helped liberate," Nancy observed, after musing over the situation.

I wasn't sure the Korean War was so much about liberation as it was about anti-Communism. She was probably thinking about Dad liberating France from the Nazis, which he also played a role in, as a younger man. And in fact Dad's tales about the Korean War, the few he told, were all about freezing almost to death in a sleeping bag and tiny tent during the winter. He'd never been colder, he said, almost shivering in remembrance. These accounts did not increase my desire to visit that particular country.

Gradually as she mulled it over in her ample spare time, Nancy began to glorify my role in Liza's possible liberation. Much as I recognized how Liza seemed to be doing a pretty good job of liberating herself, I couldn't help basking in this role of hero. When she spoke of how smart I was to be engaged in such a search and how much courage I must have to travel so far afield, I felt a slight shimmer in my hitherto rather dim aura. My search for Iris in the old days had elicited so much skepticism, teasing or irritation that I couldn't believe this even more aimless search could engender much admiration. Eventually Nancy convinced even Yuggie and Okalani of the nobility of my role in this mystery. Soon they were all three cheering me on. Turned out Okalani had a cousin teaching English in Seoul who might be willing to translate for me.

My quest was beginning to feel almost mythical. But without the name of the orphanage—I didn't even know if it was in Seoul or somewhere else—it really did feel like looking for a needle in a haystack—or like wandering around Manhattan looking for a stray cat. The capital of South Korea was a huge city.

But eventually I began to realize that I needed to get moving *somewhere*.

At first I thought Okalani's interest in me was strictly sisterly. I realized she was from a warmer culture than mine, and she was more physical with others than I was used to. She was constantly hugging Yuggie, Nancy and the twins—and, gradually, me. She was naturally affectionate and her friendliness naturally extended to me, her honey's beloved sister. But combined with a kind of hero worship tied to my writing abilities, made manifest during the Coop worker uprising, and the faux glamour of my role as a private investigator, these demonstrations of her regard were beginning to make me nervous.

Fortunately Yuggie didn't seem to notice any of this—or if she did, it certainly didn't seem to bother her. What bothered Yuggie instead— and it took a while for me to take this in—was my growing closeness with Nancy. She was used to being Nancy's main caretaker, and there was no doubt her role as such was secure. She wasn't used to sharing her with somebody else as relationally close (or distant) as I was. Yuggie wasn't just Nancy's substitute daughter, she was apparently, from Yuggie's perspective, her only daughter. Probably how she felt before I was born. How ironic that we would now be vying for Nancy's good opinion.

I couldn't quarrel with this. I had disdained any contact with Nancy for longer than Nancy had been married to our dad. I hadn't been there for her after Dad died and I certainly hadn't flown to the rescue when she had her stroke. I had absolutely no claim on her attention. And I certainly didn't want to upset Yuggie, my only root tie in the whole world. But I couldn't just blow Nancy off now that she was used to having me around. I mean, I could certainly disappear in my usual fashion, but as long as I was there, I didn't want to be rude or mean to her.

Meanwhile Okalani was trying to set me up with a friend of hers, and in the process, it seemed to me, flirting with me about it. The last thing I wanted was some blind double date with my own sister along to witness my typical awkwardness in such situations. Especially if the whole event was being orchestrated by a coy Okalani.

So I decided that the only way out of this morass of quandaries was to head for Korea. South Korea, I should explain. It's hard to imagine what North Korea is like and they'd have to kidnap me before I'd visit there. I had a passport, I had a credit card, and all I needed to do was make a plane reservation. Maybe I didn't need to know the name of the orphanage, I decided. Maybe I could track it down once I got there. So I went ahead and made a reservation for the next week. That gave me a week more of visiting with everybody, then I'd be off again. One more lesson about how I should never count on settling anywhere. Anywhere always becomes fraught, somehow, with complications.

I felt myself sliding back into my whiny, complaining self. Nothing was no good somehow. Here I was in this idyllic setting, with my beloved sister, her wonderfully fun extended family, a new mother of sorts and I still felt out of place. Why couldn't I find anywhere to belong?

Just as soon as I was packing my suitcase for the trip to Korea, Grace called to say that I was needed back in Vermont as soon as possible.

"I'm just about to fly to Korea," I protested. "Even without the name of the orphanage."

"Durga says she can't find the name of the orphanage. But it doesn't matter. Liza has contacted Marcy again. She wants to meet with you."

"With me? What on earth for?"

"She won't say."

"Why me?"

"I don't know, Xavy. I think she wants you to help her negotiate something with Durga."

"Why me?"

"Apparently she's gotten the impression you're some big hot shot."

"Me?" We both laughed.

"So, will you come back and meet with her?"

"If she's in Vermont and Durga's in Vermont, why should I come all the way from Hawaii to meet with them? Couldn't one of you negotiate whatever . . . ?"

"She's not in Vermont. She's still in some foreign country. Besides, Xavy, you're neutral. None of the rest of us are."

"I don't even know Liza."

"That's the point. You didn't know Sheila either."

"I do know Durga though."

"You knew her as Sandra. I'm not sure you really know the real Durga."

Obviously she couldn't see my shrug and look of distaste over the phone, but she could imagine it. I still couldn't help but see the reality of Sandra beneath the veneer of Durga.

"How can I talk with Liza if she's not in Vermont? Over the phone? Couldn't I do that from here?"

"She wants to talk to you in person."

"Grace, I'm not sure I'm returning to Vermont at all. It's beautiful here. I have family here. I might just make a new start here." What happened to all the complications this situation was fraught with? But wasn't the situation in Vermont just as fraught? Either I was falling in love with the wrong person or the wrong person was falling in love with me. Fortunately these days one didn't hop into bed with everybody one falls in love with, perhaps not with *any*body one falls in love with, but still—it was awkward either way.

"Well, I don't think she wants to meet us in Vermont," Grace replied, ignoring my attempts to ground myself in Hawaii.

"Us?"

"I'm supposed to lead you to her, once she lets me know where she is."

This admission made the whole prospect somewhat more appealing, but still—"So the Korean thing was just a figment of Durga's imagination?"

"I guess."

"I still don't see why I can't just talk to Liza on the phone from here"

Grace sighed. "She wants to meet with you in person."

I groaned. "So maybe she can fly from her mysterious location to Hawaii and meet me here."

"I'm afraid that would be too expensive."

"What about her trust fund? What about Durga's expense account?"

"I don't know, Xavy. That seems like a lot to ask."

"And me flying back to Vermont isn't?"

Grace sighed again, more loudly. "I thought you said you were coming back here." Grace is not usually a whiner, but I detected a hint of a whimper. Suddenly I suspected there was more to this request than met the eye.

"Well, things change. If anybody knows that, you—"

"I know, I know. And I can certainly understand why you'd want to stay in gorgeous Hawaii with Yuggie and all. But we miss you, Xavy."

"That's heartening to hear, but I don't think I was more than a blip on everybody's screen. You have your own community of folks there and I'm not a missing piece of that jigsaw puzzle, if you know what I mean."

"I miss you, Xavy. *I* need you."

Such a confession from Grace was startling. If she ever needed anybody, she never, ever would admit it. "What on earth for?" You've got Laurel, I started to add, then dropped it.

"Your presence really pulled us all out of a deep hole. I can't explain it." Clearly she'd been discussing all this with Marcy. They were both using the same line of reasoning: Xavy as savior. It was a mystery to me how I could possibly save them from anything—even more elusive than the enigma of my becoming a hero by tracking down Liza. Well, the latter role was now out, and I wasn't sure I was willing to sacrifice what I had at the moment for something as obscure as belonging to some community in a place where, if I believed the tales, winter lasted nine months of the year.

"I don't know, Grace. I'll have to think about it. There are all sorts of complications, as you can imagine."

"I understand, Xavy. Take as much time as you need. I'll tell Marcy to tell Liza that she'll just have to wait." Grace's sympathy and understanding, of course, tilted the balance in the other direction. Allowed to dawdle, suddenly I felt pressure to make up my mind. But I didn't leap to acquiescence. I accepted the time to mull it over and promised I'd call her back once I'd made up my mind. Meanwhile I cancelled my plane reservations to Korea.

Apparently sensitive to my reluctance to double date, or even to blind date, Yuggie and Okalani had conspired to have a party to which they would invite the targeted Millie. Millie, it turned out, was a vivacious blonde from Seattle, tall and slender, who loved swimming and scuba diving. She was also at least fifteen years younger than me. But the icing on the pineapple cake Okalani baked for the occasion was that Millie was not only obviously in love with Yuggie, she was a former client of Yuggie's. I felt complete empathy for her plight, having fallen in love with all my therapists, but I had zero interest in any romance with Millie.

"Yuggie," I protested when I found myself alone with her in the kitchen, "don't you see what's going on here?"

"What?" she asked innocently.

"Millie's in love with *you!*"

"No, she isn't."

"You know you shouldn't be hobnobbing with your clients, Yuggie. Isn't it against professional principles?"

"I haven't seen her as a client for at least five years. The women's community here is small. We need to stick together. We can't allow those professional distinctions to divide us."

"Now I see why Okalani wanted to set me up with her—to get her off your trail."

"Oh, Xavy, that's nonsense. Okalani just wants you to be happy here."

Someone tentatively poked her head into the kitchen, with a quizzical expression as if she sensed she might be intruding on a private conversation. We smiled and gestured her in, glad for the interruption. This someone, with her dark, curly hair and teasing blue eyes, was more attractive to me than a roomful of Millies. I made a note to find out who she was, and who she was with.

That's when I made another discovery. Watching Okalani move around the room to converse and joke with friends, I realized that her way with everybody was warm and flirtatious. Obviously everybody loved to tease with her, and almost everybody was a recipient of her hugs and occasionally chaste kisses. I was no more an object of her desires than anybody else. What hubris on my part to think she had a crush on me! What a relief.

During the party, which turned out to be a lot of fun and peopled by another community I could potentially belong to, I mulled over my options: stay here in Hawaii and face the fact that nobody is interested in me romantically, that I have no steady source of income, and that now that Liza has found herself, I can no longer be a hero in Nancy's eyes, and OR go back to Vermont and face the fact that nobody there was interested in me romantically, that I had no steady source of income there, but that I had a chance to play the role of savior in Grace's eyes and perhaps in the process help Liza out. Then there was the difference in the weather between Hawaii and Vermont. On the other hand, Hawaii had typhoons and potential tsunamis while Vermont just had a lot of snow. Maybe it would be possible to spend the winters in Hawaii and the summers in Vermont? Provided I won the Publisher's Sweepstakes or some mysterious uncle left me my own trust fund. Fat chance.

At a certain point, somewhat bored by the gossip about people I didn't know, I wandered out onto the lanai to look at the lights bobbing up and down from boats docked in the bay. A full moon was shining over the water in a mystical way, laying down a path of light from the east. Out there was California. Only a few months ago, I'd been on that shore, gazing west toward Hawaii, worrying about Yuggie and the tidal wave. West is the destination for adventure, for exploration, at least in the American mindset. East is the direction for enlightenment, for meeting the sun. No matter which way I looked I saw neither adventure nor enlightenment on my horizon. I sighed.

A voice I didn't recognize responded from a dark chair I hadn't noticed. "Beautiful, isn't it?" I startled, then looked around. I saw a sitting form but couldn't tell who it was. Somebody from the party, I hoped, not some lurking intruder. If so, this intruder had a lovely husky voice.

"Yes, it is," I said. "A lovely place."

"The full moon is gorgeous wherever you are," the voice responded. I looked closer. It was the cute woman with the dark curly hair and impish blue eyes. My mood lifted.

"Have you lived here long?" I asked.

"Coming on a decade," she replied. "But I'm heading home soon."

"Where is home?"

"Oregon."

"Ah, another beautiful place. But isn't it hard to leave here?"

"I don't know. Not when my honey isn't around. And even without her gone, it's kind of isolated here, if you know what I mean. Being an island."

Ah, I sighed inwardly, a honey in the wings. Too bad. *No woman is an island*, I thought, *entire of herself.* "No, I probably don't—I've only been here a few weeks." Any place can seem isolated, under certain circumstances. "But I can imagine—all that ocean between you and almost everybody else you know."

"Exactly. Somehow, when that tsunami hit, I began to wish for more solid ground under my feet. And more modes of transportation than flying or sailing."

"Yeah, I can see that."

"What about you? Are you planning to stay around?"

"Actually, I was on my way to Korea."

Her murmur suggested surprise, or possibly interest, I couldn't tell.

"But instead I've been called back."

"Where?"

"Vermont."

"Another beautiful place, I hear."

I nodded. I waited for her to ask me why I was being called back, and by whom, but she didn't. Instead we fell into a companionable silence, watching the moon rise and listening to the music from the party. Someone was playing a guitar and it sounded like people were singing along. After awhile, she stood up with an empty glass in her hand and went back inside, giving me a shy smile. I soon followed. So much for romance.

Some time later the singing had become so heartfelt, I felt restless, so I hopped out on the lanai again. There, again, was my curly headed friend—I hadn't gotten her name—smoking a tiny pipe.

"Want some?" she asked when she saw me.

"Sure," I said. It's the best way I know to get to whatever my own heart feels.

As I lit up, the moon slid behind a cloud. We stood there in silence, exchanging the pipe.

"You tuning into your honey?" I asked with a gesture toward the ocean east of us.

"Yeah," she said. "It's like some kind of radar connection when I get a signal. Only, from this distance, hard to interpret."

"I know. Is it a distress signal, a missing you message, or some other kind of synchronous resonance?"

"Exactly. Maybe that's why those points of connection across such expanses are so engaging. One never knows for sure."

"Even when you're actually together," I added with a chuckle, "you never know for sure. Communication is always a bit of a mystery."

"Even when she tells you for sure what she means," she said. We laughed together. "You have someone out there you're . . . ?" she asked tentatively.

"Not exactly. I wish I did."

"Be glad you don't. Love is agony. I wouldn't wish it on my best friend," she said with heartfelt irony. I smiled. Didn't I know it? So why did I still hanker after it?

Anyway, somehow, by the time the evening was over, I'd confessed to her my whole current saga: the quest for the missing daughter, the birth mother, the adoptive mother and the step-mother, the magic behind the daughter's disappearing act, the possible conspiracy, the "What the hell am I doing in Hawaii?" scenario (minus a few embarrassing details). I even confessed my crush on Kara, how it felt good to sense that shimmer again even though actually activating it was totally impossible. I didn't tell her everything. I certainly didn't reveal my hubris regarding Okalani (who was, apparently, a good friend of hers) or expose Yuggie's jealousy of me in regard to Nancy, nor did I reveal any family secrets. Nonetheless, by the time I'd listened to her tales of the angst of being in love and the challenge of hands across the ocean and had confessed to her some of my various conundrums, I began to feel a whole lot better. And she seemed, as a result, pretty perky herself. Our sharing felt like an infusion of pure empathy, like oxygen.

In fact, when we parted, in the wee hours of the morning, with a long, luxurious hug, she said, "You've saved my life and I don't even know your name."

"Ditta!" I replied. At that we introduced ourselves and exchanged email addresses. Her name was Gabi. Mine, I told her, was Xavy.

"As in Xavier, the saint?" she asked. I hadn't figured her for being Catholic. I nodded. "Ah!" she said, as if she understood something. All I knew about my family namesake was that he was a priest, a Jesuit missionary—which certainly doesn't explain my family name.

"As in Gabriel, the angel?" I asked. She nodded with a grin. The messenger angel, I realized. "Thank you so much for this conversation," I told her ardently. "It's given me a new lease on life."

"Well, good," she said with a wave as she hopped onto her motorbike and buzzed off into the balmy night.

Later I found out from Yuggie that Gabrielle is also a therapist. I figured my secrets were safe with her, even though no confidentiality clause applied to our friendly exchange. I hadn't told her I was an investigative reporter, but her revelations, as far as I was concerned, would be guarded with the privacy of the confessional. As for therapy, this time our exchange had been mutual. And, apparently, mutually beneficial.

Time, I realized, to head back toward Grace.

Chapter Twenty Three

LAYOVER

Hard as it was to leave Yuggie, Nancy, Okalani and the twins behind, I had plenty of air time to reflect upon my visit with them and to contemplate a possible relocation to Hawaii. The flight back to San Francisco and then to Chicago was long enough, but when I saw the "Flight Cancelled" on the destinations board at O'Hare, I knew I was in for a much longer transition. Hurricane Jane had put a stop to all flights to the northeast, and it wasn't clear when the storm would be over or flights would resume. It took over an hour waiting on my cell phone while standing in line to find out just about nothing. They said they'd call to let me know when my flight was rescheduled. I felt both relief and skepticism about this.

Where to go in the meantime? Last time I'd been in Chicago I'd stayed in a famous old hotel on the lake front downtown. Only it had obviously fallen on hard times. In the middle of the night I was awoken by panting and screaming from the wall behind the head of my bed. At first I feared it was torture, then I realized it was the act of intercourse (not "love-making" exactly). Three a.m. seemed a weird time for such activity but I figured it was some young tourists who'd just come in from a night on the town. Judging from the head of steam already being generated, I folded the pillow over my ears and figured it would soon be over. Less than an hour later, the same sounds bombarded my ears. They must really be hot, I thought. But by the third such event, it finally dawned on me that though the pants and groans seemed to be coming from the same feminine voice, the other tones varied. This was not a passionate young couple, this was a sex worker plying her wares. The screams were a performance. At this point, I started banging on the wall. This didn't seem to make any difference. Finally I called the front desk with a heated complaint, and eventually the noises subsided. The famous Blackwater Hotel had become a bordello. I was only too happy to check out the next morning, grateful I hadn't planned on staying a week.

My other option was my old college roommate, Mariana. We hadn't seen each other in years, it seemed our lives had diverged so thoroughly. She was married, twice, with children, had lived in the same place for all her adult life, some hip suburb of Chicago. She taught history in the community college and was a musician on the side. It was with some trepidation that I finally called her, filling up with excuses why I hadn't visited her more often.

Her voice on the phone was as warm and melodious as ever. Just hearing it brought back a flood of memories: our discussions far into the night as we assumed a variety of sitting, kneeling, and sprawling positions on our respective dorm beds, our campus pranks (mild at best, given the restrictions at Catholic women's colleges in those days), our reporting in on bad teachers and awkward blind dates.

Mariana was delighted to have me stay with her during my layover. She was caretaking her ill husband, she said, so welcomed the company. I protested that I didn't want to intrude, but she assured me he wasn't that sick, just recovering from some successful back surgery which kept him immobile. The concept of successful back surgery seemed in itself miraculous, so I didn't feel so intrusive. And I could imagine that she might like some distraction in the midst of caretaking.

After an hour's taxi ride, I found myself being warmly embraced and welcomed into a spacious kitchen for a long talk. Mariana was just as appealing as ever, her long dark hair still soft and curly around her lovely, lively face. She, like most of our generation, was bulkier than the slip of a girl she'd been in the old days, but not debilitatingly so. She told me I looked just the same as ever, which I doubted, but I appreciated the sentiment. None of us really want to admit how much older we look, but I wouldn't mind appearing somewhat wiser, and I know I'm much more hip than I used to be in our shiny, baggy polyester uniforms.

It took quite a while just to catch up. Mariana's stability, I realized, had not protected her from her share of change and loss. Her first husband died suddenly and unexpectedly of a heart attack. They'd adopted one child when it seemed she wouldn't or couldn't conceive, then were surprised by a sudden pregnancy and the birth of twins. After a long stint of widowhood, she'd remarried an old friend after their children had grown and gone off. She was now a grandmother to many.

Trying to explain my much less conventional life story was not as easy as listening to her history. It's so hard maneuvering around all the "nots"—not married, not a mother, not a grandmother, not a successful career woman. Or try to explain the complex network of relationships that still constitute the women's community, loose as it is these days. The women's movement had generated so many options and I, apparently, had opted out of all of them. And yet, I'd had a mostly exciting, mostly fun time of it so far. Not that you'd get that from all my complaints, and true, there are some serious gaps still. But I'd been blessed to be on the cutting edges of social change, I had a wealth of good friends, and my career, such as it was, took me to some challenging places. I was delighted to hear that one of Mariana's daughters was "married" to another woman, and when I asked her how she felt about that, Mariana said calmly that she hadn't been a bit surprised when her daughter came out as "bi." My, how things have changed. Knowing I was bi, she said, had helped her acceptance. I wondered how she knew—I don't recall ever telling her, but I suppose she could easily guess.

She pulled out an old album and we poured over photos of ourselves and our friends when we were still green college kids. I was shocked at how innocent I looked as well as how much hair and clothes styles had changed. I think I was wearing a Nehru jacket with some kind of fashionable upswept hairdo to distract from my chubby face. Despite my attempts to be mod, I looked like I'd just pecked out of an egg. So perky—not droopy like I feel now.

The good thing is that we are now far beyond the comparisons and envies of our youth and so could take great delight in hearing about the trials and rewards of our oh so different lifestyles as well as empathize with situations far out of our own ken. In our sharing we could see that each life has its own share of tradeoffs and sacrifices and rewards. Listening to her story helped me accept my own. Instead of feeling I had to defend or apologize for my choices, I realized that hers had been just as difficult. And guilty as I felt for not having been more supportive when her husband died, I realized she probably felt bad for not having kept in better touch with me.

Mariana, I realize now, was the first woman I fell in love with. Only I didn't realize I was in love with her until she rushed off into marriage as soon as we graduated. Having lost her own father at a young age and having only brothers, it was natural she'd jump on the heterosexual bandwagon. But I'd pined over her sudden disappearance into the institution of marriage, and sometimes wondered, after I'd more or less come out, if she ever felt anything special for me.

But none of that mattered anymore. We were both past any youthful passions, and I realized that friendship, not sex, is what really endures (not that I'm embracing celibacy, mind you). Instead, listening to her talk about her children and grandchildren, I realized this was a golden opportunity to get some advice about the Liza puzzle.

Once I'd given her the whole story, and answered her many thoughtful questions about Durga and Sheila and Liza, she just nodded. What was that supposed to mean?

"Does it sound dire to you?" I asked, somewhat pitifully, as if I were a neophyte in terms of such dynamics, which I'm not.

"Sounds pretty typical," she commented. "By dying Sheila managed to avoid that distancing which occurs around this age with some kids." I figured she was talking about her son who was on assignment in the Middle East as a photographer. "Most kids," she added slowly.

"So shouldn't Durga just stop trying to track her down? Let her find her distance without interference?"

"Maybe, but I'm not so sure. Kids that age need some resistance from at least one of their parents."

"Why?"

"It helps them keep rooted somehow so they can wander more freely. It's a paradox. You'd think that the further away the kids go, the more distanced they are from the parents. But that's not necessarily true."

"It's like that John Donne poem we read with Sister Agnes, you remember, about the compass?"

"Yes, one foot stable while the other moves."

"Durga probably doesn't realize it," Mariana said, as if all these people I was describing were her friends, "but obviously from what you say, Liza is well aware of her efforts to contain her—and as long as Durga isn't successful, that's probably good for Liza."

"But Durga isn't really doing anything—she has hired me to do it for her. And that doesn't seem right. What should I do now?"

"Well, it sounds like Liza's trying to put you into a different role, that of mediator. Maybe it's just my curiosity but my impulse is, why not listen to what she has to say? That doesn't mean you have to do anything about it."

"If I allow Durga to keep paying my way, I do."

"Well . . . ?" I recognized Mariana's characteristic tact coming to the fore here. Her hesitancy was far more effective than if she'd stated her obvious opinion—it was time for me to find another income source. I suspected Grace would agree. I wondered how they'd get along. But somehow I didn't discuss Grace with Mariana. It was kinda like they occupied the same psychic space.

Instead I turned the conversation back to her. "So maybe the deeper one's roots, the further one can wander. Your son's so far away—does that mean you have a special bond with him?"

She smiled. "I can only hope so."

"Sorry I don't have this down, but is he the adopted one?"

"No, she's the one closest to home and most conventionally married with children. He's the other twin."

"Ah, so the twins are both adventurers?!"

"Each in their own way, yes. But Johnny is the one I worry the most about." She groaned. "Why does he have to be stationed in the Middle East?"

"Probably because that's where all the action is these days. The Arab Spring and all."

"It's like a mission for him, to document these fledgling attempts at liberation. But I guess all my kids, in their own ways, are into public service." She sighed. "You must know about that, Xavy, as a journalist."

"Well, yes. We—some of us anyway—seemed to be obsessed with revealing truths, or at least the facts, of events, particularly transformative ones. I hope he comes out of this assignment with some great photos and an even greater respect for freedom."

"I just hope he comes home soon."

Even though I have not been a mother and will never be a grandmother, I could understand some of her anguish. One wants to let those one loves have the freedom to go wherever they want and do whatever they need to do for their own personal fulfillment. And yet, especially when you feel responsible, even when that life is really no longer your responsibility, it's hard to allow, much less celebrate the risks they are taking. The extended line can really pull at the heart of the anchored one.

Amazingly, during all this conversation, Mariana managed to keep her husband comfortable in their master bedroom, fixing and taking him meals, making sure his computer sat comfortably on the tray between meals, that the TV remote was within reach, and that, I assume, he felt fully tended to with whispers or strokes of endearment. I stopped by briefly to wave at him from the doorway, but since I'd never met him before, we didn't have much to say to each other. She also managed to take time out to check her email, while I reviewed messages on my cell phone, to call her oldest daughter to see about the baby's cold, and chat with the mailman. After a good night's sleep in the guest room, we walked the dog together, chatting up a storm.

I even confided my dilemma about whether to return to Hawaii or stay in Vermont.

"I just heard on the news that those are two of the safest places in the country when it comes to natural disasters," she said.

"Yeah, but Vermont has winter, which may not be a natural disaster but certainly could be a natural challenge."

She laughed, wisely just listening without giving any advice. A strategy she must've learned to employ with her wandering children. Instead she just listened to my stories about the people I knew in both places.

When the airlines finally called with my new flight information, I was reluctant to leave. Not just because Mariana was such a good friend but also because she was such a good caretaker. But then I seem to have good luck in that department—I know women who are good caretakers and who don't mind taking care of me at times. But whether in Hawaii, Vermont, or Chicago I knew better than to push my luck.

Chapter Twenty Four

SHOWDOWN

"Got your passport?" Grace asked as she greeted me outside the Burlington airport. She was keeping the car warm.

Shivering in chilly Vermont, I nodded, confused. Weren't we going home now? After my three day delay, I was eager to sink into the warm guest bed for several weeks. Was it because of the hurricane we couldn't go to Grace's house? But if the road was flooded, how did she get to the airport? I knew her house was ok from our phone conversations, but I hadn't stopped to think that the way between here and there might be blocked.

"I'm sorry, Xavy, but I think we need to strike while the iron is hot." I never understood that expression. Surely it didn't refer to that mundane (because female) occupation of ironing clothes. Even though ironing was never my favorite activity, and I was never very good at it, I never felt like I was *striking* the clothes. I looked puzzled. Blacksmithing. Time to put the shoe on the horse?

"I'm not sure how long Liza is going to be around," Grace said in her planning tone.

"Around where?" Wondering if Liza was lurking in the parking lot, I glanced around. I had no idea what she looked like, aside from the photos of her as a girl.

"Where she is now." This was beginning to sound like something out of *Alice in Wonderland*. If "Where am I?" means "Where I am *now*," I could say I'm just about anywhere, given my recent travels.

"Where is that—exactly?" I asked patiently, knowing full well that Grace was going to take me there.

"At the moment, Montreal."

"How far away is it?" I said, tossing my suitcase into the back seat, where I noticed another suitcase already stowed.

"Only a couple of hours from here," Grace replied. "That's why I thought it would be better to go right away than go home in the opposite direction for an hour."

Ah, so I was the hot iron?! Not Liza? So who was the horse and who, the blacksmith? "Makes sense," I said.

"But she's threatening to pull up stakes and head off to someplace like Timbuktu."

"Pull up stakes? You mean, all this time she's been only two hours away?"

"Three, from home," Grace admitted.

"Timbuktu?" I couldn't help getting distracted by the sound of the place. Liza wasn't the only one with itchy feet.

"You know how restless young folks are. They want to see the world in two seconds."

"You mean, she's been only two hours away from here all this time?" I repeated. *You mean to say,* I meant to say, *that I've been half way round the world looking for her and all that time she was just in your backyard, so to speak?*

As if reading my mind, Grace leapt to put the onus on me somehow, rather than apologizing as I felt she should. "Of all people, Xavy," she said with some exasperation, "You ought to understand."

"Really," I replied rather haughtily. "And why would that be?"

Somehow this particular exchange was going nowhere fast—leaving me holding the bag of my considerable disgust over how I'd been treated so far in regard to Liza's disappearance. Grace could protest all she wanted to, but I was pretty darn sure she'd known all along where Liza was.

When we got to the border, the line was long but the process was fairly quick, compared to other border crossings I've gone through. We just had to show our passports and some other ID, explain we were visiting a friend in Montreal and expected to return that same night. The border guard was friendly, with a trace of a French accent. Looking at my blank passport, which didn't even get a stamp for crossing into Canada, I realized how my world has shrunk. In the past I've traveled to Central America, through Mexico, vacationed in the Caribbean, rode trains throughout Europe, flown as far east as Israel, as far south as South Africa, as far west as California, and as far north as Alaska. Mostly on assignment, of course, which limits one's focus and depth of experience. And now I'd chickened out from traveling either to Haiti or Korea, both of which would certainly have been wild goose chases. But still I'd squandered two opportunities to discover new cultures. It seemed the new *where* for me is nowhere.

Needless to say, by the time we'd zipped into Montreal and wandered through the narrow downtown streets, I was fit to be tied, having ample opportunity to realize how I'd been led astray by people I trusted. To what extent I still wasn't sure because Grace was not the confessing type.

Not exactly the best mood with which to meet the elusive Liza. To assuage my ruffled self, Grace took me to see the famous Basilica of Notre Dame. As we walked in, I felt my spirit lift immediately in response to its beauty. The sanctuary was carved wood stretching toward a deep blue ceiling dotted with golden stars. Above us was a many flowered stained glass mandala, through which the light of the sky poured. And in the background a choir was practicing some wonderful music. It's rare that a church, even a cathedral, seems to embody the spiritual in such a natural, yet transcendent way. I'm not sure whether it evokes an aesthetic response or a religious revelation, but I had to admit just being in that place shifted my mood dramatically. As Grace must've known it would. By the time we arrived at the café where we were to meet Liza, I was feeling considerably more mellow.

The café was dark and cosy, full of enticing aromas. On one side was a boulangerie, the case loaded with loaves of bread and other bakery items. On the other side were booths. The only other people in the café at this time of the afternoon was a young couple. I was wondering if Liza was still avoiding us when the young woman stood up and approached Grace with a dazzling smile. As Grace hugged her, I realized this must be Liza. She was taller than I expected, and quite lovely. She introduced Marc, a handsome but nerdy looking fellow with dark, soulful eyes behind thick glasses, as her boyfriend. Aha, I thought. Liza is straight. When he stood up to shake our hands, I could see that he was thin as a reed and taller than Liza by at least five inches.

I wondered if Grace was surprised by this development. She didn't seem to be. She greeted him warmly as he welcomed us to Quebec with a slight accent. When the waitress came to take our order, he spoke French with her, so I figured he was a native. Although I studied French in high school, my spoken French is laughable, so I was glad to have him translate, even though the waitress also spoke English. Grace joined their conversation with her excellent French pronunciation, although I remember her telling me that people in Quebec spoke a different dialect than the one she learned in school, which was from France.

Just as I was starting to feel left out, Liza politely engaged me in light conversation, as one would a stranger. I wondered what she knew about me, and why she'd agreed to meet with me. But I wasn't sure how we could carry on this negotiation, which promised to be intense given how studiously she'd avoided it, with Marc as witness. I supposed she needed him there for support, and it did make a balance of two versus two, like a doubles tennis match, but I was hoping this exchange would not turn into either a contest or a game. But I wasn't going to take the lead in any case, so I just waited to see what would develop.

In the meantime, I listened politely while Grace managed in her graceful way to extract all sorts of information from Marc, as if she were interviewing him subtly for a job. It was not unlike how a parent might check out her daughter's potential husband. Turned out he was studying for his masters in anthropology at a local university, his family lived outside of Montreal, his father was a doctor and his mother, a nurse, he had two sisters and one brother, he'd been raised Catholic (this after we praised the beauty of the basilica), and he was obviously quite smitten with Liza. Not much not to like, I thought, from the parental perspective. I was beginning to understand why Liza brought him along.

After a leisurely afternoon's tea and pastries, Marc stood up and said he had a class to attend. Pleasant as he was, I was relieved to see him go. Now we could get down to business. Somehow I was eager to settle this whole matter, if possible, and move on with my life. I suspected Liza finally felt the same. I was ready to mediate.

"So you're Durga's agent?" Liza asked me, point blank.

I felt stricken. Or should I say *struck?* "Agent?" I exclaimed. "No, not really."

"Xavy is a private investigator," Grace jumped in to explain. "Durga asked her to track you down."

"Without much success," I added with a slight smile. "Every trail turned cold." I glanced at Grace whose face was granite. "I suspect you had a few friends helping you hide."

Liza nodded. I waited for her to explain, but she didn't. "But I don't want to hide anymore," she said. "I'd like you to convey a message to Durga for me."

"Why don't you just tell her yourself?" I asked.

She pursed her lips. "I don't know how well you know Durga, but she's not exactly open to . . ."

"I understand perfectly," I said, eager to distance myself from the stubbornly pursuing Durga.

Grace rushed to fill the gap. "Durga is really worried about you, Liza. She only wants what's best for you."

Liza rolled her eyes. How many times had I rolled my eyes about my stepmother Nancy when I was her age? How many times had Dad tried to tell me that Nancy cared about me? In hindsight he may have been right, but at the time I would have none of it. I could empathize with Liza. "She wants me to fulfill what she thinks was Mom's dream—to turn that mountain into a refuge for lesbians. I'm not gay myself, and the last thing I want to do is be stuck in Vermont taking care of an old age home for lesbians."

"To be fair, Liza," Grace said, "your mother wanted it for single mothers, including lesbians."

"Yeah, well maybe." I could tell she was feeling guilty now, and somewhat defensive. "But I grew up with her in a perfect ordinary home in Burlington, not stuck on some fancy mountain top. What about the children of those single mothers—what might *they* want?"

"Good point," I said. Grace glanced at me, alarmed perhaps at this shift in my neutrality. But since Liza hadn't, as I imagined, called me in as a negotiator, I felt no obligation to remain neutral, much less act as an "agent" for Durga.

"What do you want?" Grace asked Liza, getting to the real point of this meeting.

"I want to travel. I'm not ready to settle down anywhere—not on some mountain in Vermont, not here in Montreal, not with Marc, not *anywhere* for the present. I'd like to join an NGO along the border of Thailand and Myanmar for awhile, working with refugees. I'd like to go to Africa and South America."

"So you and Marc don't have any long range plans?" Grace asked. I could see her preparing a report not just for Durga but for the whole "extended family," especially Marcy.

"He might join me at some point. We're not sure."

So Marc's presence probably had been for support, not for Grace's approval, but maybe both.

I decided to jump in. The last thing I wanted was to be regarded as a Durga lackey. "Youth is the time to travel," I said authoritatively. "Sounds like you're pretty adventurous."

"Why not?" Liza said. I could tell she was trying to figure out which, if any, side I was on.

"If not now, when?" I added with a flourish. I glanced at Grace to see what she was thinking about my shift in perspective, but she seemed to be having no objections. She did look worried though.

"Are you having a problem with this, Grace?" Liza asked.

"No, not really. I just worry about you. When we didn't know where you'd gone, we worried. And now . . . Will you please promise to keep in touch?"

"If you promise not to send Durga, or one of her agents, chasing after me," Liza said with a hint of exasperation.

"I don't think you have much to worry about in terms of Durga," I inserted somewhat haughtily. "And I was certainly not chasing after you. I had no idea where you were." It cost a bit of my dignity to admit my colossal failure as a seeker, but to be viewed as a hovering hawk was even worse. Besides, I was pretty sure I'd been given some false leads. "I'm not sure you ever were missing, but now, as far as I'm concerned, you've been found."

Liza finally began to relax. "Will you please convey all this to Durga for me?" Her tone for the first time was more plaintive than complaining.

"Sure," I replied, although I had every intention of shifting that responsibility to Grace. I'd done my job, unsuccessful as I'd been. I wasn't quite ready to be the messenger Durga would shoot down.

"I think Durga is just trying to be loyal to what your Mom wanted for her place, for her legacy," Grace added.

"By getting me to fulfill it for her?" Liza replied with a trace of bitterness. Grace shrugged. "Well," Liza added in a hushed tone, "I've had hints from Mom with a different message."

Grace and I glanced at each other, ever curious about what the dead might have to say from, and maybe even about, the hereafter—which was of slightly more interest to me personally than what to do with Liza's mother's property.

"It was just a dream, really," Liza admitted, "but a powerful one. And she was there, radiant, telling me that I needed to move on with my life, find my own path, with her full support. I felt her blessing, I really did."

"That's wonderful, Liza," Grace said with moist eyes. "I'm so glad to hear that. And you know you have our blessing too, me and Marcy anyway."

Liza leaned across the table to give Grace's shoulder a pat of appreciation. I wanted to convey my blessing too, but who was I but an interfering stranger? "And thank you, Xavy," she added, "for your understanding. I was afraid you . . ."

"I know," I interrupted her, not eager for her to label my suddenly no longer heroic activity. "Well, I'm just glad to help."

Liza leaned forward toward me. "You remember the two deer at All Species Day," she confessed. "Well, one of them was me."

"And the other one was Hope!" Grace exclaimed, as surprised as I was. So at least she hadn't been in on that particular secret.

I laughed. "No wonder you kept darting away from me!"

"I've been going to All Species Days most of my life. I wasn't going to miss this year just because of Durga," Liza explained.

She gave us both hugs. There seemed little more to say. Grace got her to promise to keep in touch with her "family" in Vermont, and I wished her well with her travels.

We managed to scoot out of Montreal before the first wave of commuter traffic, fortified with a stash of pastries from the boulangerie.

"Well, what do you think?" Grace said, once we'd settled into the calmer roads of the Eastern Townships.

"About Liza? She's very attractive, and apparently, very stubborn. I can see why she and Durga would clash."

"About the boyfriend."

"Cute. Seems nice. But who knows? I'm sure he was on his best behavior for the elders. And it doesn't sound like they're rushing into any commitments. Which is probably good, given her thirst for adventure."

"Well, since she isn't gay," Grace said, "I can't blame her for not wanting to be the caretaker for a bunch of lesbians."

"Even if she was gay (and anybody can trot out a boyfriend for the relatives) I can't imagine her wanting to tie herself down like that. Frankly, I can't imagine wanting myself to live in such a place. We'd have to hire a lot of folks to take care of us, and who would pay for that?"

"I know," Grace admitted. "It used to be such a collective dream of ours—a place for us. But now that things have loosened up, it doesn't have such great appeal."

"I'm not sure I want to be cooped up with just old folks," I said, "much less just lesbians. Sure, it would feel great to be close to friends, but I'd like my friends to be of all ages and persuasions."

"Yeah, me too. That's one reason we run the school—to be in touch with a larger, more diverse community."

"I plan to rest my laurels on the dole, collect my social security and medicare before it runs out—I paid good money into those funds: I *am* entitled! And then sink into samadhi while others take care of me."

Grace laughed. "I suspect that's what Durga has in mind as well, only she'll have a lot more support than social security."

"How do you think she's going to take the news about Liza's intentions?" I asked.

"I dread finding out. When are you going to tell her, Xavy?"

"Me? Why me?"

"Well, wasn't that your job?"

"No, dear one, my job was to find her—which, with your help, I have. Thanks for that. It's not up to me to tell her what she probably has already figured out by now."

"Well, somebody has to tell her, and it's probably not going to be Liza. Besides, didn't you just promise Liza you'd convey all this to Durga?"

I gulped. Sure enough, I had. "I'll help you tell her, just as you helped me find her."

"Ok, fair enough," Grace said as we wound though a quaint little Quebec town, heading for the border.

It was dark by the time we arrived at Grace's house. Marcy, apparently, was at Kara's house. I tumbled into bed, asleep as soon as my head hit the pillow. Strike while the pillow is soft, I murmured to myself as I drifted off.

I woke to the sound of mewing from the upstairs bathroom. Marcy's new kitten, apparently, had already found her. When I opened the bathroom door, she scampered out, then wandered back in to climb into my lap while I sat on the toilet, her purr as loud as a small motor. She was striped grey and black with an M pattern on her forehead. At least Marcy hadn't tried to duplicate Zoom's coloring. From the moment she woke up until the time Marcy arrived home, the kitten played, leaping and running and tossing little balls and springs into the air, as well as pouncing on the dogs' tails. They tolerated these intrusions with a wary graciousness.

When Marcy arrived home later, she gave me a welcome home hug, then tossed a newspaper onto the kitchen table where I sat drinking coffee and protecting my slippered feet from tiny claws. As she scooped up the kitten affectionately, she said, "Check this out, Xavy—our local newspaper is looking for an editor."

I sat my cup down and looked at the advertisement in the paper: "Managing editor wanted." Editor? I couldn't imagine myself in such an exalted position, and yet, this was a small, local, weekly paper, and I certainly needed a job.

So the next day I sent the publisher my resume. A few lazy days later, after drifting around like the leaves which were starting to turn color and float down from the large maple trees in front of Marcy and Grace's house, helping out at the school, playing with the kitten, walking the dogs, wondering when Grace and I would meet with Durga, I got a message from the publisher, wanting to meet with me.

It was all I could do not to rush down to the office immediately, but I waited until the appointed hour and strolled casually through downtown Montpelier looking for the newspaper office which was above a flower shop. As soon as I climbed up into the suite of messy offices filled with folks huddled over computers, pouring over layouts, or talking to potential advertisers on the phone, I felt at home.

The publisher who was also the chief editor took me back into his office, his huge desk covered with piles of paper, while stacks of newspapers lined the walls. He looked like a middle-aged version of Liza's boyfriend, tall and skinny with a high receding forehead, a handsome nose, dark eyebrows, kind eyes, thick glasses, but somehow with a more English cast than French, like he'd stepped out of a Dickens novel, rather than a play by Sartre. He was very gracious, apologizing for the mess, which I suspected was chronic, and solicitous about my comfort, while clearing off one of the many cluttered chairs.

There we chatted about the paper which he had founded a decade or more earlier, my history as a reporter, what he was looking for in terms of the job. In the process we managed to investigate each other's political persuasions (both left of center but not rabidly liberal, given the journalistic code of seeing both sides of issues), lifestyles (both apparently closer than not to the poverty line), and dedication to journalism (on the same page so to speak). It was the most meandering interview I've ever had, and the most enjoyable. He seemed to value my experience and was interested in my opinions.

When I expressed some reserve about being called a "managing" editor, he offered other options, like "contributing editor," "assistant editor," or "news editor." By the time we finished talking, he was considering my suggestion that maybe he hire two editors, one for features and one for news. Oddly enough, contrary to my indignation in my early career days about being as a woman assigned "features," instead of news—the soft stuff rather than the hard—I found myself these days drawn to the features side of things. News tends to drive the reporter, but the reporter can usually drive features. In the end, when it looked like he might actually offer me a job, I decided that "contributing" might not yield a living wage whereas "assistant" editor might. When I admitted this to him, he smiled, then confessed that he'd had some trouble with previous "managing" editors because they tended to get it into their heads that they should control the whole process. It was pretty clear to me that this intelligent and sensitive man probably retained much of the control himself, and yet seemed very democratic, at least in how he was treating me. By the time the interview was over, I had been hired, on a trial basis. Seems the last managing editor had quit several months ago, and they were eager for a replacement. We shook hands and he then introduced me to the rest of the staff, an interesting crew of young and older, women and men. I could hardly wait for my first assignment, and I even dreamed of someday writing an editorial.

Since the paper was only a weekly, the job was part-time and the salary, minimal, but enough for me to live on, I figured. My plan was to find a small apartment before Grace's Laurel arrived again for one of her extended visits. Much as I loved being at Marcy and Grace's house, I knew I couldn't stay there permanently. It would be a great place to visit on weekends. But if I was going to find roots in Vermont, I needed to become more independent.

Nonetheless, as I drove home, I found myself singing "Amazing Grace." For it was Grace who'd *brought me safe thus far and Grace who'd led me home.* "Amazing Grace, how sweet the sound that saved a wretch like me. I once was lost but now am found, was blind, but now I see."

I could understand now why Grace's affections were so wide spread, not tied down to any permanent arrangement. Her serial monogamy wasn't promiscuity, it was generosity, a blessing possible only through intimacy. If she'd been married exclusively to me or Marcy or Ariel or Laurel, the rest of us might have remained wretches—me, for sure. And if I felt she belonged to me, chances are I wouldn't be able to receive fully what she gives me. Possession may be nine-tenths of the law, but it is zero percent of the spirit.

I doubt whether my inability to bond with any one person in a long-term relationship is a disguise for some secret spiritual calling on my part. But then, one never knows; the mysterious ways of providence are beyond ordinary comprehension. A flickering hope of such a possibility, at the moment, takes the bite out of self-judgment about my relational failures. I wonder how I'll feel when I see Kara again. I hope that crush is over so I can continue to feel easy with Marcy and invest my passion more profitably and honorably. But it's nice to know that such ardor can still be drawn upon.

Chapter Twenty Five

OMEGA

"You should like Omega, Xavy. It's the end of the Greek alphabet," Grace teased as we crawled along toward the retreat center in New York where Durga said she'd meet us.

We were enduring a detour from the expressway, caused we speculated by the hurricane damage of the week before, the hurricane which had occasioned my sojourn in Chicago. This hurricane was called Jane and I couldn't help thinking of a former lover of that name and her effect on my life.

As our car crawled in a line through a small picturesque town in Massachusetts, Grace, who'd been to Omega before, gave me the PR on this event, the Ecstatic Chant weekend. Ecstasy I could embrace; chanting, not so much.

"It's really amazing," Grace said, "what happens when so many people gather together just to sing."

"Singing sounds fine," I murmured, "but *chanting?*" I was wary of anything too overtly religious.

"It's when you repeat the same sound over and over until it becomes hypnotic. But not just any sound but sacred mantras which evoke the names of God. Or gods, in the Hindu lexicon."

I thought of the rosary, how Mom, Yuggie and I would repeat it over and over, following the comfort of my grandmother's voice." *Hail Mary, full of grace, the Lord is with thee. Blessed art thou among women and blessed is the fruit of thy womb, Jesus.*

"It's usually call and response," Grace explained.

Again, like the rosary. Gram said the first part of the Hail Mary and we said the last part. *Holy Mary, Mother of God, pray for us sinners now and at the hour of our death, amen.* I can't say it resulted in ecstasy, but maybe that's because we didn't sing it, we said it—on our knees. I was intrigued with how such different religions had similar practices. I was about to ask her about Jewish chanting of the Blessings when suddenly the traffic sped up and I concentrated on getting us back on the thruway, even though it was Grace driving.

"Why do you suppose Durga wanted to meet us there?" I asked. Durga seemed just as arbitrary and demanding as she ever was when she was still Sandra, but I tried to keep any tone of judgment out of my voice. "It seems like an odd and public place to give her what will surely seem bad news."

"Well, I'm not sure. It's very generous of her to pay our way, even reserving us one of the cabins on the Omega grounds." Once again, it seemed impossible for Grace to express any disapproval of Durga's quirky ways. But I couldn't complain when the same kindness tolerated my own eccentricities.

"What are the alternatives?" I asked.

"Camping or dorm style bunks."

I groaned.

"Or, I guess," she said, "staying in a motel away from the center."

Away from the center sounded pretty good to me, but not so much, I could tell, for Grace. "I still don't get it," I complained. "We could have easily met with her before this weekend."

"Except she wasn't in Vermont. She's coming from New York City. I get the feeling she is avoiding Vermont these days, I'm not sure why."

"Who looks after that fancy house of hers?"

"Oh, she has plenty of caretakers she can hire. Or friends who wouldn't mind some luxurious house-sitting."

I sighed. Not that I'd want such a fancy home, but someplace to hang my hat, so to speak, would be awfully welcome these days. Unlike Liza, my wandering days seemed to be petering out.

"I still don't understand why she wanted to meet us here, especially given how much it's costing her," I complained.

Because of the detour, we arrived too late for supper at Omega, and after settling into our cabin and grabbing something to eat at the café, we rushed up toward the hall, inhaling the sounds which poured out of it into the starry evening. After sitting in the back row for half an hour, I had yet to feel any ecstasy. It sounded more like a rock concert than a spiritual event, with a young band, pounding music more frenetic than transcendent, a certain amount of self-promotion about his latest cd from the leader of the band, and wild clapping from the crowd which emphasized the separation between performers and audience. The music was hypnotic, even orgasmic at points and when it built to a pitch, the audience rose to their feet, clapping and dancing.

It was then that Grace pointed to the front of the hall, toward the side of the band but in full view of the audience. A woman in white robes was twirling and twirling and twirling and twirling. I kept waiting for her to career into the plate glass window behind her or to trip over her whirling scarves or to stumble into the audience, but she stayed centered while spinning like a top, curving her arms to keep a balance. It seemed as if she were in a trance. I was so fascinated I couldn't stop watching.

Grace leaned into my ear and whispered, "Durga."

"What?" I looked again. Sure enough, the whirling dervish was Durga.

"It's a form of Sufi practice," Grace added with more than a note of admiration in her voice.

"I thought she was Hindu," I commented.

Grace shrugged. I reminded myself how spiritual eclecticism these days is so American—almost our patriotic duty. And who was I, who nibbled at every cuisine, to turn up my nose at such diverse accomplishments? At her age, movement of any kind is an achievement, and this kind of control and coordination, nothing short of miraculous. Durga's flowing robes, I had to admit, provided the perfect outfit for such a performance—or act of worship. They swirled around her as she spun.

We pooped out before Durga stopped rotating. After driving most of the day I was only too happy to collapse on the single bed which awaited me in our cabin.

That night I dreamt some fugitive had been trapped by the police. It looked like they were about to shoot or taser him when suddenly he bolted directly toward me, then stopped in front of me, his eyes bloodshot and angry. Moved by the spirit of the retreat center, I murmured softly, "Bless you." His response was "Fuck you!" He then pulled out a pistol and pointed it at me. I decided to wake up before he shot me. *Uh oh,* I thought, relieved to find myself in a safe bed across the room from a still sleeping Grace, *this does not bode well for this retreat.* Especially if, as my dream analyzing friends insist, all the characters in one's dream are manifestations of one's selves. I am the potential shooter? So much for blessings.

As we hurried off to breakfast before the dining hall closed, I overheard one woman saying to another, "And I'm sick of this energy conservation crap. For all we're paying—$900 for a room—they won't even give us a light bulb."

Grace and I exchanged a secret smile. I was secretly shocked at the price of the room. But the food made it all worthwhile—an array of healthy and delicious offerings with no limits on consumption. I filled my plate with scrambled eggs, roast potatoes, a bagel, cream cheese, and some fruit medley.

At breakfast there was no sign of Durga, who'd probably been up all night twirling. I entertained myself with looking at the vast array of outfits people were wearing. Although some of the dingier costumes were typical of aging hippies or young grunge guys, the predominant outfits seemed to be borrowed from other cultures, mostly Indian saris and tunics, but also Middle-Eastern (what we used to call "harem") pants, and a few African robes and turbans. Some of these outfits were obviously worn by natives or offshoots of those regions but most adorned Western followers of those traditions.

There were several women with shaved heads, whether from chemotherapy or initiation into some sacred practice, it was hard to tell. There was a smattering of tattoos, nose rings, and even some blue hair, as well as several white kids with dreadlocks. I was naturally struck (minus the hot iron) by the lithe bodies characteristic of what seemed like a bevy of woman yoga instructors of all ages, most draped with a wide array of colorful scarves, pink, fushia, bright olive, all exhibiting their toned muscles and fluid movements. While it seems that young women these days are into displaying their bodies with tops as tight as they come and skirts which barely cover their tushes, I also found myself impressed at how many tall, thin young women there were at this event—quite a few of them—standing straight and proud, moving with a grace unheard of in "my day" when anybody over five foot eight who wasn't a model was folded up like an accordion, hiding her breasts, as if trying to fit into a size 6 box. But these young women had supple, slender bodies which they didn't seem to mind showing off. At their age I was pleasantly plump, whereas now I'm just chunky—without, I'm afraid, the compensating appearance of wisdom. But perhaps being wise goes beyond appearances.

As if reading my mind, Grace pointed out the rhinestone sequined cover on a cell phone belonging to a woman probably from Manhattan or L.A. who was busy on her I-Pad during breakfast, while her table companions exchanged tips from their recent trips to Hawaii. Most participants were white, obviously well-off, and female. I was surprised to see so many women I'd consider "suburban housewives" participating in this somewhat fringe activity of Hindu chanting. I noticed the young man with sun-bleached blonde hair and dark beard, wearing a skirt, and the male staff person wearing a flowery apron, along with a number of butch women, but the range of gender-bending seemed narrow compared to our trip to Cape Cod.

One other thing I observed were communication patterns. If there was one man with several women, he held forth. If there were blonde women talking in groups with darker toned women, the blondes tended to monopolize the conversations. And if there were lesbians talking together, like the couple in line with us holding hands, the exchanges between them were almost totally *sotto voce*, while the exchange behind us between two straight women, who'd just met each other, was loud and authoritative. Obviously liberation for the marginal had yet to reach its omega.

The next morning in the hall after a few mellow songs to ease us into the day, the frenzied pounding started again. Grace, who'd been there before, tried to assure me it was going to get better. "These are just young folks grabbing their fifteen minutes of fame," she whispered. "They don't yet fully understand the sacredness of chanting. Wait for the other song leaders who are more evolved."

But I couldn't wait. It was too nice a day outside, sunny and warm. After the wind and rain of the storm, I was ready for summer again. I fled the noisy hall and wandered down to the lake where I found a hammock to swing in. As I lay there swaying, listening to the breeze stir the leaves of the trees which rose up around me and hearing the flow of the fountain in the lake, someone on a nearby bench started playing a guitar. The guitar sounded like a lute and the fellow's voice was mellow and sweet. Soon I was rocking in time to the music. His singing and playing gave me the bliss I'd been hoping for instead of the clamor in the hall.

I could have swung there forever. But I felt pressure from Grace to participate more fully in the chanting, so dutifully I popped out of the hammock, thanked the singer, and trotted up the hill, only to find Grace buying a load of cd's and books at the center's extensive bookstore. Seems the sacred always has its commercial side.

But that night everything shifted for me. First they had Ram Dass by live video stream from Hawaii, where he lives, chatting with some yogi friends among us who'd been in India with him. As a self-proclaimed "druggie" he's always been a favorite of mine with his *Be Here Now* and zest for life. He told hilarious stories about his foibles as a young person in India. I could completely identify. We laughed when he said he was drawn at the time to Buddhism which was all "spit and polish" and suspicious of Hinduism which had too many gods and made too much noise.

Now he was an old man, confined to a wheelchair because of a stroke. He spoke slowly, with long pauses, but what he said was inspiring. When we sing together like this, he said, it puts us in touch with our soul self, which is about love, not our mind self, which is from the ego. When he lived in his mind, he said, he felt a great deal of fear, fear of judgment. When he met his guru he felt for the first time unconditional love. Before that everybody who loved him had wanted something from him. Now that he lives in his soul self, he feels unconditional love for everybody—even, he said with a smile, the Republican congress which has been so obstructionist lately. Chanting the names of God, he claimed, is participation in pure love; it brings us into union with the One, and the One includes us. It's not about how well we sing, I was happy to hear, but about how all of us are seeking the inner life and sharing that exploration through chanting.

All this sounded pretty loosey goosey, I know, but I could feel the ecstasy with and through him, and had no doubt in that state that he could be in love with everyone. What really convinced me was when he said "yum, yum," in response to some illuminating insight expressed in the conversation. "Yum, yum" is not just of the mind, or even of the heart, but somehow of the whole self. He spoke so directly, so honestly, so lovingly that I had no question he knew what he was talking about. It was a rare sharing of transcendence from a nearly transcendent being.

And a great model for aging. He didn't mind his wheelchair, he accepted that he could no longer help others but had to depend on them. I thought of how sweet Nancy had become, and wished the same for my old age. In the western world he said, we fear death, but in India because of their belief in many lives, death is a total other experience. This whole event felt, as someone put it later, auspicious. Although Ram Das seemed to be balancing on the edge of mortality, the mood was celebratory.

This revelation was followed by a chant which truly felt like we were singing from the heart chakra, as Grace put it later. Everyone there—over two hundred people, I would guess—sang with one voice. The music was lovely but it was the unity of our voices that was so moving, that lifted me up from the one loving voice of Ram Dass to the one loving voice of us. I came to associate this particular chant with the spirit of blessing I experienced with that sharing, but I imagine such an exhalted moment could occur with any music.

The next day, while we were still basking in the glow of the transcendence of the night before, Durga finally made an appearance, approaching us during a mid-morning break in the chanting. Since none of us were particularly drawn to the next song leader, one of those scruffy young men who equated intensity with lyricism, we climbed together up a hill to the Sanctuary so we could speak privately. Durga's timing was exquisite, taking full advantage of our open hearts, so she could hear the report on our meeting with Liza. But even though my open heart felt protective of her, I wasn't prepared for the complete breakdown which ensued when we told her Liza had no intention of returning to Vermont, much less running a retreat place for aging lesbians. We didn't tell her at first the next revelation, which really shouldn't be such a surprise, but which might shock Durga: Liza isn't gay.

I've never seen Durga in tears before, much less sobbing so uncontrollably, and all I wanted was for her to stop. But Grace signaled that this delayed grief was more of a blessing than a curse and that we should just wait. Grace even stroked her hair, but I couldn't bring myself to that level of intimacy, given our past history together. I was, in other words, no Ram Dass, but maybe if I kept chanting, I might get there by the time I was his age. I was surprised to discover that what I had judged as her impulse to flee from responsibility was more about her conflicted desire to honor Sheila's dream about the retreat center.

"She put her heart and soul into making that place into a refuge for the marginal," she cried out. "I can't abandon it now."

"But you don't want to do it yourself?" I asked with as much compassion as I could muster.

She groaned. "I have a different path I need to follow."

"What path is that?" I asked, while Grace gave me a subtle shake of the head.

Durga burst into tears again. "This one," she said, gesturing around her. "A path of meditation and chanting. That's why I wanted to meet you here, so you could understand."

I nodded, but I still didn't understand why she couldn't do all this on top of her mountain. Grace's eyes bored into me in such a way that I knew I better not persist with my investigation. Maybe, I told myself, that's because it's not her mountain, it's Sheila's. Even though she inherited it, she hadn't exactly chosen it. I suddenly felt some sympathy for rich kids who inherited not just the family fortune but the family name, the family property, and the family expectations for it.

Grace then ventured to share the insight we'd arrived at together as we drove back to Vermont after our meeting with Liza. "You know, Durga, it may be that Sheila's dream is no longer relevant, especially in Vermont. We may still be a minority, but gays are not exactly marginalized anymore—with marriage rights and all. I'm not sure that dykes, even older ones like us, need such a refuge. Most gay people we know seem to want their own homes, like everybody else."

"Yeah," I added, "maybe Sheila's vision died with her." At this Durga burst into a new onslaught of sobs and Grace glared at me. I thought that's one of the spiritual messages we all agreed on—the impermanence of everything. *Oh well.*

"What if you—or someone you appointed—turned the property into something else?" Grace asked tentatively. "A retreat center, maybe, but not just for lesbians."

Durga perked up. "Like a school maybe? Your pre-school?"

Grace looked uncomfortable. I myself couldn't imagine parents driving up that long steep hill twice a day to drop off and pick up their kids. "It might be a bit remote for that," Grace said reluctantly, "but it would make a great retreat center."

Durga nodded for a long time. Then a look of shock came over her as she recalled something. "Sheila's dream didn't die with her," she exclaimed as if she'd just remembered what she'd discovered during her twirling. "Because Sheila isn't dead."

It was our turn to look shocked. "What do you mean?" I whispered. Could it be I'd been looking for the wrong missing person?

"When I was in a trance during my Sufi dance . . . ?" Durga said in a hushed voice. We nodded, curious but not wanting to rush her. "Sheila came to me. She was radiant. And she renewed her deathbed wish that I continue to convert the house into a refuge for lesbians."

Grace and I stared at each other. If Sheila was as blissful in death as Ram Das seemed to be in life, I thought, she ought to be open to a slight change in the agenda. But I didn't dare say that. I left it to Grace.

"I know you want to honor Sheila's wishes, and you have been most loyal, Durga, but you do have to let go and move on with your own life. I suspect your honoring her dream is also a way to hold onto Sheila, but if she is, as you say, still alive in spirit, then you can eventually communicate all this to her. I doubt if Sheila wants to shackle either you or Liza with her own worldly aspirations, generous as they have been." I was glad Grace didn't reveal that Liza's own encounters with her mother's spirit had supported a different agenda, for Liza at least. Enough was enough. For now.

By this point, Durga's grief had subsided to a few sniffles and her protests dwindled down to a few whimpers. "If I turned it into a retreat center," she asked finally, "who would run it?"

Suddenly they both turned to me. "No way!" I cried out. "I have a job." Or at least a job offer, I corrected internally.

"Frankly, I'd consider selling it if I were you," Grace said gently. Durga looked shocked. "To someone who wants to run a retreat center. That way you can more freely follow your own path to enlightenment. You're trying to let go now, but that property is like a noose around your neck. It may be time to hand it over."

Durga looked torn. I could imagine that, much as she didn't want to run Sheila's retreat center for her, she might also be reluctant to let go of such a splendid dwelling.

"It's not like you need that place to stay in touch with Sheila," Grace added. "It was here, not there, where she appeared to you."

"In the afterlife, I guess, almost anywhere can be everywhere," I commented solemnly. They both stared at me, then started laughing. I wasn't exactly joking, but I was delighted to contribute to this releasing of tension.

After this moment of connection, things fell apart, as they always do. If impermanence is one law of existence, then fragmentation is another. Durga went back to her twirling with renewed vigor, Grace drifted off into the music, and I took umbrage when one of the male song leaders kept dividing us into "the men" and "the women" in terms of singing. I stubbornly sang both parts. Admittedly, after he'd asked the men to stand and sing (what I considered the best part), then asked us all to sing together, the whole chorus was much louder. Which suggested that he was right: the men had not been singing very loud to start with. He explained that it's not easy for men to sing, but exclaimed how good it is for them to do so. Which may be true, but dividing us by gender seemed to me to undermine the whole unity thing.

Later a swami who'd gone as a penniless young man to India in search of spiritual enlightenment and ended up spending his life there explained what drew him to the Hindu religion was the feminine divine. I had to admit we westerners had nothing equivalent to Radha, the consort of Krishna. Radha, he said, was the one whose love is the source of all love in the universe. Krishna was the beloved, the receiver of that love. We had Mary the mother who loved her son, Jesus, but she wasn't considered divine by any means. I was intrigued with the fact that all these gods and goddesses were imaginary, not based in historical figures like the Buddha and Christ. And I was puzzled by how very gendered they all seemed to be. Always the male and female coupling. While viewing this sexual dimension as sacred was certainly an improvement over the Adam and Eve myth, and that wretched apple, I did wonder why Hindu culture was so gendered, compared to some indigenous systems which allowed a wider variety of genders. Was the distinction meant to assure the survival of the species in times when survival was more dicey? Or was it just the old patriarchal split? Does the threat of overpopulation in our day allow for a greater diversity of both gender and sexual preferences? If it's true that many folks are potentially androgynous and bi-sexual, then the loose distribution of roles seems more kind. But not, obviously, for devotees of certain ancient beliefs.

Does this gender tradition, I wondered, explain the glamorous outfits worn by so many of the women at this event? If the norm for femininity is a gorgeous young woman like Radha, it makes sense for women to play to that standard. Of course, if such were true, then gorgeous young men like Krishna should be the norm for masculinity, not the grizzled older western yogis who led much of the deepest chanting. All I knew was I didn't fit either the masculine or feminine norms personified in most of the Hindu gods and goddesses. Not just because I felt more androgynous than that, but also because of my age. Very few persons I've known of any age have actually fit neatly into those male and female stereotypes, or archetypes as some call them, although many have tried. My preference is Ganesh, the chunky elephant god. True, he is masculine, but not in the stereotypical sense.

So I certainly didn't feel comfortable when the same song leader started promoting the workshops he and his wife offer on tantric yoga, which as far as I know is a very gender polarized activity for heterosexual couples. The lingam and the yoni, Shiva and Shakti and all that. They called these sessions "Chanting and Panting." We all laughed, of course. But clearly he didn't seem to understand that not everybody at this gathering was straight. Soon I'd worked myself into a 'tude, translating this mood into an imagined letter to whoever ran these events, then a fantasized diatribe against polarized identities, either/ors, all those dividing lines which separate a person from her full identity, one person from another, and couples from each other. So while all this philosophy and practice wasn't necessarily divisive, and certainly, I suspected, wasn't meant to be, I found myself feeling more and more divided.

Fortunately though, the last mad dash for the best seats in the house (precipitated by a policy of keeping the doors locked until just before each session to prohibit what they called "camping out" between sessions—in other words, saving seats by leaving shawls and shirts behind) resulted in Grace and me landing smack dab between a couple from Vermont and a lesbian couple. We knew the one was from Vermont because Grace recognized the man, a tall, burly fellow with a graying ponytail, a dark mustache, and tender eyes. We knew the others were lesbians because they'd had the guts to stand in line holding hands.

Somehow, between Grace talking to the fellow about the flood damage and agreeing that it seemed to be those with the least who suffered the most and me talking to the younger 'bean about how much we enjoyed the singing and agreeing on who were the most amazing chant leaders, Grace and I had found our place in this diverse gathering without completely blending in or feeling left out.

Oddly enough, surrounded by all this neighborliness I accepted the fact that for the moment at least I was "a lesbian from Vermont." I, who eschewed labels regarding sexual preference and had never settled down anywhere before, suddenly, maybe, belonged somewhere?

This feeling of ease resulted from a sensation I've never felt before, something close to really liking who I am. Somehow, even though it was "over the air," so to speak, and completely not personal (Ram Dass couldn't even see us), I'd been exposed to the virus of "unconditional love," as if, as Ram Dass claimed, his Maharishi was really right there with us. If not that, then a transformed Mom was sending me her blessings.

Afterward, Durga met us with radiance in her eyes. "I think I've found a compromise," she whispered.

"What's that?" Grace asked.

"Turning the place into a home for orphaned or abandoned children," Durga exclaimed.

Ah, I thought, surprisingly moved. I wondered if Durga'd been an unwanted child. Or simply one who'd obviously suffered from conditional love. But the question still remained, who would take care of all these orphans, including, I supposed, Durga herself? I might be willing to help out, but . . .

I turned to Grace with this unasked question and saw that her eyes were brimming over. *Uh oh*, Grace was hooked.

No doubt I'd be called in for assistance. During my spare time, of course—there was no way I was going to turn down that job offer. I love children, but in my heart of hearts I am a journalist.

And right now I am obsessed with understanding Ram Dass's last inquiry: *"I love everybody and every thing but I am not everybody and everything like my guru is everybody and everything. Why is that?"* What does it feel like, I wonder, to be everybody and everything?

Will Ram Dass understand this fully only when he dies? Will I ever understand this? Maybe it's not, ultimately, how we are everybody and everything, but how that One is in everyone of us? Something maybe we'll eventually grasp with heart *and* mind, ego *and* soul. Anyway, as an investigative assignment, this is bound to take me through the rest of this life and into the next.

Because Marcy had called with warnings about flash flooding throughout Vermont, we decided to leave early when it started raining at Omega. Before we said goodbye to Durga, I presented her, without ceremony, the credit card she'd given me, while thanking her sincerely for enabling us to experience the chant weekend. That felt liberating.

On the way to our car, we encountered the tall burley from Vermont Grace had sat next to during the last chanting session. As we chatted about the various singers, he said that sometimes he wants to put duct tape over the mouth of the male singer whose focus on gender polarization had so irked me. It was gratifying to hear a man express this sentiment. And even more uplifting when this fine Vermonter praised one of the women singers we especially liked, saying he could imagine little angels hovering around her head. Somehow this simple exchange put everything right again for me, gender wise and heart wise.

On the way home we sailed through the pouring rain while singing to one of the chant cds Grace had bought, and we managed to get home before any flash floods spilled over onto any of the roadways we traveled.

Chapter Twenty Six

OCCUPY

You might assume, as I did, that Omega would mark the end of this verbal wanderlust—but turns out it didn't. Upon our return I received an assignment from my editor to cover the first Occupy rally in the state capital for the local paper where I was now employed. I was delighted, having been curious about the Occupy movement since its first recent eruption in Manhattan.

I wondered about its connection to the protests in Madison, Wisconsin earlier in the year, shortly before the Arab Spring. Old friends of mine had helped organize the teaching assistants' association at the University of Wisconsin, the first TA union in the country, years before, and this TAA had apparently been one guiding force behind this recent "occupation" of the Wisconsin state capital.

I was curious to see how male dominated Occupy was, and whether it was controlled by the left. I still hadn't gotten over the sting of being called a "bourgeois decadent," along with my gay friends, for practicing homosexuality. Those guys seemed every bit as rigid as Catholic bishops on this issue, their masculinity apparently just as threatened.

Ah, decadence. Oh, bourgeoise. Those were the days. It's not that I'm not middle class or self-indulgent, but no more than most of those fellows were—and probably, at least at the moment, I'd guess, a lot more underemployed. Clearly my irritation with sectarian male heavies, supported by their female lackeys, whose Marxist analysis led them to demean women, ignore the patriarchy and declare "the primary contradiction" to be between workers and capitalists was bound to color my openness to the Occupy Movement—much as I sympathized with their analysis. Suddenly I was flooded with memories of the nasty split in the Baltimore Women's Union over the rights of lesbian mothers to keep their children—which would seem, at least in retrospect, to be a progressive no-brainer.

I hoped past history wouldn't taint my journalistic objectivity. I didn't want to mess up this first, crucial assignment. But balancing my skepticism was a secret hope that another real movement had arrived to revive democracy and tackle the growing problem of the rich getting richer while the poor got poorer, which isn't exactly a new issue in human history, but recently seemed to pack quite a punch, especially to my tender stomach. I'd been lucky to be part of, or on the fringe of, some potent movements, but in the past decade or two, with the important exception of gay rights in some progressive places, progress toward equality and democracy seemed to have stalled.

I wasn't at all sure about the term "occupation" and what it invoked, from European occupation of Native American tribal lands to German occupation of most of Europe to American occupation of much of the rest of the world: empire run amok. However, "occupation" was on my mind as I searched in vain for affordable housing in Montpelier, just as another kind of occupation had been on my mind before I got this job. The tiniest apartment went for $900 a month, which might be fine in Boston or New York where higher salaries are available (for other than unemployed journalists) but here in rural Vermont, for me at least, such a rent was, for the moment, out of reach. This fruitless search fueled my curiosity about the Occupy movement which supposedly dealt with such survival issues.

So, armed with my trusty smart phone (purchased, of course, before my jobless benefits ran out) to take photos of the demo, I joined a diverse and cheerful crowd on the steps of City Hall, many carrying signs which said, "We are the 99%!" That's remarkably inclusive, I thought. Even someone like Durga, whose surplus wealth had filled my coffers for the past few months, would probably be welcome. It felt good to be part of an oppressed majority for a change, instead of just another oppressed minority. I was still shaking my head over the analysis which revealed that less than 1% of Americans owned most of America's wealth. Our much envied "middle class" was about to drop out of the bottom of the much derided "safety net," leaving the leftie heavies with no more "bourgeoisie" to rail against. Soon decadence would no longer be an option for the majority of us—lefties and heavies included.

So I expected the crowd to be mostly male and young, but was surprised to find it equally divided, and of all ages. As we marched along chanting some familiar slogans like "A people united can never be defeated," I felt a surge of nostalgia for the good old protesting days and a flush of fondness for democracy with all its messy conflicts and strategies. I was heartened by the thumbs up we received from spectators as we marched from City Hall to the State Capital (site of that amazing Council of All Beings session). I didn't notice any boos, but did see people in fancier clothing scurrying past more than a bit furtively.

Once at the Capital I expected to hear various speeches with predictable rhetoric, sad stories, and hot demands, but instead everyone gathered around a few folks sitting on the steps of the capital to hold a General Assembly. Instead of speeches, we had the "people's mic," a method of assuring that speakers could be heard by which everyone echoed, in short phrases, what that person said. Instead of VIP's lined up for speeches, we had "stack," by which a list was made to assure everyone, and anyone, could speak. At first the people's mic seemed silly, like a bunch of school kids parroting their teacher, but then I saw the delight of speakers getting that verbal confirmation they'd been heard. In my role of unbiased witness, I didn't speak, but I wanted to, just to feel my words reverberate back to me. And instead of male heavies running the show, the facilitators were mostly women—not professional women with glittering smiles and power suits but women I could imagine having a beer with in some local pub—and young men passionate about "direct democracy."

They began the meeting by explaining their process of consensus, along with the hand signals which characterized the Occupy movement: fingers up and waving to indicate approval, hands down to show disapproval, hands neutral, or hands folded across chest to register a "block." There were also signals to indicate somebody was off topic or going on too long. All this took me awhile to adjust to, but I began to see how these silent signals could increase collective participation. At this point, I put away my smart phone and my note pad and joined in, wishing I'd brought along a folding chair. I was tired of standing but was reluctant to sit for long on the hard stone steps. To my surprise, it didn't take long for folks to articulate the issues which brought us together, map out some common ground, and set up what they called "working groups." During the announcements at the end I noticed how much of a coalition this gathering seemed to be, with people representing a variety of local groups dealing with issues from workers' rights to peace protests to alternative energy advocacy to environmental protection. I wondered how gay and women's rights might fit into the picture, but true to my journalistic objectivity and propensity to hang out on the edges of organizations, I didn't ask. Perhaps out of fear of being slapped down for being bourgeois and decadent. But feeling invigorated, I headed off to the library to start writing my story. So much for Occupy, I thought at the time. That's covered.

Returning to the rest of my life, now that the so-called "missing child" had been located, I found myself still living at Marcy's house, moved now to the attic instead of the guest room but still dependent on her mercy for kitchen and bathroom access, still subject to "eviction" whenever Grace's Laurel showed up. I felt fairly successful at keeping my warm feelings for Kara hidden whenever she came over to visit Marcy. To tell you the truth, my libido has dwindled down to the slightest flutter these days, whether because of jet lag or seniority, I don't know. I can't afford to go to a doctor or an alternative practitioner for any kind of tune up, but I have to admit that sex is one of the last things on my mind lately.

In between searching for an affordable apartment in town and writing up assignments for the paper, I found myself drifting back to the Occupy meetings in an unofficial capacity. It was a relief to be amongst the clothed, even of the grungiest variety (Dress in Vermont, especially as winter creeps in, seems to raise "scruffy" to a new fashion level, layering to high art.) Of all the groups I'd visited locally, aside from the "family" group of Grace, Marcy and Kara, Occupy seemed the most intriguing, I wasn't sure why. I liked the diversity of ages and backgrounds, the tolerance for eccentricities, the fairness of "direct democracy," the sharing of roles, and the leadership provided by a number of younger (than me) women. Recalling the male dominance of the old movements like anti-war or anti-corporate dominance (usually "anti," rarely "for"), the natural leadership abilities of these women was refreshing. Maybe the women's movement had made more of a difference than sometimes, lately, it seems. Mostly I was drawn to the possibility of this new movement becoming "a place for us," the marginal. Perhaps a place where my newly found "family" could connect to the larger 99%, even more expansive than the women's movement, more inclusive than the gay rights movement.

Ever the spectator, I myself mostly listened to the various opinions, observing the dynamics, impressed by the clarity and skills of the speakers as the gathering gradually formed itself into a working organization. I enjoyed the passionate entreaties from spokespersons for various justice, environmental and energy issues. I appreciated our collective wisdom, even as I contributed none of my own.

Among the participants I noticed several women around my age, a fellow who couldn't help smiling about these gatherings, as if he'd been waiting for such a movement, a couple of even older women ardent in their support of justice, a range of opinions supporting various causes, and a healthy dose of humor.

One Saturday afternoon during the weekly General Assembly announcements, I finally ventured out of my shell to offer a few suggestions for future "teach-ins." Because fall chill had made the Capital steps less hospitable, we had moved into the basement of the public library. The meeting this day was led not by one of the several more mature and experienced facilitators but by a younger woman who seemed quite nervous about taking on this public responsibility. As it seemed we were running out of time, or at least spilling out of the time restrictions built into the agenda, she became more anxious. By the time my name rose up on stack, she could barely stand to listen to what I had to say, which wasn't much compared to speeches made by others earlier, but must have seemed interminable to her because not only did she frantically give the hand signal to "speed it up," but she also formed a triangle with her fingers to indicate I was "off topic."

Needless to say, I found this behavior more than disconcerting. Coming from other participants these signals would have been distracting; coming from the leader, they were daunting. Since this was just an announcement type suggestion, I fell into a complete muddle about how what I was saying could possibly be off topic. And to have the main facilitator (she who stood in the middle of the group conducting the meeting) signaling that I should wrap it up IMMEDIATELY, was needless to say, intimidating. As you can imagine, my words quickly drifted off to a precious few and I ended, not with a bang but a whimper.

Later I reasoned this neophyte had unconsciously abused her authority as a facilitator. Even direct democracy can provide a power trip. This experience of being hushed took me back to editorial meetings at the Globe where, as the lone woman, I would speak up, only to hear a moment of silence before the conversation continued as if I hadn't said a word. Later, often, my suggestion would be taken up by some male speaker, only to be greeted enthusiastically by the other men. It was like being invisible. This time I didn't feel invisible. She saw me, she heard me but she still couldn't listen. I felt both dismissed and empathetic. Like I was her mother! *Yee gads.* I realized it's not easy to provide that kind of leadership. You'll notice I wasn't volunteering for the job.

Oddly enough, this slight did not push me to drop out. It made me mad enough to speak out more forcefully at the next General Assembly. That shove—plus a speech by our oldest member, a woman from the International League for Peace and Freedom who proudly announced her age, 94, before entreating us to "take our lives in our own hands, to challenge imposed authority, and to breathe new hope into the belief that the people can bring about a more just society." Her vision inspired me to see that belonging to a diverse, democratic society is not about stability but about continual change—which is why we don't need another civic organization beholden to special interests, but a movement like this one which brings together strangers who are willing to explore and share common ground for the common good.

Wow, I thought, if she at her age can still believe in a new hope, then surely I can muster enough breath to join in. So participate I finally did. Not in a pushy way, of course. That's not my style. But I also refused to be intimidated by the youthful techies, by the understandably cynical older leftists, by the powerful younger feminists, by the restless young men looking to make their mark through protest, hopefully violent.

Although I'm no longer the naïve patriot who first set out to find my American dream, or the weary journalist relieved to return to this fortunate country after stints overseas where I witnessed extremes of poverty and destruction we rarely encounter, I still believe, "This land is our land." If we can take it back from the greedy, corrupt and heartless corporations and politicians, this land is *where* I belong. That's almost enough rootedness for me. As for "home," at this point it has got to be our whole planet.

Chapter Twenty Seven

WHERENESS

But *home,* I was about to discover, is not just about location—whether planet, country, state or town. And even though Grace and I were once again driving south together, where we headed was not about directions. A compass or map could not have warned us where we'd end up next.

We thought we were heading south toward Albany to attend Gloria's wedding—about which we both had mixed feelings, perhaps for different reasons. I was glad for Gloria that New York State had finally legalized same sex marriage so she could "legitimize" her 30 years relationship with her partner Maria. But we, Xavy and Grace, remained nonetheless not all that keen on wedding ceremonies or the institution of marriage.

Grace was driving, her eyes fixed intently on the road ahead, but her mind full of an old argument which had surfaced upon my return from Hawaii, where I realized, but was reluctant to admit, that maybe she'd been right all along.

"It's not that I see you as *unflappable,* Grace. Maybe it's just that you don't feel guilty about the same things I do." It's true that Grace can seem audacious at points where I might cringe. But other times it surprises me how vulnerable she is.

"Are you kidding?" Her expression, briefly turning to me, was incredulous. "I just can't believe that you still think that after all these years."

I winced, then said, "Well, it has a lot to do with what you think *flappable* means."

She just waved her hand in a gesture of dismissal which could in itself be defined as a "flap."

It's true that Grace has a certain *joie de vivre* which enables her to mask what I have recognized as anxieties as deep as my own, in some cases even deeper, if such is possible. She states her opinions, at times, with such confidence that even kings would pay heed. But as her longtime friend and former lover, I should have known better, after listening to her worries and fears in the wee small hours of the morning.

"It's all a load of Yuggie projection, Xavy," she said authoritatively. "She's the unflappable one in your life, not me. I'm the one who's never sure of her welcome."

True enough, I had to admit, after my last visit with her, Yuggie was pretty unflappable, especially these days. Living in Hawaii, except during typhoon season, would mellow anybody out. All the things which ruffled my feathers seemed to run off her back like water. But when you've known someone from the day you were born you tend to notice the slightest hints of anxiety, worry, even fear. It's inevitable that even the most easy-going, calm personality is going to feel angst from time to time, and even-tempered as Yuggie is most of the time, I could recall several incidents when she was convulsed with worry or even irritation. Need I remind myself of the time when what'shername was two-timing Yuggie? Even Grace could admit that Yuggie had her anxious moments—but nothing, apparently, as dire as what Grace, apparently, felt on a regular basis. Neither one of them, I concluded, was exactly transparent when it came to expressing certain feelings.

Nor was I, or have I ever been, the model of empathy. I have to admit I felt a great deal of remorse that I had misjudged Grace after all these years. Not admit to her, of course, not yet, but at least to myself. She was right—I had not only projected Yuggie's temperament onto her, I had glorified her ability to overcome all sorts of challenges and hurdles, brushed off her complaints, pooh-poohed her fears, challenged her to greater and greater feats of valor. (Just what some folks tended to do with Yuggie, I must add.)

This trip, for instance. I had dismissed Grace's distress over attending the marriage ceremony. I had pooh-poohed her hesitation about being with Gloria after years of separation. I had practically promised her that Gloria would be delighted to see her, even though I had only the vaguest reassurance from Gloria that such was so. I didn't even know why their friendship had fallen by the wayside ages ago.

Gloria had been Grace's best friend in college. Gloria was Yuggie's first lover, so in some closeted ways she was part of our family. Yuggie had met Grace through Gloria, and I had met Grace through Yuggie, *back in the day*, as folks are fond of saying these days. Despite their break-up, Yuggie and Gloria remained friends to this day, but Grace and Gloria had drifted apart, while I floated around somewhere in the middle of all these connections, linked to all, but very loosely tethered, if you know what I mean.

To distract Grace's attention not from the road but from this particular trip down memory lane, I tried to shift the focus to the marriage equality conundrum.

"I never thought Gloria would succumb to the argument that marriage makes us equal," I declared. Gloria was an independent and original thinker, ever skeptical about the latest popular bromide or political rant.

"Yep," muttered Grace, taking the hook, "first we demand to be in the military, then we beg to be married. Next thing we'll be asking to be embraced by the Pope."

"Aren't we already memorialized in the Sistine Chapel?" I said, referring to Michelangelo's gay propensities, and we both laughed.

"It's that old fallacy: *same* is the equivalent of *equal*. For better or worse, we have our own identity, culture, traditions, kinds of relationships."

Amen to that, I thought. As far as I was concerned, my relationship with Grace was as deep, as true, as loving as any marriage bond. But it was not monogamous, it was not exclusive, it wasn't, alas, even sexual. "Yeah," I affirmed. "Can't we be legit without being married or in the military?"

"On the other hand" she said, "I heard an interview yesterday on the radio with a gay guy who'd just gotten married in some state that just allowed it, and he said it was the first time he'd ever felt like a citizen."

I thought about it. "I've always felt like a citizen," I declared patriotically.

"I've never felt like a citizen," she replied—unflappably I might add.

We drove on, each mulling over this difference, not sure what it meant, if anything. Was my sense of belonging contained within borders while hers was more global?

Then Grace said, "The erotic between women seems different than between men and women—but is it?" She looked at me as if I might know. (Both of us had been with men, but me most currently.)

I didn't. But thinking about it later, I realize she might be onto something. I know women individually can be possessive and jealous in all contexts of sexual allure, but somehow women, even in capitalist settings, seem more communal somehow, more willing to share—or exchange perhaps. Not so many turf battles to the death.

With this we launched into our litany of complaints about the institution, not to mention the sacrament, of Marriage, which by this point fell into a familiar rhythm of call and response.

"A patriarchal institution to insure women and children remain male property."

"A false or unrealistic promise of fidelity until death do us part." I brushed aside the fact that both Grace's and my parents, had actually stayed faithful, as far as I know, until death did them part.

"Reich's research that sexual passion never lasts longer than seven years." Which was just about how long Grace and I had been lovers.

"A privileging of sexual partners over friendships." We both knew that without the network of friendship which connected our lives, we'd have fallen through the cracks long ago. Lovers who hadn't turned into lasting friends had come and gone without a trace.

"A hierarchy of relationship." Even lifelong friendships took a back seat to newfound matings, especially marital ones.

"A coupling that restricts." We sighed together over the frequent reality that in socializing, even with gay couples who weren't civil unionized or married, we couldn't relate to one without the other's presence, as if they were joined at the hip.

This led to our observation about how incompatible seemed the partners in some of the longest term gay relationships we knew. Why was it that couples who'd lasted longest couldn't be more different from each other? Opposites attract? If not gender, did converse personalities form the yin/yang of connection? Were such obvious differences a kind of magical glue, or just that extra challenge some folks relish in relationships? Or did some couples feel more comfortable with clearly delineated but somewhat traditional roles? Or was there something heroic about forging a bond across divergence?

"And is all this true or just a facile generalization?" Grace asked in her characteristically honest way.

Gloria and Maria were a case in point. Gloria was intense, thoughtful, refined. Maria was cheerful, loving, sentimental. They had different roots, different kinds of community, different personalities and different ways of being. Gloria was from a privileged but fraught family with high standards of achievement; Maria was from a large, warm family with great survival skills. They were both bright, loyal, talented; both loved family.

As it turned out, Grace had only met Maria once, early on, so I was curious what she'd think about her, as well as curious about how Gloria would receive Grace after all these years.

After circling around through Albany we finally found City Hall. It turned out to be a magnificent building which looked, appropriately, much like a church, with a tall tower and layers of peaked windows full of light. There in front of city hall stood Gloria and Maria, along with two younger women who I recognized as Maria's daughters from her previous hetero marriage. Gloria and Maria were dressed up—Gloria in an elegant shirt and pants, Maria in a colorful dress—all four of them were beaming.

After we'd parked behind the building, we joined them on the steps where Gloria, at first startled to see Grace, gave us both warm hugs, obviously delighted by our presence. Whatever tension lingered between her and Grace apparently evaporated immediately, judging from the relief in Grace's countenance. *Perhaps it was just mutual guilt at the lapse?*

The ceremony, if it even could be called that, was brief. The Justice of the Peace, a white haired man with a sour expression, seemed to be making an effort to treat this as just another marriage ceremony. But when Maria told him in her friendly way that she and Gloria had been together for thirty years, he seemed to melt, and soon was joining in the warm congratulations exchanged within our small group of witnesses. By the end he was beaming, as if somehow he had contributed to the success of this coupling. Then as the daughters presented each partner with a bouquet of flowers, bells began to toll.

"Ask not for whom the bell tolls . . ." joked Gloria, who was after all, a literary scholar.

While I racked my brain for the allusion, the Justice explained that the bells were from the carillon in the tower attached to the building and they rang every day at noon. Their timing had been auspicious.

Ah yeah, John Donne, I finally recognized: "No man is an island, entire of itself; every man is a piece of the Continent, a part of the Main." No woman either, I automatically corrected. Not even *me*.

But as we progressed out of the building, I realized this whole event wasn't about me. Nor was it celebrating a promise to be faithful. It was public recognition of a relationship which had been faithful already, longer lasting and more loving than many straight marriages. Not only was I moved to realize this, I was amazed at how joyful Gloria was after the ceremony. Maria, yes, was the marrying kind and had never been part of the women's community as I'd known it. But independent-minded Gloria, the great iconoclast? Her face was aglow with love and delight. This was an accomplishment which apparently surpassed even earning her doctorate, becoming a professor, publishing in distinguished scholarly journals. It seemed to be about more than legitimacy.

I recalled when she and Yuggie were first together, so young, hiding in the closet, deeply in love yet totally incognito as a couple. Finally Gloria—not Yuggie—came out to me. Gradually Gloria chose to come out publically—at the school where she taught, to her straight friends and family. Way before it was hip to be gay, way before it was legal. I'd always admired her courage, and wished I could emulate her, even though because I was bi I felt confused. It's hard to come out as an either/or when you tend to be a both/and.

All that angst was behind us now, and when I looked into Gloria's radiant face, my list of objections to the institution of marriage just fell away. I'd dropped into a new place, a place Buddhists call "Sympathetic Joy." Somehow my angst about relationship failures, my self-pity and loneliness, my envy over others' good fortune, all that melted away and I was left with pure unadulterated bliss shared, with Gloria.

And when I glanced over at Grace, hesitant for fear she'd feel very differently, I could see she too was in that place of sympathetic joy. *What a relief.* In that saving moment I'd never felt closer to Grace.

As we walked through town after the ceremony, Grace thanked me for once again rescuing her, this time from the separation from Gloria. Basking in the role of liberator of sorts, I started to ask Grace about the source of that particular rupture when the youngest daughter began quizzing me about my "journalism career." I was, of course, only too happy to pontificate.

On the way home after a joyous and boisterous wedding celebration in the best restaurant in town, in which we all participated whole heartedly, Grace and I revisited the whole idea of marriage.

As it turned out, as Gloria explained to us over the meal, her reasons for deciding to get married, once it was legally possible, were mostly practical. After a health scare she'd worried how Maria might get along fiscally if anything happened to her, so she decided the best protection would be a marriage contract, since her own pension and assets were more liberal than Maria's.

Grace and I agreed that, by any fiscal spreadsheet, we couldn't offer much protection for a potential mate. Although we'd both worked all of our adult years, if worse came to worst, aside from Social Security, we'd be dependent on the generosity of friends, the kindness of strangers, or complaining taxpayers.

"But Grace, what if you were in the hospital and they wouldn't let me in to see you because we're not family?"

"Just say you are my sister," Grace replied. "You might as well be."

"I might?" I was hoping for something a bit more romantic.

"Of course, Xavy. We are, at times, as close as two people can be." That sounded better.

Were we then, 'soul companions'? I wondered. Not sole, of course, but soul. Had I been admitted to that august company? But here I studiously avoided anything like a piteous or begging tone. If this gift was offered to me, I wasn't going to whine about it. "Of course we are," I asserted with the utmost confidence—but then couldn't help but add ruefully, "I wonder why we didn't last as a couple."

"Depends on what you mean by 'couple'," she said. "The deep bond between us is an unbroken line, even when we've been apart. So in that sense we've always been a couple, even though we haven't always been together. But if by 'couple' is meant the one and only major line, then of course we aren't a *couple* since we're also connected by other lines to other folks." I imagined two linked webs, one for Grace, one for me, with other lines weaving out in many directions.

"So maybe that's the difference between a couple and a marriage? But isn't everybody connected that way to lots of others, not just one's mate?"

"Perhaps. The fact that she's married doesn't erase the lines between Gloria and Yuggie, Gloria and you, or even Gloria and me. It just means she hasn't built her life around living with any of the rest of us as she has with Maria. Building a life around one other person can be a foundation for family. And family provides stability for children and for elders."

I realized I'd still forgotten to ask Grace what the estrangement had been between Gloria and her in the first place. In fact, what their connection had been. Had they been lovers?

But at that moment I had to let that line of inquiry fall by the wayside lest I lose the thread between Grace and me we were unexpectedly exploring. For Grace to confess to feeling a deep bond with me was a clue I wasn't about to let disappear. What did it mean? Was it anything I could count on *now*? I do not need to stress at this point that neither Grace nor I have the stability of family—at least not beyond siblings, not into a new generation. Not that kind of home.

"Funny," she said, "how this marriage equality campaign has turned out. It's meant to give gay and lesbian folks the ability to be accepted for who we are by providing us legitimacy for our relationships and lifestyle, or at least our fiscal interdependence. But, despite all those categories, each one of us is so different in terms of expectations, preferences, identities, life trajectories. There's always some of us who are going to fall between the cracks of any liberation." She paused to mull over what she'd just said and to bring it home. "But indirectly it has helped you and me recognize even more fully who we are not."

"What's that?" I asked, some tiny part of me still hoping for a belated proposal.

"The marrying kind!" she said.

I laughed. Of course this was true of both of us, but somehow I still wanted some assurance that if she married anybody, it would be me. "If we'd have stayed together back in the day, do you think we'd be getting married now?" I asked.

She looked at me curiously, then shrugged. "Maybe, Xavy, maybe . . . but then what about . . . ?"

And internally we both ticked off the list of soul companions who'd entered Grace's life, and the "almosts" in mine, since the demise of our romance. Not to mention those we hadn't even met yet.

"So I guess I'm just a *has-bian*," I said woefully. I'd recently read that "grace," in the spiritual sense, is unexpected, undeserved, and ephemeral.

"You're an always and forever, Xavy."

"For *you*?"

"For me, with me, till death do us part—and beyond."

What an unexpected, and probably undeserved, blessing. I was aflutter with images of our next lives together, mixed with wonderings about our past lives together. But instead of heading for that detour, I smiled and suggested we co-write a play called "The Occasional Couple" which could span several lifetimes.

Grace loved the idea. "We could call it *'When?'!*"

As we played around with the plot line, I had to admit, in terms of legacy, I wouldn't want to be known as the person who deprived anybody of the whereness of my abiding but occasional dear soul companion, Grace. And, perhaps, in her generous way, Grace recognized that some folks might need the independent whereness of Xavy from time to time.

As for whereness itself, I continued to ponder my "place in the family of things." I knew only too well that "you can't go home again." I was painfully aware that belonging someplace is tricky—like trying to root in the sands of an hourglass. Perhaps I was a citizen, but of a country I hardly recognized anymore. Where is my where? I still wondered. Vermont? U.S.A? Earth? (*Not for long.*)

Then Grace showed me a poem by her friend, the poet S.B. Sowbel, which said all I need to know for now:

"MAP

There are places that have lost their way.
If you are lost in those lost places
the loneliness is all flesh-razored shame.
One friend says Pittsburgh is despair.

Another says Fresno's roads
disintegrate in the heat.
Guidebooks say Detroit is still
waiting to be found.
I say, *Go to the Green Mountains*
though there is no signage to point the way
and thickets abound. Your travel
will be a slow bear ambling up
a steep mountain
where you will find
honeybees
thrive
There
even degradation
can disrobe among
the meadows.
Search for the compass rose,
find a sly pond where herons
stand and beavers trim trees
of all greenery for staffs
that can walk you out
of heartbreak
to home."

Other Books by Margaret Blanchard

The Rest of the Deer: An Intuitive Study of Intuition (Portland, Maine: Astarte Press, 1993), ISBN: 0-9624626-7-5.

Restoring the Orchard: A Guide to Learning Intuition, with S.B. Sowbel (Baltimore, Md.: Tara Press, 1994).

Duet: A Book of Poems and Paintings, with S.B.Sowbel. (San Antonio, Texas: M&A Editions, 1995), ISBN: 0-913983-13-6.

From the Listening Place: Languages of Intuition (Portland, Maine: Astarte Press, 1997), ISBN: 1-885349-05-X.

Hatching (a novel) (Lincoln, Nebraska: iUniverse, 2001), ISBN: 0-595-17695-X.

Wandering Potatoes (a novel) (Lincoln, Nebraska: iUniverse, 2002), ISBN: 0-595-26155-8.

Who? (a novel). (Lincoln, Nebraska: iUniverse, 2004), ISBN: 0-595-32472-x.

Queen Bea (a novel). (Lincoln, Nebraska: iUniverse, 2005), ISBN: 0-595-36338-5.

Change of Course: the Education of Jessie Adamson (a novel). (Bloomington, IN: iUniverse, 2008), ISBN: 978-1-4401-0290-5.

This Land (a novel memoir). (Bloomington, IN: iUniverse, 2010), ISBN: 978-1-4502-2262-4.

Water Spies (a novel). (Manchester Center, Vt: Spires Press, 2012), ISBN: 978-1-60571-145-4

Photo by K.A. Herrington

Margaret Blanchard has lived in central Vermont for many years after sharing land in the Adirondack woods and living in the city of Baltimore. A writer, stained glass artist, and educator, she has published books on intuition and creativity as well as poetry and fiction. She has been active in movements for civil rights, peace, women's rights, gay rights, as well as union, community and environmental organizing. Retired from teaching in the M.A. program of Vermont College, she is currently engaged with Restoring the Heart of Democracy Circles, Courage and Renewal Retreats, Walk in Beauty Retreats, Occupy Central Vermont, and the Northern Lights Singing Group.